The Seven Year Scratch

S0-ARO-347

The Seven Year Scratch

Teresa McClain-Watson

sepia
★BET
BOOKS

BET Publications, LLC
http://www.bet.com

SEPIA BOOKS are published by
BET Publications, LLC
c/o BET BOOKS
One BET Plaza
1900 W Place NE
Washington, DC 20018-1211

Copyright © 2005 by Teresa McClain-Watson

All rights reserved. No part of this book may be reproduced, stored in a retrieval system, or transmitted in any form or by any means without the prior written consent of the Publisher.

If you purchased this book without a cover, you should be aware that this book is stolen property. It was reported as "unsold and destroyed" to the Publisher and neither the Author nor the Publisher has received any payment for this "stripped book."

All Kensington Titles, Imprints, and Distributed Lines are available at special quantity discounts for bulk purchases for sales promotions, premiums, fund-raising, and educational or institutional use. Special book excerpts or customized printings can also be created to fit specific needs. For details, write or phone the office of the Kensington Special Sales Manager: Attn. Special Sales Department, Kensington Publishing Corp., 850 Third Avenue, New York, NY 10022, Phone: 1-800-221-2647.

BET Books is a trademark of Black Entertainment Television, Inc. SEPIA and the SEPIA logo are trademarks of BET Books and the BET BOOKS logo is a registered trademark.

ISBN: 1-58314-462-5

First Printing: July 2005
10 9 8 7 6 5 4 3 2 1

Printed in the United States of America

ACKNOWLEDGMENTS

I wish to thank God Almighty for the gift of writing and the enjoyment it brings.

I also wish to thank numerous supporters, including Gregory Bullard, Bartholous Woodley II, Shavonne McClain, Sherman McClain, Jr., Marilyn Enos-Upthegrove, Minnie McClain-Hogan, Marion McClain, James McClain, Danny and Nancy Watson, Donald Watson, Annie Ruth Brookins, Annette White, Betty Gainous, Deborah Lee, and Steven Murray.

I wish to thank Glenda Howard, my superb editor.

And, of course, John T. Watson, my beloved husband.

I also wish to thank my readers. God bless you indeed!

Visit me at *www.teresamcclainwatson.com*

MAKES ME WANNA HOLLER

"*Ask Sister J.* This is J. What's up, Miami?"

It was the last caller of the afternoon and Jazz Walker was already scribbling down notes for tomorrow's program: less love-gone-wrong calls, more inspirational stories. She, after all, had been hosting this same, tired radio program for over five years now, and it was time, she felt, that she moved the conversation to a higher level. Her callers, however, didn't seem to want to cooperate.

"Is this Sister J?" the caller asked as if she had no clue what number she had just dialed.

Jazz, who did not suffer fools well, rolled her eyes. "Yes, it is. What's up?"

"It's my husband, Sister J. He's been acting so weird lately and I don't know what to do."

"Weird how?"

The caller, a soft, female's voice, hesitated, which usually meant the truth was about to be revealed. "I think he's having an affair."

"And you're probably right, girl."

"Excuse me?"

"You're probably right. Don't try to sugarcoat it. Don't try to convince yourself that it's all in your imagination and those phone numbers you found or that lipstick on his collar are just innocent coincidences, because chances are, they aren't."

"But he denies everything."

"*Duh.*"

"And what phone numbers and lipstick? I didn't find any phone numbers or lipstick."

"I can feel that. But you found something or you wouldn't be calling me. So what's the story? What did you find that's got you so concerned about your man's fidelity?"

Again the woman hesitated. Jazz underlined the words *no more love-gone-wrong callers* on her notepad and wrote in three exclamation points for emphasis.

"He was in bed with this woman," the caller said, "but he declares nothing happened."

Jazz shook her head. What did she think he was going to declare? "Did you see the two of them in bed?"

"Yes."

"You saw them with your own two eyes?"

"Yes, I saw them."

"Do you know the woman?"

"No."

"But she was in bed with your husband?"

"Yes."

"Were they above or beneath the covers?"

"Beneath."

"Were they clothed completely, semicompletely, or nude?"

"She was nude but he wasn't."

"But she was?"

"But he wasn't. He still had on his boxers."

"And he says nothing happened?"

"That's right. He said she was just a friend of his who had some death in her family or something and he was just comforting her."

"In the nude, under covers, in bed?"

"He wasn't nude, Sister J. He still had on his boxers. He hadn't even removed his boxers."

"But he had removed everything else?"

"Well, yeah."

"Just not his boxers yet?"

"You don't know my husband, Sister J. He's no liar. He don't swing like that. And he was so sincere, you should have seen him. He insists to this day nothing happened."

"Because you walked in on his ass, lady, who are you kidding?

Something would have happened, if, in fact, it hadn't already, if you hadn't have shown up! For the love of truth don't get pitiful on me, sister."

"You just don't understand. He wouldn't lie to me."

"He was in bed with another woman! He ain't got to lie, he ain't got to tell the truth, he ain't got to say a word! His actions should have been all you needed to hear!"

"So what are you saying? Are you telling me to walk away from my husband, from my marriage?"

"Not walk. Run! Fly! Get away without delay! Because I will tell you, dear sister, you only saw the tip of the iceberg. It will not get better."

"How can you say such a thing? You don't even know my husband."

"You don't either, apparently."

"Are you married, Sister J?"

There it was, Jazz thought. The question. The one ace-in-the-hole question the callers loved to flip the script and ask anytime Jazz's honest assessment was, in their view anyway, over the top. "Not at the present, no."

"Have you ever been married?"

Another pause. Jazz thought about telling the sister that it was none of her business, but she didn't go there. She did, after all, put herself out there as some super advice maven. The least she could do was accept that every caller wasn't going for that advice. "Yes," Jazz said.

"Once?"

"Thrice."

"*Three times?* You've been married *three times?* Why should I trust you? You're no love expert. You're a failure!"

"I'm a sister who knows when the jig is up. I'm a sister who knows how to let go and move on."

"You're a sister who can't keep a man. I'm just trying to hold on to my man, that's all I'm trying to do."

"No matter what?"

"He says he didn't do anything, Sister J. So excuse me if I prefer to believe my husband, a very good man by the way, instead of you."

"Fine. Believe him. Believe fairy tales, too, while you're at it. But not with Sister J!"

Jazz quickly flipped off the switch, effectively disconnecting her last caller of the day, and then she bid a hearty farewell to her listen-ing audience. "Until we meet again, Miami. Peace!"

The closing music roared on and Jazz folded her arms and leaned back in the swivel chair inside the recording booth. She wore glasses, a stylish pair of square-rimmed Liz Claibornes, and with some degree of anger she pushed them up on the bridge of her thin nose. Gerald, her show's producer, a tall man with a small head and small, slanted eyes, hustled into the room. He was relieved, not just because the show was over but because there were no major glitches to report.

"Thank God," he said as he walked in.

"What an asshole!" Jazz said.

"It was a great show, Jazz, come on. Don't let that last caller spook you."

"I'm a failure, she says. I can't keep a man, she says. Where does she get off?"

"Why don't you take five and we'll start the postproduction meet-ing after that?"

"I could keep a man if I wanted to. But only if I'm willing to trade in my own self-respect for that man, as she's so willing to do."

Gerald looked at Jazz and smiled. She was a goddess in his eyes, a thirty-four-year-old stunner who wasn't conceited in her beauty but did everything she could to conceal it as if determined to keep men at bay. From the purposefully baggy clothes she favored to the wild-styled Afro she donned, her every move seemed to scream disinterest. It didn't work with Gerald, however, because her style itself turned him on, but other brothers didn't seem to share his enthusiasm. In the five years he'd worked with Jazz, first as a station assistant and then as her show's producer, he had yet to see a steady man in her life. Of course Thomas Drayton, the well-known attorney, was in her life, but he was supposedly her best friend, not her boyfriend, al-though Gerald wondered about that, too. They were a little too tight, he felt, to be just friends, and every time Drayton came around Jazz seemed to forget Gerald even existed. She was quick to blame the three bad marriages she endured as the reason for her refusal to give Gerald or any other man a chance, but Gerald kept sensing that it was Drayton, that his overwhelming presence in her life kept her from launching out.

He leaned against her desk and glanced down at the notes she had scribbled earlier. "I still say it was a good show," he said. Then he looked up from her notepad. "No more love-gone-wrong callers?" he asked. "You're kidding, right? That's all we get. And it's been a good ride, Jazz, despite that last caller."

"She calls in for advice and then gets offended when I give it to her. But she'll believe that butt-naked husband of hers, and probably any other sorry excuse for a man. Now she'll listen to anything they have to say."

"Now, now, Jazz," Gerald said with a slight smile on his face, "we aren't all cheating dogs."

"I didn't say all of you were. Thomas certainly isn't. But he's about it."

Gerald hesitated, wishing to God that she could have as high of an opinion of him as she did of Drayton, and in his hesitation Jazz realized her slight. "And you, too, of course," she quickly added.

Gerald smiled, although he knew she didn't mean it.

The nasal voice of Beatrice, the receptionist, could be heard over the booth's intercom. "Phone call on line four, Jazz."

"Thanks, Bea," Jazz replied as she grabbed the phone and pressed four. "This is Jazz. What's up?"

"Jazz, hi. It's me. Paula."

Jazz, who had been swiveling nervously in her chair, stopped. Paula was Thomas Drayton's girlfriend, a woman who actually believed she had the inside track to his heart after only three months in his life. A woman Jazz could not stand. "Hello, Paula."

"I caught your show."

"Did you?"

"Yes, I did. Quite impressive. Especially that last caller."

"Yeah, I thought you'd like her."

There was a slight pause, as if Paula fully understood the snide remark. "So," she said, deciding to ignore the remark, "how have you been?"

Jazz knew that Paula Scott wasn't any more interested in her well-being than she was in Paula's. But she was too intrigued by the phone call itself to not play along. "I've been good," she said.

"Glad to hear it. So have I."

Another pause. Then the point. "I won't keep you, Jazz," she finally said. "I was calling to invite you to dinner tonight."

Jazz almost smiled. "Come again?"

"Yes, that's right. Thomas and I are meeting for dinner at Solesby's tonight and I would love for you to join us."

"You want *me* to join *you* and Thomas?"

"If you can make it, yes."

"What did Thomas say about this invite?"

"He was all for it. You know he loves your company."

Jazz hesitated. Either Paula's relationship with Thomas was becoming more serious than Jazz had thought possible and they wanted to make Jazz, as Thomas's best friend, aware of the new development, or this was all Paula's doing and the relationship was going south. Either way, Jazz would just as soon stay out of it.

"Jazz? Are you there?"

"Yes."

"Then you'll come?"

But then again, Jazz thought, Paula's game may allow Thomas to finally see her for the snake she really was and he just might dump her tonight. And that was definitely worth the price of admission. "Yes," she said. "I'll put in an appearance."

"Wonderful, Jazz. Fantastic. I'll see you tonight then. At eight."

"Eight it is," Jazz said. Then she looked at the phone as if it were some strange object and hung up.

"Who was that?" Gerald asked her.

"That was Paula."

"Paula?"

"Thomas's latest. She's invited me to dinner."

"I thought you and his girlfriends didn't get along."

"We don't."

"So what's up with that one?"

Jazz exhaled. "Apparently something," she said, and after a brief moment of reflection where all sorts of possibilities roared through her head, she got up and hurried out for a cigarette break.

He had a reputation for ruthlessness, seen as a man you didn't want to cross if you had any hopes of keeping your own reputation intact, and Joe Carter knew it. As he and Greg Myers sat in the elegant conference room at the Drayton law firm and waited, often impatiently, for Thomas Drayton to arrive, he tried to impress upon his client that very point.

"He won't like it, Greg," Carter said. "He's a man of his word and he's not going to be easily persuaded to back down from that word."

"Then you've got to work harder to persuade him, don't you, Joe?"

"It's just a difference of two thousand dollars, Greg, come on."

"Yeah, two thousand dollars of my hard-earned money every single month. That's twenty-four grand extra every single year! No way, partner. You don't know Lydia. She won't be bleeding this brother dry."

Carter leaned back. Greg Myers was a depth-chart number-two wide receiver for the Miami Dolphins, and although he earned more than enough to easily cover the agreement, Carter knew he wanted to stick it to his soon-to-be-ex wife just to make her squirm. It was a game of save face, and Carter could appreciate that. He only hoped Thomas Drayton, a man so relentless in his pursuit of winning that not only your client but your very reputation could be ruined if you rubbed him the wrong way, could appreciate it, too.

And when Thomas Drayton finally arrived with Lydia Myers— Greg's beautiful wife—Carter, in a lame attempt at making it clear to Drayton that this was all his client's doing, moved swiftly, too swiftly, Greg felt, to shake his hand.

"Thomas, hi," he said smilingly as he stood and extended his hand.

"Hello, Joe," Thomas replied with a smile and handshake of his own. "You remember Mrs. Myers?"

"Of course." Carter said this as he shook Lydia's hand. But his small eyes riveted back to Drayton. Drayton was a tall, muscle-tight man with a firm handshake and an easy smile. And although his large body and commanding presence seemed to fill the room, causing even an experienced attorney like Carter to pause in admiration, there was still something soothing about Thomas Drayton, something compassionate even, that could lull many an unsuspecting opponent right under his spell. Even down to the simple things, like the calm manner in which he presented his arguments in court, or the elegant suits he favored, such as the blue periwinkle pinstripe that adorned his well-formed body today, everything about the man seemed to personify cool.

But Carter knew better. He knew that underneath that placid demeanor was no lightweight happy-go-lucky but a fierce competitor, a cold, calculating, will-stop-at-nothing master manipulator. He won you over with his smile, a stark, white, beautifully enchanting smile that was so easily displayed, and he kept you under his spell with that earnest, almost sedulous look in his eyes. But Carter had heard too much about Drayton to be fooled. He knew that if you messed with Drayton you'd better be willing to fight him every step of the way, unwavering, because as soon as he found your weakness he'd go in for the kill. But to look at Drayton, a man of such easy manners and contagious charm, made Carter wonder if all of that talk could possibly be true; maybe the man's reputation had nothing to do with the man himself.

But after all formalities were over and they finally sat down to business, Carter's initial assessment of Drayton was quickly realized. Drayton didn't like the change in plans one bit. Carter and his client had agreed to the terms of the divorce just two days ago, he reminded them, and already they wanted to renegotiate? He stood up on his muscular six-foot-two frame and walked away from the conference table. Carter was still talking, still trying to explain why his client suddenly didn't feel his estranged wife and his kids were worth fifteen thousand a month, but he could tell his argument was as hollow as brass.

"The bottom line is simple," Carter finally said. "My client believes thirteen is more than adequate and would be a very fair settlement."

"Fair my foot!" Lydia said, forcing her husband, Greg Myers, to speak up, too.

"You won't bleed me dry!" Greg yelled. "All about the dollar, that's all you're about!"

"We had an agreement, Joe," Thomas said calmly as he stood with his back against the wall.

"I understand that," Carter replied, less confidently this time. "But my client believes . . ."

Thomas shook his head. "We went through this over and over again, week after week after week. And we finally reached a settlement. Now you come in here with this new proposal? Forget it, Joe. Your client needs to either back off this nonsense now or be willing to face the consequences. My client is not changing, not one iota, what has already been agreed upon."

"I'm not giving that witch no fifteen thousand dollars a month!" Greg yelled. "She either takes thirteen or she can face the damn consequences herself!"

"We have evidence." Thomas said this almost too low to be heard, and both Greg and Carter looked at him.

"What evidence?" Greg asked, far less stridently.

Thomas, however, leaned his head against the wall and stared at them, his strikingly handsome face and athletically imposing body almost serene against their sudden distress.

"What evidence?" Carter asked nervously.

"The gambling."

"The what?" Greg asked, his rage attempting to return.

"The gambling. The associations. The infidelities."

"What the hell are you talking about, Drayton?"

"You aren't just a football player, Mr. Myers. You're a respected member of this community. Kids especially look up to you, because of that reputation. You've received good money from endorsements because of that reputation. But if you want a messy, public divorce, you'll get one."

Carter exhaled. Drayton's ruthlessness at work, he thought. Greg, on the other hand, looked at his attorney. He didn't know if Thomas Drayton was full of it or on to something. But he was a practical man, and he knew for a fact that the last thing he needed was negative press.

"We don't know what you're talking about," Carter said carefully, staring at Drayton, knowing that this was undoubtedly just the beginning because Drayton would never reveal his trump card this soon.

"Mr. Myers knows what I'm talking about," Thomas said. "So let's cut the nonsense, okay? And agree to terms."

Carter looked at Greg. Greg, albeit reluctantly, exhaled and then nodded his head.

"All right," Carter said. "Fifteen it is. But three child support and twelve spousal."

"Ten and five as agreed, Joe," Thomas said.

"Oh, Thomas, for crying out loud! What's the damn difference?"

"You know the difference. If my client remarries that twelve spousal is over. Ten and five as agreed."

Carter exhaled. "You're a hard man, Thomas Drayton," he said. "But all right. Ten and five."

"And the house and cabin?"

"Yes, yes. Everything as agreed."

Thomas nodded. "Okay."

Greg stood from his seat, glared at his irrepressible wife, and walked angrily out of the conference room. Carter stood up, too, but made certain to shake Thomas's hand before he hurried out after his unhappy client.

Lydia looked at Thomas and smiled for the first time. "Yes!" she said with a fist pump. "We got that bastard good!"

Thomas, however, didn't say anything. He walked to the conference table and began shoving papers into his briefcase. Lydia watched him. She watched the way his muscular arms pulsated lightly underneath the suit he wore as he grabbed huge stacks of papers in his big hands; the way his face, his wondrously appealing face, never showed any kind of emotion; the way his pure black eyebrows and uncommonly long eyelashes gave an enthrallingly dark definition to his big brown eyes and velvety brown skin. He was a delicious hunk of man, she thought, with a body so perfectly chiseled that she could hardly wait to get her hands on it. But in all the time they'd spent together, going over their strategy to take Greg Myers for as much as she could get, he never once came on to her. Not once! Since the work was now over and he'd gotten her exactly what she was after, she decided that such a pitiful fact just had to change.

"Isn't it wonderful, Thomas?" she said with great elation. "We hit him where it hurt. And I mean hard! Thank you, Thomas, thank you so much!"

"Okay" was all Thomas would say, refusing to match her elation. He felt sickened, not elated. His client was willing to decimate her husband in public, the man she once professed to love, the man who is the father of her children, just to gain a few extra dollars. Thomas was a thirty-nine-year-old divorce attorney who'd never even been married, and females like Lydia were the reason why. They knew how to pull the plug. They knew how to make that great, high-flying romance, where the sky was supposed to be the limit, take a sad, twisted nose-dive.

Lydia rose to her feet and perused, once again, Thomas's big body. When he returned her gaze, she smiled. "Would you like to have dinner with me, Mr. Drayton?" she asked expectantly.

Thomas looked at his excited client. He would rather eat nails, he wanted to tell her. "Can't," he told her instead as he locked his briefcase. "I have a dinner date already."

IN THE SHADOWS
OF LOVE

Thomas Drayton parked his teal-blue Bentley Arnage on a side street off Meridian Avenue and made the block-long walk to Solesby's restaurant in short, easy strides. The heavy night air in South Beach was calming, and the sidewalk was cluttered with young women in string bikinis, young men in extra-long Bermuda shorts, and skateboarders of both genders maneuvering their way through those bodies as if they could lose control at any moment. Thomas was dressed comfortably, too, in a loose-fitting pair of cornmeal-white casual pants and a long, matching shirt with an open V-collar that revealed his thick, hairy chest. He also had a pair of sunglasses hanging at the V, more out of habit than need given the evening hour, and he wore a pair of Gucci loafers perfect for slow walks. Females gave him looks of approval as he walked past, and he returned their favor with a smile of his own, but his mind wasn't on them—it was on this meeting with Jazz that Paula insisted they have.

That meeting remained at the forefront of his mind when he entered the heavy double doors of Solesby's, where it was just as crowded as the sidewalks of South Beach. The maitre d' approached him as he looked around, ready to tell him, undoubtedly, that he could not possibly add another name to the list of those waiting to be seated, and that was when he saw them: Paula Scott, his girlfriend of three months, and Jazz Walker, his best friend. They were sitting together and talking, no doubt about him, in a booth near the back of the restaurant.

He notified the maitre d' that he saw his party and then headed in that direction.

Although Thomas was pleased to see his girlfriend, it was seeing Jazz that caused his heartbeat to quicken. There was always something about Jazz, although there was nothing he could point to that was special about her that night. She was dressed in her familiar jeans and jersey, with a biker emblem on the back of her shirt; her fashionable eyeglasses were perched on her nose, giving her that almost unapproachable attractive look; and her hair was in its usual wild-cut, square-trimmed, bouncy Afro style that gave an incredibly sexy shape to her small head. She was even puffing on one of her beloved cigarettes, a habit of hers that Thomas despised, although he'd been known to take the occasional puff himself. But he always loved seeing her and hearing that deep, sultry voice of hers, the perfect radio voice, as Gerald loved to say, and looking into her beautiful eyes, eyes so dark brown they looked black, eyes that drooped into a beautiful, almost sensual curl that gave her the look of somebody not thrilled with the world, but bored by it.

Thomas met her almost seven years ago, before she even had a radio show, when she was a canvas painter going through her third divorce. One of the attorneys in his law firm represented her but became increasingly frustrated when she refused to seek a dime from her wealthy, soon-to-be ex. It became so bad that the lawyer asked Thomas, his boss, to intervene. "What's the point of representing her," the attorney asked Thomas, "if she's contesting nothing?" But Thomas didn't argue with Jazz. He, in fact, found her independence refreshing. Here was a woman, he thought, who could tell her old man to go screw himself even though she didn't have a dime to her name. She didn't want his money, houses, or land. All she wanted was her freedom. Instead of trying to dissuade her as his colleague had attempted to do, Thomas encouraged her and even took over her representation himself.

But working closely with the quirky Jazz Walker only made her more attractive to him, and he began talking to her with every intention of eventually having sex with her. But the more time he spent with Jazz, including great days where he had the time of his life and dark nights where he helped her overcome a burgeoning alcohol addiction, the more afraid he became of messing up a good, needful friendship by injecting sex into the mix. So he didn't. And Jazz didn't.

And now, nearly seven years later, including six years of complete so-briety for Jazz, the only lasting relationship either of them had been able to sustain was the very friendship they had decided to protect.

"There he is!" Paula said with a grand smile as Thomas approached their table. Jazz looked, too, at the unquestionably gorgeous man coming their way. He was a head turner to be sure, she thought, a man who was never cocky with the spell he put on women, but he appeared to her to be burdened by his gifts, as if the last thing he wanted was to be the center of somebody's attention. But how could he not be, she wondered, given the way he looked, and the way his big body moved, and the way his lips, his sweet, rich, sensual lips, began to part and open up a smile to charm birds from trees, a smile that just had to reveal itself and the cares of the world seemed to lessen; a real man, right before them, and although she knew they'd decided years ago to keep it on the friendship tip, she couldn't help but get goose bumps whenever Thomas Drayton entered a room.

"Hello, ladies," he said, lively himself as he leaned down and kissed Paula on the cheek. Then he leaned over to Jazz, placed his arm across her narrow shoulder, and kissed her on the cheek as well, his lips burrowing into her soft skin and resting there far longer than they had on Paula's cheek and then pulling off slowly, in a suction that lifted her skin into his mouth, her into him, if only momentarily. They looked into each other's eyes as he pulled away, as his hand slid ever so gently across her thin neck and caressed the nape as it departed. And the cologne that seemed to permeate every inch of his white clothing and big, muscular frame stayed in Jazz's nostrils like a sweet-smelling salt, and she wanted to close her eyes and fully experience the smell of him, but she couldn't. Paula was there. And she was watching Jazz like a hawk.

When Thomas sat down next to Paula at the table, in front of the drink she had audaciously ordered for him, he could tell, just as Jazz had when Paula first invited her to come along, that something was up. He looked at his girlfriend, who still looked pretty to him but not in that sexy way that drew him three months ago. Now she was aw'ight, as Jazz would say, because of her steadiness, because of her willingness to please him in bed—although she was no dynamo in bed, as he had always suspected Jazz was. But Paula was a reliable lay, somebody who once turned him on mightily but now, like a movie he'd seen over and over again, just didn't give him that same kick of excitement she used to give. He knew it was his problem. He knew it had been only three months and his sudden boredom with her body said more about him than it ever could about her. But what could he do?

Paula's smile was wide and grand but oddly staged, Thomas thought, as if she was being forced to smile, and when he looked into her small, contact-green eyes, he could see the pain.

"How was your day, honey?" he asked her, deciding that some things were better left unsaid.

"My day. Yes, well. It was a day."

"Don't tell me all of your beauticians didn't show up again?"

Paula owned a hair salon, and normally she loved it when Thomas showed some interest in her work, but her job was the last thing on her mind. "All but two," she said. "But their customers didn't show either, so it worked out."

"Good. Glad to hear it." Thomas said this and then looked at Jazz. His heart fluttered when her droopy eyes returned his gaze. "And what about you, Sister J? How did your day go?"

Jazz picked up her glass of ginger ale. "It was aw'ight," she said with a smile.

He couldn't help but smile, too. "It was aw'ight, was it? I caught your show. Some interesting-behind callers you had on your hands, girl."

"Interesting my foot. Crazy. Off the chain. Deaf, dumb, and blind in love. I couldn't tell those heifers nothing today."

"Don't beat yourself up," he said firmly. He knew her like a book. "You definitely got through to a few of them. You always touch somebody's life."

"Think so?"

"I know so. Hearing the truth is what those callers need. And you give it to them. You're hope for the hopeless, Jazzy. A friend to the friendless. And not just the crazies either."

"Did you check out that last caller?"

Thomas laughed. "Oh, yeah."

"She caught the man in bed with the woman, Thomas, in bed with the woman! But she still believes nothing happened."

"Yeah, and I'm Santa Claus."

"These ladies need to get a grip, boy, I'm telling you. I mean, that sister amazed me. Truly amazed me. That husband of hers could have told her anything. He could have told her that he wasn't a naked, cheating dog as it seemed so obvious that he was. Oh, no. He was a streaker, you see." Thomas laughed as Jazz continued. "He was naked, yes, he would admit that. But he wasn't naked for sexual reasons, that was the last thing on his mind. He was naked because he had to go streaking up the boulevard for political reasons, for the sake of civil disobedience. And I guarantee you girlfriend would have believed him."

"Would've probably asked if she could come along," Thomas added.

"I'm telling you," Jazz said with a smile. "Of course that naked woman in his bed should have given it away, but hey."

"You know better than that anyway, Jazz," Thomas said. "That naked woman wasn't his sex partner, she was his streaking partner! Now any fool could see that."

Jazz laughed. "True that," she said, then shook her head. "Yeah, they were streaking all right. But only it was more like stroking. Up and down and around and around." Jazz said this by boldly demonstrating the movements with her hands and hips, causing Thomas to laugh out loud.

Paula, however, failed to see the humor. "Y'all missing the point," she said. "It wasn't that she believed everything her husband said. She just didn't feel that Jazz, of all people, was equipped to be lecturing her. Not a woman who can't keep a man herself. I mean honestly. She understood there were problems in her marriage, of course she did, but she wasn't about to let the likes of Jazz Walker, after three failed marriages of her own, tell her a thing. And who could blame her?"

Jazz took a slow drag on her cigarette and looked out of the restaurant's window, her droopy eyes only mildly interested in the never-ending swirl of activity on the streets of South Beach. Thomas's heart dropped as he watched her, because he could tell she was hurt by Paula's put-down, but then Jazz smiled as he was hoping she would and looked back at him. "I almost fell out of my chair when she said nothing could have happened because he still had on his boxer shorts," she said.

Thomas shook his head. "And she seemed to believe it, too, poor kid. Believed it with all her heart. The gullibility of some people astounds me still."

"You? Please. I could write a book."

Thomas laughed again and Jazz tapped the ash off of her cigarette and rested her elbows on the table. "But enough about me," she said, looking adoringly at her dearest friend. "What about you? How was your day?"

"You see!" Paula said accusingly, and both Thomas and Jazz looked at her. "This is the reason. This is exactly why I wanted Jazz here tonight."

"You mean it wasn't because of my winning personality?" Jazz said this lightheartedly, but Paula frowned.

"Don't be coy," she said. Then she looked at Thomas. "There have got to be some changes made."

Thomas leaned back, staring at his glass of wine rather than Paula. Here we go, he thought. "Paula, what are you talking about?"

"I'm talking about you and Jazz. I'm talking about the way you show more interest in her job than you ever show in mine. The way you laugh so heartily with her when nothing's even funny. The way you *kiss* her."

Thomas glanced at Jazz, who quickly looked away from him, and then he smiled his wonderful, bright-white smile as if he had no clue what Paula was trying to say. "I'm sure I don't understand what you're trying to say," he said without guile. "I'm certain of that."

"Y'all too chummy, Thomas, you understand that? Way too chummy for my comfort zone. I've put up with it for three months now. Her calling for you all times of the night even when you're with me and she knows you're not available. You're always at her house, she's always at your house, as if the two of you can't get enough of each other. I put up with it. But not anymore. She's not your girlfriend, Thomas. I am!"

Thomas's smile remained constant, as he didn't quite know how to respond to Paula. And Paula, caught up in her own emotions, didn't give him a chance. "This is the deal," she said, to make herself perfectly clear. "Either Jazz goes, or I will. I mean look at me. I am too good a catch to have to take a backseat to anyone."

Thomas took a sip from his drink and glanced, once again, at Jazz. She was uncomfortable with this, maybe even worried, because once again Thomas had to choose between his latest girlfriend and his friendship with her—it always came down to this—but Thomas wasn't concerned. He even wanted to tell Jazz to relax, that she never, not as long as there was breath in his body, had to worry about losing him, and they made eye contact as if to confirm that reality. Jazz, his big, brown eyes made clear, had a handful of aces and needn't worry about a thing. Paula, however, had overplayed her hand.

"Jazz and I are just friends," he finally said.

"Good," Paula replied. "Then this decision should be easy for you. Because we're more than friends, Thomas, and if you value me in your life then you'll have no trouble telling your little friend to hit the road and stay out of our affairs."

Thomas's smile began to weaken. He had experienced Paula's brand of ultimatum many times before, from previous girlfriends jealous of his close ties to the eccentric but drop-dead-gorgeous Jazz, and he knew from experience that when they take on that attitude you can't even reason with them anymore. Now it was Paula's turn. She, like them, felt comfortable enough in the relationship to gamble. She, like them, didn't understand the stakes.

Jazz looked at Thomas, who, to her eyes, didn't seem conflicted at all. That gave her some comfort. But the look on Paula's face kept her edgy. Paula had become less confident just that fast, and Thomas's unresponsiveness made it even more painful to watch. Jazz looked away.

"What's it going to be, Thomas?" Paula asked. "Me, who happens to be your girlfriend by the way, or Jazz?"

Thomas sighed and looked at his girlfriend. A feeling of regret overtook him, of what could have been if only she would not have let jealousy overshadow her faith in him. "Do what you need to do," he said to her.

Paula hesitated in stunned pause. "What's that supposed to mean?" she asked him.

"Do what you need to do."

"But what does that mean, Thomas?"

Thomas didn't respond. Paula swallowed hard as fear caught her breath. "So what you're telling me, what you're saying to me, is that you choose Jazz? Is that what you're telling me?"

"I'm not ending a perfectly fine friendship because you have problems with my friend. Jazz hasn't done anything to you."

"She takes up all your time, Thomas. She keeps you so preoccupied with her life that you don't have time for a life of your own."

"That's nonsense and you know it."

Paula shook her head. "You choose her over *me*? How can you choose her over me? I thought . . ."

Paula could not finish. She looked at Thomas, and she was devastated. She never dreamed, not in a million years, that this would be the outcome. She thought he loved her. She thought she had made all kinds of inroads to his heart. Then she looked at Jazz, whom she never liked, whom, it seemed to her, always had the look of somebody who thought she had it all figured out because she was more beautiful and smarter and far more clever than any simple-minded *hairdresser* like Paula could ever be. And to make matters worse, Paula thought, Jazz seemed to be bored by the conversation. Paula's very life was in the balance, and Jazz was bored. Paula shook her head. She always hated Jazz Walker, she just never knew, until now, how passionately. And the thought that Thomas would choose that witch over her was more than she cared to believe. But she stood up anyway, and without saying another word she hurried out of the restaurant.

After a painfully quiet dinner, where neither of them seemed able to muster the will to even small talk, Thomas walked Jazz to the parking lot across the street. Unlike Thomas's stylish Bentley, Jazz drove an old '88 Ford Pinto, dark green, with a missing rearview mirror and only half a front bumper. Thomas hated the car and thought it wasn't a safe enough mode of transportation for Jazz, who loved to be out and about at all times of the day and night, but he had tried unsuccessfully too many times to convince her to at least let him buy her a car if she wasn't willing to give up the cash herself. But Jazz wouldn't hear of it. Her Pinto was fine, she insisted, as it got her from point A to point B most of the time, and she wasn't about to let him or anybody else spend a dime of their hard-earned money to remedy a problem that, in her mind, didn't exist. So he gave up, as he often found himself doing with Jazz, and could only pray that the heap she called an automobile didn't let her down.

Not that the car was the problem. It wasn't. Jazz was. She was the worst driver he had ever known, somebody who was constantly in minor traffic accidents as if she had no clue what she was doing. He had once hoped that if he bought her a new car she'd be more careful, given the money involved, but he knew now that was wishful thinking at best. And that was why, when he walked toward the car and noticed a fresh dent on the otherwise beat-up Pinto, a dent he knew wasn't there previously because, given Jazz's driving record, he always paid attention to such things, he was more upset than surprised.

"Not another accident, Jazz," he said, his face frowned with worry.

"What are you talking about?"

"That dent."

"What dent?"

Thomas didn't respond and just stared at what he was talking about. And that worried look on his face unnerved Jazz. He worried too much, she wanted to tell him. "It wasn't my fault," she said instead, her hand waving as if to brush it off as grossly insignificant. "I had the right-of-way."

Thomas looked at her. "What happened?"

Jazz leaned against the door of her car and pulled a cigarette from her oversized shoulder bag. "Nothing happened," she said. "Just a fender bender. A little, nothing fender bender. And it wasn't my fault."

"What happened?"

"Nothing, Thomas. Nothing happened. How many times do you want me to say it?"

"Did anyone get hurt?"

She rolled her eyes. "I know you didn't ask me that. Don't you see that dent? It's barely visible!"

"Did anyone get hurt, Jazz?" His voice was stern but in control.

"No!" she said, her patience with his mother-hen act quickly wearing thin.

Thomas didn't like the tone of her voice, and anger rose into his chest like a thunder clap. But he maintained his cool. "Was the police called?"

"Will you knock it off? I told you it was nothing. I told you it wasn't my fault."

"It wasn't?"

"No."

"That would be a first, then."

"Whatever, Thomas, all right?" Jazz said this with a snappiness to her voice that made him look away from her. Sometimes he felt like a sap around Jazz, like the brother who was all gung ho about a party he wasn't even invited to. His position of power in Miami was secure, as his success and influence and natural authoritarian style made men far stronger than Jazz quake in their boots. But Jazz had a way of cutting him down to size, as if he was little more than a nuisance to her, a pest even, and she'd be more than grateful if he'd just leave her alone.

"You okay?" she asked as his thoughts seemed far away from her.

Thomas sighed. Okay was the last thing he was. "I'm fine," he said.

"I think our friendship is costing you too much, Thomas. Too many lost opportunities."

Thomas frowned and looked at her. "Well, what do you want me to do? Keep Paula but get rid of you? Is that what you want?"

Jazz didn't know what she wanted, so she didn't say anything. Instead, she lit her cigarette and took a slow drag, the nicotine shooting down just what she needed after Paula's little hysterics. But she could feel Thomas's disapproval. When she looked at him she knew what was coming next.

"Jazz?"

"Yes?"

"Do you have to smoke?"

"Yes, Thomas, I have to."

Thomas threw his hands in the air. What a night, he thought. "Okay, fine. Smoke. Kill yourself. Why the hell should I care?"

Thomas released a heavy exhale and looked away from Jazz. She sighed, too, because she felt horrible. His girlfriend had just dumped him, all because of his refusal to give up his friendship with her, and she was as bitchy as she'd ever been. Thomas could be in love with Paula, for all she knew, his heart could be breaking at this very moment, and she was treating him as if she couldn't care less. She wanted to say something to him, to let him know that it was all an act, that she cared more than he would ever know. But she couldn't bring herself to say a word. Their relationship was strong because it was more about unspoken devotion, actions rather than words, and given her track record with all of her prior relationships, she was terrified of doing anything different to upset what they'd been able to maintain.

Thomas looked across the highway as busy Meridian Avenue

began to become even more cluttered with youthful, scantily clad bodies, kids who thought life was as easy as a Tuesday night out, and only one thing was clear in his mind: he was tired of starting over. He was tired of bouncing from relationship to relationship as if he wasn't a man about to turn forty who should have his love life together by now. And all because he chose to befriend Jazz. All because he had yet to meet a female who was secure enough within herself to accept that his best friend was possibly the most beautiful woman in the world. He looked at Jazz, at her biker jersey and bored eyes, and he smiled.

"I guess I'd better get going," he said.

"Already?"

She was acting as if she didn't want him to leave. Which would be news to him. "We can't exactly hang out in this parking lot all night," he said. "Unless you want to go somewhere else?"

"No," Jazz said quickly, not about to yield to any temptations tonight. "I'm tired anyway."

Thomas nodded, disappointed.

"Call me tomorrow?"

"Will do," Thomas said obediently and then leaned down and kissed her gently on the lips. Although it was brief, nothing more than a peck, Jazz closed her eyes. Thomas leaned into her, just enough to feel the tips of her breasts against his chest, and then he backed away.

As he walked away, Jazz got into her car, but she couldn't take her eyes off of Thomas. She watched him, with some degree of odd pride, as his tall, athletic body strolled along the avenue, heading for his expensive Bentley, as if he owned the night. The females knew it, too, taking sly glances at him as he passed, and Thomas seemed to enjoy the attention of the ladies for a change. He probably needed it, but, to Jazz's delight, he didn't entertain any of them and kept on walking. It had been years since Jazz had been with a man, opting to rely exclusively on Thomas's friendship for her companionship, because she thought their platonic relationship was more than enough for her. But lately, like tonight, she wasn't so sure.

It definitely wasn't enough for Thomas. She found that out a long time ago. He wasn't the celibate type by a mile, and since they both agreed that Jazz wouldn't be giving it up to him, she knew that he would always be romantically entangled with some woman. Which, she also knew, was his right. And although she wasn't crazy about that right, she wasn't worried about it either. Because she felt fervently that at the end of the day, when all of his romantic interludes were over, she, not one of his girlfriends-of-the-moment, would continue to be the number-one female in his life.

COMING TOGETHER
TO FALL APART

"Get out of my house and stay out!" Larry Lindsey yelled at the top of his lungs as he grabbed Alex Mailer by the arm, shoved her pocketbook against her chest, and heaved her and her suitcase out of his apartment in Key Largo, once and for all he declared, slamming the door bitterly behind her.

First she was shocked, as she stood there far longer than she knew made any sense. And then she got into her Saab and hit the road. He had some nerve, she thought as she drove those sixty-two miles from Key Largo to Miami, her high-revved sports car like a restless cannon darting across the Florida turnpike, the top down, her long, straight, jet-black hair blowing briskly in the wind. She didn't exactly love Larry anyway, before he showed his behind, and now she loathed the man. She even smiled as she drove, trying desperately to convince herself that she was glad to be rid of him, money or no money, sugar daddy or no sugar daddy, once and for all!

Nikki, her kid sister, had phoned earlier that day begging her to come, that she had some heavy news she just had to unload, and Alex agreed to make the journey to Miami to help her sister out. But Larry didn't want to hear it. She was going on a rendezvous to meet some man, he said as if it were a fact, that was why she was always running to Miami. Going to see about Nikki had nothing to do with it. He even decided that Nikki was Alex's cover, the phone call that spurred the plan into action. Alex told him he was being ridiculous, that if she wanted to be with another man she could think of a helluva better excuse than going to the aid of her kid sister, but Larry knew her. She'd cheated on him before. She was just a gold-digging user, he yelled, somebody who wanted to bleed him for all she could get and then move on to her next gold mine. He wasn't having it.

And Alex wasn't either. And that was why, when he told her to either stay home or not bother coming back, she gladly headed for the bedroom to pack her bags. His normal routine would have been to hurry behind her, kissing the nape of her neck and quickly apologizing. "I didn't mean it, baby," he'd say. What stunned her was when he didn't come. What shocked her was, while she continued with the charade of packing her bag and preparing to leave, he lashed out at her even more, his anger flaring like a sudden bolt of lightning and boring down on her. She was going to be with another dude, wasn't she? he kept asking, until she was tired of saying no and decided to remain silent. Her silence, to him, said it all, and he threw her out of his apartment as if he was throwing out the trash.

Now she was on her own again, with nothing more than a suitcase filled with clothes, a not-so-impressive bank account filled with the money Larry had given to her throughout their time together, and her aging but beloved Saab, with its convertible top that she let down for the drive. Her sister thought she was coming to her rescue once again, coming to get her out of yet another jam, but Alex knew better. She was coming together with Nikki because she had no choice, because something as crude as a change of heart from a man who claimed to love her beyond words, a man she could barely stomach anyway with his nauseating bragging and boring-behind life, had put her in the position of having nowhere else to go.

Twenty-two-year-old Nikki Mailer lived in a condo in Miami's trendy South Beach, a condo that looked more appealing outside than in. Outside it stood as part of a white, ten-floor monument to elegant living with small but functional balconies, always working elevators, friendly doormen, and slick cars of all makes and models stationed like leased image protectors around the front and side. Inside it looked like a pigsty, with clothes spewed about, dirty dishes in the sink, and newspapers and magazines and old romance novels in every nook and cranny of the small, two-bedroom home.

Nikki, in fact, was lying on the sofa watching the soaps when the doorbell rang. She was angered by the interruption, because the

Drucilla character was about to come clean, but when she looked through the peephole and saw that it was her big sister Alex, she flung the door open and fell into her arms.

Alex, who was five years older than Nikki but was considerably shorter and twenty pounds lighter, nearly fell back from her sister's embrace and had to make considerable effort to push her way inside and close the door. By now Nikki was crying, which disturbed Alex mightily because Nikki never cried. "What's happened?" she asked nervously.

Nikki looked at her. "What took you so long?" she asked.

"Larry started trippin', girl, I'll tell you about it. But what's going on, Nick?"

Nikki exhaled and walked back to the sofa, to get off her feet when she told the news but also to see if Dru really went through with her confession. Alex, who knew her sister all too well, decided not to press. She walked around the small condo that could have been right cute if Nikki knew anything at all about good housekeeping, but Nikki, Alex had concluded long ago, was their mother's daughter, a woman who would dress to kill every time she stepped out the door but who would have to blaze a trail through the filth just to get back inside that door.

When the soaps conveniently went to a commercial break, Nikki turned off the TV and looked at Alex, at the sister she grew up wanting to be just like. At five foot five Alex was exactly the right height, Nikki thought, and she had all the right curves and angles to turn on men, and she had those beautiful hazel eyes, the silky, jet-black hair, and a face, although similar to Nikki's in its small, round shape, that was far more sexy because her eyes were larger and her lips fuller and her forehead didn't have that protruded look the way Nikki's did, but smoothed down into arched eyebrows that looked natural on Alex. Nikki, on the other hand, saw herself, at five foot nine, as this towering figure, somebody who was only minimally attractive because of her slender body, but facewise and heightwise was generally more awkward than sexy. She admired her sister sometimes, envied her many times, because she had it all, Nikki thought, and knew it every time a man crossed their path.

"I'm listening," Alex said as she walked over to Nikki and sat down.

Nikki shook her head and then leaned it back. "You ain't gonna believe it," she said.

"What?"

"I just wanna put it out of my mind. I wish I could put it out of my mind."

"Nikki, what?"

Nikki exhaled and looked at her. "Ray Ray died."

"What?"

"He's dead, Alex."

"Damn, Nikki. When? *How?*"

"It happened last night. The cops say he was shot down in a drug deal gone wrong, shot down by some undercover cop, but I don't even believe that. I didn't find out about it until this morning when one of his boys came and told me. That's when I called you."

"Damn. Ray Ray's dead? Damn, Nick."

"I didn't wanna tell you over the phone."

"Ah, man, Nick, I'm so sorry." Alex said this and hugged her kid sister. Then she looked at her. "You okay?"

"Yeah. I will be."

Alex shook her head. "I hate to say this, girl, but this was bound to happen. I told you not to be fooling around with no drug dealer."

Nikki frowned. "He ain't no drug dealer, aw'ight? Yeah, he used to be. But Ray Ray been got his act together. He wasn't doing that shit no more. He's been legit for months now."

"Nikki, please. What legitimate work has Ray Ray ever done?"

"He don't be telling me his business, okay? And why you getting all hot with me? I wasn't selling no drugs."

"But you were benefitting from the sales. Ray Ray put you up in this condo. Bought you that Trans Am outside. You knew where that money was coming from, Nikki, ain't nobody that naive. And I told you a long time ago it was gonna end in tragedy, I told you that."

Nikki leaned forward, and the tears returned. "What am I gonna do, Alex?"

"You're gonna move on, girl, and live your life. That's what. I know it sounds cold, but you don't have no choice. Now I'm sorry about Ray Ray, I really am, but brothers like him dying everyday. It's the lifestyle, Nick."

Nikki paused. "He has a wife."

"What?"

Anguish overtook Nikki's small, round face. "He's got a wife,

Alex. I just found out today. All these months he's been kickin' it with me, I was just the other woman. She's got papers on his ass!"

"I don't believe this. Damn! Does she know about you?"

"Yeah, that heifer knows. She had some buppie come 'round here this morning talking about Mrs. Raymond Kravitz doesn't want me to attend the funeral of her beloved husband."

"No, she didn't."

"Yes, she did. But that's not all. She also expects me to turn over the keys to this condo and to the Trans Am as soon as possible because both are in Ray Ray's name and are, therefore, as her mouthpiece puts it, hers."

Alex could not believe it. First Larry kicks her to the curb and the only landing pad she had, Nikki, was about to crash herself. This was too much. She looked at her kid sister.

"So what are you gonna do?" she asked with grave concern in her voice.

"What you think I'm gonna do? I'm not about to be turning over no keys to nobody, and you know I'm attending Ray Ray's funeral, I don't care what some female I don't even know says."

"Now wait a minute, Nikki. Let's think about this for a minute. We don't want to antagonize his wife . . . ."

"Bump that bitch!"

"We've got to think this thing through, Nick, that's all I'm saying. I told you Larry was trippin', didn't I?"

"Yeah, you told me. Trippin' about what?"

"He thinks I'm cheatin', you know him. But he kicked me out today."

"Kicked you out?"

"Oh, yeah. He had a field day with my emotions, girl, you should have seen his sorry ass. But the point is, I ain't got a thing and now, neither do you. So we've got to hold on to the little you do have as long as we can. Your benefactor just died, my benefactor just kicked me to the curb, we've got to think more than one way, Nikki. And going up in that funeral of Ray Ray's ain't gonna get us nothing but a 'vacate immediately' notice."

Nikki leaned back and shook her head. "I can't believe this is happening. How can Ray Ray be dead? He didn't come home last night, but that wasn't no big deal. He almost never came home every night. But when his boy told me this morning, it was like unreal, sis. Ray Ray is dead? *My* Ray Ray? It was like I couldn't believe it. I still can't. Then that skank-ass female come laying down some law to me. The man's body ain't even cold in the morgue and she telling me what I got to do. Turn over the keys, she said. Yeah, I got her keys! And then she tells me I can't attend my own man's funeral? I didn't know his ass was married, why she trying to punish me? Why she taking it out on me? So yeah, I'm going up in that funeral, okay?"

"But, Nikki!"

"But, Nikki, nothing! Don't even try that, Alex! I will be going to my man's funeral, yes I will. And I will most definitely put on a show!"

Jazz Walker didn't realize it, but she was doing exactly what Thomas had begged her on many occasions not to do: she was speeding. This time ninety in a forty-five zone. The road that led to her home outside Miami, in Homestead, Florida, was dark, the night now descending like a swooping shadow, making it not only difficult for Jazz to see but even more difficult since she was not only driving too fast but was also fumbling with her car's radio as she did. She had been to an art gallery all evening, where she displayed some of her paintings to the proprietor who, at first, seemed interested, but ultimately bought nothing. Now she was antsy. She didn't like to waste her time, and hanging around for somebody to tell her thanks, but no thanks, was definitely a waste.

She wanted music to calm her back down, and she was looking for something, anything, other than those rap and hard-rock stations she kept turning to. A Latin station, playing an upbeat salsa tune, finally won out. But by the time she turned her attention back to the task she had almost forgotten she was doing, that is, driving, she saw a sudden movement in the road. It appeared to be a squirrel but she had to push her glasses up on her nose and squint her eyes because she wasn't sure. Something furry with a tail. She suddenly swerved her car—the idea of being responsible for the demise of the little fellow wasn't even a consideration to her—and it was a successful maneuver since the squirrel lived. But as she moved to straighten back her wheel she overcorrected in a panic, the feeling that she was losing control quickly becoming a reality, and not only did her now-swerving car wipe out the once lucky squirrel but it also ended up on two wheels, and then broadside, and soon her old Pinto was gliding across the dark highway as if it were some out-of-control toy of a car, sliding with no end in sight, until it finally came to rest with a glass-shattering slam into the mighty trunk of a lonely, wasn't bothering anybody, oak tree.

DON'T WANNA
BE LONELY

He thought he was in dreamland when he heard the ringing of the bell. He woke up with a start and then quickly reached for his phone. But when the ringing continued, and then the sound of knocking commenced, he realized that he was not dreaming but was being roused from a deep, peaceful sleep by some uninvited guest who aimed to be heard.

He got out of bed, threw on his red silk robe and house shoes, and hurried downstairs to his front door. His housekeeper and assistant, Henry Bonner, was also pulling on his robe and hurrying to the door from his room downstairs, but Thomas waved him off. No need for both of them to be disrupted, he thought. But when he looked through the peephole and saw that it was Paula standing there, he almost called Henry back.

"Hi!" she said grandly after Thomas reluctantly opened the door.

"It's almost midnight, Paula," he said as he leaned against the doorjamb, his entire body screaming for more sleep.

She glanced at his hairy chest and then looked into his sleepy brown eyes. "I know it's late," she said. "But this couldn't keep. May I come in?"

He wanted to tell her no and effectively end this nonsense, but the look in those hurt eyes of hers made him sigh in anguish—it was too damn late for this—but it also made him step aside and allow her passage in.

Paula entered looking, as she still couldn't get over the beauty of

Thomas's home. There was the winding staircase, the exotic African sculptures, the Tiffany lamps, the Queen Anne lowboy desk and side chair, the hundred-year-old Persian rug, and the original classic artwork, including a painting by Jazz herself that Paula could only describe as a bunch of lines and designs and hung at the top of the stairs. It was a home that took Paula's breath away when she first saw it, a home that she wanted to possess almost as badly as she wanted the home's owner. And both were once in her grasp. Both were hers for the taking. And she couldn't rest, she couldn't sit back and go on with her life, until she got back what was rightfully hers.

After she settled in and Thomas finally closed the door, they just stood there, neither saying anything, until he felt compelled to offer her a seat.

"I know you're wondering why I'm here," Paula said as she sat on the white leather sofa in the large, quiet living room. Thomas sat across from her in a chair. "I'm wondering myself, to tell you the truth. But I thought I should apologize, Thomas."

Thomas crossed his legs and allowed his hands to rest limply on the arms of his chair. He stared unceasingly at Paula, studying every inch of her face. He never knew her to be the impulsive type, and this late-night visit certainly qualified as impulsive, but he didn't expect her to be the type to hand out ultimatums either.

Paula continued, as it was clear to her that Thomas was not above making her work for his affections. All she could think about, as soon as she left Solesby's last night and at the salon all day today, was how wonderful he could make her feel whenever he touched her, whenever his big arms would ease their way around her and crush her to him, and how she was in serious danger of never experiencing that ecstasy again. "I want to apologize for the way I behaved at Solesby's," she said. "I was wrong to put you on the spot like that. I'm sorry."

Thomas still didn't speak. She was traveling down a dead-end road as far as he was concerned, and he wanted to tell her so. But he didn't. He stood up, went and made two drinks, handed her one, and then sat back down. He sipped slowly from his glass, deciding deliberately to wait her out, certain that in her babbling she herself would realize the futility of her last-ditch effort.

"I thought we were on the same page, Thomas," she said, gripping her glass of wine. "I thought you loved me the way I love you."

She said this and looked at him. But he still wouldn't respond. He cared about Paula, in a lot of ways he thought the world of Paula, but *love* wasn't a word he lightly tossed around.

"I thought you wanted this relationship to work," she continued. "Not because of me, but because you said yourself you was tired of starting over. Well I'm tired, too, Thomas. I'm forty years old. I'm not a kid anymore. I'm tired, too. That's why I came here. I think what we had is worth saving. I think we can get back to where we were."

"We can't, Paula."

"Don't say that. Don't say we can't, Thomas. We can. Unless . . . unless there's someone else."

Thomas wanted to roll his eyes. "There is no one else."

"Is it my age then?"

He was not in the mood for this. "Don't be ridiculous," he said. "You and I are practically the same age."

"Then what is it? I thought we were happy."

Thomas exhaled. She was overlooking the obvious. "What about Jazz?" he asked.

"I know she's your friend and she means a lot to you. And yes, I admit I'm jealous of her, okay? She seems to put a sparkle in your eyes I've been unable to match and of course it bothers me. But I promise I won't interfere ever again in your friendship with Jazz, because I trust you completely, Thomas. You're the best man I've ever known."

Thomas sipped from his drink and attempted to close his robe, which had gapped open almost to his navel, and it took all he had just to stay awake. This meant everything to Paula, if the expression on her face was any indication, but for Thomas, whatever she was selling, he wasn't buying.

Mainly because of Jazz. She would always be a major part of his life and he had yet to meet a woman who could handle that. And Paula, he decided, with her blatant insecurities, could handle it least of all. "I care about you, Paula," he said. "I think you're a good woman who can make a man very happy. But . . ."

"But what, Thomas? Please don't say but."

"But I think we need to go our separate ways."

Paula closed her eyes. It was the last thing she wanted to hear. "Thomas, I love you."

"I know that. But I'm not going through this again. My relationship with Jazz isn't going to change. She's my closest friend and she will always be my closest friend. And you've already made it clear that you can't deal with that."

"Yes, I can! I can now. I just didn't realize how much she meant to you or I would have never even suggested you choose between us, Thomas."

"You don't like her. Face it."

Paula hesitated. Lying had never been her strong suit. "Okay," she said, "I don't. I think she puts on this act like she's so above the fray, like she's so different from everybody else, when she's nothing more than one of those slick females who's been trying to sabotage our relationship since the day I met you. Yes I do feel that way about her. But I love you. Isn't that enough?"

Thomas exhaled. "It's not going to work, Paula."

"I can learn to like Jazz. I can learn to care for her."

"That's not it."

"I won't so much as mention her name again, Thomas, honest I won't."

"It's not about Jazz, okay? I just don't want the relationship any-more."

Paula knew he was lying. How could any man not want her? It was unthinkable. "How can you say that? You know you don't mean that."

"So you know what I mean now? You can read my mind now?"

"I know that Jazz has twisted up your mind so much that you aren't thinking straight."

"Okay, whatever," Thomas said as he stood to his feet. "I'll walk you to the door."

"Thomas—"

"Paula, don't do this. I mean it."

"Okay. I'm not going to beg you, if that's what you're thinking. That'd be absurd."

"Right."

Paula didn't like the tone of his voice but she knew she was fight-ing a losing battle tonight. The phone began ringing as she slowly gathered up her purse. Thomas, annoyed once again by these late-night interruptions, moved swiftly to the phone on his bar counter and slung it to his ear. When he realized it was Carmella's voice on the other end, his anger lessened into a sudden pang of anxiety. "What's happened?" he asked her.

Carmella hesitated on the line. She was Jazz's friend, a fellow artist who also happened to be a tenant on Jazz's property, somebody who couldn't afford to get out of Jazz's good graces. "She didn't want me to call you," she said quickly. "She didn't want you to find out."

"What's happened, Carmella?"

Another hesitation. "She's been in a bad car wreck, Thomas."

A sudden, heart-stopping terror stabbed at Thomas as those words he'd been dreading to hear echoed in his ears. He held on to the phone with both hands, as if the next responses were crucial to whether he'd breathe another breath. "Is she all right?" he asked slowly, nervously.

Carmella exhaled. "She seems to think so," she said.

"But you don't?"

"It was a bad accident, Thomas. Real bad. Her car was totaled and she was even knocked unconscious for a while. So she can't be all right. But you know Jazz. Against the doctor's advice, my advice, a two-year-old's advice, she's checking herself out of the hospital."

Thomas frowned. Jazz was the most stubborn human being he'd ever met. Damn her. "Where is she now?" he asked Carmella.

"Still here, at Baptist, but not for long. She's getting dressed to leave even as we speak. Her car was totaled in the accident, that's how bad it was, yet she's getting ready to go. She wants me to drive her home."

"You aren't driving her anywhere." Thomas didn't mean for this to come out as harsh as it did, but he needed Carmella to understand him. "Stall her as long as you can, Carmella. I'm on my way."

He hung up the phone after she agreed and then began the painful process of getting Paula out of his house. She still wanted to talk, still wanted to convince him that they could actually make it if they tried, but he wanted no part of it. He also didn't want to hurt Paula; she didn't deserve to be treated badly, but he couldn't think for worrying about Jazz. He knew how pigheaded Jazz could be. He knew she could be half-dead and still insistent on doing things her way. That was why, when Paula finally left, when she finally came to the conclusion that she wasn't convincing anybody tonight and walked on out of Thomas's door, he hurried upstairs, dressed quickly in a pair of jeans and a sweatshirt, and drove like Jazz to the hospital.

* * *

They had a screaming match at that hospital as Jazz refused to even entertain the idea of staying a moment longer, let alone all night, and Thomas couldn't believe how a woman of her mighty intellect could be this dumb.

"You need to stay for observation, Jazz."

"I said no."

"Just overnight, Jazz. That's all they want."

"I don't care what they want. I'm not staying here."

"But they haven't ran a single test yet, woman!"

"I don't care what they haven't run. And don't you call me that!" Jazz said this bitterly and Thomas, so beside himself with frustration that he didn't know what to do, threw his hands in the air and shook his head.

"Pardon me for calling you a woman," he said.

Carmella, who was also in the room, smiled.

"And why they need to be running tests on me anyway?" Jazz asked, anxious to move on from the silliness of her last statement. "I told you I'm fine."

"You were just in an accident that could have killed you, Jazz. It totaled your car. Remember that bit of information? They need to observe you."

"I'll go home and observe myself, thank you very much."

Thomas was livid but he knew he had to calm down. Jazz wasn't about to budge, she never did, so he may as well realize it and chill. "I understand you were unconscious for a while," he said calmly, hoping that his change in tone would slow her down. He was wrong.

"That doesn't mean anything," she said.

"It could mean something, Jazz."

"I told you I'm fine."

"Let them decide that."

"No."

"One test, Jazz. Just let them run one test."

"No. Goodness, Thomas! Stop making a big deal out of nothing!"

Thomas placed his hands on his hips and exhaled. Why does he even bother, he wondered. He looked at Jazz, his sad, pitiful, self-reliant Jazz, and he softened. "I just want you to be all right," he said, and he said it so heartfelt, and so out of the blue, that his words alone stopped Jazz cold in her tracks. And for the first time since his arrival at the hospital, she found the courage to actually look into his eyes, those expressive eyes that always told the story for him. And the concern she saw was wrenching.

"I'm all right, Thomas," she said with a sudden need to reassure him.

Thomas paused as he stared back into her eyes. "You sure about that, Jazz?"

"Positive."

"You told Carmella you had a headache."

"Yeah, I thought I did, but I don't."

"Don't lie to me, okay?"

And those words put the fire back in her voice. "Don't you call me a liar!" she said. "And I don't care if I had fifty headaches, I'm not staying here for observations or anything else. I know all about their observations. It's just a code word for easy money. A nurse comes to my room once in the middle of the night, while I'm dead asleep, and then they're charging me ten thousand dollars! Please. I'll observe myself in the comfort of my own home and it'll be free of charge and, if I might add, far more efficient."

Jazz then turned to Carmella, who was staring at the two angry friends. No two people could be more different, she thought, or more meant for each other. "Are you finally ready to drive me home, or do I need to call a cab?" Jazz asked her.

Carmella, a red-haired beauty with large, coal-black eyes and a short, man-cut Afro, a thirty-year-old woman from the island of Saint Croix whose accent was far less pronounced than many of her countrymen, shook her head. "My friend," she said, "I think you ought to listen to Thomas."

"Answer my question, Carmella. Are you giving me a lift home or are you not?"

Carmella looked at Thomas, who, it seemed to her, looked just about ready to either harm Jazz or hug her. Thomas hesitated before speaking, as if he was weighing in his own mind if he wanted to even bother. "She's going with me," he finally said, in a calm but firm voice. And oddly enough, at least from Carmella's point of view, Jazz didn't argue with him.

*   *   *

Thomas opened the passenger door of his Bentley and Jazz plopped down on the leather seat as if the last place she wanted to be was in his car. It smelled like him for one thing, with that sweet cologne smell that always seemed to settle in her nostrils and make her almost groggy, and it was always so damn neat, with a tray filled with the ash of those Macanudo cigars he occasionally smoked as the only visible messiness. Yet she was inwardly relieved that it was Thomas instead of Carmella taking her home; she somehow felt that she needed him tonight, but she was also determined to never for a moment let him know it.

He drove her home slowly, as if he wanted to show her how it's done, and the animated conversation that had taken place at the hospital was now replaced by a quiet affirmation of a truce. It was a hot, humid night in south Florida, and since Thomas didn't seem interested in turning on his AC, Jazz pressed down the passenger window and allowed the wind to blow through her already bouncy hair. She didn't remember much of anything about the accident, except the sound of sirens and muffled voices, and when she finally did come to, at the hospital, the first thing she heard was one of the paramedics tell the doctor that she kept asking for somebody named Thomas.

Thomas, she thought, as she took a sly, almost peripheral look at him. Easily the most handsome man she'd ever known, with the profile of a movie star, his big hands and big body seeming to her to be tensed and uneasy as he drove along the Florida Turnpike slowly, and she hated herself for the way she behaved at the hospital. He was terrified that she was hurt, it showed all over his face when he first arrived at the hospital and laid eyes on her, and all she could do was yell at him for showing up at all. One day he was going to realize, as she suspected everybody else already had, that she wasn't worth all of this upheaval after all and leave her, too.

Thomas glanced over at her just as she was glancing at him, but she quickly looked away. He reached out and placed her hand in his, to help relieve the terror that was still in her eyes, and for a moment she allowed the contact and even slid her fingers between his in an intimate interlace. But as if such a move exposed some deep weakness in her, she just as quickly removed her hand. Thomas looked at her, and without returning his glare she could feel his disappointment, but he didn't say a word.

His car eventually turned off of the dark highway and onto the long, graveled driveway of a brick-front, ranch-style home. He kept driving, past the home, to a detached garage in the backyard. They were now in Homestead, Florida, a small, wooded community on the border of the Everglades, some thirty-four miles outside of Miami, and Jazz, although she owned the entire property, rented out her house to her friend Carmella and lived very simply in the loft-style apartment above the garage. She initially rented out her home and moved into the apartment because, after her third divorce, she was flat broke and needed the money. Now, some seven years later, it was a matter of convenience rather than money. She was comfortable in the loft. The studio where she produced all of her paintings was in the loft. Carmella loved the house and took excellent care of it. There was no practical reason, it seemed to Jazz, to change a thing.

She looked over at the dark house as Thomas's Bentley lumbered by it and she could see that Carmella's car, an older Honda Accord, hadn't made it back. She was probably attempting to salvage what remained of her evening, Jazz thought, after being so rudely interrupted with a phone call Jazz now regretted making. But she knew she was in no condition to drive herself, was even terrified of some stranger, including a cab driver, driving her at this point, and if she didn't call Carmella to help her out, she would have to call Thomas. And she wasn't about to call Thomas.

Thomas could see that stubbornness of hers in full bloom as she got out of his car before he could open the door for her, and then she walked swiftly up the side stairs to her apartment as if she was trying to elude him. Why she hated him to see her in any vulnerable state was beyond him, but it was a fact. Whenever Jazz was in a bad way, even if it was something as insignificant as a head cold, she avoided him.

He followed closely behind her anyway, because after an accident like the one she'd endured he knew she couldn't possibly be a hundred percent. She was content, of course, to pretend that nothing was wrong and Thomas, as usual, was overreacting, but Thomas decided to overreact anyway.

When they made it up the stairs and to her front door, she turned toward him, as if a few words were going to get rid of him. "Thanks again for the ride," she said. "Good night."

She tried to smile, to keep up that *all is well* routine of hers, but the anguish Thomas saw beyond her smile told another story. He took the keys from her small hand and unlocked the door, their bodies standing so close that their stomachs touched, and Jazz quickly, but barely noticeably, backed away. Thomas smiled, she noticed, as he pushed open her front door and motioned for her to go inside.

She gave up. If he wanted to play the hero tonight, so be it, she decided. But she wasn't about to play the helpless victim. She walked through her small living room, past her small studio where all of her artistic endeavors—finished paintings and unfinished paintings—were stored, to her bedroom, closing the door behind her. She would lounge in the tub for an hour, she thought, and if he wasn't gone by then, she'd just go on to bed.

But her body wouldn't cooperate. She was wearing a T-shirt and a pair of jeans, a T-shirt that could only be removed by pulling it over her head. Her range of motion, however, was next to nothing, as the stiffness in her joints made it impossible for her to lift her arms beyond her chest. She tried, Lord did she try, but it was a fruitless battle. She felt so helpless, so stiff, so damn achy all over, that she knew she had no choice but to seek out Thomas's help.

He hadn't gone, thank God, she thought, as she walked into her small kitchen, where he wasn't all hot and bothered by her rude behavior but was preparing, undoubtedly for her, some herbal drink. He knew better than anybody that, although she'd been sober for six years, she was still a recovering alcoholic, somebody who couldn't be trusted in that department to so much as take a single sip, and he would always bring over odd, all-herbal drinks for her to try. In fact, he was so into his brew that she was able to come up behind him long before he realized she was even in the kitchen. His back was strong and straight and his backside tight underneath those jeans, and when he turned toward her, when his beautiful, cheerful face revealed itself to her, causing her heart to leap, she once again backed up. He smiled that devastatingly charming smile of his. "Hey," he said cheerfully, as if he didn't feel offended at all by her unexplained fear of him, "I thought you'd like something hot."

"I have coffee."

"That'll keep you up. This won't."

She paused, as if she just dreaded asking him for help. "I can't take off my shirt," she said.

"You what?"

"I can't take off my shirt."

Thomas, who was just about to hand her a cup filled almost to the brim with all kinds of herbs, sat the cup back on the drainboard and turned to her. "Come here," he said.

She moved closer to him but immediately felt at a disadvantage. He was so much bigger than her, for one thing, and when his hands began lifting up her shirt, he moved her closer to him in such a definite way that she could not resist his pull. "How far can you lift your arms, honey?" he asked her.

"Just to my chest," she said.

He lifted her shirt over the back of her head to the front, where she could then slide it off of her arms. She did, revealing an aqua-colored lace bra snugly protecting two large breasts. Although he tried to keep his eyes on Jazz's face, a face that seemed almost embarrassed to ask for help, he couldn't pull it off. His eyes trailed down her thin neck to her now beautifully enticing chest, and he could feel a surge of desire swish through his body. He'd seen his share of bras, more than his share, but never one worn by Jazz. He almost wanted to smile at how a man of his experience could get turned on this mightily just by seeing a woman in a bra.

But when she turned her back to him, revealing her beautiful, practically bare back, he was so enamored with what he was seeing that he didn't immediately realize what she was doing. Jazz, who hated that she had to tell him that, too, sighed. "I can't reach back and unfasten it," she said. Thomas, finally understanding, quickly unsnapped the two-prong closure and watched as Jazz allowed the bra to slowly slide down her thin arms. For both their sakes Thomas hoped she wasn't planning on turning around. He also prayed that she would.

But Jazz just stood there, as if too paralyzed to move. He didn't realize she was crying until he saw her small shoulders lift up and heard the sound of a muffled sniffle come out. And it was he who grabbed her by the shoulders and quickly turned her around, her breasts bouncing from the force of the turn. The tears that were in her eyes, undeniable, painful tears, broke his heart. "Honey, what's the matter?" he asked. It was the first time, absolutely the first time, that he'd seen her cry.

"My paintings were destroyed," she said.

"You had paintings in the car?"

"Yes. They were destroyed."

Thomas, however, doubted that the loss of a few paintings would be enough to make Jazz cry. She was an artist who created more work than she could sell and who never became emotionally attached to anything she created, believing that even the idea of an attachment to an abstract piece of art was the height of narcissism. No, he decided. It was a far deeper pain that was tearing at her.

But she wasn't telling. Thomas held her by her shoulders, as she stood before him naked from the waist up, and all he could think to do was stare deep into her beautiful dark brown eyes, eyes that didn't appear bored anymore, but pained. And he placed his hand under her chin and lifted her face to his. "Honey, what's wrong?" he asked her.

When she closed her eyes and opened them again, the tears that had been stationary puddles in her eyes began to roll down her cheeks. "I lost control of the car. I was trying to avoid hitting a squirrel, a squirrel, and lost control of the car. That's what happened." There was a pause, and then she added, "I hate losing control. I just hate it!"

She said this with such pain in her voice that Thomas quickly pulled her against his chest and wrapped her in his arms. At first she resisted him, as she placed her hands in front of her and tried to pull back, but he would not let her go. She stopped fighting, she was tired of fighting anyway, and allowed him to pull her closer, tighter, against his body.

They stood that way for a long few minutes, neither moving nor saying a word. Then Thomas began stroking her hair, as the feel of her bare back against his hand and her naked breasts pressed rigidly against his chest was becoming more than he could continue to ignore. She turned him on in ways no other woman could, and although he knew she was in pain, he couldn't help how his body was feeling at the mere thought of her in his arms. And Jazz could feel his heat, too, as his arousal hardened against her, but she could only stand there with regret that she hadn't met him sooner, before hubby number one, and then number two, and then number three effectively disengaged her heart.

She pulled away from Thomas. He looked down, at her big breasts and then into her eyes. She looked almost apologetic as she stood there, her shirt and bra in her hands, and when she said "thank you" to him, his heart melted. When he first met her nearly seven years ago, she was a battered woman. Not physically; none of her three husbands beat on her. But they had cheated on her and lied to her and misused every inch of her once free-giving heart and devastated her. Back then she drowned her sorrows in drink. But once Thomas became fully planted in her life, bartenders at her favorite hangouts started phoning him at all times of the day and night to come and get her when she had drowned those sorrows too much and could hardly walk, let alone drive, herself home. Carmella would get in touch with him, too, on those days when Jazz was too drunk to even get out of bed, and Thomas would drop everything and be right there. And he'd yell at her for not realizing the harm she was doing to herself, a harm far greater than any of those three scumbag husbands of hers could have ever done. Then he'd hold her and apologize to her for getting upset in the first place. Then he'd pour out every drop of liquor in the apartment. He even did an intervention and got her some rehab. But nothing worked. She was still drunk almost every weekend, painting horrendously bad works that weren't selling a dime, and on a sure road to ultimate self-destruction. But it wasn't until one moment in time, when she disappeared on a three-day drunk only to be found in some cheap motel by a private investigator Thomas had hired, and she didn't have a clue how she got there, that Thomas finally accepted the fact that his presence in her life wasn't helping her at all. He threatened to leave her, to put an end to their friendship for good if she didn't get it together. At first she didn't, she couldn't, but then, amazingly to Thomas, she did eventually pull herself together, turning to the church and AA for guidance, and she never took another drink.

Now she still drowned her sorrows, not in liquor or any other artificial stimulation, but in anger and defensiveness and constructed walls of self-preservation designed for the unexpressed but undeniable purpose of keeping her heart at bay.

He looked at her as she stood before him. She didn't attempt to hide her nakedness, as he fully expected she would, but she allowed him the uncommon pleasure of looking at her, staring at her, *wanting* her. But the walls were still there. Although he didn't see them, he felt them every time he even entertained the idea of Jazz finally opening up to him. And from his vantage point, it was a shame.

It was a shame to Jazz, too, because she knew she should trust

Thomas more. But the memories of her past were the haunt of her existence, and after three strikes where she thought each at-bat would be a home run, she personally declared herself out. And she wasn't about to swing at anymore balls of hope and promise, that ultimately landed foul, ever again.

She finally turned away from Thomas and his heartrending gaze and walked out of the room.

THE LAST RITES (AND RIOTS, TOO)

Alex's only hope was that Nikki would behave. Nikki loved Ray Ray after all, she thought, and the last thing she should want would be to turn his last rites into a sideshow. That was Alex's hope anyway. But when Nikki's Trans Am pulled up to the Mission Light Baptist Church in Miami's Carol City, and a group of females so hoochie-looking they gave prostitution a bad name came up to the car as if thrilled to death to see Nikki, to see that the show was still on, Alex's hope was gone.

Alex looked away from the females and back at her sister, who, in a dress so inappropriately short and tight, not to mention red, also had the nerve to put on dark shades as she prepared to exit the car.

"All right, Nick," Alex said. "Behave."

Nikki smiled. "You know me," she said coyly as she stepped out of the car. Her friends, the egg-on committee in Alex's view, started high-fiving her as soon as she stepped out. They knew Nikki, too. They knew that if the least situation rubbed her the wrong way, she would forget everything and go nuts. They were, in fact, counting on Nikki to be Nikki. Alex was praying for Nikki to be anybody *but* Nikki. And as Nikki and her homegirls hurried for the church's entrance, stepping high like foot soldiers gearing up for battle, Alex jumped from the car and hurried behind them. If anything goes down, she thought, she was grabbing her kid sister and making a run for it, she didn't care how uncool it looked.

The family of Raymond Kravitz, the "official" family that is, had not yet arrived when they made their way into the small church with its plywood pews and high altar. Nikki's movements became decidedly slower as she walked up to the casket and stared at the lifeless body of the only man she had ever truly loved. He looked like a bloated, bald-headed, hunched-up butterball to Nikki, and she wanted to get angry because she just knew his so-called wife had probably allowed the undertakers to make him look bad on purpose, but she surprisingly contained herself. She still loved Ray Ray, despite his betrayal, and she suddenly didn't feel like making a scene anymore. What would be the damn point?

Alex, too, could sense surrender by Nikki as they took a seat in the pews behind those reserved for family members. Nikki all but started ignoring the aggressive chatter of her homegirls. She was serene, hurt, the truth about Ray Ray's death a reality now. Alex relaxed, too, and began looking around as others strolled into the church and made their way up to the casket. One man who made such a stroll, a tall, thin brother around twenty-six, twenty-seven years old, in what Alex would quickly see was a nice but poorly fitting suit, locked his small eyes onto hers as he moved away from the casket. He, in fact, seemed unable to stop looking at her. Even when he sat down in a seat some five pews behind her, he kept his eyes on her. Alex could feel his stare, but she would not turn around until finally, when the audience was asked to rise and receive the bereaved family, she did glance his way. He wasn't exactly gorgeous, she thought, but rarely were the men who wanted her most, so she smiled at him all the same. And he smiled back. And that was all it took. Before the Kravitz family could even begin their procession into the church, he was standing beside Alex.

"I'm Conrad Baines," he said in greeting and extended his hand. "I was Raymond's attorney. One of them anyway."

Alex smiled. Ray Ray definitely got into his share of trouble and had probably utilized every criminal lawyer in Miami at some time or another, but somehow this Conrad Baines character didn't appear to Alex as the type to be the lawyer of a drug dealer. "Hello, Conrad," Alex said as she shook his hand. "I'm Alexandria."

Conrad smiled. He could see she was beautiful and exotic, but with a name like that he knew she was. "Alexandria," he said, his thin hand resting comfortably in hers as he unconsciously licked his thick lips. "How lovely."

"Everybody calls me Alex. They tend to find Alexandria a bit too much to say in one breath."

"Not me," Conrad said. "I just love that name."

Alex smiled, although she was obviously unimpressed. He was a little too eager for her tastes, she thought, as she gladly looked away from him and toward the entranceway. The family, led by Ray Ray's widow and her pastor, entered the church slowly. The widow was a small woman, around Alex's height and build, with a pretty face and large, dark eyes. Alex looked at Nikki. Nikki was watching the female as hard as she could, as if comparing herself to the widow and sadly discovering that there was a reason she was Mrs. Kravitz and Nikki was not. Ray Ray once told Nikki that she wasn't "wife material" and they had a knock-down, drag-out when he said it, but he would have never said such a cruel thing to a sister like the one making her way up the aisle. She was wife material, Nikki thought, down to the simple black but elegant shift dress that draped her petite body, down to the understated scarf that gathered around her thin neck. And the more Nikki looked at the widow, and saw her for what she truly was—the wife, the chosen one of the man she loved—the more her contained anger bubbled to the surface like grits in a frying pan.

"Some damn nerve," she kept saying under her breath as they all sat down and the choir sung and the preacher preached and the body of Raymond Kravitz seemed more and more like the elephant in the room. It wasn't about him, Nikki thought bitterly, but all about the wife. How patient she was. How understanding she was. How long suffering she was. Speaker after speaker stood up, but instead of eulogizing Ray Ray, they were heaping praises on Beth—her name, as Nikki finally discovered. Beth Kravitz. The good wife. The loving woman. The saint.

But by the time speaker number eight had said his two cents, once again praising good-old Beth, Nikki had had enough. She bolted from her seat and hurried for the front of the church. Alex tried to grab her arm as she swished by but Nikki moved way too fast for Alex's reflexes. The homegirls almost leaped in anticipation as Nikki moved away. And by the time she made it to the front of the church, standing there in all of her red-dress, hoochie-mama glory, Alex looked at Conrad and smiled and then sank further down in her seat.

"What the hell is the problem here?" Nikki frowningly asked the stunned congregation. "Y'all heard me! What's the damn problem?

Ray Ray is dead. Dead! A good man is gone. And what y'all doing? Y'all ain't praising him, y'all ain't even talking about him. No. Y'all too busy praising the wife, praising this bitch!" Nikki said this and pointed directly at Beth.

To her credit Beth didn't jump up. But other members of her family did, particularly the females who knew all about that illicit affair Ray Ray was carrying on with Nikki Mailer, and they bum-rushed Nikki and started pointing fingers at her. That got Nikki's girls up, who ran to the front as if the funeral was a rap concert, and bum-rushed those who were bum-rushing Nikki. The men in the church tried to keep the women apart, and they nearly succeeded, until one female, a big one they called Big Meek, slapped Nikki hard across the face.

It was the slap that changed the entire mood in the church. Everything stopped. And then it was on. No more talk, no more respecting the occasion, no more words. The line that took them from forced civility to an uncivilized free-for-all had been crossed. Chairs started flying, fists started flailing, and Alex jumped from her seat and hurried to Nikki's aid, which prompted Conrad to run to Alex's. The pastor, who almost seemed like a passive observer at first, was now beside himself with anger. "Cut it out, people!" he was shouting. "Cut it out!"

But nobody was listening. The pastor, it seemed, was as insignificant a player as Ray Ray in the casket, a casket that, eventually, was knocked over, too.

They made it home, in one piece, Nikki and Alex both still reeling from what was anything but a peaceful home going for Ray Ray. Conrad followed them home in his Jeep Cherokee, just in case, he said, those females had some ideas, but no one bothered to follow Nikki. Not even her own girls, who ended up with messed-up hairdos, torn clothes, and battered faces. More, they thought, than they had bargained for, especially since Nikki got off without a scratch.

Conrad handed Alex his business card as she stood by his car and thanked him for his concern. He wanted to come in, she could tell, but she wasn't about to allow it. The last thing she needed was some solicitous man like Conrad in her life right now.

"My office number is on the front," he said as Alex accepted his card. "My home number's on the back. Call anytime."

"I will," Alex said assuredly and smiled that charming smile of hers as Conrad got into his car and drove away. Alex then rolled her eyes and hurried to see about Nikki.

By the time she made it up the elevator to Nikki's condo, Nikki was reclining in her living room, but she had the nerve to laugh. Alex could not believe it.

"It's not funny, Nikki," she said with some degree of bitterness and plopped down on the sofa. "You've got that witch 90-hot. She'll probably kick us out tomorrow for sure now!"

"She's got to give me thirty days notice—she can't just kick me out! And it is funny, I don't care what you say. I showed that uptown bitch what downtown looks like!"

"Yeah, you showed her all right. Showed yourself, too."

"What's that supposed to mean?"

"Nothing, Nikki. Nothing at all."

There was a long silence as the two sisters, seemingly exhausted, sat quietly in the living room. And although tears began to come into Nikki's eyes, she quickly wiped them away. She looked at Alex, whom she knew was genuinely worried that their gravy-train days may be nearing an abrupt end, and then she looked at the card in Alex's hand. "What's that?"

"You've got to find a replacement, Nick," Alex said, ignoring her question. "And I mean like right away. This is no joke. We're in trouble."

"What are you talking about? What trouble?"

"Ray Ray is gone, okay? Your provider, a reasonably good one by the way, is gone."

Tears reappeared in Nikki's eyes. "He was so good, to me. He was good, period. That's why I had to do something at that funeral. It was wrong how they were trying to act like that woman was a saint for putting up with Ray Ray. I had to do something."

"Yeah, you did something all right. Expedited our demise, that's what you did."

"What?"

"The question is: What are we going to do?"

Nikki exhaled. She had no idea.

"I'll tell you what we won't be doing," Alex added. "We won't be sitting around here crying our eyes out over some dude who is long gone now, we most definitely will not be doing that. Ray Ray is gone and Larry, that weasel, has dumped me. Sad, but true. But unlike Mama, who called herself too in love with some scrub to move the hell on, we will be moving on, Nikki. Just got to find us some replacements."

"It's not that simple, Alex."

"I didn't say it was. But we've got to do it. Because the alternative, baby sister, would require a revolutionary move. Like getting our behinds a job."

Nikki actually laughed, and so did Alex. "I don't mind working," Nikki said.

"That's not the issue. No nine-to-five is gonna allow us to live in the lifestyle to which we've grown accustomed, so that's not even the issue. We're two beautiful sisters . . ."

"Please."

"You are beautiful, Nick. And we've just got to put our prowess to work and entice some nice, unsuspecting sugar daddy once again."

Nikki frowned. "How can you say that? That sounds horrible. Ray Ray wasn't my sugar daddy. He was my boyfriend, a man I loved. And I don't wanna replace him, all right? Nobody can replace him."

"Okay, keep talking. See how much of that talk is gonna pay your bills."

"What about Conrad?"

Alex looked at Conrad's business card still in her hand, then she looked at Nikki. "What about him?"

"He seems like a nice dude. Maybe you can try to win him over."

"Don't even try that."

"I'm serious. He likes you."

"And? He's just a young, upstart lawyer, Nikki. That's all. He can barely take care of himself. He's nowhere near the kind of sugar daddy I'm talking about. Because trust me, girl, a buppie like that? Please. We can do way better than him!" Alex said this emphatically as she tossed Conrad's card into the wastebasket.

WHERE DO BROKEN HEARTS GO?

The Drayton law firm was located on the forty-first floor of the RCN building on Biscayne Boulevard, in the hub of downtown Miami. Paula Scott, her gorgeous apple-red pantsuit fitting her like a glove, walked off of the elevator and moved swiftly through the elegant lobby and up to the smiling receptionist. But when the receptionist told her that Thomas Drayton wasn't in, Paula's own smile faded.

She removed her shades. "What do you mean he's not in?"

The receptionist hesitated. She thought she had been clear. "Mr. Drayton is not in at this time, ma'am. Would you like to leave him a message?"

"Leave him a mess . . . Oh, my God. Excuse me, but do you know who I am?"

The receptionist, a short, twenty-something woman with long, weaved hair, looked away from Paula. Having to deal with a drama queen this early in the morning wasn't her idea of a great way to start the day.

"Well, do you?" Paula asked again.

"I sure don't," the receptionist said with a little attitude of her own.

"Excuse me, but I'm Paula Scott. Mr. Drayton's girlfriend, okay? And I'm telling you your job is on the line, lady. So I would strongly suggest you pick up that little phone of yours and inform Mr. Drayton that I am here."

The receptionist sighed. It's too early for this, she thought. "Just a moment, ma'am," she said as she picked up the telephone.

Paula smiled. She knew that girlfriend line would get their attention. Now she would get some respect around here. Now they knew who they were dealing with.

The receptionist's voice became indiscernible as she spoke softly to someone on the phone. Paula assumed it to be Thomas. But by the time she had taken her sunglasses and slipped them into her Gucci bag, readying herself to greet him with a big bear hug, a female with a glide-like walk and a decidedly less friendly disposition was heading her way. The woman looked toward the receptionist, who nodded toward Paula.

"May I help you?" the woman asked Paula.

Paula held her hand up as if to halt the woman's speech, and then she looked her up and down. "May I help *you*?" she replied.

"I'm Janet Williams, Mr. Drayton's executive assistant."

"You're his secretary. I see. Fine. Now what is it that I can do for you?"

Janet glanced at the receptionist. The receptionist shrugged her shoulders. Janet then looked back at Paula. "I understand you're here to see Mr. Drayton."

"Your boss, yes. I'm his girlfriend."

"I'm sorry, but he's not in at this time."

"Bullshit!"

Paula said this so loudly that both Janet and the receptionist looked around at the same time. The office was fairly quiet, as most of the attorneys that worked for Thomas Drayton were either in court or in conferences, but some were still there and a few began to look their way.

"I would suggest you watch your language, ma'am," Janet said in an almost hushed tone. "We've told you that Mr. Drayton isn't in. There's nothing more we can tell you. Now if you want us to give him a message . . . ."

"Is she here?" Paula asked as she began looking around.

"Is who here?"

"Is she here, don't play games with me. Is Jazz Walker here? The great Jazz Walker."

Janet looked confused. "Miss Walker?"

"Yes! Is she here?"

"I don't understand."

"Is Jazz Walker in this building, woman, don't try me like that!"

"No. She's not here."

"She's supposed to be his friend, you know. His best friend. But I know better."

Janet just stared at Paula. She didn't know what to say.

"Look," Paula said loudly, causing many of the attorneys to look toward the reception area again. It was an office in the round, and the reception area was the center of the circle. "I don't know who you think you're dealing with and I don't care. Thomas is here, I know that much. He has no court appearances scheduled for today because I checked, all right? So why wouldn't he be here? Now I'm giving you two minutes. Just two minutes to inform him of my presence. And then you'd better pray that I don't tell him to kick all your asses to the curb."

Something was wrong with this woman, Janet thought as she gave the receptionist a look that made the receptionist quickly pick up the phone. Within a minute Wade Cobb, a tall man in his late forties, was coming toward the desk. He was smiling greatly as his eyes locked onto Paula's. He was the most senior member of Thomas's firm, but he'd never seen this so-called girlfriend of Thomas's in his life. Either the woman was lying, he decided, or it was just another testament to the way Thomas zealously guarded his private life. "Hello there!" Wade said as he extended his hand. Paula, to everybody's surprise, did shake it. "What can I do for you, beautiful lady?"

"Excuse me, but who are you?"

"I am Wade Cobb. I work for Thomas. Now what can we do for you?"

"I'm here to see him."

"Is that right? Well, gosh, dear, I'm afraid he's not here."

"Yes, he is. I'm his girlfriend. I know these things."

"And I'm sure you do. You've known Thomas long, have you?"

"She's back there, isn't she?"

"What?"

"Is that why you came out instead of Thomas? Because of her? But you know what, forget you!" Paula brushed past Wade and began moving hurriedly toward the offices in the back. She had never been to Thomas's firm before; he wouldn't allow it. He believed that mixing his private affairs with his business was a lethal combination. So now Paula was only guessing her way around.

She began opening doors and, satisfied that Thomas wasn't in a particular office, slamming them shut. Attorneys who hadn't given the commotion outside their offices a second thought suddenly came out to see just what all the fuss was about. Wade looked at Janet. "Call security," he ordered. And before Janet could react, the receptionist was doing just that.

One of the attorneys who came out of his office to witness Paula's performance was Conrad Baines. Conrad and a few of the other lower-level staff attorneys looked at each other and smiled. Their boss, who was extremely discreet, didn't even appear to have a love life from what they saw day to day. Now some woman shows up angry as hell, demanding to see Thomas Drayton or else, as if she's some jilted lover, and the attorneys couldn't help but laugh.

It was no laughing matter, however, when security came. Two men, big and beefy, had to literally chase Paula around the office until they were able to pin her against the reception desk. Wade, who didn't know what to make of Paula, was concerned enough to go up to her after the guards had her sufficiently subdued. The pathetic look on her face softened him. "He's not here, ma'am," he said with all sincerity, and Paula, as if suddenly realizing what a fool she was making of herself, closed her eyes. Wade motioned for the guards to release their hold on her. They did. And Paula, finally getting the message, didn't hesitate to leave the building.

Conrad shook his head and went back into his office. Love was crazy, he said to himself. And he started thinking about Drayton and how above the fray he always tried to present himself, when he was deep down in it just like the rest of them. It felt refreshing to Conrad actually, to know that even Thomas Drayton had weaknesses.

His desk phone began ringing as soon as he sat down. It was Mandy, his ex-wife. And the conversation was familiar. She and her new hubby wanted to take Ricky, their six-year-old son, somewhere special this weekend. This time it was Disney World. Only problem: it was Conrad's weekend to have the boy. Conrad was disappointed as hell, and quick to say so, but his ex promised to make it up to him. "I'll give you an extra week, Connie, come on," she said. Conrad exhaled. Ricky had been to Disney World probably seven or eight times already in his short life. But it was a place Ricky loved. And Conrad still loved his ex, he always would, and he could never say no to her. So he leaned back, understanding exactly how that woman who was desperately seeking Drayton must have felt, and gave in.

At the radio station Jazz was attempting to prep for her show. But the stiffness in her joints was making the task almost too difficult, causing her to spend most of the morning taking nicotine breaks rather than taking care of the business at hand. Gerald, who was also preparing for the show, could see it, too. But Jazz, being Jazz, wouldn't admit for a second that she was in pain.

"We can always run a tape, Jazz, and you can go home and get you some rest."

"I'm fine, G."

"You don't look fine."

"A matter of opinion."

"More than that."

"Yeah, well, what can you do?" Jazz said this as she reached for a pile of program notes on the desk. The grimace on her face, as that range-of-motion problem showed itself once again in her aching shoulder joint, caused Gerald to hurry to her side.

"You okay?"

"Yes! Just a little stiff, that's all."

Gerald shook his head. The woman was nearly killed in a car wreck just three days ago and she was back at work, in full force, as if nothing ever happened. But what else, he thought, should he have expected from Jazz?

He sat down his coffee cup and, without asking Jazz a thing, began massaging her shoulders. At first Jazz tried to pull away from Gerald, but it felt too good. She even leaned back and closed her eyes, her body relaxing under his gentle hands. Gerald loved it, too, as the feel of her fragile flesh caused him to want her more. He was, in fact, so into the massage, and Jazz was, too, that neither one of them noticed when Thomas Drayton entered their domain.

He leaned against the doorjamb and studied them intensely, his hands in his pants pockets, his expensive brown suit no worse for wear given that he'd just flown in from Arizona. Jazz was enjoying the massage immensely, she undoubtedly needed it, but Gerald appeared to Thomas to be enjoying it more. The way his hands seemed to rub her more than they massaged her. The way his eyes couldn't stop looking so adoringly at her long, slender neck. The way his body pressed against the back of the chair as if he was pressing against her. Gerald had a thing for Jazz, anybody could see that, but he was harmless enough. Yet Thomas couldn't bear to see even Gerald touching her so intimately.

He had been out of town on business the last couple of days and hadn't seen Jazz since the night of the accident—when he saw quite a bit of her. He went by her house as soon as he got back in town and when he didn't find her there, he just knew she was at the station, back to work far sooner than they had agreed, but he knew Jazz. It wasn't soon enough for her.

Yet Jazz's stubbornness wasn't the only thing on Thomas's mind. That accident had worried him greatly, as the thought of losing Jazz made him ever more mindful of his feelings for her. But seeing her now, as she allowed the hands of another man to relax her, made him more than just worried. If he could barely handle seeing Jazz with harmless Gerald, a man he'd known for years, how in the world was he going to handle that inevitable day when a man with far more on his mind than massaging her came into her life?

Gerald was the first to see Thomas when he finally looked up and saw a reflection in the Plexiglas. He withdrew his hands from Jazz quickly and turned around. "Thomas!" he said as if he'd been caught red-handed.

Jazz opened her eyes then. And when she saw Thomas, looking gorgeous, she thought, in his dazzling suit, and when he smiled that slaying smile of his, she wanted to leap from her chair, run to him as fast as she could, and fall into his big arms. But she didn't so much as attempt a move.

"Well hello there, stranger," she said, her voice heavy, raspy. A voice that warmed Thomas's skin.

"Hello yourself."

"When did you get back in town?"

"Just got back."

Jazz nodded. He came looking for her first, before he even went to his office. It pleased her and made her uneasy at the same time.

"It's good seeing you again, man." Gerald cleared his throat. "Where you been keeping yourself? It's been a while since I've seen you around here."

"How are you, Gerald?"

"Good. Real good. The ratings are moving on up there and management is pleased. I've got no complaints."

"The ratings are up? That's nice to hear."

"They're better than ever. We found out this morning, which makes me a very happy man. It's all thanks to Jazz, of course. Since she's been back—"

"When did she come back?"

"Don't you have work to do, Gerald?" Jazz suddenly interjected.

"Plenty," he said to Jazz and then turned back to Thomas. "Yesterday. Two days after the accident. I was stunned to see her, to tell you the truth. We could have easily ran old shows the rest of the week, but you know Jazz."

"Yeah, I know her," Thomas said with a frown on his face. He looked at her. "Two days after the accident, Jazz? You were supposed to give yourself a week, at least a week to recuperate. But you couldn't even do that."

Jazz looked at Gerald. "Thanks a lot," she said to him.

He smiled. "I talk too much, don't I?"

"Yes, you do."

"No, you don't," Thomas said. "She couldn't lift her arms above her chest, she couldn't undress herself without assistance, but she could come to work."

"Carmella helped me, Thomas, dang. I felt better the next day. If you would have bothered to give me a call and check on me in the whole time you were out of town, you would have known what was going on."

He wanted to call her. Every hour of each day he was away. But he assumed he'd only be annoying her, so he didn't bother.

"I'll be in my office if you need me, Jazz," Gerald said, as he could feel the temperature rising. "Later, man," he said to Thomas as he began leaving the booth. Thomas nodded, but he kept his eyes on Jazz. When Gerald was gone, he began moving further in.

"So you feel better now?" he asked her.

"Yes," Jazz said, although it wasn't completely true. "Much. In fact all."

Thomas nodded. Then he grabbed a small chair and pulled it beside Jazz's. When he sat backwards in the chair beside her, the smell of him, that wonderful scent she missed, made her smile.

"What are you smiling about?" he asked her, suddenly smiling, too. "I'm serious about this."

"I know. How was your trip?"

"Oh, the usual."

"Business or pleasure?"

Thomas was somehow offended by the question. "Business," he said. "I wouldn't have left town the morning after your accident, Jazz, if it could have been avoided."

"You don't have to explain anything like that to me. You have a business to run, I understand that. You have clients all over the country. You don't have time to be calling me and checking on me."

It was the second time she had mentioned his not phoning her, and it was odd to Thomas. He didn't know what to make of it. Maybe it was the accident. Maybe it was the fact that he had seen her crying—and half naked—when they'd never been quite that intimate before. But could Jazz Walker possibly have missed him? Could *his* Jazz Walker be going soft on him? The thought of it made him want to laugh. But it was too disturbing to be funny. Because if it was true, and Jazz was indeed attempting to let down her guard a little, it would certainly put an unexpected wrinkle in their relationship.

"I didn't see the point in calling," he said. "I knew you were fine. You're always fine." He said this rather snidely and looked at Jazz. Although she was disturbed by his comment, he couldn't tell it by looking at her. She simply reached once again for her program notes, this time refusing to show her pain, and began reading the notes. She was also biting her lower lip, a routine Thomas knew she did only when she was worried sick about something. But watching those lips of Jazz's, so soft and brown and sultry, made him want to kiss her. When he suddenly realized that he hadn't, in fact, kissed her hello, he smiled. He had an excuse.

"Anyway," he said, leaning toward her, "I'm glad you're okay." Jazz could feel his sweet breath against her neck as he placed his hand under her chin to get her attention and turned her face to his. They looked into each other's eyes in such a longing way that when he placed his mouth on hers, her entire body stiffened.

Thomas felt just as virile when he kissed her. And he wanted to do more than kiss her lips; he wanted to French kiss her, but in all their years together, and all the hello and good-bye kisses they'd shared, Jazz had yet to open her mouth to him and allow more intimate contact. She wanted it, every time his lips touched hers, but she didn't see the point. They had decided to be friends, not lovers, and she never wanted to complicate that decision.

But she loved when he kissed her. She loved even his little pecks. This morning was certainly more than a peck. He was kissing her with a lingering, pressing kiss, and it lasted long enough for him to remove his hand from her chin and place it on her shoulder, pulling her closer to him. Jazz could do nothing but close her eyes. Why did he have to smell so good, and feel so warm, and kiss so lovingly? But when she heard him groan as he kissed her, in that lusty, hoarse way of his, she opened her eyes quickly and pulled back.

"Where did you go?" she asked him, determined to stay composed. He was still remembering the taste of her and looked as if he had no clue what she was talking about. "Your business trip," she added. "Where did you go?"

"Oh. I went, where did I go? Phoenix."

"That far?"

"That far."

"Everything worked out then?"

"Inasmuch as it could."

Jazz nodded. And silence fell.

"How did you know I was here?" she finally asked.

"I went by your house after my plane touched down. No answer."

"So you just assumed I was here?"

"Yup."

"I am too predictable."

Thomas smiled weakly and stared at Jazz. She was dressed in a split-neck tunic top and a pair of baggy cargo pants. She was a sexy, shapely woman, he thought, wondrously shapely, but you wouldn't know it to look at those clothes she loved to wear.

"What's the matter?" Jazz asked him, feeling suddenly very conscious of his stare. She nervously pushed her glasses up on her thin nose.

"I thought we agreed with the doctor that you should take it easy for at least a week, honey."

"You agreed with the doctor."

"Jazz."

"I didn't commit to anything, Thomas. I can't stand doctors. I'm fine."

"Sure you are."

"I am."

Thomas gave up. He knew arguing with Jazz was like arguing with a brick wall, so he stopped trying. She seemed to realize it, too, as she turned and looked at him.

"I'm all right, Thomas," she said with some exasperation, because she knew that look of his all too well. "There's nothing wrong with me."

That conversation, as far as Thomas was concerned, was over. "How have you been getting to work?" he asked.

"Cab."

"Why didn't you call to see if I was back in town?"

"Because I knew I would have to listen to a sermon first. And I wasn't in the mood."

Thomas exhaled. "You make me sound just awful, Jazz."

Jazz smiled. "You're hardly awful, Thomas. Just overbearing at times."

Thomas didn't like the sound of that either. He shows a little concern for his friend, his best friend, and that made him overbearing? He stood up. "I'd better get going," he said.

"Now you're upset."

"I'm not upset."

"You are, Thomas. I know you pretty well, remember?" Jazz looked over her shoulder at him when she said this. Thomas looked into those big, droopy eyes of hers and exhaled.

"I assure you I'm not upset," he said. "I just need to check in at the office and get my behind some rest. I'll be back later this afternoon to pick you up. Would I do that if I was upset?"

"I've got to get another car, you know."

Thomas sighed. "We've been through this already, Jazz."

"And I still say it's ridiculous. You can't drive me around forever. I don't look like *Miss Daisy* to me. Besides, why don't you want me to have a car?"

"Oh, that's easy. Because you can't drive. Because you're the worst driver I've ever seen. Because every time you get behind the wheel of a car something happens."

"Not every time."

"Every other time then. Just humor me, honey, all right? Let's recover from the last accident first before we start worrying about the next one."

"If that squirrel wasn't in the road . . ."

"And if you weren't doing ninety, Jazz."

"Okay, okay. I'm not the most attentive driver. But eventually I'm getting me another car, now that's all there is to it."

Whether you like it or not, Thomas knew she wanted to add. "I'll see you later," he said as he began to leave the booth.

Jazz swerved her chair completely toward him. "No good-bye kiss?" she asked rather brazenly for her. She'd upset him, when that wasn't her intention at all. She was trying to make amends.

He hesitated. Sometimes he felt like a wind-up toy around Jazz. But she was one lady he could never so much as offend. That was why he walked back up to her, leaned down, and gave her a soft peck on the lips. When he looked into her eyes, his heart seemed to skip a beat. "It's just that I want you around me, Jazz, not wrapped around some tree somewhere."

She smiled a smile so warm that Thomas moved closer to her before he realized he had.

"I plan to avoid anymore tree trunks for a while," Jazz said. "I promise you that."

Thomas smiled and Jazz looked adoringly at his mouth. She wanted him to kiss her again. He, instead, placed his hand against her cheek, smiled once again, and left.

But he didn't go far. Down the hall, near the water cooler, was Gerald's office. He rapped lightly on the door and then peered inside just as Gerald was standing up to head out.

"I was just going to see if you and Jazz were done yet," Gerald said grandly. "We need to go over some production notes before showtime."

Thomas, known as a man who always got to the point, motioned his head toward the booth down the hall. "What was that about?" he asked.

"Excuse me?" Gerald asked, but when Thomas didn't respond he knew he had to drop the pretense. "She complained of stiffness, Thomas. That's all, man. I was just giving her an innocent massage."

Thomas nodded, still staring at him. Both men knew the real deal.

Both men knew that not a day goes by when Gerald wasn't wishing, hoping, praying that Jazz was his. "Okay," Thomas said and then, after another long stare as if to remind Gerald that he was watching him, so he'd better watch out, Thomas left.

Gerald, immediately afterwards, walked up the hall and into the booth, mumbling to himself. And when Jazz looked at him and asked him what was wrong, he fumed.

"He's got some nerve," he said.

"Who's got some nerve?"

"He can sleep around with any female in his path and that's absolutely fine. But let a man innocently lay a hand on you and he's ready to have a case. He's ready to fight somebody. Please."

Jazz shook her head. He was talking about Thomas. Thomas had apparently mentioned something to him about the massage. "He just wants to make sure you aren't up to no good," she said with a smile, playing off the seriousness. It worked. Gerald smiled, too.

"And what if I am?" he asked.

"Then heaven help you because what Thomas doesn't do to you, I will!"

Gerald laughed, although he could sense, from experience alone, that Jazz wasn't playing at all.

Thomas's Bentley made a U-turn in the middle of the road and headed for Carol City. He had just gotten word from Janet, his assistant, that Paula, identifying herself as his girlfriend, had been to the office earlier, "creating a stir."

"What kind of stir?" he had asked her.

"She wanted to see you and wouldn't take no for an answer. Security had to be called."

Thomas thanked Janet and then slammed his car phone down. He never, not ever, allowed his private life to become fodder for the gossip vine at work, and Paula wasn't about to change that fact. That was why he broke all speed limits getting to her. She knew better. Every girlfriend he'd ever had was carefully instructed on what he would and would not tolerate when it came to his public life, and Paula knew exactly how discretion was the most essential part of it. But just in case she'd forgotten, Thomas thought as he drove into the parking lot of the Elegant Touch beauty salon, he was just about to give her an unforgettable reminder.

The salon was located in the predominantly black Carol City on the northwest end of a, to say the least, rough neighborhood. Thomas, however, was oblivious to his surroundings as he parked in the street-side parking lot and hurried inside. Her staff greeted him warmly, although they had seen him only once before, and one female, the oldest one, told him that his "sweetie" was in her office in the back of the parlor. Thomas could only imagine the lies Paula had told them about the state of their relationship, but he didn't bother to correct their misguided perceptions. He simply hurried to the back office, knocked first, and then entered. His anger was palpable, but he was somehow able to maintain control. Paula, on the other hand, was all smiles.

"Hello, dear," she said. "I was hoping you'd come by. Have a seat."

Thomas, however, remained where he was: leaned against the door as if it were wedged to him, staring at this woman who was beginning to become a serious problem.

"You were at my firm this morning," he said matter-of-factly.

Paula wanted to deny that ghastly scene, but she knew she couldn't. "Yes, dear, I went by there. Just to see how you were doing. And before you get in a tizzy, I know you would prefer that your employees not know anything about your private life, including, apparently, your girlfriend's name, but I just find such an idea ludicrous. You come by my place of business all the time, I thought. Why can't I go to his?"

"This is only the second time I've been to your place of business, Paula, for one thing. You're not my girlfriend anymore, for another."

"Don't say that," Paula said painfully. "Stop saying that." Then she stood up and walked from behind her desk, the sudden desperation on her face unnerving Thomas. "I am your girl, Thomas. We're so good together. You can't just throw that away."

"I have thrown it away. Okay? It's gone! Now I'm warning you to stay away from me and my office or it'll be more than security that's called the next time."

Paula hesitated. The look in Thomas's eyes startled her. He wasn't understanding. He wasn't sympathetic to their plight. He was angry. And that angered her. "You need to get a grip, Thomas, all right? You need to leave me alone."

"Leave *you* alone?"

"Coming to my job like this. I can't come to yours but you can come to mine? Yeah, right. Do it again. That's all I'm saying. Do it again and I'll be the one calling security!"

Thomas could not believe his ears. He'd never seen Paula in such a pathetic state of denial. But he didn't argue with her. He merely looked at her and shook his head. "Good-bye, Paula," he said and hurried away from her.

Paula continued to stand in the middle of her office long after the door slammed shut. And as a smile slowly crept onto her otherwise expressionless face, her hands clenched into fists and her nails dug deeply into her palms, so deeply, so tightly, that she drew blood.

DOWN AND OUT IN
SOUTH BEACH

Thursday night on the town, a night out to cheer up Nikki after Ray Ray's unexpected death, and all hell broke loose again. It started early on, when Alex and Nikki arrived at a club so packed with wall-to-wall bodies that dancing was next to impossible. But Nikki managed; the bump and grind didn't bother her. Alex, however, wasn't interested. She found a table against the wall and stayed there, turning down offer after offer from young men anxious to get a piece of her. Those jokers weren't getting any feels off of her tonight, she decided. She ordered a drink instead, vodka, and decided to watch the action from afar. And she was actually beginning to enjoy the view. Until Nikki came hurrying to her table, removing her jewelry as she came.

"What's the matter with you?" Alex asked her.

"One of those females who jumped me at Ray Ray's funeral up in here."

"What?"

"That hussy up in here! Like nothing never happened!"

"Now, Nikki, hold on. Let's think about this."

"Yeah, I'll think about it all right." Nikki said this as she tossed her jewelry to Alex and began hurrying away.

"Nikki, wait a minute!" Alex demanded, but Nikki wasn't trying to hear her. She moved like a hungry animal through the crowd of bodies, her small eyes fixed on the woman they called Big Meek. Alex wanted to run to Nikki's defense, to tell that fool to stop being so damn rash about everything, but she was tired of running to Nikki's defense. If Nikki's mind was on fighting, no devil in hell could change that mind. And Alex knew it. Her only prayer was that cooler heads would prevail, that the sudden shouting match that began as soon as Nikki made it up to Big Meek's table wouldn't escalate.

It escalated, however, when Big Meek, just as she did at the funeral, got tired of talk and leaned back and slapped Nikki hard across the face. Alex jumped up as soon as the slap occurred, and without giving a second thought to her earlier decision to just stay out of it, she moved like a streaking panther to Nikki's side. But she got there too late. Nikki at first smiled at Big Meek's slap, as if she was expecting a better hit than that, and then she balled her fist and knocked Big Meek completely over the table. Nikki jumped over the table and landed on top of Meek, her fists burrowing into the big lady's flesh as if she was a boxer and Meek was her boxing bag. Alex tried to pull Nikki off of the female, and so did others around them, but it took two heavyset bouncers to wrestle control of Nikki. By the time they managed to pull her up and physically remove her, along with Big Meek, past all of the gawking club-goers to the exit doors, where they then slung them outside of the club and against the wall, the police who regularly patrolled the Art Deco district were already on the scene.

After some private conversations between the bouncers and the cops, Alex was horrified when one of the officers began slapping cuffs on Nikki but not Big Meek.

"What are you doing?" Alex shouted. "She hit Nikki first!"

But nobody wanted to hear it. Alex even tried to run up to one of the cops, to get his full attention, but the bouncers pulled her back. The facts surrounding the fight weren't the issue anymore as far as they were concerned. Getting that hell-raising Nikki Mailer away from their establishment was.

Nikki knew it, too. That was why she was resisting the cops with every ounce of strength she had. "Why y'all arresting me?" she kept asking them as the cuffs gripped into her wrists. "Because I won the fight? Y'all gonna arrest me because I beat her ass?"

"Just come on!" the officer said impatiently as he pulled her toward his patrol car.

"Oh, my God!" Alex said. "Nikki?"

"Get me out of this, Alex!" Nikki was yelling, trying to turn around. "Get me out of this!"

Alex was too stunned to do anything. She just watched in disbelief as the patrol car hurried away with Nikki in its backseat, hurrying away to avoid the riot-like atmosphere everybody was now claiming was all Nikki's fault. Alex looked at Big Meek, who was smiling at her, and she lunged at her, to finish what Nikki started. But the bouncers wouldn't let her budge. And they told Alex, not Big Meek, to stay away from their club.

Alex yanked herself out of the grasp of the bouncers and walked angrily away from their precious club. Her Saab was parked some four blocks away, and the walk in the heavy night air gave her time to think. Nikki needed a lawyer, she decided, or a bail bondsman or something, she wasn't sure what. But what she did know was that she didn't know any lawyers or bail bondsmen. And she also knew she couldn't exactly afford either. But Nikki, though wild she might be, wasn't jail material. They'd have her up on new charges just from her bad attitude alone. Alex knew that she had to get Nikki out of there, and the sooner the better.

Her only choice was to phone Key Largo and her ex-boyfriend Larry Lindsey. A horrible choice since she didn't want to have anything more to do with him, and he undoubtedly felt the same way about her, but where Nikki was concerned she was willing to make the sacrifice.

When she got into her Saab, she pulled the cell phone from her purse, ready to swallow her pride and beg Larry for help. And that was when it hit her. He was a lawyer. That sap of a brother at Ray Ray's funeral who couldn't seem to take his eyes off of her was a lawyer. And he gave her his card with his office and *home* numbers on it. But she had thrown it away, tossed it into the wastebasket as if it was of no earthly good to her. Now it was priceless.

She shifted her car into gear and drove as fast as she could to Nikki's condo. Nikki's place was still a mess, she knew, and she'd be stunned if the wastebasket had even been emptied yet. But she also knew her luck of late, and it would be just like Nikki to have decided that the one particular wastebasket she now needed intact was the one pile of mess she decided to clean out in the otherwise hurricane of a home.

*   *   *

Conrad was at home, in bed, talking happily with Ricky, his six-year-old son, when a beep signified a call waiting.

"I'd better answer it, sport," he said to his son. "It's past your bedtime anyway."

"Love you, dad."

"Love you, too, son. I'll call you in the morning."

"Okay," Ricky said and hung up the phone. Conrad quickly answered his other call and was stunned to hear that voice again.

"This is Alex," the voice said, just as sexy as Conrad had remembered.

"Alexandria," he said with a smile. "Hello. You were beginning to worry me. I thought you'd never call."

"I'm sorry about that, Cur, I mean Conrad. It's been a crazy week."

"No doubt, no doubt. How's your sister holding up? I understand she and Raymond were pretty tight."

"Yes, they were very tight. And she's not doing good at all, Conrad. That's one of the reasons I'm calling you." Alex swallowed hard. "She's been arrested."

"Arrested? What for?"

"One of those girls who jumped her at Ray Ray's funeral was at a nightclub and they got into it again. But the cops only arrested Nikki when she didn't even start the fight."

Conrad hesitated. One day he was going to find a woman who had no ulterior motives, who called him because she wanted to get to know him better, not get what she could out of him. But his weakness was good-looking women, like his ex-wife, like Alex, and their motives for wanting him almost always took a backseat. "Give me her full name," he said. "I'll see what I can do."

It was almost eleven at night when Nikki and Conrad finally arrived at Nikki's condo. Alex opened the door and threw her arms around her kid sister. Nikki, however, pulled away, her anger unabated. "I need a bath," she said. "You should have seen that cell they put me in. Like I'm some criminal. I wanted to cuss every single one of their asses out."

Alex rolled her eyes as Nikki moved swiftly toward her bedroom. Conrad shrugged his shoulders.

"I tried to cheer her up," he said with a smile, "but she wasn't interested."

"Thank you, Conrad," Alex said, heartfelt. "Thank you so much."

"You're welcome."

"I don't know what her problem is. It's as if she never thinks before she acts. She just do it and worry about the consequences later. And she's always been that way."

"She's the younger one?"

"Oh, yeah. She's my baby sister."

"Some baby."

Alex laughed. "I know what you mean."

There was a pause. Alex wanted her thanks to be enough, but she suspected it was nowhere near enough. "Would you like to come in?" she asked Conrad. It was no mystery, the way he lingered outside her door, that he was itching to get inside.

But he declined the offer. There would be time, he decided. "No," he said. "It's late and I know you want to be with your sister. Maybe another time?"

Alex smiled. "Yes. That would be nice."

"A week from tonight, for instance?"

Alex hesitated. Everybody got game, she thought. "Excuse me?" she said.

"Thomas Drayton, he's my boss, is having this big-deal dinner party at his house next Thursday night and all of us lowly staff attorneys have been invited. This is my first invite to the big man's place so I'm like really hyped, you know? But it'll be an honor if I could show up with someone as beautiful, and as kind, as you on my arms."

Alex smiled. The brother was a trip, she thought. But she also thought of Nikki and how she was going to need a lawyer more than just tonight, and payment, at this point, was out of the question. So for Nikki's sake . . . "Okay," she said. "I accept your invitation."

Conrad stood erect. He hadn't expected such a quick answer. "You sure your calendar can bear it?"

"It'll bear it."

Conrad smiled. "Well good. Great. Thank you."

"No, Conrad, thank you. You've been a tremendous help to us tonight."

"Anytime, Alexandria, you know that."

"Do I?"

"Yes. I mean it."

"Okay now. I'm gonna hold you to your word."

"Please do," Conrad said. Then he smiled. "This is, this is fantastic. You as my date. This is . . . I am above all men most richly blessed."

Alex smiled again. She could kill Nikki for putting her in a position to have to deal with some geek like this.

"So," Conrad said, believing he had won the day, "I'll pick you up at eight. Eight sharp. Next Thursday night."

"Thursday night it is," Alex said, and then, upon wishing him a good night, slowly but anxiously closed the door.

WAKE UP CALL

Carmella Crane came out onto the porch of the house she rented from Jazz and handed Jazz a cool glass of lemonade. It was already a hot day, eighty degrees before eleven a.m., and they both could feel the waves of heat against their skin. Carmella was dressed in a sheer, light blue sundress and seemed particularly uncomfortable, whereas Jazz, in a pair of green shorts, a pink cotton T-shirt, and a pair of dark green prescription sunglasses, appeared more relaxed. And it wasn't that she didn't feel the heat—she did—but she was apparently a little more accustomed to it than Carmella.

"I'm from the islands," Carmella said as she sat down on the bench swing and swatted away a fly, "but island heat is not like this heat. No breeze, no shade, no nothing. This heat is insufferable."

"It's hot, Carmella," Jazz said, sipping slowly from her lemonade, "that's why they call it heat. And eighty degrees is eighty degrees, I don't care where you're from."

"Not so. That is not so. It can be a hundred and ten in Saint Croix, but it feels like fifty compared to this."

Jazz laughed. "Yeah, right."

"On this I do not kid, Jazz Walker. There is a decided difference, no question about it."

"Well," Jazz said as she lifted her cold glass and placed it against her face, "it's hot as hell today, that's all I know." And as soon as she said this, the wide grill front of Thomas's beautiful blue Bentley turned in to the gravel driveway and began a slow ride up to the front porch. Carmella smiled.

"Gorgeous is here," she said.

"So he is."

Carmella knew Thomas even longer than Jazz did, when she saw him roaming around an art festival in Little Havana, and when Jazz needed a tenant for her house, Thomas recommended her. She and Jazz were both artists, he said, although Carmella viewed her job of postcard illustrations as hardly art, and would probably hit it off well. And as time has told, Carmella thought, he was right.

"I was checking him out at the hospital the night of your accident," she said, "and oh my goodness gracious. I almost went weak in the knees. That man gets finer every time I see him, Jazz. And he's so sweet, too. But you, of course, treats him like a stepchild."

"When he starts that mother-hen routine, you better believe I do. Like he was going to make me stay at that hospital. Please."

"You couldn't even dress yourself the next day, Jazz. He had a point."

"I didn't see any point. And point or no point, I wasn't staying at that hospital."

Carmella shook her head. "How the two of you became best friends is a mystery for the ages."

Jazz smiled and raised her glass in an imaginary toast. "I'll drink to that," she said.

Thomas's Bentley pulled up alongside the porch and he pressed down the car's window. "Hello, Carmella," he said as he removed his shades, his soft brown eyes glistening against the Florida sun. "How you doing this morning?"

"Just trying to beat the heat," she said with a smile. "What about you?"

"I'm all right. Hot, but all right." Carmella smiled. Thomas looked at Jazz. "Hey."

"Hey."

"Where're your paintings?"

"They're up here," Jazz said, and Thomas unbuckled his seatbelt and stepped out of his car. Carmella found herself moaning in admiration of his body as he began walking up on the porch. He wore a pair of brown shorts, a white polo shirt, and sandals, but all Carmella could see were the muscles, from his biceps to his thick thighs to his hairy legs. All muscle, she thought. All *man.*

"Where are they?" Thomas asked and Jazz pointed to the five paintings of various sizes that she had leaned against the porch rail next to her chair. Thomas placed his shades back over his eyes and moved in that direction. Jazz stood up just as he came near her and they kissed each other on the lips.

"You okay?" Thomas asked as he removed his lips from hers and squeezed past her.

"Yeah," she said and handed Carmella the half-empty glass of lemonade.

As Thomas carefully grabbed the paintings and headed for his car's trunk, Carmella kept smiling so much that Jazz couldn't help but smile, too.

"What is your problem?"

"You and he, the two of you, are still just friends, right?"

"Right."

"Kissing friends?"

"What kiss? That was just a peck."

"Yeah, girl."

"It was."

"Okay. Pecking friends then. You and he are just pecking friends then?"

"You can say that, yes."

Carmella shook her head. "You are out of your mind, Jazz," she said.

"What are you talking about?"

"I'm talking about Thomas Drayton! That beautiful muscle man loading those paintings in his beautiful Bentley. Women dream of having a man like that one. They would kill to get him. You have him and don't want him."

"Here we go again."

"Yes, here we go."

"Thomas and I have a great relationship, Carmella, the best relationship either one of us has ever enjoyed. And contrary to popular opinion by people who generally don't know a damn thing anyway, we are quite content with our relationship just the way it is. We aren't about to mess that up with romance, we don't care what people think. Got it?"

"Okay. I get it. But just to be clear: what you're saying is that he's your best friend but not your boyfriend. That's what you're saying, right?"

"Right."

"So what you're also saying is that if I want to go after him, since he's not your man, then by George I can. Right?" Carmella said this and looked at Jazz. Jazz, however, didn't say a word. Carmella nodded and sipped from her glass of lemonade. "Uh-huh," she said. "Thought so."

The Cumberland Gallery was quiet at noon as Thomas browsed the displayed artwork and Jazz talked softly with the proprietor about the possibility of selling him some of her paintings. She didn't like consignment; she found that entire process too unnecessarily involved. Her preference was outright buys. Abram Boranski, the owner of the gallery, a short man with a curved mustache, knew Jazz for many years and was well aware of her eccentric demands. He was also aware of her great talent, although, on this particular day, he was quoting prices to her that were way too low.

"I'm not in this for my health, Abe," Jazz said as if she couldn't believe the nerve of him.

"I thought you, like most artists, were in it for the love of your art," Abram replied. Jazz laughed.

"Yeah, right," she said. "Let's get serious, okay? You know any painting of mine will make four times what you're quoting me today, come on."

"Yeah. You're probably right. If it sells."

"It'll sell."

"If you want to do a consignment, fine. We'll split the difference. But an outright buy? I've got to hedge my bets, Jazz. We're in a recession now. People can't afford to be as careless with cash as they used to be. And so cautious they are! So I've got to be cautious, too."

Jazz shook her head. She'd been doing business with Cumberland for over five years now and never once did she leave them dangling with a painting of hers that didn't sell. It wasn't the money exactly. She painted because she had to paint, because she felt as if she would die if she didn't have that outlet. But it was the money, too, because fair was fair and she and Abram both knew he was being anything but.

"Let me talk to Thomas," she said and began walking away.

"Yeah, you talk to Thomas," Abram said in such a derogatory tone that Jazz turned back and looked at him. He was smiling, as if it was all an act she was putting on, but she turned back around and kept walking. She was a pro at ignoring rudeness, so she opted to ignore him.

Thomas took off his shades and placed them on his shirt just above the button-up when Jazz walked over. He moved in closer to a lithograph of an Italian village, undoubtedly to get a better look, and Jazz smiled. "Thinking about buying something, Thomas?" she asked.

Thomas didn't move an eye from the lithograph. "Remarkable, isn't it?"

Jazz looked at it. Then Thomas looked at her. "It's aw'ight," she said. Thomas smiled.

"It's aw'ight, huh?"

"I've seen better."

"I'll bet."

"Thomas, Abe's offering six."

"Hundred?"

"Yeah."

"No way."

"I know, but, I don't know, we are in a recession."

"We're always in a recession. Tell him no thank you if he can't do better than that, and then pack up your paintings and let's go."

"I hate leaving empty-handed, Thomas."

"Forget it, Jazz. He'll pay you what you're worth or he'll never be straight with you."

Jazz exhaled. He was right, as usual, but the idea of lugging around those paintings again wasn't turning her on either. Paintings are to be seen, not bundled up in a loft somewhere. But before she could mention this fact to Thomas, she looked over his shoulder and almost had to do a double take. "I don't believe it," she said.

"What is it?"

"Didn't you say Paula dropped by your office the other day?"

"Yeah."

"Well guess where else she's dropping by?"

Thomas turned quickly, because he had to see it to believe it. And it was true. Paula Scott, dressed ever so conservatively in a blue skirt suit, was standing in the Cumberland Gallery perusing a postcard display. Thomas let out an anguished sigh. "What is wrong with her?" he asked.

"She doesn't want to let you go," Jazz said.

Thomas shook his head. Then he moved toward Paula swiftly, his every step hostile and tense. "I thought I was clear, Paula," he said to her before she could turn around. When she turned around, his heart sank. She was hurting. He could see it in her eyes.

"Excuse me?" she asked.

"Why are you following me?"

"Following you? Why are you following me?"

"So I'm to believe that this is nothing more than a coincidence?"

"You can believe anything you want. But I know it's not. I think you're following me on purpose."

Thomas would have laughed if she didn't look so serious and so wounded. "It didn't work out, Paula. I'm sorry, but it didn't. So you need to just back off and go on with your life."

Paula, however, did laugh. "You have some nerve. Is this how you expect to win me over? With this reverse psychology nonsense? You stalk me and then blame it on me? Is that your game, Thomas? Well, I'll have you to know that you'll have to do a lot better than this to regain my affections. A lot better. I'm not that naive."

Thomas stood there stunned, his every instinct telling him to make a scene, to make it undeniably clear that he's done with her. But he couldn't do it. She still believed she loved him. She still believed that what they used to have will return intact if only he would believe it, too. He folded his arms. She couldn't be that delusional, he decided. "It's over, Paula. You know it and I know it. So let's cut the charade, all right?"

Paula quickly tossed a postcard she had been browsing back onto the rack. "Fine," she said. "I don't like games either. So this is the deal. If you want to come see me tonight, I'll be at home. We can talk then. Maybe have a nice quiet dinner together. Otherwise, I want you to leave me alone. I am too good looking and too good a catch to even consider giving you more than this one chance." She said her last line in almost a whisper, then she turned away from Thomas, brushing against him as she did, and walked out of the gallery. Thomas just stood there, staring after her. Even Jazz coming over to him didn't break his stare.

"What did she want?" Jazz asked. "Other than the obvious, of course."

"She wants me to stop stalking her," Thomas said and then looked at Jazz. Jazz quickly let out a great laugh. The best Thomas could manage, however, was a faint smile.

Jazz, eventually, went back to her negotiations with Abram and Thomas continued his browsing. He still couldn't stop thinking about Paula and how serious she seemed, as if her crazy insinuations about him wanting her were actually true. She seemed nothing like the woman he thought he knew. That woman was thoughtful and mature and sweet. This new woman, however, was almost mind-boggling.

But not so mind-boggling that he didn't notice another woman who continually took peeps at him. Although women gave him peeps all of the time, and he was accustomed to it, this particular woman with her long, attractive face and big, pretty eyes, looked familiar. And when she finally began walking toward him, he knew he had seen her before, may have even gone out on a date with her before, but he couldn't recall her name or any of the circumstances regarding their past encounter.

"Hi," she said with a soft voice. He remembered that voice.

"How are you?"

"Good." There was a pause. "My, it's been a while."

"Yes, it has."

"I never thought I'd see you again. How have you been, Thomas?"

"I've been okay. You're certainly looking good."

She didn't respond. She just stared at him.

"The weather's been holding pretty consistent of late," he said, seeking to lighten her mood. It worked.

"Yeah," she said with a weak smile. "That's south Florida for ya. Hot and hotter."

"And with no end in sight."

She tried to respond to that, to keep the conversation moving, but no words would come. And then silence fell. After a long few moments of such uncomfortable quietness, the woman's once warm smile took on a cynical look. "You don't remember me," she said as if she was just coming to the realization herself, "do you?"

Thomas swallowed hard. She was somebody he should have remembered. But for the life of him, he couldn't. "No," he finally said.

She nodded, and as if they had been waiting there all along, tears suddenly appeared in her eyes. "That's rich," she said.

"Excuse me?" he asked.

"You broke my heart, and you don't even remember my name. Now that's rich." She said this as if it were some hard truth and then, before Thomas could say a word, could offer an apology, could find out for himself who the heck she was, she moved away from him as if he had a contagious disease and hurried out of the gallery.

First Paula. Now her. Thomas suddenly felt as if karma was knocking at his door at the most inopportune time in his life. All the women he'd known; all the break-ups and disappointments; all the decisions he'd made to just disappear from their lives, as if leaving them was best for them, seemed to be coming back at him in spades. As if it was his time to anguish. As if it was his time to feel the flip side of all of those supposedly thoughtful decisions of his to end the relationship before it had a real chance to go south on its own. It was his time now. That was why, as emotions he didn't care to entertain attempted to lay some claim on him, he turned quickly and then around again, in search of Jazz.

By the time they loaded Jazz's paintings back into the trunk of the Bentley and were on the road again, Jazz couldn't help but notice Thomas's somber mood.

"Who was that woman you were talking with?" she asked him.

He shook his head. "I don't know."

Jazz smiled. "You don't know? How could you not know? She was crying, Thomas."

"Yes, she was."

"Then who was she?"

"What did I say, Jazz? I don't know." He said this snappily and then glanced at his friend.

Jazz, at first, started to ignore him. He was in a pissy mood, then fine, she thought. See if she cared. But she did care.

"What's the matter?" she asked him. But he didn't respond. "What's the matter, Thomas?"

"I didn't know her name."

Jazz hesitated, as if she'd missed something. "Say again?"

"That woman. I didn't know anything about her. I broke her heart, she said, and I don't have the slightest idea who the hell she is." He slung his Bentley around a winding curve and then let out a great sigh of exasperation. "I'm getting too old for this craziness, Jazz," he said. "I can't keep living like this. I need to get myself a wife and settle my behind down."

Jazz looked at her friend, and now she was stunned. She'd never heard him speak this way before. A wife? For Thomas? That didn't even sound right. Because how could she remain the number one female in his life, or in his life at all given the closeness of their relationship, if he was to get a wife?

THE THOMAS DRAYTON AFFAIR

Alex and Nikki plopped down on the sofa, exhausted, and looked at the room around them. Nikki smiled. "It looks so different," she said.

"This is what cleaning up can do," Alex said, as if Nikki didn't understand. "The clutter's gone. It's livable again."

"All the good it'll do us. Ray Ray's so-called wife has given me thirty days to vacate the premises, remember? Like she owns something."

"Well, technically, Nikki, she does." Then Alex shook her head. "I can't believe you didn't make Ray Ray put your name on the deed, girl. What were you thinking?"

"I didn't think he'd be dead, that's for sure. And maybe, I don't know. Maybe I didn't want all that responsibility."

"All what responsibility?" Alex asked frowningly. "It would have beat the hell out of moving, finding another place to stay, when you ain't got a dime and my savings are dwindling fast."

"I still can't believe he's gone, Alex. I loved him so much."

"I know you did, Nikki, I know you did. But you need to back up a minute and listen to what I'm saying. You cannot afford to sit up in here pining away over no Ray Ray. Okay? Now I know you loved him, and I know you're grieving his death. But you have got to snap out of it."

"It's not that simple."

"Yes, it is! Remember Mama? Remember Carlton? She loved him

to death, too. And when he hit the road she had nothing left—nothing but a broken heart. Just like you right now. And for the rest of her life all she could do was wait for that sorry-ass Carlton to return, as if he was worth a damn. Instead of moving on and finding her a real man to take care of her, she was waiting on Carlton. *Carlton,* Nikki! Please."

Nikki shook her head. "We're no better than hookers," she said before she realized she had said it, and Alex gave her a harsh, cutting look.

"What did you say?"

"The way we rely on men for support. The way a man got to take care of us. What's the difference between us and hookers?"

"Plenty, Nikki, don't even try that. We don't be on nobody's street corner begging no man, okay? Hell, they be begging us! And yeah we make them put up the cash, this ain't no welfare we handing out. Ain't nothing free here. We give them our heart and they pay for the privilege. They pay for it, that's right. That's the least their asses can do!"

Nikki mumbled something too low for Alex to hear and Alex gave her another sharp look.

"What was that?"

"Nothing."

"What, Nikki?"

"You said we don't be begging on no street corner."

"That's right."

"You ain't got to stand on no street corner to be a ho, Alex."

Alex just stared at Nikki, her anger attempting to emerge, but she contained it. "We're not hos or hookers or anything like that, all right? We're smart, resourceful businesswomen."

"Businesswomen?"

"Yes! This is a business we're in."

"But I loved Ray Ray, Alex. I can't help that. It wasn't about business to me. And I don't want another man, not right now."

"So it's Mama all over again. First Carlton did it to her, now Ray Ray's doing it to you. Ray Ray of all people. A man who was married, by the way, and you didn't even know it; a man who cared so much for your ass that he made no provisions whatsoever for you! Now his wife, that's right, his *wife,* is about to take your house and your car and put your grieving behind on the street. Where you gonna go? What you gonna do? You haven't worked on a job since tenth grade, Nikki, let's get real here, all right? You have zero skills! Mama ended up poor, alone, and brokenhearted. She forgot that love was a business, not an emotion. Love is our family business. She forgot all about that. But I'll tell you this, Nikki, it'll be a cold day in hell before we forget!"

Alex said this and leaned back. Nikki leaned forward, unable to stop the tears now. She knew everything Alex said was true. She knew she couldn't live the kind of life she was now accustomed to living, not if it was left up to her skills. But she also knew she was devastated, and she couldn't deal with another heartbreak. She wasn't like Alex. She couldn't have a man she didn't love. She always fell in love! Even with a man who chose another woman to be his wife.

The doorbell rang. Nikki wiped her tears away and Alex went to answer the ring. "Who the devil is this?" she asked as she hurried for the door. When she saw that it was Conrad, she rolled her eyes. But she opened the door.

He smiled and licked his large lips. "Hello, pretty lady."

"Hey," Alex said with little enthusiasm.

Conrad looked down at Alex's casual attire. "You forgot?" he asked her.

"Forgot what?"

Conrad could have dropped the smile, that's how disappointed he was, but he didn't. "I told you my boss was having a dinner party tonight. Remember?"

"Oh, yeah," Alex said, vaguely remembering.

"You agreed to go with me."

She did, when she was grateful for his help with Nikki. But he'd already managed to get the charges dropped on Nikki, convincing the prosecution that very next day that taking such a flimsy case to court, where there were no injuries, no reportable damage, and different witnesses telling different versions of who hit whom first, would be a total waste of the state's time and money. He'd therefore already fulfilled the purpose Alex needed him to fulfill. So now, she felt, she could afford to be honest with the brother. "I really don't feel like going anywhere tonight, Conrad," she said. "Me and Nikki just chillin' and that's all I wanna do."

Conrad was extremely disappointed. He had done nothing but think about this night since she accepted his invitation. That was

why he worked so hard to exonerate Nikki. That was why he purchased this expensive suit Alex didn't even seem to notice. "I think
you'll enjoy yourself," he said almost halfheartedly.

Alex smiled. "I doubt that."

"I don't know. You might. That'll be a live band and great food,
and some of the most influential folks in Miami will be there."

"I told you I don't . . ." Alex finally heard what Conrad was saying. "Influential?"

Conrad, sensing that he was on to something, perked up. "Very,"
he said. "Mr. Drayton is well respected in this town. I've never been
to one of his parties, I've never been invited before to tell you the
truth, but I've heard he puts on an elegant show."

Alex hesitated and then said, as if thinking aloud, "You know
what? It may just be interesting after all. And elegant, too? Yeah, I
can see where it might be well worth it. Besides," she added, perking
up herself, "I can use a night out. Come in. Come on in, Conrad!"

And Conrad gladly went in. For him, it was going to be the perfect date. A woman like Alex on his arms. A woman too beautiful for
words. For Alex, it wasn't what she'd call a date at all. In her mind,
it was going to be more like the perfect fishing expedition.

The cab drove slowly up a long, winding driveway that led to a
circular curve. Jazz paid the driver and quickly stepped out. She looked
up at the Drayton home, at the elongated steps leading up to an elongated porch that whirled around to either side of the house; at the
big, fat columns out front and the gazebo-style windows upstairs; at
the brick front of a home that reminded Jazz of a bank. And all she
could think to do was shake her head. All this house for one man,
she thought, while she lived in a hovel. Men, she thought, as she walked
up the steps. Whatever they had, it had to be *big*.

She rang the doorbell, smiling at the numerous chimes just one
ring could make. Henry, Thomas's fifty-something, able, but often
nervous assistant, smiled when he saw that it was Jazz. "Thank God
it's you," he said. "I thought you were an early arriving guest. We
aren't nearly ready yet."

"How are you, Hank?"

"I'm very well, Jazz. Come in."

Jazz stepped inside amidst a flurry of activity, from caterers to
flower people to maids and servers alike, dropping vases and running

into each other and yelling across the room, as if Thomas's house was a veritable zoo. "It's crazy up in here," she said with a smile.

"This is calm compared to earlier," Henry said. "Trust me."

"Dang. I hated to see it then. Where's Thomas?"

"Upstairs."

"Good," Jazz said as she hurried toward the winding staircase, glad to be out of the way of the nerve-racking scene.

Up the stairs, past one of her paintings Thomas so proudly displayed at the top, the master suite was next to last down the hall. She could smell his cologne before she even made it to the closed door. It relaxed her, his smell, and she couldn't understand why. He was just a friend, for crying out loud. Yet every time she so much as sniffed his presence her entire body chemistry changed. And instead of easing up as the years came and went, it was getting worse. Far worse. Sometimes she even found herself waking up in the middle of the night sniffing for Thomas.

She rapped lightly on the door and Thomas yelled "Yes?" in what she discerned as a slightly irritated voice.

"Police, open up!" she yelled back, unable to match his annoyance.

"Jazz, come on in," he said the way she liked it, softer and more affectionately, and she opened the door of his bedroom and walked in slowly. She had to walk around a wall before she saw him. Then she saw him. And she smiled.

He was standing on the opposite side of his big poster bed, talking on the telephone. He waved her in as he talked, standing there in only a dress shirt and briefs, and Jazz felt suddenly skittish as she moved toward him. He was engrossed in some conversation, making it clear that he disagreed with whomever he was talking with, and he motioned for her to sit down.

She sat down on the bed in front of him and crossed her legs. Thomas looked at those legs as soon as they crossed, those gorgeous plump legs that she often had hidden from sight, this time by a pair of army fatigue pants. Such an attire would be vintage Jazz, except that she wore a nice green jacket and heels for the occasion, which was about as dressed up as it got for her. Thomas smiled. She would easily be the most casually dressed of his guests, that was for sure, and probably no man would come within ten feet of her because of her boldness. But God was she beautiful, he thought.

"You're early," he said as he finally hung up the telephone.

Jazz looked up at him and pushed her glasses up on her nose. "And you're feisty," she said. "Who was that?"

"One of my business partners. Nobody."

Jazz smiled. "They're going crazy downstairs."

"I know. I have one of these parties four or five times every year and every time Henry acts as if he'd never heard of such an affair."

"Hank's cool. I like him."

"He's a nervous Nellie."

"I still like him."

Thomas nodded as he stood there, his intense gaze trailing her up and down. Then he took her by the hand and pulled her to her feet. "Stand up and let me get a look at you," he said.

"For what?" she asked as she stood up.

"It's not every day Jazz Walker wears a jacket. I'm honored that you would choose my humble get-together for the occasion."

"It's nothing, trust me."

"Let me be the judge of that," he said as he looked her over and then turned her around. He laughed, however, when he saw the back of her jacket.

"What's so funny?" she asked, looking over her shoulder at him.

" 'Woodstock '69' is nicely stitched on the back of your dinner jacket, dear."

"I told you I wasn't dressed up."

"Point taken," he said as he twirled her back around to face him. As soon as he saw her eyes, eyes that drooped down into an almost drowsy look of sexiness, he pulled her against him. Then he wrapped his arms around her in a warm embrace. "I'm glad you came anyway, baby," he said softly in her ear. "Woodstock and all."

Jazz smiled as she relaxed in his big arms. His body was rock hard, especially the bundle inside his briefs, and he kept pressing it harder against her, as if he wanted her to feel it, too. She knew she should back away. But she couldn't.

"You've been smoking," she said, as she could smell the hint of cigar smoke mingled with his cologne.

"I'm sure you have, too," he replied, his eyes tightly shut as he held her.

"I smoke all the time. You only smoke when you're upset."

Thomas's eyes flew open. Sometimes he sensed that Jazz knew

him better than he knew himself. An uncomfortable proposition. He removed his arms from around her and walked toward his pair of pants hanging from his closet door. "Now why would I be upset?"

Jazz began rubbing her arm, as she suddenly felt shivery away from his embrace. "I don't know," she said. "Why would you?"

Thomas slipped into his dress pants quickly. He didn't answer her because he didn't know how to say it. He certainly couldn't tell her the truth, that he was antsy because he hadn't been laid in over a month now and he got a hard-on every time he so much as looked in her direction. No other woman turned him on like that, including Paula, whom he stopped bedding weeks before their break-up. And that was why he was more temperamental, more impatient, more in need of the occasional cigar than usual. But if he was to tell it to Jazz, he knew he'd be in for it. She'd preach to him nonstop about the blessing of friendship and the devastation of romance gone wrong and how a good friend was too hard to find to even think about taking such a gamble. She, would, in other words, turn Sister J on him and tell him everything he'd already told himself a thousand times before. But damn if it wasn't frustrating the hell out of him. He knew he had to do something, and soon, or he was positively going to explode.

"Well?" she asked. "What's the matter?"

"Nothing," he said as he removed his suit coat from the hanger. "I'll just be glad to get this evening over, to tell you the truth."

Jazz laughed. "For a man who loves to put on the party, you don't love to put on the party."

Thomas smiled. "Now you know all my secrets," he said. And he couldn't stop staring at her.

Alex and Conrad arrived to a lively party at the Drayton home. Alex was immediately impressed with the home itself, and the fancy cars outside, and the smell of money oozing in the air as soon as she darted through the big, double doors. Surely, she thought, at least one sugar daddy had to be somewhere amongst them. And she didn't want a chump like Larry Lindsey either. She needed somebody who didn't want any more from her than she wanted from him. Just long-term companionship for him, a high-flying lifestyle for her. Somebody confident, well-off, and as uninterested in her moral core as she would be in his.

But as the evening progressed it began to seem next to impossible to find such a man. All of the potentials, as far as she could determine—and she had a trained eye—were either too old, too young, too faithfully married, or too something. None of them would do. And these were supposed to be the cream of the crop? *These?* She was disappointed beyond words. If she couldn't find a potential among this group, then what were her chances of ever finding the right man? And it wasn't as if she had all of this time. She and Nikki were going to be virtually homeless in two weeks if something didn't happen. Something drastic. But it wasn't happening here, she concluded, and she was just about to go over to Conrad, who seemed to be having the time of his life, and suggest to him that they leave. Until she saw him standing there.

He stood away from the center of things but was more to the side, and people seemed to come to him, rather than the other way around. Women especially were constantly in his face and standing beside him and rubbing ever so lightly against him, but Alex could see his displeasure. He wasn't thinking about them. He even appeared annoyed by the contact. His eyes, instead, kept looking over in the direction of some butch-looking, trapped-in-the-sixties-dressing female in army fatigues and a green Woodstock jacket, but Alex just knew he couldn't possibly be attracted to *that*. The woman had more than likely crashed his party, she figured, and he was wisely keeping an eye on her.

But damn if he wasn't gorgeous. And powerfully built. And when he smiled, Lord have mercy. Alex wanted to swoon. She'd seen her share of good-looking brothers before, but he took the prize. And he was single, too, Alex decided, or his wife would be beside him. No self-respecting woman would let a hunk like that out of her sight. Not with other females around. Alex also knew instinctively, based on his look alone, that he just had to be Thomas Drayton.

She found Conrad, who was laughing it up with some other geeky-looking attorneys, and coaxed him away from the crowd.

"Having fun, beautiful?" he asked her.

"When are you going to introduce me to your boss?" she asked.

"My boss?"

"Yes, Conrad. We're here at his house, aren't we?"

"Well, yeah."

"He invited you here, right?"

"Yeah, he invited all of his employees."

"Then don't you think it would be rude if you didn't introduce your guest to him? I am, after all, in the man's house."

"I hear what you're saying, Alexandria, but I thought I'd wait around until he came over to me."

Alex wanted to roll her eyes. *Chump,* in the dictionary, would be a picture of Conrad. "Why in the world would he come running over to you, Conrad?"

"Not running over. But I don't want to antagonize the man, that's all. This is my first invite. I don't want it to be my last."

"Why would it be your last? What are you talking about?"

"He doesn't like blatant ambitiousness. He might think I'm trying to curry favor or something, Alexandria, it's complicated."

That did it. Alex's look turned hard. "You'd better take me over there to meet that man now, Conrad, or I'll do it myself."

Conrad hesitated. He knew an iron will when he saw one. He began looking around the room, looking for Thomas Drayton, until he saw him. It wasn't his style to kiss butt, or to be all up in somebody's face, but Alex was probably right. How could anybody misconstrue a gesture as innocent as introducing your companion to your boss? His ambitious-as-hell coworkers, that's who, he thought, all of whom were jockeying to become the next senior associate at the firm, a required step before partnership. But he looked at Alex and the determination on her beautiful face. He swallowed hard.

"Okay," he said. "Let's go."

They ended up standing behind an older couple who seemed determined to tell Thomas everything they could about their expansive résumés, as if they were at a networking convention rather than a party. They were obnoxious, in Alex's view, just insecure people who had to continually laud their accomplishments for eternal remembrance when it was clear that Thomas Drayton probably wouldn't even remember their names when they walked away from him. And finally they did walk away. And then Alex and Conrad stood before him.

Conrad kept his hand on the small of Alex's back as he introduced her. Thomas took her small hand into his big one and squeezed lightly, but it was enough to make Alex feel the heat. She smiled. Grandly.

"It's an honor to meet you, Mr. Drayton. I've heard a lot of wonderful things about you. And this is a very lovely party."

"Is it?"

"Oh, yes."

Thomas didn't say anything. He simply stared at Alex as if he was staring through her, and then he looked at Conrad. "How's it going on the Apek case, Baines?"

"Good," Conrad said nervously. "Pretty good, anyway. We hope to settle by the end of next week."

Thomas nodded. "That'll be best," he said firmly.

"Yes, sir," Conrad replied and Thomas, once again, looked at Alex. "Nice meeting you, Miss . . . um?"

"Mailer. Alex Mailer."

"Miss Mailer. I hope you and Conrad continue to enjoy yourselves."

"Thank you," Alex said with a wide smile. Conrad attempted to politely pull her away—he knew a shove off when he heard one and Drayton, he believed, was definitely bidding them farewell—but Alex wasn't satisfied yet. She decided to take a chance.

"Your party is lovely, the setting, that is," she said to Thomas, "but your guests are the pits."

Conrad couldn't believe his ears. He even looked at Alex, to make sure she had said what she had. Thomas hesitated—even he seemed thrown—but only momentarily. "Are they?" he asked.

"Oh, yes. Utter bores. Like that couple that was talking to you before we came up. Good grief. What was their problem? Like you wanted to know all about their accomplishments at a party. Please. I wanted to tell them to shut the hell up myself." She said this and laughed. Thomas managed a faint smile.

"Well, we'll just get out of your way, Mr. Drayton," Conrad said, "and thanks again for the invitation."

Thomas nodded and Conrad, not so politely this time, pulled Alex along with him as he moved as far away from his boss as he could go. Alex looked back at Thomas as another couple hurried up to him, hoping that he'd be looking her way, too. But he didn't appear to be giving her so much as another thought. She suddenly felt extremely disappointed, as if she had blown a golden opportunity, and she felt suddenly very sad.

Sad? she thought. Why in the world should she feel sad? It was obvious that Thomas Drayton didn't know a good catch when he saw one or he would have been all over her. So why should she feel bad because of his poor insight? But she did. She couldn't deny it. She felt as if she'd failed.

"Have you lost your mind, Alex?" Conrad asked as soon as they were safely on the other side of the big room.

"His guests are boring. I told the truth. So what's the big deal?"

"My career is the big deal! You don't know that guy. He doesn't like that sort of thing."

"What sort of thing?"

"Your behavior. Calling his guests names. What was the damn point, Alexandria?"

Good question, she thought. Because now she wasn't so sure. She had tried to distinguish herself from all those other females tripping over themselves to get to him by proving that she was different, that she wasn't about to grovel to him or anyone else. She had thought, just by watching him, that he was the kind of self-secured man who could appreciate honesty. She, apparently, thought wrong.

"Let's just go," she said to Conrad, her frustration with him and with her failed attempt too much for her to digest.

"Now?" he asked.

"Yes, Conrad, let's go."

Conrad sighed. What a mistake bringing her here, he thought. "Okay. Let me say good-bye to a few of my friends and we'll be on our way."

Alex nodded; she didn't exactly have a choice. And it took him too long, by her estimation, but instead of arguing with him when he did finally return, she began walking ahead of him toward the exit doors, the gaiety of the crowd suddenly nauseating her.

"Mr. Baines?" a voice yelled out just behind them. They both turned at the same time.

"Yes?" Conrad said as Henry hurried up to them.

"Hello, Mr. Baines, I'm Mr. Drayton's assistant. He would like to speak with you and Miss Mailer after the party. If that's all right?"

Conrad hesitated. Why would Thomas Drayton want to see him? He'd worked for him for nearly two years and he'd yet to have a private audience with the man. It had to be, he concluded, because of Alex's big mouth. "Tell Mr. Drayton we'll be delighted to meet with him," Conrad said with a smile.

Henry gave a slight nod to both Conrad and Alex and then walked away. Alex looked at Conrad.

"Why would he want to meet with you?" she asked.

"I don't know," Conrad said.

"Good news maybe?"

"Maybe. But that's not how it feels."

. Jazz had had enough. She'd asked that band over and over to put some variety in their tunes, but they continued to ignore her request. Now she intended to demand their compliance.

The bandleader, a tall, husky man named Firth, at first didn't even look her way. He continued waving around his baton to the beat of yet another big-band sound tune as if he didn't hear her. When the song concluded, and before the next one could begin, Jazz spoke up louder.

"Would you please play something else?" she pushed her glasses up on her nose and asked, yet again.

"We haven't played one song twice, lady, so I don't know what you're talking about."

"We're in the twenty-first century, guys. The best of Benny Goodman ain't cuttin' it, all right?"

"What we're playing is appropriate to the occasion."

"What you're playing is boring the tears out of everybody in the room. I mean, come on. It's not as if I'm asking you to start spinning rap tunes, but at least something more up-to-date. I'd even take Motown, man."

"Will you please move?" Firth said to Jazz.

"Not until you play something else."

"We're not playing anything else. Now if you don't like it, then I strongly suggest you leave. I strongly suggest you let the door hit'cha where the good Lord split'cha and get the hell out of my way."

Giggling could be heard just to the right of Jazz and she looked in that direction. A group of females, the same females Jazz remembered couldn't stop making little sly remarks about her attire, were looking and laughing. Unbeknownst to all of them, however, Thomas was looking, too, farther away, only he didn't look to be as accommodating as Jazz. He began moving in that direction.

Jazz looked back at Firth. "You don't have to get nasty," she said to him.

"Look, lady, why don't you get out of my face so I can get to work. I'm being paid to play, not run my mouth with you!"

"Is there a problem here?" Thomas asked as he moved alongside Jazz.

Firth, startled by Thomas's sudden presence, quickly started smiling. "No, sir," he said. "Not at all."

"What's going on, Jazz?"

Jazz decided to back down. "Nothing," she said.

"Don't tell me nothing. What's the matter?"

"I guess you can call it an artistic disagreement."

"What did you want them to play?"

"Something far different than what they're playing, but it's not worth getting into a lather over."

Thomas looked at Firth. "Play whatever she wants," he said.

"Yes, sir," Firth replied obediently. Thomas looked at Jazz again and kissed her lightly on the cheek. Then he glared at Firth again as if to warn him that this one was not to be disrespected and walked back to entertain his other guests.

Jazz looked at the giggling females. They were still staring, but they weren't laughing anymore.

Firth obviously hated the position he was in, but he knew he had no choice. "What do you want us to play?" he asked Jazz.

Jazz had to think about this. She didn't exactly have a particular song in mind. " 'Fernando' would be nice."

Firth looked at his band mates and then back at Jazz. "Fer-who?"

" 'Fernando.' By Abba. You know."

Firth sighed. "No, lady, I don't know."

"Okay. You don't have to get testy. What about 'I'm All Out of Love'?"

"You're all out of love?"

"Yes. Air Supply?"

Firth folded his arms. "Try again, lady."

"All right, Motown then."

"Which Motown song?"

"I don't know. What's that one called about some unplanned wedding on a hill or something?"

Firth looked at his band members and then back at Jazz. "We have no idea," he said.

"Well I don't know what to tell you. I've never heard of such an unknowledgeable band. I know. Play some Tracy Chapman. 'She's Got Her Ticket' will do."

Firth gave her another blank stare.

"Just play whatever, all right?" Jazz said and walked away from the bandstand.

Conrad and Alex sat quietly on the living-room sofa while Jazz, who, by tradition, was always the last guest to leave from one of Thomas's parties, sat in one of the two wingback chairs. Alex thought it odd that a strange woman like Jazz, with her wild-cut Afro and unfashionable attire, would be hanging around, but she didn't say anything. She certainly didn't see her as a threat of any kind since she looked too butch, Alex felt, to be Thomas Drayton's type. So she relaxed.

Conrad was certain that this invitation to stay afterwards meant nothing but bad news for him, but Alex wasn't so sure. She saw the way Drayton looked at her, although he absolutely didn't give off any overt signs of interest, but if her experience was her guide, she wouldn't be stunned if he came on to her before the night was out. Stunned, she thought. She'd be delighted.

"So, where's Mr. Drayton?" Conrad asked Jazz. "Do you know?"

"He's seeing Judge Millburn out. He'll be here."

Conrad nodded. His nerves had him jittery. "Did he mention to you what this is about?" he asked Jazz and Alex looked at him before Jazz could answer.

"Why would he discuss that with her?" she wanted to know.

Conrad tried to smile, to minimize the harsh, condescending tone of Alex's question. "Jazz Walker is Mr. Drayton's best friend, Alexandria. And she also happens to be the host of *Ask Sister J* from the radio. So if he discussed it with anybody, it would probably be with her."

"*Ask Sister J?*"

"Yeah. From the radio."

"Oh," Alex said. "So you're the lady with all that big advice?"

Jazz didn't say anything.

"But I like your show."

Jazz nodded slightly. "Thank you."

Alex smiled. If this weirdo was Drayton's best friend, she thought, then she'd better be careful to maintain a good impression. "You don't be playing, do you?" she asked Jazz.

"I try to tell the truth."

"I know that's right. That's what I be saying. Why lie? The truth is what those silly women need to hear."

Again, Jazz didn't say anything. She just stared at Alex. She didn't see Alex as any particular threat, not with that phony smile of hers and overeagerness to please. She was obviously too devious and gold-digging to be of any long-term interest to Thomas. Besides, Conrad seemed to have staked out that territory for himself, the way he clasped his hand into hers and wouldn't let her remove it even when she tried. The fact that she was trying to remove it, however, did concern Jazz—but just a bit.

And Alex did remove it, with considerable but determined effort, by the time Thomas returned into the house and headed in their direction. Alex smiled so grandly when he arrived and sat down beside her that Jazz wondered if the sister was crazy.

"I hope my guests didn't bore you all evening, Miss Mailer," Thomas said as he crossed his legs.

"They would have, but I refused to let them."

"Good for you," Thomas said, whose big body next to Alex's short, petite one made a towering impression. From his vantage point he could see perfectly the cleavage her low-cut dress was designed to reveal. Her breasts were about half the size of Jazz's, however, he noted.

"And what about you, young man?" he looked past Alex and asked Conrad, who sat on the other side of her. "Was it a bore of an evening for you, too?"

Conrad slightly unloosened his tie. "Oh, no, sir. Not at all. I enjoyed myself immensely. Thanks for the opportunity."

Alex frowned. "What opportunity?" she asked the nervous Conrad.

Conrad glanced at Thomas, then he tried his best to keep smiling. "The opportunity to be here, Alexandria. The invitation. That's what I was thanking him for."

"I like your work," Thomas said and Conrad looked at him.

"You don't?" he asked. "I mean, you do?"

"Yes. Very thoughtful. That's why I wanted you to hang back. To thank you for the good work you've done for the firm, Conrad. Consistently high caliber. I've noticed."

This time it was easy for Conrad to smile. He licked his lips as if relieved. "I love what I do," he said. "Thank you for noticing."

Thomas then looked down at Alex, and she, as if on cue, crossed her short, curvy legs. "You have a beautiful lady," he said to Conrad in a voice somewhat lower than his regular speaking voice. Jazz looked at him.

"We're just friends," Alex quickly responded before Conrad could say a word.

Thomas nodded. "I see," he said, his eyes unable to release their lock on her legs. But then he stood up, and Conrad and Alex quickly stood, too.

"We'll talk more, Conrad," he said and then began walking toward the door. "I'm so tired I can barely keep my eyes open right now."

"I can understand that," Conrad said as he and Alex walked hurriedly behind him. Although Alex was disappointed to be leaving Thomas's side, she felt rejuvenated, because she was now certain that he was interested, too. Why else, she wondered, would he mention anything about her beauty? He was just testing Conrad, to see what kind of claim he had on her. In fact, by the time they said their good-byes to Thomas Drayton and were heading for Conrad's Jeep, both feeling great for totally different reasons, Alex was convinced that the entire after-party get-together was just a ruse by the handsome Mr. Drayton, not to get to know Conrad better, but because he wanted to know about her. And if she played her cards right, she decided, as Conrad opened his car door for her, he will soon know more than he ever dreamed.

Thomas stood at the front door of his home watching as Conrad and Alex got into Conrad's Jeep and quickly drove away. She was a looker all right, he thought, and a tease if ever he'd seen one. But she had one thing right: his guests were bores, even to him.

"I guess I'd better call myself a cab," Jazz said as she walked up and stood alongside Thomas. He looked at her.

"Did you enjoy yourself?"

"No."

"Me either."

Jazz smiled and shook her head. Thomas continued staring at her, and she knew what that meant. At first she tried not to look at him at all. But she did.

"Sorry about the band," Thomas said.

"They eventually came around."

"And my guests."

Jazz nodded, remembering all the nasty little comments she constantly heard behind her back.

Thomas's staring wouldn't let up. Then he said the words they often said when one or the other didn't want to be alone. "You may as well stay here tonight," he said.

Jazz looked at him, with that nonverbal language they'd mastered, and then looked back outdoors.

Conrad took the elevator with Alex up to Nikki's condo. He wanted to come in, for a nightcap, but Alex said no.

"I'm too tired," she said as they stood at the door and Alex pulled out the set of keys Nikki had given her. "But thanks for taking me to the party. It was nice."

Conrad smiled. "I thought you hated it?"

"It wasn't particularly exciting, no, but it had some good points."

"I'm still reeling from Mr. Drayton. He notices the work I'm doing, he said. Isn't that something?"

"Yes, he is," Alex said in an almost absentminded mumble.

"What was that?"

"Oh, nothing, Conrad, I'm just tired. I'll see you later. Okay?"

Conrad nodded. "Okay, okay. I get the hint." He said this with a smile. "Good night, Alexandria."

"Good night," Alex said and unlocked the door.

Nikki, who was lying on the sofa watching late-night TV, didn't even glance her sister's way when she walked through the door. That, however, didn't stop her curiosity. "How did it go?" she asked at the sound of the entry.

Alex leaned against the door and couldn't stop thinking about that gorgeous hunk of Thomas and what a perfect catch he would be. A man with it all for a change. Not just money and power, she was used to those. But great looks, too. Tall, muscular, perfect, she thought.

"Well?" Nikki asked as she finally pulled her attention away from the TV and looked at her sister. "How was it?"

Alex smiled an all-knowing smile. "It was fantastic," she said.

*   *   *

Thomas was in bed, wearing a pair of pajama pants but no top, talking on the telephone and trying like mad not to fall asleep. He was talking with Marlene, an old friend and business associate, as she cried out to him about her failing marriage. He tried to be encouraging, but he could tell she was only half listening.

He was so out of it, in fact, that he didn't notice Jazz when she came out of his bathroom wearing one of his big white shirts, her eyes transfixed on him as she moved slowly toward his bed. Every time she stayed the night at his house she always slept with him, but lately it was becoming more and more unnatural to her. He was just a friend, but her heart wasn't behaving the way it used to behave. Even just looking at him lying in his bed, with his six-pack abs and thick, muscle-tight arms uncovered, tensed her body. She used to react to him the way a friend would to a friend, because she needed his friendship just that badly, but lately, like now, her body wasn't cooperating.

She slid into his bed, pulling the cover up to the pit of her arms, her back turned to him, and it was only then that he noticed her presence. He looked at her, in his big, long-sleeved shirt, and he smiled.

"Listen, Marlene," he said into the phone, "I'm dead tired, girl. But call me tomorrow. We'll talk then."

Jazz's muscles tightened as she listened to him say good night to yet another one of his lady friends. She knew Marlene from seeing her a few times with Thomas, and she knew that Marlene was a lawyer, too, but that was all she knew about her.

Thomas hung up the telephone and turned toward Jazz. "That was Marlene," he said.

"I gathered."

"Her old man's acting a fool and she needed some advice."

"I see."

"You do?"

"Certainly. Who, after all, would know more about marriage than a divorce attorney who's never been married?"

Thomas laughed. "You've got a point there."

"Tell her to call *Ask Sister J* tomorrow. I'll straighten her out."

Thomas laughed again and then leaned over toward Jazz. "You'll straighten her out all right," he said, in a low, husky voice, and then he began sliding her toward him, which caused her to start laughing, too.

She turned on her back to face him. "You don't have a lot of faith in my advice either, do you?"

"Of course I do. If I was young and dumb and didn't know what the hell I was doing. Marlene's none of those things."

A tinge of jealousy swept across Jazz, which surprised her. She looked at Thomas. He leaned up on one elbow, his soft, kind face within inches of hers. "How long have you known her?" she asked him.

"About, I don't know, ten years or more."

"Is it serious?"

"Is what serious?"

"You and her."

Thomas smiled. "No," he said. "She's just a friend."

"Just a friend, huh? Like you and me?"

"No. Not like you and me. You're my best friend." He wanted to add more, a lot more, but he didn't.

Jazz smiled. "Has she ever slept in your bed before? As a friend?"

"No. Friends don't usually sleep together, honey."

Jazz didn't like the implications of that statement one bit. And she knew she should have just ended the conversation where it was, but she felt playful for some reason. "Then why do I always end up in bed with you?" she asked him.

He smiled, too. "Because of our ground rules. When I ask you to stay over, or when you ask me to stay over, it's already understood that we want company, somebody close by. What would be the point of you staying over and sleeping in another room? We could talk on the telephone if that was it."

Jazz nodded. She knew.

"Besides," he added, "how could I listen to you snore if you're in another room?"

"I do not snore, Thomas."

"You keep me up half the night, girl, don't even try that."

"I do not snore!"

"You snort then."

Jazz laughed. "You're wrong for that, Thomas." She said this in such a playful way that he laughed, too. Then he looked deep into her eyes and couldn't seem to break his stare. And then, as if being beckoned, he leaned down and kissed her. She, at first, just laid there and allowed his lips to probe hers with short, sweet kisses, his usual fare, but then he was kissing her cheeks, and then her neck. It was inappropriate, they both knew it, but neither bothered to stop it. And when he moved back up to her lips and his tongue began to attempt entry, she, for the first time ever in their relationship, parted those small, soft lips of hers and allowed him in. She wrapped her arms around his neck as he leaned into her, kissing her so hard and so forcefully that she could hardly contain the joy she felt. Her entire body was tingling, as his hard arousal pressed against her thigh, even his pajamas not thick enough to shield his heat, and his tongue pushed farther and farther into her mouth. He'd never French kissed her before, she'd never allowed it, but now, as he pushed into her, as the bundle inside his pants became bigger and bigger, harder and harder, she knew she was powerless to stop him. It terrified her, the thought that they would be tossing away nearly seven years of a friendship they both depended on, and it apparently terrified him, too, because he was the one, not her, who pulled back.

He was breathing heavily as he removed his lips from hers and looked into her eyes, his bare chest rising up and down in near hyperventilation. He could take her, over and over again, and she'd let him. Tonight she'd let him. But tomorrow, he thought, when the reality of what they'd done crept in, would be another story. As he looked into Jazz's clear, beautiful eyes, eyes that melted with warmth and kindness, he felt angry. He wished to God he wasn't so jaded. He wished he hadn't seen as much as he'd seen. All of those weddings he'd attended. All of those divorces he'd handled. Not one of his friends had a good marriage. Not one of his clients had an amicable divorce. He'd handled too many divorce cases, that was the problem, too many cases where two people were once so in love, as if they just knew they'd found the answer, only to end up despising each other, hating each other, wanting nothing more to do with each other. God help him, but he'd seen too much.

Jazz didn't have to see it; she experienced it three marriages in a row, and she knew firsthand exactly what Thomas was feeling. That was why she didn't pull him back to her. That was why she fought back tears, too. They couldn't risk it. Not for all the passion in this world, they could not take that chance.

Thomas embraced her again, pulling her against him as close as he could, his eyes closed tightly to ward off that overpowering feeling of oncoming emotion. Then he pulled away gently and moved back to his side of the bed. "Good night, Jazz," he said.

Jazz swallowed hard, praying that her voice wouldn't quake when she spoke. "Good night," she replied.

FOOLS RUSH IN

Alex stepped off of the elevator and into the lobby of the law offices of Thomas Drayton. She was immediately struck by the swirl of activity as attorneys moved swiftly from one office to the next, one meeting to the next, as if their very lives depended on speed. Alex, however, decided to take it slow as she stood patiently at the reception desk and waited for the young woman to get off of the telephone. She had all the time in the world, she felt, because, in time, once Thomas Drayton understood the gravity of the gem he had within his reach, all of *this* would be hers.

"Yes?" the receptionist said. "May I help you?"

"Yes, you may," Alex said. "I'm here to see Conrad Baines."

"Do you have an appointment?"

"No, but I think he'll want to see me."

The woman hesitated, as if Alex was invading some territory she had hoped to claim, but then she smiled. "Your name?"

"Alex. Alex Mailer."

"If you'll have a seat, Miss Mailer, I'll let Mr. Baines know you're here."

Alex looked at the leather couch against the back wall, thanked the receptionist, and then walked over to it and sat down. She crossed her legs and began looking around, wondering which office could possibly belong to Thomas Drayton, or if his office was even on that floor. She didn't have to wonder long, however, because before she could adjust herself in her seat, the elevator doors across the hall slid open and Thomas Drayton, along with two other attorneys, entered the lobby.

Alex's heart raced with anticipation as Thomas stood near the elevator talking with his colleagues, his tall, muscularly lean body a sight to behold. And when he glanced her way, when his lovely dark brown eyes finally looked in her direction, she wanted to smile, and wave, and hurry to his side. But as he stood there watching her while listening to his talkative colleagues, his intense expression seemed to discourage it, as if he would not appreciate the gesture one bit.

So she just looked at him, without appearing to gawk, although she found herself doing exactly that. He wore a double-breasted brown suit where brown, she thought, had never looked so good. And when he laughed at some joke one of the other men told and revealed that drop-dead sexy smile of his, she almost forgot to breathe. She was looking for a sugar daddy, somebody to bankroll her lifestyle, but with Thomas Drayton she'd be getting so much more. More sugar than daddy, perhaps, which would be a first for her, and that was why her plan of action had to work. And it was working like a charm so far, she thought, because the focus of that plan, the man himself, was now in the house.

"Miss Mailer?" the receptionist said, and Alex finally removed her eyes from Thomas, who had not looked at her again after his initial peep, and turned toward the sound of her name.

"Yes?"

"Mr. Baines will see you now."

Alex stood quickly and the receptionist pointed to the second office to the far left. As soon as Alex walked into the small office, Conrad grabbed her by the hand, smiling greatly, and gave her a small peck on the cheek.

"What a way to begin the day," he said as Alex took a seat.

"Nice seeing you, too, Connie. I can call you Connie, can't I?"

"You can call me anything, sweetheart," Conrad said and sat in the chair beside Alex. "Don't you look great today. All pretty in pink."

Alex smiled. She wore a short, pink dress and matching pink-and-white heels. Loud but tasteful. She knew what she was doing.

"So," Conrad said, "to what do I owe this privilege?"

"I just dropped by to thank you for last night. It was a wonderful evening."

"It was?"

"Yes, Connie, it was. All in all it was a very good night out."

"Well I'm glad you thought so. I know I thought so. Especially after Mr. Drayton proved that I was on his radar screen and all those other kiss-butts aren't fooling anybody."

"Funny you should mention that."

"Mention what?"

"Mr. Drayton. I was thinking, just now, that it could do wonders for your career if you invited that nice boss of yours to dinner."

Conrad hesitated. "You're joking, right?"

"Think about it, Connie. He likes you, that's why he asked you to stay after the party last night. And he said himself he wanted to talk with you some more. He's probably waiting for an invitation. He's probably waiting for you to invite him to your place, for dinner."

Conrad smiled. "I doubt that."

"I don't, Connie. It's called networking. He's used to it. But don't make it elaborate, he wouldn't go for that. Just something small and intimate. You and me—I'll be glad to be there—and him. That's it. It'll be a business get-together with a friendly touch."

Conrad shook his head. His amazement wasn't that Alex was asking him to invite his boss to dinner but that she was serious about it. "I don't know, Alexandria—"

"Alex. Please."

"I don't know. He's a smart man. He'll see right through such a blatant act of ambitiousness. I figure I'll make progress by not being like everybody else. I don't kiss up to him. I think he likes that about me."

"Nonsense," Alex said derisively. "Why do you think he had that little conversation with you last night? Because you went up to him earlier and made your presence known, that's why. As I recall you didn't even want to do that. But it paid off. That's what got you on the map, Connie, that's why he praised you last night. So let's just go to his office and invite him. That's all we've got to do. He can say yes or he can say no, but I guarantee you he'll appreciate the gesture."

Connie exhaled. He continued to disagree with Alex, but it was no use. She was a smart, savvy, beautiful woman who was winning his heart more and more each day. He could not say no to her.

* * *

"Hello?" Jazz's raspy voice said into the telephone. Thomas smiled when he heard it.

"It's me, sweetie. Up yet?" He was in his office sitting behind his large desk. Stacks of papers awaited his review, but the only thing on his mind this morning was Jazz. "Jazz?"

"Um?" she said. He knew she was barely awake.

"It's time to get up, babe, or you're going to be late."

"What time is it?"

"Almost ten."

"That late? Dang. Why didn't you wake me this morning before you left?"

"Because you had tossed and turned all night and were finally resting peacefully. I wasn't about to deny you that."

"I tossed and turned?"

"All night. I held you, and that helped a little, but you still didn't sleep well."

Jazz sighed. "I hope I didn't disturb your rest."

"Impossible."

"It's not impossible, Thomas."

"You didn't disturb me."

"Well, anyway, I'd better get up. Thanks for the wake-up call."

"You know you're welcome."

There was a pause. The thought of his tongue in her mouth still haunted him. "Well, I won't keep you. Just wanted to make sure you got up in time."

"Thanks again."

"Sure."

"Bye."

Jazz said this and hung up quickly. That was her style and Thomas knew it. He hung up, too. The idea of her still in his house, wearing his shirt, made him smile. But it was a bittersweet smile at best, because she was only temporarily there and wouldn't be there at all when he made it back home.

"Mr. Drayton?" his secretary's voice bellowed through his desk intercom.

"Yes, Pamela?"

"I was waiting for you to get off the line, sir. Attorney Baines and a Miss Mailer are here to see you."

Thomas exhaled. What in the world would Baines want? he wondered. "Send them in," he said.

Conrad and Alex walked swiftly through the double doors of Thomas's huge office and then walked slowly up to his desk. Thomas stood up, out of deference to Alex, and invited them both to sit down. "I'm afraid I only have a few minutes," he said as he sat down, too.

"Oh, we know, sir," Conrad said quickly. "We'll just, I'm here to invite you to dinner tomorrow night, if that's not too inconvenient for you. Of course we'll, I'll understand if you can't make it. I'm not giving you any real advanced notice. But if you can make it we, I'll certainly appreciate it."

Thomas didn't say anything. He didn't like the nervousness in Conrad, the way he was so easily intimidated. Such a problem could prove fatal in court. He'd talk to the young man, he decided. But alone. Definitely alone.

Alex's heart was in her shoes as Thomas seemed ready to turn Conrad's offer down cold. She had to intervene, and fast. "We promise you, Mr. Drayton," she said with a grand smile, "it'll be a night you'll never forget."

Talk about a seduction, Thomas thought, as he looked at Alex. She looked ridiculous in all that pink, he thought, like some overgrown Barbie doll, but he couldn't exactly discount her not-so-veiled offer. It had been a while, he had to admit, since he'd had some action, and holding Jazz all night had his body aching for some. But he wasn't all that certain if he wanted to go down that road with somebody like Alex Mailer, somebody easily not his type.

"You'll love the food, the wine," Alex said, "everything. Trust me."

Thomas glanced at Conrad. Apparently she wasn't his woman just as she had said last night because he was still sitting there smiling as if a robbery wasn't taking place right before his very eyes. Thomas decided then to accept. Not just because of Alex's offer, although that was probably the main reason, but because this dinner apparently was important to Conrad, too. And he liked Conrad. "What time tomorrow night?" he asked, and Alex and Conrad, for very different reasons, smiled.

Jazz was at her loft painting when Thomas made his way through the living room and into her small studio.

"You should lock your door sometimes, Jazz," he said.

"When I'm not here it's locked," she said. She was sitting on the floor, her painting a large canvas in the middle of the room, and she wore a denim work jumper that was smeared in small paint splatters. Thomas, still wearing his double-breasted brown suit, kneeled down where she sat and studied the painting.

"What is it?" he asked her.

"I haven't decided yet."

Thomas smiled and looked at Jazz. Even with a paint smudge on her nose, she looked beautiful to him. She pushed her glasses up on the bridge of her nose and returned his glare. And without saying a word they kissed each other with a quick peck on the lips. Nothing nearly as elaborate as the kissing they'd done the night before, but it was obvious by their body language that they both remembered it well. Jazz even avoided looking into his eyes when their lips separated and he backed away.

"So how was your day?" she asked him.

"Tolerable. Yours?"

"Same. Did you catch the show?"

"No, I was in court. What happened?"

"Your friend Marlene called."

"Did she?"

"I couldn't believe it."

"You told me to tell her to call the show if she wanted answers to her troubled marriage. So I told her."

"I know. That's what I couldn't believe."

"How did it go?"

"Like it always goes, Thomas. She heard me and she didn't hear me. I'm so tired of those love-gone-wrong shows I don't know what to do. But that's all my callers seem to want to talk about."

"Love is the deal, Jazz. That's what everybody wants."

"Yeah, well, it sucks to me."

Thomas laughed. "You are so romantic, girl."

Jazz smiled. "What can I say?"

Thomas shook his head. One of a kind, he thought. "Conrad came by to see me today," he said.

"Conrad Baines. I like him."

"He invited me to dinner tomorrow night."

"No sweat? That don't even sound like Conrad. I always pictured him as the quiet, unassuming type."

"Sometimes people change."

"And sometimes they don't."

"That's true, too. But it's not a big deal. He just probably wants to make a pitch for a more senior position at the firm."

"Maybe so," Jazz said and then picked up the cigarette she had smoldering in an ashtray nearby. "Will his woman be there, too?" she asked.

"Yes, as a matter of fact," Thomas said, remembering Alex was the main reason he accepted the invite. "And she's not Conrad's woman."

Jazz looked at Thomas as she took a slow drag on her cigarette. "That doesn't appear to be Conrad's impression," she said.

Dinner was eaten quietly, as both Conrad and Alex seemed at first to be intimidated by Thomas's mere presence in the hardly glamorous apartment, an apartment that appeared too small to contain him, but they relaxed more when they retired to the living room. Thomas, dressed casually in a pair of khakis and a tucked-in, button-front shirt, sat on the sofa and pulled out a cigar, feeling antsy for some reason, and Alex moved quickly to sit down beside him. So close, in fact, that their shoulders touched. Then she crossed her legs underneath her miniskirt, a skirt so short it revealed her thighs almost up to the forbidden zone. Thomas glanced at those thighs and then asked if anyone mind if he smoked.

"Not at all, Mr. Drayton," Conrad said as he walked over by the television set.

"Oh, Connie," Alex said. "I think we can dispense with formalities now. Don't you think so, Thomas?"

"Absolutely," Thomas said as he lit his cigar.

"I thought we'd watch a movie, guys," Conrad said. "What do you think?"

Alex wanted to laugh. "A movie?"

"Yes."

"A movie, Connie?"

"What's the name?" Thomas asked.

"*Chicago.*"

"With Queen Latifah? I'd love to watch it."

Alex couldn't believe her ears. But it was true. Thomas seemed just as excited as Conrad as Conrad slipped in the DVD and they all sat around watching a movie. This wasn't exactly what Alex had in mind—she would have preferred more conversation—but when Conrad killed the lights and darkness permeated the room, with only the slit of brightness from the television screen giving off any illumination, she took that wonderful opportunity to move her body closer to Thomas's.

Thomas, however, never cared for those silly seduction games, and he leaned his body forward, away from Alex's. Alex was disappointed, and she hadn't expected such a reaction, but she remained hopeful. The timing just wasn't right, she decided.

But everything changed when Conrad received a phone call. They were still watching the movie, still laughing at certain scenes and yelling at other scenes, when the phone rang.

"Excuse me, folks," Conrad said warmly as he moved quickly to answer his phone.

"I didn't mean to scare you," Alex said to Thomas in a low voice. Thomas looked back at her.

"Scare me?"

"My move to get closer to you. I didn't mean anything by it."

Thomas looked into her eyes. They were a beautiful hazel, just stunning against her smooth, caramel skin, and as he looked down to her small but shapely breasts, he knew there was no way he was going to resist her tonight. Jazz was the one he wanted, there was no denying it, but he couldn't have Jazz. She was his best friend, off limits, too precious for the complicated, unregulated mishaps of romance, and they had to keep it that way. But his need was becoming an inferno in his body, and it had to be extinguished. Using Alex to cool him down wasn't the best idea, he knew, but she was so ready and willing. And so available. And too stuck on herself, he'd concluded, to ever fall in love with him and muck it all up.

Conrad hung up the telephone and hurried for his car keys on the desk in the foyer. "I've got to go," he said apologetically. "My son's had another asthma attack and he's at the emergency room."

Thomas stood up. "You okay?"

"Yes, sir. Thank you."

"Thomas will take me home," Alex volunteered quickly as she

stood up, and both Conrad and Thomas looked at her. Then Conrad looked at Thomas.

"Will that be okay, Mr. Drayton?"

"That'll be fine, Conrad," Thomas said. "You just go on and see about your son."

Conrad smiled. And as they all headed for the front door, Thomas looked at the opportunistic Alex, who seemed as if she had just won some contest, and he began to wonder just who was using whom.

Alex marveled at Thomas's Bentley but kept her admiration to herself as they drove along the busy streets of Miami heading for Nikki's condo. Alex couldn't seem to stop looking at Thomas as he drove, and she found herself admiring his profile even more than his car. She loved the strong curve of his forehead and the straight shape of his nose and the perfect line of his lips. Even his hair, his low-top fade, appeared to glisten with softness. And as he put the cigar he'd been smoking to his lips and puffed twice before removing it, his eyes focused like a laser beam on the dark road outside, she couldn't help but wonder if a man like him could ever truly love a woman like her. Her former boyfriends loved her dearly, but they were all pretty pathetic in one way or another, and this man, this statue of David sitting before her, didn't seem to have a flaw to his name. He could have anybody he wanted. *Anybody,* she decided. And that was why she knew she had to be careful, and methodical, and stick to the plan no matter what.

Thomas parked his Bentley across the street from Nikki's condo and by the time they made it up to the apartment, an apartment Alex made sure the day before would be empty of Nikki for the rest of the evening, Thomas began to feel a sense of urgency. Alex was walking in front of him and the way she sashayed those hips of hers, teasing him mercilessly, had him nearly sick with lust. He wanted her in the worst way, but he knew she was a game player from way back and would insist he play along first. That was why he never cared to date younger women. The games they played, the silliness they seemed to possess, turned him off more than it turned him on, but he knew, in this case, he would have to endure it all if he expected to get some tonight.

Alex was expectant, too, not to get her groove on but to get his desire stirred. She hadn't planned on Conrad's son getting ill. She thought she would have to manipulate Conrad into letting Thomas take her home, using the line that it would be more practical since Thomas had to drive anyway, but the illness certainly helped make her plans easier to implement. And when Thomas made it into the condo, and they sat together on the sofa talking small talk, it was apparent to her that the timing she felt was a little off at Conrad's house was perfectly synchronized at hers.

He kissed her. Which she allowed. And when he began kissing her neck and cupping her breasts and pulling her closer to his rock-hard body, she allowed that, too. But as soon as his hand moved up her short skirt and reached inside her panties, she hated to do it but knew she had to. She placed her hand on his and stopped his progress.

Thomas, who had thought of Alex as an easy lay, did not immediately pull out of her underwear. He was as stunned as he was disappointed. "What's the matter, Alex?" he asked her in a husky, hoarse voice, his loins pulsating with desire.

"I'm sorry," she said sadly.

"Don't tell me that."

"I can't do it."

"Yes, you can." He was frustrated as hell at the thought that she would use this time, this very crucial moment, to play some game.

"You don't understand," she said. "I just got out of a bad relationship, a really bad relationship, and I'm not at all sure if I'm ready to take the plunge again."

Thomas removed his hand and leaned forward. He was so disappointed he was almost angry. He wanted to tell her that it wasn't a plunge, it was just a night of sex, but he couldn't bring himself to do it. He looked at her. Maybe the hot-to-trot had some morals after all, he decided. He didn't think so, the way she tried to throw herself at him over at Conrad's, but anything was possible. He stood up.

"You don't have to go now," she asked in her best soft voice. "Do you?"

It had its desired effect because Thomas's gaze softened, too. "I'm just . . . tired, Alex, that's all." Her sweet hazel eyes were staring up at him. "I respect your decision."

"You sure?"

He smiled. "Yes. I'm sure."

Alex smiled and stood up, too. "I'll come around," she said. "I just don't want another bad scene."

Thomas nodded. Given the trouble he'd been having with Paula, he certainly didn't need any himself. "I'll talk to you later."

"Promise?"

Thomas hesitated. Something about her was beginning to unsettle him, as if he had read her completely wrong. "I promise," he said.

Alex smiled and hugged him. Although he was taken aback by her almost childlike show of affection, he felt he had no choice but to hug her, too. And oddly, as he stood there holding her, his antsyness, something he'd felt since the night began, seemed to disappear.

When he disappeared, when they finally said their good-byes and parted ways, Alex closed the door and laughed. She was so happy she was giddy. "Perfect!"she yelled. *"Per-fect!"*

WHAT EVERY MAN SHOULD WANT

Carmella walked out of the loft and met Thomas at the bottom of the stairs. Thomas smiled when he saw her, but Carmella did not return the courtesy.

"What's up?"

Carmella took a second to calm herself down, as Thomas, in a beautifully tailored charcoal-gray suit that seemed to highlight the brightness in his brown eyes, looked too relaxed for her to remain so jumpy. But just thinking about that Jazz Walker made her want to scream.

"She's driving me crazy," she said. "No, I take that back. She's driven me crazy."

"What happened?"

"That in-home art show of hers isn't for another week, Thomas, another whole week, but Jazz is acting like it's going to take place in about an hour!"

Thomas shook his head. He knew what she meant. But he still had to defend Jazz. "She wants to be super-prepared, Carm," he said.

"Super-prepared my eye! She wants to torment me, that's what she wants to do. You should see her barking out orders! I'm an artist, too, I reminded her. She ain't the only temperamental bitch in the barn, but does she even consider how I feel? No. Not Jazz Walker. Not Sister J. I tell you I'm done with her!" Carmella said this in her best island accent and then stomped on down the stairs and kept on moving.

Thomas watched as she left. He handled Carmella's divorce, from some loser actor, and they hung out a few times until she moved onto Jazz's property. What he most liked about Carmella then was her ability to keep her mouth shut. Her discretion was legendary. But now, watching her all worked up over Jazz being Jazz, he knew breaking it off with her all those years ago was the absolute right thing to do. She'd grown as hot-tempered as Jazz now, she may even have Jazz beat, and that was saying something.

He went on upstairs and knocked lightly on Jazz's screened door. Her front door was wide open. "Jazz?" he yelled as he walked in.

"I'm in the studio!" she yelled back and Thomas followed the sound of her voice.

Carmella was right. Jazz was fit to be tied. Scurrying around in a pair of shorts and a tube top, she was raging on about the lighting, and the space, and even the appropriateness of her paintings. Rambling on unlike Thomas had ever seen her. At first he just leaned his big body against the doorjamb of the studio and watched her rant and rave, deciding against saying anything to her, but when she dropped a punch bowl and nearly went ballistic over that minor matter, he exhaled.

"It's only a show, Jazzy," he said.

Jazz looked at him. She nearly stopped cold when she saw him and how gorgeous he looked in that gray suit. "Only a show?" she managed to say. "This is my first in-home show, Thomas. My first. It's not just a show and you know it!"

"You need to settle down."

"Ah, forget you!"

"Watch it, Jazz."

Jazz hesitated. He didn't understand. Nobody understood! Then she shook her head in sheer frustration and began walking out of the studio, past Thomas, but Thomas grabbed her by the arm and wouldn't let her pass. She tried to fight back, slinging from him, but his hand only gripped her tighter. When she finally gave up, when her body finally relaxed under the pressure of his hold, he moved up behind her and placed his arms around her waist, her back against his stomach.

"I want you to calm down, Jazz," he said in a soft voice.

Jazz exhaled. The tension that was tightening every fiber of her being had little to do with that show, and she knew it. And by the way Thomas held her, she could only conclude that he knew it, too. "I just want this to be right," she finally said.

"It'll be fine, honey," Thomas said. "It's always right when you're involved." He said this soothingly, and if his goal, by holding her against him, was to relax her, it was beginning to work. She even closed her eyes and leaned her head against his chest.

Thomas knew he was flirting with danger; he knew, given his forced celibate state, that he had no business getting this close to a woman who just had to look at him to turn him on, but he pulled her closer anyway. He loved the smell of her, as he ran his nose through her soft hair; she always smelled as if she had just bathed in oils and perfume. And just smelling her made him relax, too. He even began swaying side to side with her, as if they were dancing to unheard music, and she didn't mind that at all either. She felt his arousal, and was even grinding against it as he rocked her, as those floating-on-air feelings only Thomas could elicit from her caused her not to worry about a thing.

Thomas, however, was going mad with worry as Jazz grinded against him, his entire body nearly limp with desire. But when his hand slid up from her waist to her exposed stomach and gently touched the part of her tube top shielding her breast, his thumb lightly rubbing across her nipple, reality struck suddenly and Jazz opened her eyes and quickly removed her backside from his now mammoth-sized front.

"So," she said as she began walking around her studio, her voice raspier than normal, "how did it go last night?"

Thomas sighed a great sigh of frustration. "Fine," he said as he pulled out a handkerchief and began to absently wipe his hands.

"Was the food any good?"

"What?"

"The food. How was it?"

"Oh. It was okay."

"What did he serve?"

"Chicken."

"Chicken? Good for him. At least he wasn't trying to overly impress."

"Yeah." Thomas suddenly felt a need, not to hurt Jazz, but to put her on notice that there just may be another woman on his horizon. "His son became ill and he had to hurry to the hospital."

Jazz looked at Thomas. "The hospital? Is the kid all right?"

"He's fine. I talked with Conrad this morning. He had an asthma attack, but nothing too serious."

"Thank God."

"Yeah. So I drove Miss Alex Mailer home."

Jazz almost stopped in her tracks. But she didn't. She kept busying around, as if he hadn't said a word about that devious Alex Mailer. She wanted desperately to ask if anything happened between he and Alex, since Jazz just knew that gold digger wanted her hooks in Thomas badly, but she couldn't bring herself to ask it. His personal life was his personal business, she decided. "I didn't know Conrad had a son," she said instead.

Thomas sighed. He would have much rather talked about Alex. But that wasn't the kind of friendship they had. He nodded. "Yeah," he said. "He has a son."

After Thomas left Jazz he had dinner with his friend Marlene, subjecting himself to more of her complaints about her estranged husband, a man not worth sweeping out the door in his opinion, and then he made it home. He pulled into his curved driveway behind a car already parked there. It was a Lexus, white in gold trim, and he knew immediately that it belonged to Paula. He shook his head. Will the woman ever let up? he wondered.

He wanted to jump from his car in unrestrained anger and let her have it once and for all. No more Mister Nice Guy. No more worrying about her precious feelings, because she obviously didn't give a damn about his.

But he decided to take a deep breath instead and get control of himself first. Causing a scene with Paula wasn't going to help anything. Given her behavior of late, he wasn't so sure if she wouldn't find his bad mood sexy or something. So he sat there, in his car, until he was certain he could face his ex-girlfriend without reeling in rage.

Paula sat erect when Thomas got out of his car and walked up slowly to her passenger side door. And when he opened the door and sat inside, she smiled.

"Hey," she said.

"What do you want, Paula?"

"Where were you?"

Thomas leaned his head back. "Paula, Paula, Paula," he said with deep exasperation. Then he looked at her. "What are you doing?"

"I thought I was talking with you."

"It's over, Paula. Understand? It's over. I don't want to have anything to do with you."

Paula looked forward, out at the black night in front of them, and then she nodded her head. "It's Jazz," she said. "I know it now. She's the reason. And I know why."

"Jazz has nothing to do with this. I'm the reason, Paula. It's me. I don't want you. I don't want to be with you. I don't love you!"

Paula's heart dropped as those words left Thomas's lips. But she knew better. She looked at him. "It's not your fault, Thomas," she said. "Jazz has worked roots on you."

"Oh, for heaven's sake, woman! Did you hear a word I said? This isn't about Jazz. It's me. I don't want you, Paula. Period. Jazz has nothing to do with this!"

Paula reached over and placed her hand on Thomas's thigh. "I'll do anything you want, Thomas. *Anything.*"

Thomas took Paula's hand and slung it off of him. "I may be hard up, sweetheart," he said, "but I'm not that hard!"

He moved to get out of the car. Paula lashed back. "Yeah, you run along now," she said. "Run on back to Jazz. And stop bothering me, all right? Y'all can just leave me out of it!"

Thomas turned and looked at her, his eyes seared in disbelief. "There is something wrong with you," he said. And then he got out of the car and slammed the door.

Paula immediately slammed on the gas pedal and sped away from Thomas's house, the tears in her eyes undetected by the tint of her windows.

Thomas was stunned. He hardly recognized Paula, this woman he once cared for deeply. Now she was a shell of the woman he once knew. He'd had stalkers before, women who kept calling him well after the jig was up, but nothing like this.

He hurried inside his home and phoned Jazz. She had all of this great advice to dispense to strangers, he could use some himself for a change. Now it was his time, he decided, to ask Sister J.

*   *   *

Alex waited outside of Thomas's office for nearly thirty minutes before he could see her. She stood up slowly, straightened her too-short, bright yellow miniskirt, and then walked calmly into his office.

Thomas sat behind his desk but stood up when she walked in, and she smiled greatly because she knew she had her work cut out for her. She had given him a week, a full week after he took her home from Conrad's, to give her a call. But he hadn't called. Now she knew she had to make the next move.

"Good morning," she said as she walked toward his desk. He was dressed in shirt sleeves and suspenders, and the muscles that bulged from his white shirt, as if reminding all of the power behind the man, made Alex almost doubtful that she could pull this off.

"Good morning," he said with far less enthusiasm.

"I hope I'm not interrupting anything."

"No, not at all. Have a seat."

She sat down in the chair in front of his desk and immediately crossed her legs, a maneuver, she'd discovered, that always got his attention.

Thomas leaned back. "How have you been, Alex?" he asked her.

"Pretty good. Trying to stay out of trouble."

Thomas smiled. "I hear that."

"I just came to apologize, Thomas."

Thomas hesitated. "Oh, yeah?"

"Yes. I guess I sounded like some old tightass the other night. I didn't mean to. I just, I don't sleep around, you see."

She was up to something, Thomas could tell. All of this *little Miss Perfect* routine was just an opening for what she really wanted. Why she would think that such a lame game would work on him, however, was what worried him. "Well," he said, "I'm glad to hear that."

Alex laughed.

"And contrary to popular opinion," Thomas added, "neither do I."

"Oh, Thomas, I didn't mean to imply that you slept around, I was just . . . Well, it's different for a woman, you know that."

Thomas nodded. "I know."

"Good. I'm glad you understand. So we're still friends?"

This was almost laughable, Thomas thought. Friends? He barely knew her. "Sure," he said.

"Good, because I really like you. You were such a gentleman the other night. Most men would not have backed off."

"Well," he said as he stood. Enough of this, he thought. "I wish I had more time, but . . ."

"Of course," Alex said as she stood up, too. "I fully understand. You have a very busy schedule. I won't keep you any longer. I just really dropped by to apologize, like I said, but also to ask if you would like to come to my housewarming party."

They now had a house, Nikki and Alex, thanks to Nikki's new sugar daddy. His name was Earl, an older gentleman that Alex felt was perfect for Nikki, since Nikki had a tendency to fall in love with every man she'd ever had. But Earl was rude and crude and wealthy, somebody who wasn't interested in being loved and therefore didn't campaign for the job. He just wanted a beautiful woman to fulfill his occasional needs and he'd in turn take care of hers. A perfect sugar daddy. Alex, in fact, would have easily chosen him for herself in normal circumstances. But she had already met Thomas Drayton. Possibly the man of her dreams. And she wasn't about to mess that up.

But Alex did take the lead in urging Earl to do certain things for Nikki, including getting her a new place to live, away from what she told Earl was the ghost of Nikki's former boyfriend. Earl agreed and within one day had rented out a three-bedroom home for Nikki on Melrose Drive, a beautiful crib that reminded Alex of the house from the "Golden Girls" TV show, but Nikki still wanted to turn Earl down. Alex's will prevailed, however, although it was only after a bitter argument, with Nikki even insisting that she didn't need Earl, that she was going back to school to become a teacher and thereby take care of herself. It was always Nikki's dream and she believed it was time to get on with it. Alex agreed, but she also told Nikki to be practical. They were within days of being kicked out of Ray Ray's condo with no other prospects readily at hand. Earl was there, willing and able, and Nikki had to understand that. But when Nikki continued to balk, Alex lost it and told her kid sister in no uncertain terms that she could enroll in school if she wished, and dream all she pleased, but she'd better not even think about turning down Earl.

It worked, and now, two days later, Alex couldn't wait to invite Thomas over. "I know it sounds weird," she said, "having a housewarming party when I'm barely moved in myself. But I just wanted to invite a few friends over."

Thomas delayed his response, mainly because he never cared to participate in games, but also because he wondered just how young Alex really was that she would even try to run such a ridiculous game on somebody with his experience. He'd assumed her to be in her mid to late twenties. Now he wasn't so sure.

"How old are you?" he decided to ask her.

She smiled. "What?"

"How old are you?"

"I'm twenty-seven," she said. "How old are you?"

Thomas smiled. He hadn't expected that comeback. "I'm . . . not twenty-seven," he said.

"That's good enough for me."

She was old enough to know better, but she was intent on seducing him anyway. It was surprising, maybe even admirable, he thought. "Okay," he said, "you win. I'll be honored to attend your party, young lady. When is it?"

"It's tomorrow night. Seven sharp."

"Ah, I'll probably be a little late. My friend Jazz Walker will be showing her art tomorrow and I wanted to be there with her."

"I see. But I'll tell you what. I will simply push back the start time and that way you'll be on time."

"I couldn't ask you to do that."

"It's no problem at all, Thomas. Seven is too early anyway. Besides, I know Miss Walker is your best friend, Conrad told me so. Me and Conrad are friends, so I can respect that."

Thomas was pleased by Alex's easy acceptance of Jazz, although he also knew that everything was easy until it was fully understood.

"Will Conrad be in attendance?" he asked.

Alex paused. He was testing her, she thought. He was trying to see just how badly she wanted him. "Of course," she replied. And then, after leaving Thomas's office, she hurried to Conrad's to invite him, too.

LADIES' NIGHT

"You're tired of me, aren't you?" Marlene Vinson asked as she looked across the table at Thomas.

"I just think you should move on," Thomas said as he placed the papers Marlene had signed into his briefcase. "You can do better than Steve any day of the week."

"You're so sweet, Thomas, and I have moved on. Steve showed me what he was about. It just still hurts, that's all."

Thomas nodded and looked around at the sparse crowd in Solesby's. It was four o' clock, a little early for the dinner crowd and far too late for the lunch folks, but perfect timing to discuss business. He and Marlene co-owned some real estate that they were preparing to sell. But she couldn't stop talking about that estranged husband of hers and Thomas had to interrupt her twice to get her to sign the necessary documents.

"Hurt doesn't help," he said, "but it can hurt if you don't get a grip."

She smiled. "You sound like Sister J."

Thomas laughed. "I guess I do. But you know what I mean, Marlie. You're an attorney and a businesswoman. You don't need this kind of distraction."

"Agreed. But that doesn't ease the pain."

Thomas decided to leave it alone. She was throwing herself a pity party and she didn't need him to tell her to wrap it up. Besides, he thought with a smile, what did he know?

"Excuse me, sweets," Marlene said as she stood up. "I need to go to the little girls room."

Thomas stood up partway as Marlene left. She was a rare beauty, he thought, one of those sisters with the perfect combination of looks and brains. But stubborn as a mule.

He pulled out his cell phone and called Jazz, the personification of stubbornness. Carmella answered.

"I was just checking in," he said to her. "How's the show going? I'm coming over after I wrap it up here."

"The show couldn't go any worse, Thomas," Carmella said.

"What's happened?"

"Nothing. That's the problem. Nobody's shown up."

"Nobody?"

"Not one soul."

"I thought Jazz said all of her art-gallery friends would be there?"

"They told her they would. But I guess they were lying."

Thomas sighed. He knew how much that show meant to Jazz. "I'm on my way, Carmella," he said. "Stay there with her."

"I will."

Thomas flipped off his phone and then called for the check. By the time Marlene returned from the restroom he had paid the bill and was tossing a twenty tip on the table.

"Leaving so soon?" she asked.

"Jazz's show isn't going well. I'd better get over there."

"Understood," Marlene said, although she was sorely disappointed. Since her breakup with Steve she had been hoping, foolishly she was sure, that she and Thomas might just make a hookup. She knew he didn't mix business with pleasure, it was a religion with him, but she was wishing for an exception. They had so much in common, after all, and they seemed to enjoy each other's company. But it wasn't happening today, not if Jazz needed him. Marlene was Thomas's friend, too, and she'd known him longer than most all of his current acquaintances, but she knew, when it came to Jazz, she could forget it.

A car drove up the long, graveled drive, past the house, and up to the garage apartment. Carmella, inside the apartment, hurried to the window. She smiled when a female got out and began walking up the side stairs. "Finally," she said to herself. "Jazz!" she yelled aloud.

Jazz came out of the kitchen, where she'd been helping herself to some of the hors d'oeuvres. She had on her narrow-frame glasses and was carrying a pile of papers in her hands. "What's up?"

"Customer," Carmella said.

"Quit playing, girl."

"I don't play, at least not like that. A sister's on her way up now."

Jazz actually was relieved. Her prayer was that somebody would show up. They didn't have to buy anything, she'd gladly give them a painting or two, but just that it wouldn't all have been in vain was the point to her.

Her relief, however, was short lived when the door was opened and Carmella warmly greeted someone she thought was a customer. It was actually Paula Scott.

Jazz shook her head. All she needed, she thought. "Hello, Paula."

"Good evening."

"He's not here."

"I didn't say he was."

"Don't tell me you're here for the art."

"Don't be ridiculous. What art?"

"Look, Paula, I can feel your hurt and all that. But I'm not up for this today."

"Up for what? Honestly! As if you're some goddess everybody has to bow down to."

Jazz frowned. "What?"

"I take it you two know each other," Carmella said, intrigued by the odd woman.

"Oh, yes," Paula said. "Jazz and I are quite acquainted. Aren't we, Jazz?"

"What do you want, Paula?"

Paula smiled then sat down on the sofa. "I want to make a deal," she said.

Carmella looked at Jazz, as if she was dying to hear the details, but Jazz didn't take her eyes off of Paula.

"You heard me," Paula said. "Let's make a deal."

"No thanks."

"You haven't heard the deal yet."

"Yeah," Carmella said, sitting on the arm of a nearby chair, "let's hear the offer first."

"Okay, fine. What's the deal?"

Paula paused and then sat erect. "I'll let you have Thomas," she said to Jazz, "if you let me have him, too."

Carmella smiled. It sounded freaky to her, which was a joke since she knew Jazz didn't swing like that.

"You need to get a grip, Paula," Jazz said, "and I mean like now. It's over between you and Thomas and you know it."

"Ain't nothing over!" Paula yelled, her deceptively cool demeanor beginning to unravel. "Yeah, you want it to be over. But ain't nothing over! We were so happy, he was so happy with me. And you couldn't stand that. Oh, I saw how you looked at me with those big-behind eyes of yours. You never wanted him to touch me. But he did. Many times. And you hated it. And you kept feeding lies to him about me. Lies, lies, lies! It's all been you, Jazz, I know it now. You and your roots. Probably some potion you cooked up with your island friend here. That's why I don't have my man anymore. Because of you. But I got something for you, sister. It's over all right. He's through with you, that's what's over."

Carmella, understanding clearly just how crazy Paula was, rose to make a mad dash to the nearest telephone, but Paula quickly but calmly pulled a gun out of her small purse and pointed it at her. "Sit down," she ordered Carmella, and Carmella, nobody's fool, quickly obliged.

Jazz, however, was stunned. "What do you think you're doing?" she asked Paula, her eyes now staring at the gun.

"I'm getting rid of my problem, that's what I'm doing. I'm about to make some drastic changes in my life. Beginning with you."

Paula stood up. Jazz's heart dropped.

"Wait a minute, Paula."

"Nope."

"Let's make a deal, okay? Let's talk about this."

"Oh no," Paula said, waving the gun around, "you don't want to make a deal. Thomas doesn't want me, remember? And he probably doesn't, as long as you're around to feed him all those lies about me."

"But it's not like that."

"It's exactly like that! It took me some time to figure it out. Why was he treating me like this, I kept asking myself. Why was he breaking up with me?"

"But you dumped him, remember? You're the one who gave him an ultimatum."

"Stop lying on me!" Paula yelled this as she stood directly in front of Jazz and pointed the gun right at her head. "You keep lying on me," she said in a softer voice. "All I did was love Thomas, that's all I ever did. You were supposed to be his friend, just his friend, but that wasn't good enough for you. You wanted him as badly as I did. And you was going to stop at nothing to get him. But I was in your way. So you had to make up tall tales about me, anything you could think up, to turn him against me." Tears began to come to her eyes. "You turned him against me, Jazz. Now he looks at me with such hate! He used to love me. But he doesn't anymore. And it's all because of you. But if I get rid of you, then he'll love me again."

"He'll blame you, Paula," Jazz said desperately, staring down the barrel of the gun. "Think about it. If something happens to me he'll blame you. He'll hate you more."

"No, he won't. He understands what's going on. He knows it's all your fault. He won't blame me, because he knows what you're up to."

"Paula, please put the gun down."

"No!"

"It can go off, Paula. Please aim it away from my head."

"No! Stop it! It's always about you, isn't it? Jazz, Jazz, Jazz. Always all about Jazz. But not anymore. You have done some bad things, Jazz Walker. Some terrible, terrible things. And now you've got to pay."

Paula placed the gun closer to Jazz's skull just as the front door flew open and, to everybody's astonishment, Thomas appeared. He had seen Paula's Lexus downstairs and he was hot. He was ready, absolutely ready, to settle this once and for all. But when he saw the gun, and the barrel of that gun against Jazz's head, *Jazz's* head, he froze.

"Paula," he said as if he could not believe what he was viewing.

Paula turned quickly, which caused the gun's barrel to reposition away from Jazz, which caused Jazz to let out a sigh of relief that almost took her to her knees.

There was a sudden hush in the room, as everybody seemed frozen by the gravity of the horror. Thomas, however, was thinking so hard he was getting a headache. He knew he had to calmly coax that gun out of Paula's hand. He knew that much. But the erratic way she'd been behaving lately made him also know that she was far more dangerous than he could even imagine.

"Paula," he said again, but this time calmly, "I was looking for you."

There was a stunned hesitation by Paula. "You were?"

"Yes! Yes, I was. I wanted to tell you how much . . . how much I loved you and how I couldn't wait to be by your side again."

Paula stared at Thomas. "Really?"

"Yes, honey. I'm so glad you're here. I want to take you to dinner and talk with you."

Paula was too confused for words. He couldn't stand the sight of her earlier, and now he wanted to take her to dinner? Even with Jazz still around? Her hopes tried to soar. But when, peripherally, she could see Jazz backing away from her, she immediately regained her defensive posture and quickly aimed the gun at Jazz once more.

Thomas panicked. "Paula, listen to me," he said, moving a step closer.

"I can't."

"Yes, you can, Paula. Yes, honey, you can."

"What about her?" Paula said this as she waved the gun in front of Jazz. "We can never be happy, Thomas, never, with her in our lives."

Thomas's heart pounded as he walked slowly toward Paula. "I know exactly what you mean, honey, I really do. That's why I was coming over here. To tell Jazz that I can't see her anymore."

"But that's not enough. I see how you look at her. You'll want her again."

"No, Paula, no. Look at me. Paula, look at me." Thomas stood beside her as he said this. Paula turned and looked into his eyes. That faraway look in hers stunned him. "You're the one I want," he said. "You understand me? Jazz doesn't mean a thing to me. It's you, Paula." He said this calmly, staring deeply into her confused eyes. Then, as she continued that almost-otherworldly look at him, he slowly, without taking his eyes off of hers, removed the gun from her hand. As soon as he did Carmella bolted from her seat and ran into the kitchen to call the police. Paula turned quickly, which allowed

Thomas to push her down on the sofa and away from Jazz. Paula was stunned as she looked up at Thomas. Thomas, however, was staring at Jazz.

"You okay?" he asked her.

Jazz, however, could only manage a nod. She walked back, until her back was against the wall.

Thomas walked the last police officer to the door and then talked a few minutes longer with Carmella on the porch before he returned to Jazz. She was slouched down on her couch, her small glasses perched on her nose, her legs spread apart and weightless as she stared at a sitcom on television. Thomas, now in shirt sleeves, sat down beside her. He was emotionally exhausted, and it was still draining him. From the police to the gun to Paula's hate-filled defiance as she realized he didn't mean a word he had said to her, the events of the day seemed to have taken a heavier toll on him. Jazz looked up at him, at the hurt that still showed in his eyes, then leaned against him as he put his arm around her. She'd never been so scared in her life, and it bothered her, because she froze in the face of Paula. She didn't know what to do or say. She felt helpless and frightened and so completely out of control.

"Was the gun loaded?" she asked Thomas.

Thomas hesitated. "Yes," he said.

Jazz closed her eyes. "Jesus. I didn't think Paula was like that."

"Tell me about it," Thomas said as he began unconsciously running his hand up and down Jazz's back. "She became desperate after we broke up, for reasons I'm sure had little to do with me, but she decided to make me the object of her desperation."

"Her eyes looked dead. Like she was far away from here. It was so weird." Then Jazz paused for a long time as she contemplated saying what she was thinking. Then, after much reflection, she decided to speak. "If we weren't so close," she said, "none of this would have happened."

Thomas frowned. "What?"

"You know what, Thomas," Jazz said as she removed herself from his embrace. "She asked you to end your friendship with me, but you wouldn't do it. So she took matters into her own hands."

"She's a nutcase, Jazz. And she would have been a nutcase regardless of my decision. I'm not going to sit up here and let somebody like Paula convince me that I did something wrong. She can't make me love her."

"I know that. But . . ."

"But what?"

"All I'm saying is maybe we need to just cool it for a while, you know? This relationship, this friendship is costing you too much, Thomas, and I can't keep letting it happen."

Thomas leaned his head back. "Don't do this, Jazz."

"Every girlfriend you've had, every one, has left you because of me. That should tell us something."

"Yeah, it tells us that you're hot and they can't deal with that."

Jazz managed to smile. "I'm not hot."

"Yes, you are."

"Yeah, me in my baggy jeans and glasses. I'm sure they're real jealous of me."

"They are."

"Thomas, please. I'm sure that's not it."

Thomas looked at Jazz. She had no clue how beautiful she really was. No clue at all. "Come here," he said to her. She hesitated—it sounded too commanding to her—but the warmth of his arms around her felt too good lately for her to resist. She moved back over to him. He did place his arm around her, but then he lifted her on his lap. At first she thought to get up, he was going too far, but she didn't. She wasn't sure if she could.

Thomas pulled her closer to him and embraced her gently. The thought that something could have happened to her, that he could have lost her today, unnerved him. He closed his eyes as she laid her head against his chest. She was blaming their friendship. Not Paula and her craziness, but their friendship. No way was he losing her, he thought. Because that friendship that nobody seemed to want them to have was slowly becoming the very reason he got out of bed every day.

He held Jazz in his lap for hours. She dozed off twice, he dozed off once. She felt light on his lap, and he snuggled her closer to him. He had erection after erection, as she sat on top of him, but he fought the urge to even kiss her. The pain he saw in her eyes, when he finally got that gun out of Paula's hands and they both realized what could have been, made her too vulnerable now. And it was too painful to think about. But that was all Thomas thought about as he held Jazz, as he felt the ache in every breath she took. She was his, he thought, as he kept pulling her closer to him, and nobody, not crazy ex-lovers, not their friendship itself, was going to ever take her away from him.

By the time Jazz woke up for the second time, Thomas's arm was numb. But when she looked up at him with those droopy eyes of hers and then smiled, he didn't even care.

"Weren't you suppose to have dinner with what's-her-name?" Jazz asked him.

Thomas smiled. "Her name is Alex. And I wasn't going anywhere."

"What time is it?"

Thomas lifted his arm and glanced at his Rolex. "Almost eleven," he said.

"Eleven?" Jazz said with shock in her voice and jumped out of his lap. "You've got to be out of town first thing in the morning, Thomas, what are you doing? You've got to prepare for that conference in Tampa tomorrow. You should be home in bed getting your rest."

"I'm fine, Jazz."

"But you've got to give a presentation as soon as you hit town, Thomas. Why didn't you wake me up and go home?"

"I told you I wasn't going anywhere. Not until I was sure you're okay."

Jazz grabbed Thomas by the arm and helped him to his feet. "I'm okay, all right?" she said. "Now get your jacket and go home."

Thomas laughed as he grabbed his suit coat off of the back of the sofa. "You are so ungrateful!"

"Right," Jazz said as she pushed him toward the front door. "Just go home."

When they made it to the door Thomas began putting on his suit coat. Jazz helped him. "But for real, Thomas," she said, "I'm all right."

Thomas nodded and looked at her. "You can always come with me."

"No thanks."

"Four days away. It'll do you good."

Jazz shook her head. "No thanks. I'm not about to be following you around as if I'm some basket case. I'm fine."

She wasn't, but he knew she would die before admitting it to him. "Well at least let me stay here with you tonight."

"Not necessary, Thomas. Really. All I want to do is take me a hot bath and go to sleep. And you need to do the same so you'll be fresh for your presentation tomorrow."

"Then come over to my house tonight."

"No."

"Just for the night."

"No way, Thomas. I'm staying right here. Alone. Okay?"

Thomas shook his head. "You win, Jazz," he said reluctantly. "You always win."

Jazz didn't know if she liked the way he said that but she decided to let it pass. It had been quite a day for both of them, and they were both edgy. They stared at each other a few moments longer, as if trying with their eyes to reassure the other, and then he leaned down to her, and she lifted up to him, and they kissed. She was so welcoming of the kiss that she opened her mouth immediately and allowed his tongue in. Thomas, surprised by the allowance, wrapped his arms around her and lingered in his kiss. He pressed her against the door as he kissed her, his loins so hard that he couldn't stop himself from jamming her. And when she responded by holding him tighter, he placed his hands on her behind and lifted her slightly until her sex was against his sex in such a tight lock that even her jeans and his pants couldn't stop the heat from penetrating. And when he took one hand and unbuttoned and then unzipped those jeans, they both seemed to realize simultaneously what a bad idea that would be, especially after a day like this, and they stopped kissing immediately. They had enough on their plates as it was, their sudden withdrawal seemed to say.

"I hope you have a safe trip," Jazz said as she reassembled her clothes. Her breathing was so irregular that she could barely speak.

"I'll see you when I get back," Thomas said, breathing heavily, too. They stood there momentarily, saying their good-byes, as their bodies slowly began to cool down from the heat they had generated. They knew they couldn't keep going down this dead-end road, where frustration was always the final stop, and they both looked into the other's eyes as a reminder. Because both of them, no matter how they tried to smile as they said good night, no matter what kind of spin they tried to put on their ever-increasing passionate kisses, were beginning to become two exceedingly frustrated people.

NOTHING ON ALEX

Alex arrived at Thomas's law firm early the next day, anxious to find out why he was a no-show at her housewarming party. She had it all planned out, down to his spending the night with her, and he didn't even show up. And when the receptionist informed her that Thomas was out of town on business and wouldn't be back for another four days, anxiety gripped her.

She hurried to Conrad's office. He was her saving grace. But even he was reluctant to help.

"I'm not being difficult, Alexandria," he said as he walked from behind his desk. "I just don't understand why you need to know where Mr. Drayton went."

"I told you, Nikki needs to know."

"But why?"

Alex shook her head as if frustrated with Conrad's questions. Actually, she was trying like mad to think up something as she went along. "He promised to give Nikki some valuable legal advice about a personal family matter, Conrad," she said, finding her way, "and Nikki desperately needs to talk with him."

"If it's about that assault charge from the nightclub, that's over with."

"No, it has nothing to do with that. It's just something Nikki needs to talk to him about."

Conrad leaned against his desk and folded his arms. "I wish I could help, kid, honest I do. But I'm too far down the food chain around here to know anything about Mr. Drayton's travel itinerary."

"You can ask somebody, Conrad, come on."

"It's not that simple."

"Make it that simple. Please." She said this and moved closer to Conrad. And she smiled. Conrad stood up.

"I'll check around," he said. "But I can't promise you anything."

"Just do it, please."

"All right."

"I'll wait right here."

"Not now, Alexandria. I've got to be in court in thirty minutes."

"This won't take you two minutes, Conrad, if you go on and do it."

Conrad laughed to himself. What a chump he must be to her. "All right," he said. "I'll be back."

Alex waited so nervously that she paced the floor the entire time. She couldn't wait four more days to see Thomas, not after he didn't show up for her party and didn't even bother to call and cancel. There must be another woman. That was it. He must have some bitch on the side who suddenly appeared and now he doesn't feel a need to bother with her anymore. That was why she pressed. She had to change things. She had to convince him, and quickly, that no other woman on the face of this earth could give him what she had in mind.

It took five more minutes but Conrad finally returned. Mr. Drayton, he informed her, was in Tampa for the next four days and he was staying at the Radisson. He even managed to get Thomas's room number. Alex smiled greatly, kissed Conrad on the lips, and hurried out of the door as if her life depended on it. Conrad touched his lips and smiled. She either loved her sister very much, he thought, or he was the biggest fool this side of living.

The conference wrapped up by six p.m. and Thomas made it back to his hotel room a little after seven. He laid on top of the bed and dialed Jazz's number. He'd been thinking about her all day, and that passionate kiss they shared, and it took every ounce of strength he had not to pick up his cell phone to give her a call much earlier. The last thing she needed was to feel burdened by his desire for her, a desire that neither booze nor cigars nor anything else seemed able to wash away. But now, as the night descended and the memories of Paula with that gun and the fright in Jazz's eyes crystallized again, Thomas had to call her, to make sure she was all right.

"I'm fine," she said immediately, as she could hear the concern in his voice. "I did my radio show and had a very good postproduction meeting, so all in all it was a good day."

"How did you rest last night?" he asked. "I barely got a good hour in."

"I slept like a log," Jazz said. It was a lie, and he knew it, but he also knew she wasn't about to say anything different.

"Well, I was just calling you, to make sure you were okay. I worry about you, you know."

"How was the conference?"

Thomas sighed. She'd rather talk about anything than the real thing. "It was good. Got a lot done."

"And your presentation? Was it good, too?"

"I think so. I was told it was excellent."

"Well, congratulations. You'll be president of that bar association yet again this year if you aren't careful."

"I'm careful. I'm not taking on that job again. But listen, Jazz, I've been thinking about your art show."

"Don't. It was a fiasco all around and that's all there is to it."

"Because it was an in-home show, in a small studio, and in Homestead of all places. I was thinking if I was to rent you a gallery for an evening or two . . ."

"No thanks, Thomas."

"Convenience for your customers is important, Jazz."

"I know that. And if I want to put on a gallery show, then I'll put on a gallery show. But that wasn't what I wanted."

Thomas exhaled. "I'm just sorry it didn't work out."

"I know."

There was a slight pause. "What's that noise I hear?"

"TV. I'm watching the news."

"Anything interesting going on?"

"Nothing. And I mean nada. But no news is good news, right?"

"That's what they say. I hadn't heard from you all day, so I assumed you were all right. But Lord knows I was dying to hear your voice again."

There was a pause from Jazz that, Thomas knew, meant that his little words of affection had gone too far. "Anyway, Thomas," she said, "I'd better get off of this phone."

"What's the hurry?" he asked, although he already knew.

"I'm not hurrying. I just wanted, I plan to do some painting tonight and I wanted to get started."

Thomas closed his eyes. "Okay," he said. "Call me if you need me."

"I will."

"Good night."

"Night," she said and hung up the phone.

Thomas laid there momentarily, with the dead line in his hand, and then he hung up, too.

He got out of bed and headed for the bathroom. By the time he had showered and changed into his robe, he was beginning to feel sleep coming on. Good timing, he thought, because he certainly didn't have anything else to do, having turned down all offers from his colleagues to go out or have dinner or just hang around. He wasn't in the party mood tonight. Not after yesterday, and the trip today, and the exhausting presentation and conference that sapped the little energy he did have. Now sleep was a pleasant thought. But just as he turned his covers back and removed his bedroom shoes, knocks could be heard on his hotel room door.

Thomas frowned. It was probably a colleague who'd decided not to take no for an answer, and he slipped back into his shoes and hurried for the door.

He slung it open, so whoever it was could readily see his displeasure. But it wasn't a colleague as he had assumed. It was Alex.

"Hi," she said with a smile so grand he would have normally smiled, too. But he was too stunned to smile.

"What are you doing here?" he asked her, the frown that had fixed on his face still remaining.

It wasn't exactly the response Alex was hoping for, but she continued smiling anyway. "I was just in the neighborhood . . ."

"Alex!"

"Okay. I heard that you were here in Tampa and so I thought I'd pay you a visit."

Thomas paused, his face unable to stop staring at her. She was dressed in her usual loud colors, this time a hot-lime miniskirt with matching blouse and heels and a purse with a streak of lime also. She looked like a pack of Kool-Aid to Thomas. But her smile was endearing and her face, pretty in the classic sense, wasn't exactly something to frown upon. But she was here, in Tampa, following him around as if she was aiming to pick up where Paula left off. And he wasn't having it. "Why?" he asked her.

"Why what?"

"Why are you paying me a visit?"

Alex was crushed. He was treating her as if she was some stalker or something. But she refused to stop smiling. "You didn't show up for my housewarming party, and I wanted to know why."

Thomas smiled. And then he laughed. He couldn't help himself. Because he knew it was true. Because anybody who would wear a lime miniskirt for all the world to see would also journey all the way to Tampa just to get an answer to a question.

"Come in," he said, between laughs, and Alex, though unsure of the joke, gladly walked in.

As soon as the door shut behind them, Alex didn't waste another minute. She moved closer to Thomas and put her arms around his waist. His entire body tensed up by the closeness of the contact—he was horny as hell—and by her assertiveness. "You're one aggressive lady," he said as he looked down at her, his voice lower than before.

"If you think this is aggressive," she said, her voice softer, too, "get a load of this."

She raised up on her tiptoes and kissed Thomas on the lips. It was a sweet kiss, warm and simple, with none of the kick he felt whenever his lips touched Jazz's. But she did it again, and this time with her tongue going down his throat, a move that made him as if by reflex place his arms around her and pull her closer to him. She tasted sweet and smelled perfumey, and just the idea of a warm body against his was enough to dull his senses. He didn't know if he wanted Alex Mailer, he didn't even know if she really wanted him, but he needed her tonight. He needed her taste and her touch and her smell to warm his bed tonight. And that was why he returned her kiss with an even more passionate kiss and ended up walking her backwards until he had her on his bed.

He undressed her, all of her lime colors floating down like deflated balloons on his floor. And as he looked over her naked body, a body so small and soft, so feminine and young, he kissed her again. She reacted to the kiss by pulling him on top of her, but he pulled away. Kissing was not enough. Not tonight.

He reached for his wallet, pulled out a condom, and then mounted her without removing his robe. But she removed it, as he put on his condom and entered her and as her body arched with the pleasure of him going in. At first he eased in and moved slow, but then he slapped hard against her, the long overdue release causing him to lose all restraint, and she matched his forcefulness, thrust for thrust. The sound of pounding flesh echoed throughout the quiet bedroom, as the sweat built up and the feelings intensified, until neither could hold on any longer and they both came. Alex came first with a scream, and then Thomas. Thomas jerked as he came, his muscular frame going weak, and then he collapsed on top of her, his body feeling sated, his mind settling back into a rhythm of rationality, and his heart, his heavy, hungry heart, wishing to God that it was Jazz.

The next morning Thomas was sitting in a chair smoking a cigar and watching Alex as she slept. She had it all, he was thinking: the looks, the body, some prowess in bed. But will she get along with Jazz? Will he open up his heart to her only to have to deal with yet another ultimatum? He could set some ground rules. He could make it perfectly clear, up front, that their relationship is going nowhere if she can't handle the fact that Jazz is, and will always be, his closest, dearest, best friend. But who was he kidding? Every girlfriend he'd ever had thought the world of Jazz early on, before the relationship intensified. But as soon as feelings got in the way, they became threatened. They knew how much Thomas cared for Jazz, they probably could see it all over his face, but they were convinced that he'd acted on those feelings. He hadn't, he'd never been unfaithful to any of his girlfriends, but trying to get them to believe it was impossible.

Now Alex wanted a go of it. She said as much last night. They could be great together, she said, and she all but begged him to give her a chance. He watched her as she moved around in his bed, her little hands wrapped around the pillow as if it were her security. She was younger than he would like, and her body was a little too small and fragile for his style of lovemaking, but there was something refreshing about her. Her silly seduction games were over—they weren't going to be successful anyway—but he admired the fact that she would even try something like that on a man like him, a man who could write a book on seduction.

He rubbed his cigar across his tongue as he stared at Alex. He was tired of starting over, tired of dumping one woman and picking up another one as if any of them would ever completely satisfy him. But with Jazz off limits, he knew, unfortunately, that he would continue to start over until somebody showed him a lot more than he'd been seeing.

And as if she could read Thomas's mind, Alex opened her eyes. And then she smiled.

"Good morning," he said.

"Good morning," she said, and she said it lowly, as if she was embarrassed. "You okay?"

Thomas smiled. "Yes," he said. "Come here."

Her smile increased as she kicked the covers back, her naked body nothing to her, and got out of bed. When she got up to Thomas he placed his arms around her waist and looked at her. Although she was standing up and he was sitting, they were practically eye to eye. "Did you sleep well?" he asked her.

"Oh, did I. I haven't slept this good in years."

"I've got a conference this morning," he said, "but we'll have lunch."

"Can I stay here, or will I need to get a room?"

Thomas hesitated. He wasn't sure if he wanted to go down this road, but he didn't see where he had a choice now. "Of course you can stay here," he said.

Nikki wasn't ten minutes back home when Earl was calling her cell phone again. She wanted to toss the darn thing out the window. She knew she should have never hooked up with a joker like him, not when she was trying to get her own act together, but Alex insisted. They needed somebody to use, in other words, and Earl, with his selfish behind, was willing.

"Yes, Earl, what is it?" Nikki said as she sat down on her living-room sofa and answered the ringing phone.

"Where were you all morning?"

"I told you I had to register for classes today, Earl."

"Classes? What kind of classes?"

"Earl, I told you I had enrolled at Miami-Dade, I told you that. And I had to register today."

"College? Please. You expect me to believe that?"

Nikki rolled her eyes. "Yes, as a matter of fact, I do expect you to believe that."

"Just using me, that's all. Taking my money and laughing at me. But keep on, okay? Stop being around when I'm looking for you. I'll snatch that house from under y'all in a Miami minute, keep trying me!"

"Whatever, Earl, all right?" Nikki said angrily and tossed her cell phone aside. She leaned her head back and exhaled. He couldn't take the house, Nikki's name was on the lease agreement—thanks to Alex's insistence—but if he pulled his financial backing it'll be just as good as taking it. The little money Alex had saved up barely covered the utilities and food bills and even that wasn't going to last forever. She could only hope that Alex's little trip to Tampa proved more fruitful or they were going to just have to get off of their behinds and get jobs.

Which was all right with Nikki, her sugar-daddy days were numbered anyway, but her skill level was the problem. She doubted if Mickie D's would hire her. But she'd scrub floors before she kissed Earl Hunter's behind.

The doorbell rang. When she peeped out of the bay window and saw that it was Conrad, she smiled. She liked him, he seemed like such a good guy, although Alex treated him like her doormat.

"Conrad, come in," Nikki said excitedly and Conrad, along with his son, six-year-old Ricky Baines, walked in.

"Hello, Nikki," Conrad said. "I want you to meet my son, Ricardo Baines. Better known as Ricky."

"Ah, what a handsome little man." Nikki said this and then kneeled down to Ricky. "Hey, little man, how you doing?"

"Fine," Ricky said with a smile.

"How old are you?"

"Six."

"Wow, you'll be full grown any day now."

Ricky blushed. Nikki stood up. "He's great, Conrad," she said.

"Thanks. I love him." Conrad said this and put his arm around Ricky's shoulders.

"Y'all have a seat, I'm just getting in good. I had to register for classes."

"Oh," Conrad said as he and Ricky walked over to the sofa. "You're going to school now?"

"Yeah. Well, only at Miami-Dade, but I hope to transfer to Florida Memorial as soon as I get my AA."

"Good for you," Conrad said, and he and Ricky sat down. Nikki, seemingly pleased with their company, sat down beside Ricky. "A good education is the key to success," Conrad added.

"That's the truth. That's why I'm doing it. I don't want to have to depend on anybody anymore."

"Like Raymond."

"Right. I mean, don't get me wrong, Ray Ray was a good provider. But he wasn't right, you know? He had a wife I knew nothing about. The drugs. I'm tired of all of that."

"You can do bad by yourself."

Nikki laugh. "I know that's right."

"So," Conrad said, looking around, "where's Alexandria? She promised to meet my son today."

"Oh. Really? Well, I'm sorry, Conrad, but she's not here."

"She's not?"

"No. I'm sorry."

"Man. When do you expect her back?"

"I don't know."

Conrad nodded. "I see. Well. I was hoping she'd be here."

Nikki felt bad. Why he wouldn't just forget about Alex and go on with his life was beyond her. Any fool could see the mismatch. "I'll tell her that you came by, though," she said.

"Thanks."

"And that doesn't mean you have to rush off now. I was just about to fix me some lunch. Why don't you and Ricky join me?"

"You sure, Nikki?"

"Positive. After what you did for me, getting those charges dropped and all, man, please. It'll be my pleasure to fix you lunch."

Conrad smiled. "Thanks. We appreciate it."

Nikki stood up. "You and little man just make yourselves at home. I won't be a minute."

"Oh, Nikki, were you able to reach Mr. Drayton?"

Nikki hesitated. "Was I able to what?"

"Did you get in touch with Thomas Drayton? Alex said—"

"Oh, yeah, I got in touch with him. Thanks for asking."

"You're welcome," Conrad said, and Nikki, so tired of Alex and her nonsense, hurried out of the living room to avoid further lies.

Noon time in Tampa and the restaurant Thomas had selected was crowded, but the waitress managed to find them a cozy booth in the back, away from the deafening noise of the bar crowd. Alex was smiling, a little too much for Thomas's taste, and her outfit, a purple-and-red shorts set, made him wonder if she owned any grown-up clothes. He had on a brown suit, very sternly conservative, and they looked as mismatched as humanly possible. But she didn't seem to mind his style of dress, which he was sure didn't suit her any more than hers suited him, so he decided to stop worrying about hers.

That was easy to do. She was a burst of energy and cheerfulness, he thought. And she knew how to keep him upbeat. That was why, after their drinks arrived and she asked him what he thought was an odd question, he couldn't help but smile. "Of course I believe in God," he said. "Jesus Christ, too. I'm not foolish enough to think that I was responsible for waking myself up this morning. And who sustains me day in and day out? Me? So yes, Miss Alex, I most definitely believe in God."

Alex smiled. "Just checking," she said. "The way people are nowadays you never know."

Thomas nodded. The fact that she would be concerned about his religious bent surprised him. He didn't take her for the type. But there was nothing about Alex Mailer, he was beginning to discover, that was what it seemed. When he first saw her at his dinner party, he just knew she was some hot-to-trot looking for a good time, somebody he wouldn't trust as far as he could throw. But when she turned him down because she didn't want to suffer again, and when she actually apologized to him for that night, it touched him in a way he didn't think possible. She wasn't a good girl, the sister was too aggressive all around to not have been around herself, but she wasn't the easy lay he had took her for either. This was one he had to play by ear, he decided.

"So, Alex," he said, leaning back, "tell me about yourself."

"Not much to tell. I was born in a small town called Palatka. It was just me and my sister and my mother. Never knew my daddy. We moved to Miami, though, when I was like ten. My mother was a good mother, she just fell in love a lot, and me and my sister, her name is Nikki, she's my baby sister, we sort of just took care of ourselves. Then my mother died. So we were on our own for real. I grew up, did some modeling work, then moved to Fort Lauderdale, where I met this guy who was supposed to be the answer to my prayers."

"Of course he wasn't."

"The understatement of the year. But it broke my heart. So I came back to Miami. I guess I'm between careers right now. Making it off of my savings right now." This was the opening Alex had hoped for, the chance for her to mention her dire financial situation within the flow of the conversation and the chance for him to offer to help her out. But Thomas was unlike any man she'd ever met. He never took the bait. "And that's about it," she said, when it was clear he wasn't biting. "What about you? Are you originally from here, or, as most folks, you got here by way of somewhere else?"

"Texas, actually. I'm originally from Fort Worth. I moved to Miami after law school, with no particular plans to stay very long."

"And you never left."

"That's right."

"And I know this is an odd time to ask this question, but are you married?"

Thomas laughed. "No, I'm not married."

Alex exhaled. "Good. I didn't want to be a part of the adultery thing."

"I second that."

"And you have no children? Or do you?"

"No, no children. You?"

"None. And I'd better hurry up, too, because I'm almost thirty."

Thomas smiled. "You're twenty-seven, Alex. You're still a baby."

"Yeah, right. I just couldn't see myself having no children from the kind of men I'd been hooking up with. They were all right, you know, but none of them were what I'd call father material. Present company excluded, of course."

Thomas smiled weakly. She was seriously getting ahead of herself, he thought. He was still trying to decide if he even wanted to see her again, and she was talking about kids.

"So there's nobody?" she asked him. "No parents, no sisters, no brothers?"

"My parents are dead. I have a brother in New Hampshire but we don't keep in touch. So, there's really nobody else. Except Jazz." Thomas said this and looked at Alex. Alex smiled.

"She seems like such a nice person," she said, not meaning a word of it. "I didn't get a chance to really talk with her, but she seemed to be a very smart, impressive woman."

"Yeah," Thomas said, "she's a special lady."

"How long have you known her?"

"Six, no, almost seven years now. I was her divorce attorney."

Alex laughed. "That's a good way to meet girls."

"Not really. But I met Jazz that way. And we've been friends ever since. Of course a lot of females don't think it's possible."

"They don't think what's possible? For a man to have a woman as a friend only?"

"As his best friend, yes."

"That's stupid. Of course a man and a woman can be friends. I think it's a good thing, actually."

"Jazz is very close to me, Alex. Extremely close. And nothing, and I mean nothing, is going to come between my friendship with her."

We'll see about that, Alex wanted to say. "I can really respect that, Thomas," she said instead. "I really can. Because that's exactly how I feel about my relationship with Nikki. And I'm not trying to say that our relationship is going anywhere, I'm not trying to put any pressure on you or anything like that. But let me be clear: I will never let you interfere in my relationship with my sister, just as I won't ever interfere in your relationship with Jazz. I know what it's like to be close to somebody. And I'll never mess that up."

Thomas stared at Alex. She certainly gave the right answer. The perfect answer in fact, because she knew what it was like to have a special person in her life. And although he was admittedly optimistic, and her differentness was giving her the edge, he still wasn't throwing caution to the wind just yet.

COME SATURDAY MORNING

Jazz waited in the airport for Thomas to round the corner. His plane had already touched down and she wanted to surprise him as soon as he showed up. She hadn't heard from him since his first night in Tampa, when he phoned to see if she was all right, and she felt that she'd been less than kind to him even then. This was make-up time. He was her best friend, after all, the man she couldn't live without, and she treated him like crap.

She stood there, in a tunic top and baggy cargo pants, her small-frame eyeglasses perched on her nose, her oversized hobo bag hanging from her shoulder. She glanced at herself in the line of mirrors against the wall. She looked like a nerd, she thought, like somebody so steeped in her artist world that she didn't have time or inclination for glamor. But Thomas thought she was beautiful. And other men, too, as they loved to hit on her. But every time she looked in the mirror she didn't see the beauty. Yet the fact that Thomas did was good enough for her.

She smiled as soon as he walked from around the ramp and entered into the airport, his broad shoulders holding up his carrying bag with a firm grip. He had on Dockers and a white banded-bottom shirt, and he looked so sexy that she wanted to run to him and throw her arms around him, and she would have. But he stopped and turned as if he was waiting for someone to catch up. When Jazz saw Alex Mailer hurry around that corner, walking up beside Thomas as if she belonged by his side, she almost puked. She knew Alex had designs on Thomas, but damn, she thought. Thomas didn't usually mix his business with pleasure. Not ever. What was so special about Alex, she wondered, to make him break his own rules now?

Thomas put his free hand on Alex's lower back, as if to guide her along, and Jazz knew it was a sure sign that they'd slept together. Which was fine by her. Thomas was, after all, a free man. But damn, she thought.

When Thomas finally managed to look away from Alex and check out his surroundings, he nearly stopped in his tracks when he saw Jazz. He couldn't believe his eyes. She'd never met his plane before, not even on the few occasions when he asked her to, and her unexpected presence alone caused a grinding ache to come into his heart. God, she was beautiful, he thought, as she stood there in her baggy pants and glasses, and although she was just a friend, although Alex was walking right beside him, he couldn't help himself. He pulled away from Alex and hurried to Jazz. He felt as if he would die if he didn't hold her, and feel her lips on his one more time, regardless of how it looked and what people thought. That was Jazz standing there waiting on him. *Jazz.*

He slung his carrying bag off of his shoulder and dropped it to the ground as soon as he reached her side. She tried not to smile. She tried not to encourage what she could tell was certain to be an emotional response from Thomas. But seeing him again, close to her, evoked feelings too strong. She couldn't help but smile.

"Hey," Thomas said as he put his arms around her and pulled her against him. He took her chin in his hand and lifted her face up to his. "Miss you," he said.

Jazz smiled. "Me, too," was the most she could manage to say. But that was enough for Thomas as he rubbed his mouth across her lips, over and over, and when he kissed her he let out a moan inside her mouth that made her heart flutter. Then he pulled her once again against his hard, muscular body, causing every inch of her to tingle with desire.

Alex walked up behind them but was careful to stay a slight distance back. Thomas obviously cared for the weird woman, she thought, even if the woman was probably butch and could offer him nothing more than maybe a little intelligent conversation perhaps, but even that was suspect to Alex. She'd heard Jazz's show, that *Ask Sister J* nonsense, and the way Alex saw it Jazz was using that show as nothing more than a forum to throw down on men, as if men were the cause of all of her troubles. But she seemed to just love Thomas. She had her eyes closed and her hands around his neck as if she was enjoying him holding her, even though he was a man, too. Alex didn't know what the deal was, but she was beginning to understand why Thomas made such a point of talking about his friendship with Jazz and how it meant the world to him. He was preparing her for this, for his public display of affection toward Jazz that was going on way too long and was far too intimate for Alex's liking, especially since Jazz appeared to her to be as slick as the men she seemed to hate.

But Alex didn't say anything, and when Thomas finally released Jazz from his grasp and turned enough to remember that Alex also happened to be there, she smiled.

"Hello, Jazz," she said. "It's so nice to see you again."

Jazz, who was still reeling from her close contact with Thomas, didn't know what to say. She had forgotten, just that fast, that Alex was even there.

"I listened to your show the other day," Alex continued, refusing to fall prey to what she perceived as Jazz's natural rudeness. "That show be good, girl. All of that advice you give. I wish I was half as talented as you are."

"I'm sure you are," Jazz said and then smiled when it was obvious that Alex didn't get the put-down.

Thomas got it, however, and gave Jazz a harsh look. Then he attempted to change the subject. "How long have you been waiting?" he asked.

"Not long."

"I'm surprised to see you here. Delighted, but surprised. This is a first."

"Yes, it is," Jazz said. "In more ways than one." Jazz said this and looked at Alex.

"You remember Alex, don't you?" Thomas asked her as he picked back up his carrying bag.

"Oh, yes," Jazz said, and Alex smiled. Alex also eased up so close to Thomas that he had no choice, it seemed to Jazz, but to place her hand in his.

"We met at Tommy's party," Alex said, unable to suppress the joy she felt when Thomas took her hand.

"Yeah," Jazz said. "*Tommy's* party. I remember."

"Well, ladies," Thomas said, knowing all too well the sarcasm in Jazz's voice, "shall we?"

"Sure," Jazz said and stepped aside as Thomas and Alex began heading for the exit. Jazz pulled up the rear on purpose, and Thomas glanced back at her, but she wasn't about to interfere with what was obviously a perfect coming-out party for Alex.

The ride from the airport was a jubilant one as Alex gabbed on and on in the front seat and Thomas drove his Bentley, laughing all the way. Jazz sat in the backseat and stared at him. What was so damn funny, she wanted to know? Alex was brutal in her sense of humor, picking at people just because they dressed differently, or looked odd, or were standing on a Miami street corner minding their own business. The novelty of it, that Alex was livelier than most, had to be the attraction for a sophisticated man like Thomas, Jazz thought, and she had every intention of broaching the subject with him privately after they dropped off Miss Thang.

But she didn't get the chance because Thomas, to her shock, dropped her off first. Jazz was stunned. He'd never done that before, no matter how long he'd been dating the woman. Now he just met this Alex Mailer and things were changing already.

Jazz, however, didn't say anything. There will be another day to talk, she decided. Like Saturday, for instance. Saturday was the seventh anniversary of the day they first met, and they always did something special on their anniversary. So she just let him open the back door of his Bentley for her and quietly walk her up the side stairs to the front door of her loft. But when Thomas did not even mention Saturday, not even in passing, Jazz's hope began to turn into bitter reality. He had, apparently, forgotten.

He did thank her, however, for meeting his plane.

"It was nothing," Jazz said, pulling out her door keys.

"It was a nice gesture."

"It was nothing, Thomas, okay?" She said this harsher than she meant to and she could see Thomas's jaws tighten. One day he was going to walk down those stairs and never return, and it'll serve her right, she thought. No wonder he was dropping her off first now. He probably couldn't wait to be out of her sight.

He kissed her very lightly on the cheek, not on the lips as he'd been doing lately, and the change also disturbed Jazz.

"I'll see you Saturday," he said as he removed his sultry lips from her cool, smooth cheek and turned to leave.

"Saturday?" she asked, as excitement began to build up inside her again.

Thomas turned back around, but it was obvious that he wasn't excited but annoyed. "Yes, Jazz, Saturday," he said. "You asked me to take you to that new art gallery on Collins. Remember?"

The elation left. "Yeah," Jazz said. "I remember. But you don't have to do that."

"I know I don't have to do it. Did I say I had to do it?" He exhaled. He didn't mean to lose his cool. He had been trying to contain his disappointment. "I'll see you Saturday, Jazz," he said again and then hurried on down the stairs.

Jazz moved toward the top stair, as if she wanted to apologize to him, but she held her tongue. She went to the airport because she felt he deserved better treatment from her—he was, after all, the most important human being in her life—but man did that little gesture blow up in her face. But forget it, she thought, as she wrestled with her keys and unlocked her front door. She entered her apartment attempting to get on with her day. She even kicked off her shoes and headed for her studio, ready to paint her anxieties away.

But as the silence of the room crept in, and as that look of disappointment that seared Thomas's face crystallized in her mind, she couldn't go on with anything. She walked over to the window and watched Thomas's Bentley as it slowly backed out of her long, gravel drive. And her heart sank. What was her damn problem?

Alex smiled. "She's looking out the window at us," she said to Thomas.

Thomas was staring in the rearview mirror, concentrating on backing up his car, when Alex spoke. He immediately looked up at Jazz's large, upstairs window, the window inside her studio, and there she was, staring at them as if she were some kid wishing she could come outside and play. Thomas had to fight every urge to sling his car out of reverse and head back up to Jazz's loft. She spoke to him sometimes as if she couldn't stand him, so why would he want to run back to her side? For what? More abuse? But watching Jazz, watching her bite her bottom lip the way she was prone to do when something worried her, made him want to do just that. Run back to her. Hold her. *Feel* her.

And he would have done so easily, but Jazz, as always, was the one who set the rules. She turned and left the window. Thomas's heart sank.

"I know she's your friend, Tommy," Alex said smilingly, unable to resist a put-down of Jazz, "but don't you think she's just a little . . ." Thomas looked at Alex, and his look was so hard, so intense, that she decided to soften the word she really wanted to use.

"A little what?" he asked her.

"Off center," she said.

Thomas glared at Alex for a death-defying few seconds, then continued backing out of the drive. "No," he replied flatly.

She invited him in. He was reluctant, and tired, but he went in anyway. Alex, relieved that Nikki wasn't home, took Thomas by the hand and began showing him around. "I call it my Golden Girls retreat," she said as she took him into the kitchen, into the hall, into bedroom number one, then number two (Nikki's), and then number three (hers). She tried to linger there, showing him the bathroom and the tile inside the shower, but Thomas merely nodded and began heading back up front. He still couldn't get Jazz out of his mind, the way she never let up, the way she always had to put up that wall between them.

"Would you like something to drink?" Alex asked him as he took a seat on the living room sofa.

"No, I'm good," he said and stretched out his long legs.

Alex hated the mood Jazz had put him in. On the plane coming home he was wonderful, laughing and talking and having a ball. But as soon as Jazz came around he was all uptight and snappy and unable to even fix his mouth into a smile. Alex decided that she had to change that quickly. She had to get every thought of that foolish Jazz Walker out of his mind.

She walked up to him and, instead of sitting beside him, sat on top of him, her face facing his, her legs straddling him. Thomas laid his head against the back of the sofa. "I'm too tired, Alex," he said.

"Good," she said, "because I don't need you to do a doggone thing." She said this and then slid down to the floor. She sat on her knees between Thomas's legs. Then she unzipped his pants and attempted to do more, but Thomas grabbed her hand. She looked up at him.

"I said no," he said.

"It'll make you feel better, Tommy. I promise."

Thomas looked at Alex, at that wide-eyed look of hers, at that eagerness that showed even in her body language, and his heart dropped. By sleeping with her he had committed himself to her, but he couldn't help wondering just how seriously committed he really could be with Jazz always on his mind, always clogging up his day, always there, even if not physically. He was beginning to care for Alex now—after four days of bliss in Tampa with her he felt he had no choice—but he also knew that the intensity of his feelings for her wasn't nearly where it ought to be. He couldn't bear the thought of breaking somebody else's heart, not after Paula, not after that mystery woman in that art gallery that time, a former lover whose name he couldn't even remember. He knew he had to work harder in his relationship with Alex, for her sake but also for his. He knew it was high time he settled his behind down, even he could see that he was getting too old for the chase. And this Alex, this excitable, pleasant Alex Mailer, was apparently going to have to do.

He gently lifted her from the floor and sat her on his lap. She was worried that she had pressed too hard, but when he smiled that clear, angelic smile of his, she relaxed. "You don't have to do that, honey. Okay?"

Alex smiled. "I wanted to."

"I know. But we're okay."

Alex wanted to ask him what exactly did he mean by that, but she knew not to push it again. She, instead, leaned against his thick chest and closed her eyes. He rubbed her long hair and pulled her closer to him. He closed his eyes, too, but Jazz's face appeared in the darkness, standing at that window of her loft, so he quickly opened them again. Just as he did, the front door of the condo was opened and Nikki came barreling through. Thomas removed Alex from his lap, although she would have preferred staying as they were, and then he stood up. Nikki had only to turn the corner of the foyer to see them, and when she did, she smiled.

"Well, hello there," she said, glad to see Alex back, and with a man.

"Hello, Nikki," Alex said. "I want you to meet Thomas Drayton."

Nikki was immediately impressed. Based on what Alex had told her she expected a good-looking man, but nothing like this. She smiled as she walked over to Thomas and extended her hand. "So you're Thomas Drayton?"

"Yes."

"Don't mind her, Tommy," Alex said. "She's just my silly sister."

"Nice to meet you, Nikki."

"Likewise, I'm sure."

Alex rolled her eyes.

"Well, Alex," Thomas said, "I'd better be getting home."

"So soon?"

"Yes. I'm afraid so."

Alex didn't like his decision to leave but she didn't argue with it, either. She smiled and then placed her arm around his waist as she walked with him to the front door. Once at the front door he gave her a peck on the lips.

"What's your schedule like tomorrow?" she looked up at him and asked.

"Tomorrow's Friday. Which means it's tight. I have to be in court probably most of the day and I have a dinner engagement later that evening."

"Dinner? With who?" Jazz? she wanted to add.

"A client."

"That doesn't sound like a very exciting evening."

"I know."

"What about Saturday?"

"No, I'm taking Jazz to that new art gallery on Collins and I don't know how long that'll take. But I'll call you."

Yeah, Alex thought, just as he promised to call her before and never did. He just didn't sound like somebody hungry to be by her side. She tried all she could to turn him on in bed, but she could tell it wasn't the best he'd ever had by a long shot. She even wondered sometimes if he wasn't just going through the motions when he was with her. But that was why she had to stay up in his face. That was why she had no intentions of waiting for him to make the next move. She was going to make him love her, by the strength of her will alone, if that was the last thing she did.

"Good night, Thomas," she said and kissed him on his lips. She wanted to tongue kiss him, but he wouldn't open his mouth. He simply removed his lips from hers, smiled one more time, and then left. If Alex was a betting woman she'd bet that he was done with her. And maybe he was. But she wasn't done with him.

"He's gorgeous, Al," Nikki said as soon as Alex walked back into the living room. "Did you see the way he smiled? Damn! I'd never seen such a sexy smile, girl. I wouldn't mind having that brother for myself."

"You ain't touching him," Alex said as she sat down on the sofa and drew her legs up under her butt. "He's mine, all right? At least he will be. And I know exactly how to snare him, too."

"Oh, yeah?" Nikki asked, sitting down. "School me then, girl. Because I know a brother like that is not about to fall for one of your lame games."

"I know what he likes. He's not looking for no good girl, he's had enough of them. He wants a rebel, an aggressive woman who knows what she wants and won't stop until she gets it. You should have seen the way he looked at me when I showed up at his hotel room in Tampa. Your boy was stunned, Nikki. And excited, too. It was like he couldn't get me to that bed fast enough."

"So y'all . . ."

"Hell, yeah. He ain't no choir boy and I ain't no choir girl. My job is to keep him good and satisfied so he don't even have a chance to think about all those other females waiting in the wings to get a piece of him."

Nikki exhaled. "You're gonna have to move fast, girl."

"Why you say that?"

"Earl's trippin' big-time."

"Oh, Lord. What's happened?"

"While you were in Tampa wooing the good lawyer, Earl was here in Miami cussing my ass out. Oh, you should have seen him.

He's just convinced that I'm not going to the junior college like I told him. He just knows I got me a man I'm going to meet."

"He sound just like that Larry Lindsey."

"I know it."

"Dang. So what's the bottom line?"

"He said he wasn't giving me another dime on rent, that's the bottom line. And he means it."

"Damn, Nikki! I told you that ridiculous school nonsense was gonna get us nothing but trouble. Now look what's happened. How in hell are we gonna afford a place like this, Nick? We ain't got a damn thing!"

"Ask Mr. Drayton to help us."

"He ain't down like that."

"How do you know?"

"Because I kind of hinted that I could use some help when we were having lunch one day and he didn't offer a dime. Not one red cent. So the brother's tight with the cash, ain't no doubt about it. We ain't gonna be able to use him like that. He's a long-term, not a short-term solution. Earl was short-term. That's why we needed Earl."

"Well Earl is old news now."

"But you can get him back if you apologize to him."

"No! I don't want him back, his insecure behind. I don't want any more gravy trains from any more men, Alex, I don't care what you say. Ray Ray was the man of my dreams and even he didn't take care of me right. That's why I'm taking care of myself. Going back to school, getting me some education. And if it means getting on public assistance . . ."

"Public assistance?"

"Yes, Alex. They call it welfare."

"Girl, you out of your mind. And where do you think that'll get you? Some trailer in a shotgun trailer park somewhere? Or maybe some hell-hole housing project. Child, please. You need to get on from 'round here with your crazy talk."

Alex said this and left the room. She couldn't even begin to understand what wild Nikki, of all people, was trying to prove. So she didn't even try. She just went into her bedroom and fell across the bed. She had to take matters into her own hands, that was what she knew she had to do. And she'll begin tomorrow. No. He was too busy tomorrow, he wouldn't appreciate the intrusion. She'll begin Saturday, she decided. The day Thomas was supposed to take Jazz to some boring-behind gallery. She smiled at the prospect. She could kill two birds with one stone if she waited until Saturday. She could get closer to Thomas, that would be her number one goal, but she could also rain down like a monsoon on Jazz Walker's parade. Goal number two.

A COLD DAY IN HELL

It was early Saturday, the morning of their seventh anniversary, and Jazz was sitting on the porch of the main house, waiting patiently for Thomas. Seven years ago today, on a warm morning not unlike this one, Jazz and Thomas saw each other for the first time. The attraction was so strong, right off the bat, that Jazz felt it necessary to decline Thomas's offer to take over her case—her divorce number three case. But Thomas was Thomas, always insistent, and he took over anyway.

She took a slow drag on her cigarette and crossed her legs. She was comfortably dressed in a pair of cuffed shorts, a sleeveless cotton blouse, and nondescript tennis shoes, a pair she picked up from Payless. Her bouncy, manageably wild Afro was freshly cut, and she felt fresh, too, all for the occasion. She didn't hear from Thomas at all yesterday, and that was a big disappointment for her, and she could only hope that her less-than-best-friend-like treatment of him of late hadn't driven him away for good. She never lasted long in any relationship, except this one, and it'll break her heart, she was coming to realize, if her own problems with affection caused this one to collapse, too.

That was why she couldn't wait to see Thomas. She was going to smother that brother in affection, just shower him with it. Then she smiled. She wasn't going to do a darn thing and she knew it. But she certainly planned to let this day be a new beginning, a chance for her to prove to him that he was her world, too.

But he didn't show. Not at eight thirty, his normal time, not a nine, not even by nine thirty. As ten began to roll around she pulled out her cell phone. Her heart began to pound with the possibility that he had no intentions of taking her to the gallery today or celebrating their anniversary with her. She had wondered if he'd forgotten about their anniversary, and now she was beginning to feel certain of it. That line that she was always edging toward, the line of his limitations, may have already been crossed.

Thomas woke up quickly and answered his ringing phone. "Yes, hello?" he said irritably, hating to be roused from sleep so suddenly. When there was no response on the other end, somehow his instincts told him that it was Jazz. He glanced at the clock on his nightstand. It was almost ten o'clock. And he immediately remembered. Damn, he said to himself, and then he got up. "Jazz, I'm sorry," he said into the phone. "I've overslept. I'm on my way."

The phone on the other end clicked off, without a word being said, and Thomas hung up, too. He paused for a moment, thinking about Jazz and how hostile she'd been behaving lately. Paula's mess didn't help the situation, he knew, but he also knew that Jazz's behavior was changing long before Paula started tripping. Thomas wondered if she was trying to tell him something, that maybe his affection for her was getting too strong. He was, after all, kissing her passionately every chance he got, as if she was his woman, and maybe it was driving her away. She didn't want to be his woman and he needed to get that through his thick skull, he decided. He also decided to start acting as if he got it.

He showered and dressed quickly, in a pair of jeans, a green polo shirt, and loafers, and had his keys and wallet in hand as he hurried for the front door of his big, somber house.

He was astounded, however, when he opened that door and Alex was standing there.

"Alex?"

"Good morning!" she said cheerfully.

"How long have you been out here?"

"Not that long. I didn't want to be banging on your door and disturb you."

Thomas didn't know what to say. There she was, Alex Mailer,

looking decidedly pretty, he thought, in her flowery sundress and sandals. He didn't know, however, if he was glad to see her or mad as hell at the idea of her just showing up at his home, *his* home, like this.

"I hope I haven't startled you," she said when it was obvious that Thomas was trying to make up his mind about her sudden appearance.

"I'm not startled," he said. "I just don't understand what you're up to."

Alex smiled. She had to lay on the Southern charm and lay it on thick. "I'm not up to anything, why, Mr. Drayton. I just wanted to see you this morning. That's all."

Thomas smiled at her exaggerated Southern belle act. "Well. I guess I should be flattered."

"You should be."

"And I wish I could spend some time with you, Alex, but I'm afraid I can't. I'm already late picking up Jazz. I promised to take her to an art gallery this morning."

"Oh, yes, that's right. You mentioned that. I adore art galleries, you know. My." She hesitated, hoping he would invite her along. When he didn't speak, she pressed. "Would it be an imposition if I were to come along, too?"

Thomas shook his head and smiled. What was he going to do with this hot mama? "Why not," he said with a shrug of his shoulders, and then Alex moved closer to him.

"But first," she said, her small body managing to push his back into his home, "I want to show you a little art of my own."

Thomas allowed her to push him back into his home, as he was suddenly turned on by her, by her soft hands on his cheeks, by her fresh breath blowing against his chin, by her brashness. And when she kicked the door shut behind her and backed him against the wall of his foyer, he facilitated her intentions by placing his hands on her waist and pulling her up against him. She lifted up on tiptoes and began kissing him, her tongue circling his at first and then plunging in, and he immediately lifted her closer to him and returned her affection. And before he could come back up for air, she was stepping out of her underwear, her dress lifted up to her waist, his hand moving down to cup her soft bottom. Kissing was fine with him, but he knew she wanted more, he could feel it in the tension in her limbs. So he accommodated that, too. She was his woman now, by default if nothing else, and he aimed to please her.

In what seemed to her to be almost one extended motion given the quickness with which he moved, he had unzipped his pants, pulled out a condom from his wallet, and then tossed the wallet to the floor. She wasn't so far gone in lust, however, to notice that his wallet was cash heavy, because it hit the ground hard, with a thump rather than a thung.

But Thomas didn't notice anything of the sort. He was too busy sliding on his condom, his sex big and throbbing now. Then he lifted her up to where her legs wrapped around his waist, and he shifted her around, until it was her back that was now against the wall. And then he entered her, gently, staring at her as he did, as if looking to see just exactly how she responded to his penetration.

She responded well. Her face lit up as he entered her, and when she began bucking her pelvis into him, encouraging him to force the issue because she knew he liked it like that, he thrust into her hard, deeper, and moved in and out forcefully, over and over again, until she was shaking in his arms and screaming in unbridled passion.

It took many more thrusts to rattle him, as he had to fight to keep focused, but he came, too, stronger than he had remembered in a long time, so strong that he had to lean against her little body when his big body stopped convulsing with the feeling and left him drained. He was breathing heavily as he rested against her, and she loved the feel of his warm breath against her face. She was smiling, because she couldn't believe it. She actually loved being like this, with him, where she didn't have to fake orgasms, because he knew how to please her. No other man, in all of her twenty-seven years on earth, had ever been able to make her feel this good.

But then again, she thought, she'd never been with a man like Thomas. He wasn't so old that he was ancient, or so unattractive that she could barely stand looking at him but had no choice because she needed his money. She'd go after Thomas even if she didn't need a dime. He was older than her, which she felt was a good thing be-cause she could use her youthfulness to her advantage, and he was so handsome and strong that she was proud to be around this man, not embarrassed as she had been with all those other sugar daddies in her past. Oh yes, she thought, as her arms held him tighter, and she leaned her head against his chest, this was one sugar daddy she aimed to keep.

Thomas looked at her, at the smile that seemed fixed on her face, and he kissed her peck-style on the lips. Then he slowly pulled out of her, still unable to stop staring at her, as if there was something about her he was trying his darndest to get a handle on, and then he stepped back from the warmth of her soft body and allowed her feet to touch ground again.

Jazz could not believe it. Not only was he late, which was bad enough, but he was pulling up in her driveway with that floozy in his car. On their seventh anniversary, on the day she had decided to show her kind, considerate side, he brought another woman along. And not just another woman, but that Alex. She doused out her cigarette angrily. Where does he get off? she wondered.

Carmella, who was, by now, sitting out on the porch of the main house with Jazz, was wondering, too, as Thomas stepped out of his car and Alex eagerly followed suit. "Who the hell is that?" she asked in a voice just loud enough for Jazz to hear.

"A character out of a James Bond movie."

"A what? Which character?"

"Gold digger," Jazz said, and Carmella laughed.

"I think that's Goldfinger, Jazz," she said.

"Whatever," Jazz replied.

"Good morning, ladies," Thomas said as he began slowly making his way up the steps. Alex was careful to stay as close to him as possible because Jazz, she felt, had to understand that Thomas belonged to her now.

"Good morning," Carmella said. "Don't you look scrumptious in your jeans."

Thomas smiled that smile of his that made both Carmella and Jazz want to swoon. Carmella even placed her hand to her chest. It was a sin to look that good, she thought.

Thomas immediately looked at Jazz, at her legs first and then her face. "Hey there," he said to her, unable to resist giving her a special greeting.

"You're late," she said and stood up, her face hard and unforgiving.

Thomas's heart tightened. It was obvious that she didn't want to have anything to do with him, why the hell was he even there? And the way she phoned this morning and didn't think enough of him to at least acknowledge that it was her angered him, too. And he knew it was her because it wasn't the first time she pulled that little stunt. She'd done it many times before. Any time he was late, any time he didn't jump at her command, she was calling and saying nothing, because she knew him like a book. He'd complain, but he'd comply. He didn't let anybody treat him the way Jazz did. Not anybody. His reputation around every other human being on the face of this earth was everything he wasn't around Jazz: strong, ruthless, uncompromising, hard. But when it came to Jazz, when all she had to do was look his way and his heart skipped beats, he was as soft as cotton.

That was why he chose to ignore her smart remark rather than risk a confrontation with her, because he knew her, and he knew she'd refuse to go anywhere with him, which in turn would make him want to beg her to forgive him even though he knew it wasn't his fault. Forget all that drama, he thought. "Carmella," he said instead, "I don't think you've met Alex."

Alex smiled. She was wondering when he'd get around to acknowledging her. "Hello," she said as she extended her hand to Carmella. Carmella shook it very reluctantly and said "good morning" so harshly that Alex couldn't help but smile.

When it was obvious to Thomas that the ladies weren't about to hold any kind of conversation with Alex, not even small talk, he looked at Jazz again. "Ready?" he said.

"I been ready," Jazz said and began walking toward Thomas. She fully expected him to do as he always did and give her a hello kiss, and she desperately wanted his kiss because she felt she needed it to help take the edge off, but when he took a step back as she approached him, as if he had no intentions of touching her, her heart dropped. He'd never before denied her his affections, even when she was in worst moods than this, and she looked into his eyes to find out why. He didn't, however, return her gaze. He just went and retrieved the paintings that were lined up on the porch and, with Alex following closely behind, took them to his car's trunk. Jazz almost told him to forget the whole thing, that she could find her own way, but she didn't say a word. Something was different about Thomas now. As if he made a decision and Alex, for some unfathomable reason, was the lucky beneficiary.

He placed Alex in a different category than all of his previous ladies, it seemed to Jazz, and that revelation alone astounded her. Alex had been the first girlfriend of Thomas's that Jazz didn't feel threatened by in the least. The first one she had dismissed out of hand as so obviously devious that no way was she going to lose Thomas over *that*. The first one, she was now coming to realize, who had managed to sneak up like a thief in the night and blindside her.

The ride to the gallery was painful for Jazz. Alex sat in the front seat alongside Thomas talking up a storm, her pretty little head bobbing up and down as if she was having the time of her life. And Thomas was totally engaged, listening carefully, nodding, laughing— oh, how he laughed. Jazz used to be the only person who could put a smile on that sometimes stern face of Thomas's, but not any longer. Alex had topped her by leaps and bounds. She had the man practically in stitches. And it wasn't even funny, not to Jazz anyway, not that nonsense she was gabbing on about. But Jazz also knew it didn't have to be funny. It was the way Alex said it. The way she seemed so put off by everybody different, everybody who wasn't like her. "They crazy," she'd say like some ghetto-fabulous sister, and Thomas would laugh, not at the fact that whomever may or may not have been as Alex had said, but it was all in the way she said it.

And when they arrived at the new gallery on Collins Avenue, a large, dome-shaped building that reminded Jazz of the entranceway to a Las Vegas casino, Jazz stepped out quickly, anxious to get as far away from Alex as possible. It wasn't lost on Jazz that Thomas hadn't even mentioned their anniversary, hadn't even mentioned it, as if his mind was a million miles away from what she used to think was very important to him.

Jazz and Alex ended up side by side initially, however, as they walked into the gallery, Thomas too much of a gentleman to go in ahead of any woman. Jazz felt awkward as hell, because she was a good three inches taller and seemed to tower over the shorter Alex. She looked at Alex, who seemed to be perfectly proportioned in every way, who seemed so much prettier than her, and younger, and somebody she now could easily see Thomas falling hard for. Why she didn't see it before astounded her now. She seemed to have been so secure in her friendship with Thomas that she just knew it was going to go on forever, with no bumps, no close calls, no Alexes in sight. She looked back at Thomas, expecting to take an unnoticed glance, but, to her shock, he was staring at her, as if he could read her emotions, as if he was telling her with his gorgeous eyes that she should have grabbed him while she had the chance because now, for better or worse, he's taken.

She could feel the hot heat of tears trying to press their way into her eyes, but she'd die before she'd let the likes of Alex Mailer see her cry. She broke away from them like a running back, moving in the complete opposite direction of their trek, and her feet wouldn't stop until she was clean across the gallery, near the watercolors. She stared at the display, willing herself not to cry, reminding herself that Thomas was just a friend and any fool should have known that he'd eventually find somebody to love.

She kept staring, kept dismissing, kept trying with all she had to keep her composure. But then she heard his voice. That voice. "You okay?" he walked up to her and asked.

She couldn't turn to look at him, because she knew she'd lose it. "I'm fine," she said, her back to him.

Thomas stared at her back, and he knew she was a long way from fine, but he also knew she wasn't about to tell him about it. They were best friends in an unspoken kind of way, friends, not because of the secrets they share, but because of the strong feelings they had for each other, feelings so intense sometimes Thomas used to wonder if he could contain them. "Jazz," Thomas said, but she quickly interrupted him.

"I'm fine, Thomas, okay? Can you just, can you get the paintings out of the trunk?"

Thomas exhaled. Why did he bother? "Sure," he said and walked away.

The paintings were taken to the back of the gallery and the proprietor, a large, middle-aged man with squinted eyes, studied them carefully. Alex pulled Thomas away almost immediately and Jazz could not believe it when he forgot his customary role of advising her on prices and, instead, played around with that trifling Alex. First he forgot their anniversary, now he wasn't even trying to be of any assistance to her. By the time he finally made it back over to her side, his hand interlocked with Alex's, it was too much. Jazz couldn't take it anymore.

"You guys can leave now," she looked at Thomas and said.

Alex smiled. "Excuse me?"

"I won't take up anymore of your time."

"What did we do?" Alex asked, but Jazz ignored her.

"What's the matter, Jazz?" Thomas asked, his face stern, hard.

"Nothing's the matter. I'll catch a cab back. You guys can go."

"What is it, Jazz?"

"I told you nothing."

"I was a little late picking you up, I'm sorry, but it happens. I thought I apologized. Now you're angry again. What's going on here?"

"Nothing's going on, all right? Nothing at all. So will you just leave me the hell alone for once?"

Thomas stared at Jazz with an angry glare of his own, and he felt, for the first time in a long time, that he didn't know her at all. "Yeah, I'll do that," he said, and he and Alex left the building.

Alex came out of the dressing room of the large department store and twirled wildly in front of Thomas. He sat in an armchair against the wall and stared at the short-length, bright yellow dress she was showing off, but even she could see that his mind was miles away.

"You don't like it, do you?" she asked.

"Yeah, it's okay."

"Just okay?"

Thomas didn't respond.

"What don't you like about it?"

"It's fine, Alex. I didn't say I didn't like it."

"But you didn't say you loved it either."

Thomas looked at her with an angry glare and then stood up. "I'm going outside to smoke," he said.

Alex sighed as he walked away from her. That Jazz Walker had upset him again, she thought. The way she snapped at him like he was some child. *Y'all can leave*, she said, like she was the mother earth. Now all of Alex's plans were probably shot to hell because she was certain he wasn't about to be bothered with her much longer. Not today anyway. She turned and walked back into the fitting room. She had her work cut out for her and she knew it. She also knew that, eventually, Jazz Walker had to go.

Alex's spirits didn't lift much at all, however, after Thomas drove her to his place to pick up her car and didn't even offer to let her in.

He had some business to take care of, he suddenly declared. Alex nodded—she could only imagine what kind of business he had to take care of—and she got in her car and left.

But when she drove to her house on Melrose Drive and saw a white Town Car in her drive, her ex-boyfriend's car she was certain, her spirits dropped through her shoe.

She hurried out of her car and nearly ran across the grass to the front door. And sure enough, Larry Lindsey was coming out of her house just as she was walking in.

"I was wondering when you were coming home," he said dryly, trying to smile, trying to act as if he didn't kick her out of his Key Largo apartment and tell her to take a hike. She almost wanted to tell him that she had a real man now and didn't need his trifling butt anymore, but she was too smart for that. She knew the deal. She knew that she and Nikki had no rent money for next month and this month was coming to a close fast. Thomas Drayton may wine and dine her, but he wasn't giving up the cash. He was accustomed to dating females who could take care of themselves, who didn't need sugar daddies, and he therefore didn't understand the role. That'll change, of course, Alex was certain of that. But in the meantime . . .

"Larry, hi," she said with a grand smile. "It's so good to see you again. Don't tell me you're leaving already?"

"I've been here for nearly two hours," he said in his old testy way.

"Oh, I'm sorry about that. I went shopping. Come on in." She said this and slid her arm around his, not giving him a choice in the matter. He hesitantly moved aside and let her in.

"Have a seat," she said. "Would you like something to drink?"

"No."

"Where's Nikki?"

"In her room. She said she had to study."

"Study?"

"Yeah. Like I'm supposed to believe that."

"So she just left you out here alone like this?"

"Yes, she did," he said, as if he still didn't like it at all.

Alex sighed. What was Nikki thinking? "I'm sorry, Larry," she said. "I don't know what's wrong with Nikki lately."

"I don't either. But she need to get it together."

"Oh, she will. And she'll be apologizing to you, too. Let me go get her."

"Yeah, you do that," Larry said in his old familiar voice of contempt and Alex rolled her eyes as she hurried to Nikki's room.

Nikki was lying across her bed attempting to do her math homework. She was just getting started at the junior college, and even the basics were giving her fits. The last thing she needed was an interruption, but already she'd gotten two. First from that trifling Larry Lindsey, who found out where Alex was staying and came on over without even bothering to call and ask if it was okay, and now from Alex herself.

"I'm trying to study, Al," she said with a tinge of anger.

"Have you lost your mind?" Alex asked as she closed the door, her anger more than a tinge. "That's Larry, Nikki. Larry Lindsey from Key Largo!"

"And? I know who he is. I don't care who he is."

"You are so dense, you know that?"

"How am I dense? Because I'm studying instead of entertaining his butt? I didn't ask him to come barging over here."

"Nikki, the man is a blessing to us right now. Unless you've forgotten, and I don't see how you could have, we ain't got no money for the rent that's coming due. Not a dime. Or does your college brain not think about such trivial matters?"

Nikki blew a deep sigh of disgust and laid on her back. "So what are you saying? You're back with Larry now? The same dude that didn't wanna have nothing to do with you a couple months ago? The same dude that kicked you out on your ass?"

"This ain't got nothing to do with that, Nikki. We need Larry right now."

"But what about Thomas Drayton?"

"It ain't about Thomas Drayton either. It's ain't about Larry. It's about us and how we're gonna survive up in here."

"But Thomas Drayton would be perfect for you, Alex. He's everything you need. Tough, strong, the kind of man who wouldn't put up with your bs. He's somebody you could love and marry and you wouldn't need any more sugar daddies like Larry Lindsey. You could have children, Alex. A family. Everything we used to want. I thought you was falling for Thomas. Why you wanna mess that up?"

Alex covered her face momentarily and sighed. Will Nikki ever get it? "I'm not messing nothing up, Nick, are you listening to a word I'm saying? Even if I am falling for Thomas Drayton, that's not the point. Business is business and Thomas ain't giving up no cash. You hear me? Larry will, if I treat him right, and that'll help to keep our heads above water until I can wrangle Thomas. But in the meantime, we've got to keep Larry around and you have got to go back into that living room and apologize for being so damn dumb."

When Alex finished her little speech, a smile began to appear on Nikki's long face. Alex couldn't believe it. "This isn't funny, Nikki," she said.

"So it's true," Nikki said.

Alex sighed and shook her head. "What are you talking about? What's true?"

"You're falling in love with Thomas Drayton. My big sister is falling in love for once in her life. I cannot believe it!"

Alex, however, didn't say a word, because, in truth, she couldn't believe it either.

IF YOU CAN'T
BEAT 'EM...

An old-fashioned cargo van drove up to the porch of the main house, and Carmella, sitting on the porch, stood up. From the looks of it, with its bright blue color and the words *Mount Moriah Primitive Baptist Church* written on the side panel, Carmella figured it was a wrong turn problem, that the driver had lost his way on the main road and needed directions. She moved closer to the porch's rail as the van came to a stop, more than happy to offer her assistance. It was easy to get lost out here in the boonies where she lived, in little Homestead, and often she found herself on many a Sunday morning pointing out the right way home. But when Jazz Walker of all people got out of the van, waved good-bye to the few folks on board, and the van backed out and left the scene as if it had just dropped off an old saint from way back, Carmella laughed. Jazz, however, looked at Carmella as if she was not the one to be bothered with and then began a slow ascent up the porch steps.

"Don't start, Carmella," she said as she walked.

"Start what? It's a beautiful Sunday morning. Am I not allowed to laugh?"

Jazz ignored her comeback as she sat on the porch's top step and looked at the woods across the street. She was right about it being a beautiful day, Jazz thought. She only wished her unable-to-shake-the-doldrums mood could match it.

And Carmella wasn't helping, as Jazz could feel her stare. She turned and looked at her. Carmella smiled.

"What?" Jazz asked without cracking any smile, fake or otherwise, of her own.

Carmella sat down in the chair on the porch and crossed her legs. "What what?" she asked, as if dumbfounded.

"What's so funny, Carmella?"

"You."

"What about me?"

"Mount Moriah Primitive Baptist Church, Jazz?"

"That's right."

"Come on."

"Come on what?"

"That's where you were all morning?"

"That's right."

Carmella shook her head. "You're weird, you know that?"

"I'm weird? Because I go to church? No, you're weird because you don't."

"Whatever."

"Yeah, whatever." Jazz said this and looked back across the street. Carmella continued to stare at her. She wore a brown skirt of modest length and a white blouse, an outfit even Carmella couldn't complain about, but when she looked down at Jazz's shoes and saw that they weren't nice dress shoes appropriate for her little church visit, but sneakers, Carmella laughed again. And Jazz, once again, gave her a harsh glare.

"Okay, what is it?" Carmella said, tired of the game.

"What are you talking about?"

"Come on, Jazz. I know your lil' butt. Going to church. Looking like you've lost your best friend. Let's have it. What's going on?"

Jazz leaned back against the railing on the side of the steps. "Nothing's going on," she said.

"Then why the long face? What's got you so depressed and impatient that you can't even smile anymore?"

Jazz sighed and looked out across the street as the wind began to pick up strength and toss around the wooded landscape. Peaceful one minute, in danger of being uprooted the next. The story of her life, she thought.

"What is it, Jazz? Is it Thomas?"

Jazz smiled within herself. Carmella, she decided, was either psychic or so damn nosey that she always found a way to hit the hammer on the nail. She looked at her. No point in obfuscating any longer. "We had an argument a week ago."

"Okay."

"On the seventh anniversary of the day we met."

"Um. Okay."

"And I haven't heard from him since."

Carmella paused. "Now that's unusual."

"I know."

"You guys argue all the time, it's the hallmark of your relationship, but you always get it back together."

"I know."

"So what's up? What was so bad about this last argument that would keep him away from you for an entire week?"

"It's not the argument. That was nothing. I just got kind of testy with him, that's all. But I think . . ."

"You think what, girl?"

"I think Thomas might be falling in love."

Carmella smiled. "That's great news, Jazzy! That's nothing to be depressed about. I told you a long time ago y'all were meant for each other."

"I'm not the one."

"What?"

"He's not falling in love with me. I'm not the one." Jazz said this unable to conceal her sadness. Carmella leaned back.

"Oh," she said. "I see. Then who?"

Jazz looked at Carmella.

"Not gold digger?"

"Yep."

"You have got to be joking. *Gold digger?* What could he possibly see in that young thang?"

Jazz shook her head. "Thomas thinks he's getting old."

"Well, he is."

"He's at a point in his life where he feels it's high time he settled on down."

"Which makes him prime bait for a barracuda like what's-her-name."

"Right. And her name is Alex." Jazz folded her arms. "I don't know what to do, Carmella. I feel like I should do something, you know? I don't see how I can just sit back and let Thomas make the biggest mistake of his life, and believe me, if he falls for that sister it'll be a disaster. She doesn't love him, just what she can get from him."

"Girl, you ain't got to tell me that. I saw so many dollar signs in her eyes I couldn't see her eyeballs. And I only met the chick once."

"I've got to do something. I just don't know what. And it's eating me alive."

"Have you told Thomas how you feel?"

"Of course not. Whom he chooses to fall in love with is his business. I'll look like a fool telling somebody like him that he's being duped. Maybe he wants to be duped for all I know. Besides, our relationship isn't like that."

"Like what? He's your best friend, Jazz. You're telling me you can't discuss something this important with your best friend?"

"It's not my business. I've never questioned what he does in his personal life and he likes it that way. He'll have a fit if I try to interfere."

"Then don't interfere. Just tell him the truth. Tell him you don't feel any woman, except yourself, is good enough for him."

Jazz quickly swung around to Carmella. "What are you talking about?" she asked angrily. "I don't want him! I just don't want some good-for-nothing like Alex Mailer taking advantage of him, that's all I want!"

"Okay, Jazz."

"I don't want him. He's just a friend. Got it?"

"I got it."

"I want that to be perfectly understood."

"It's understood. Damn!"

Jazz settled back down. She was protesting too much and she knew it. She decided to move on. "I've never interfered with Thomas's love life before and I don't see how I can interfere now."

Carmella didn't say anything. She just shook her head.

"What's that supposed to signify?"

"You are so slow," Carmella said beneath her breath.

"Say again?"

"You are so slow," Carmella repeated herself, this time loudly.

"Slow about what? I told you I don't want Thomas."

"And I heard you loud and clear. Man, did I hear you. You don't want him. Fine. You supposedly don't want the best-looking brother this side of living, not to mention the nicest, and that's perfectly all right. It's your life. But what you do want is to get him away from gold digger, right? To get his mind away from dollar girl, right?"

"Right."

"Then distract him, Jazz, don't you see it? If somebody's looking at one thing, and you would prefer he look at something else, then you've got to give him something else to look at."

Jazz considered what Carmella had just said, but she concluded that Carmella's meaning was too vague. She frowned. "I guess I am slow because I don't know what you're talking about. You think I should distract him away from Alex by finding another woman who can catch his attention?"

Carmella stared at Jazz. She was slower than she thought. "Not another woman, that'll be too risky. It'll have to be you."

"Me?"

"Yes, Jazz, think about it. Thomas likes you. You say it's because y'all are friends. I think it's more than that, but that's just my opinion. But we both agree that he likes you. If he's falling for gold digger like you claim, then another woman will not work because you and I both know that Thomas is not the type to sleep around on somebody he cares about. But if you're the distraction, Jazz, he'll pay attention. You've just got to give him a taste of his own medicine."

"By distracting him?"

"Right."

"And what kind of distraction am I supposed to be, Dr. Ruth?"

"The same kind Alex has become to you."

"You want me to *seduce* Thomas? Please."

"No, Jazz. It's just a matter of making him a little jealous, that's all, in the same way that you're jealous of Alex."

"I'm not jealous of that little witch!"

"You know what I mean. She's endangering your friendship with Thomas, that's what I mean. And that's got you all concerned, let's face it. But that's why you've got to flip the script. You haven't been with a man in so long that Thomas no longer appreciates what a catch you really are. He hasn't had to deal with another man touching you and hanging all up under you the way you've had to deal with him and his women. He'll probably pass out if he sees another man touching you, Jazz. And it won't be because you want him or he wants you," Carmella quickly added, although she didn't believe it herself. "But it'll be because he'll feel, like you feel about Alex, that this other man could really harm his place in your life. And I guarantee you, Sister J, that he'll realize then that little Miss Alex is nowhere near worth losing you over. Not that heifer."

As Jazz thought about it, and then thought about it some more, she managed to smile. It was a plan that sounded so devious, and so unlike her in every conceivable way, that she could only conclude that it just might actually work.

The doorbell continued to ring as Alex made her way out of the bedroom. It was Sunday and she had every intention of just sleeping in all day, but now this. She looked through the living room window and saw Conrad's Jeep on her drive. She rolled her eyes, but she opened the door.

"I can't see you today, Connie," she said before he could say hello. He was dressed in his Sunday best and Alex could tell right away that he was just back from church.

"May I come in?" he asked, his smile unwavering.

"No. I'm still in bed."

"I see." Conrad said this as he perused the terry-cloth robe she wore.

"What is it that you want, Connie?"

"I just want to see you. Can't a man want to see his lady? I haven't seen you in quite a while, Alexandria. It's probably my fault, I've been working too hard, but I thought today I would make it up to you."

"You don't have anything to make up to me."

Conrad smiled. "I thought maybe a picnic in the park could . . ."

"Okay, that's it," Alex said. "I didn't want to go there, but you leave me no choice. You and me are not boyfriend and girlfriend, Connie. Okay? I am not your woman by any stretch of the imagination. I never was and I never will be. You've been a good friend and I hope we can maintain our friendship, but a love affair between you and me? Uh-uh. It ain't gonna happen. Now I suggest you go on with your life and find you somebody else because you're a very nice young man, but you need to leave me alone because I am not interested."

"Now."

"What?"

"You're not interested now. But when you needed my help you were extremely interested."

Alex's temper flared. "You know what," she said, "just get off of my property, okay? That'll show you how interested I am now, then, and forever more!"

Alex said this and slammed the door. Conrad stood there momentarily, knowing that his words were the harsh truth and all the door slams in the world weren't about to convince him otherwise. He walked to his Jeep, got in, and drove hastily away.

At the bay window of the living room, Nikki, now awake, watched him as he left.

Two days later, Thomas and Alex were seated at a quiet booth in Solesby's eating dinner. Alex was doing most of the talking as Thomas was tired from a long day, but even Alex shut her mouth when Jazz walked into the restaurant. They both were surprised, as Jazz rarely frequented restaurants. They weren't robbing her blind, she always told Thomas.

"What is she doing here?" Alex asked, immediately suspicious.

"She apparently needs to see me about something. We haven't seen each other in a while."

"Well how did she know you were here?"

"My answering service probably told her. They know Jazz."

Alex cut a nasty look at Thomas but, for the most part, she didn't take her eyes off of Jazz. Especially when Jazz didn't even think about coming their way but moved to a table of her own away from theirs. Alex smiled.

"She doesn't appear to want you at all, Thomas," Alex said with some satisfaction. Thomas, however, ignored her. And when he stood up without saying a word to her, and began walking toward Jazz's table, Alex's great smile quickly fizzled. That oddball Jazz Walker was going to be the death of her plans yet, she thought, but she also knew there was no way she was going to let that happen.

Thomas's heart tightened as he walked toward Jazz. She sat there, looking so out of place, he thought, as she ordered some nonalcoholic beverage and then watched the waitress as she walked away. She was dressed comfortably in a white pullover shirt that amplified her big breasts, it seemed to Thomas, and a pair of nicely fitting capri pants. Her eyeglasses were sitting purposely down the bridge of her nose and her hair had a shorter look to it. She looked fresh, he thought. But when she looked up and saw him coming her way, she appeared startled. He immediately smiled and threw up his hands.

"Didn't mean to scare you," he said lightheartedly.

"No, not at all," she said. "What are you doing here?" She knew he would be here, but he didn't know she knew.

"Just having dinner with Alex," he said. "Care to join us?"

"No," Jazz said quickly. "I'm expecting someone. But thanks anyway."

Thomas nodded. Then stared at her. "It's good seeing you again, Jazz."

"You, too."

"It's been a while."

"I know."

"You've been taking care of yourself?"

"Yeah, I've been doing okay."

"How do you get to work?"

"Gerald insists on picking me up."

Thomas hesitated. "Does he?"

"Yep. Or Carmella will take me in. Or one day both. I'd just as soon catch a cab, but they won't hear of it."

"I see."

"Yeah, I don't have any transportation problems whatsoever." In other words, Jazz thought to herself, your little absence from my life hasn't hurt me at all. It was a lie, of course, but Jazz felt it needed to be conveyed.

"Well, anyway," Thomas said, getting the message loud and clear, "I'd better get back. You know how Alex can be."

"Yeah, I know how Alex can be."

Jazz said this so harshly that Thomas hesitated. Then his light brown eyes met up with her droopy dark ones, and his heart sank. He had missed her more than she would ever know. Missed her so badly that he couldn't half sleep at night for thinking about her. But she was tired of him, that little scene in the art gallery proved that, and he felt it best if they spent a little time away. But now he wanted back in and Jazz was behaving as if she wasn't ready for that yet. So he decided not to press.

He could not deny himself a kiss, however, as he seemed unable to stop his eyes from roaming down to her sweet lips. But when he leaned over to kiss her on those lips, it was Jazz who did the denying. She turned away as soon as he moved toward her and allowed him to kiss only her cheek. Although he was disappointed, he nonetheless kissed her cheek, slowly, allowing the soft skin of that cheek to linger in his mouth longer than necessary, but even after that he still wanted her. Badly. And suppressing it was killing him. But as he stood up and looked at her again, it was obvious to him that she not only didn't want him, but she more than likely didn't really want any contact with him. He sighed. She was breaking his heart.

"Well," he said, "I'll see you around."

"Okay." Jazz said this and looked up at him, and if Thomas didn't know any better he'd declare he saw a sudden flash of great sadness in those eyes of hers. It caused his heart to drop and confusion to reign, and he found himself unable to leave.

Jazz looked away from him, afraid that her pain was beginning to show, and she wished to God he would just leave. But he just stood there. She looked at him again.

He tried to smile, but he couldn't pull it off. "Who're you meeting here, Jazz?" he asked. It was none of his business but he didn't see where he had anything to lose.

"Excuse me?"

"You said you were meeting someone here. Who is it? Gerald?"

"Gerald? No. I'm meeting Pierre."

Thomas hesitated. "And who is Pierre?"

"A friend of mine. A very nice man. He's an accountant."

"Oh. It's a business meeting then."

"No, not really. I don't have any business to discuss with him. At least none that I know of."

"I thought you said he was an accountant."

"He is. But he's not *my* accountant."

"Oh. I see. So do I know this Pierre?" Thomas tried to say this lightheartedly as he smiled and placed his hand in his pants pocket, but it was easy to see that he was mortified.

"I don't think you know him, no," Jazz replied.

"You just met him, then?"

"I wouldn't say that." Actually she could have said it because she'd only known Pierre for a day. Yesterday, to be precise, when she saw him in a bookstore. He kept eyeing her, obviously finding her attractive, and then he finally got up the nerve to ask if she would like to have a drink with him. Normally she told guys who tried to pick her up to take a hike, but she remembered her discussion with Carmella and agreed to go out with him, but at a time and place of her choosing. He was interested, so he accepted her terms. Carmella had planned to fix her up with one of their lets-make-Thomas-jealous dates, but Jazz decided that Pierre would be better. More authentic. And by the way Thomas kept questioning her about the brother, she was convinced that she was right to pick her own distraction.

"Well, good-bye," Thomas said smilingly, although his heart was shattered, and when Jazz nodded her good-bye to him he headed back for Alex. Jazz watched Alex as he arrived back at their table. She immediately placed his hand in hers and began kissing on him, as if he'd just been through an ordeal and she had to comfort him. She even cut her eyes over at Jazz when he returned her passionate kiss, to rub it in, but Jazz knew how to handle females like Alex. She smiled and waved. That managed to stop Alex cold. And she turned her unwanted attention away from Jazz.

But Thomas didn't. He continued taking quick peeps at her every chance he got, as if he was just drinking her up with his eyes, and this annoyed Alex greatly. But she knew not to say anything. From what Thomas told her about his more recent past relationships, they all seemed to fall on the question of his friendship with Jazz. The other females couldn't handle it. She had to handle it, at least until she was firmly in his stable; then she'd get rid of Jazz herself.

Pierre finally arrived, after nearly ten minutes of Jazz just sitting there, but she was so relieved to see him that she managed a big smile. He was a good-looking man in his late thirties, with a bald head and a nice physique, although he dressed like a stereotypic nerd, down to the bow tie he wore. But he was a man and he smiled when he saw her and when she glanced in Thomas's direction she could see that she had his undivided attention. If the point of this date was to distract Thomas away from Alex, then it was working even before it really got started, Jazz thought.

It began to unravel quickly, however, when Jazz realized that Pierre was not alone. Walking up behind him was a woman who looked to be in her sixties, a harsh-featured woman who walked with a cane and who was mumbling something as if she were arguing. The young lady walking even further behind Pierre and the older woman was apparently the target of the old lady's venom because the teenager was busy rolling her eyes and mouthing off something, too. Jazz couldn't believe it. She just knew this couldn't be right. Pierre could not have possibly brought them along!

"I'm so sorry I'm late, Jill," he said.

"Jazz," Jazz corrected him.

"Right. Jazz. But you called on such short notice this afternoon that there simply wasn't enough time."

Jazz looked beyond Pierre at the two women bringing up the rear. They began sitting at the table without so much as a hello, even forcing Jazz to slide over, and it was only after drinks had been ordered for all did Pierre realize his error.

"Oh, my goodness," he said. "Where's my manners? This is my mother, Jazz, I'm sorry, and my niece Ferdicky."

Fer-who? Jazz wanted to ask. But she didn't bother. Why Ferdicky and Mama were there at all was what she wanted to know.

But Pierre wasn't telling. He was too busy arguing with Mama and Ferdicky about everything under the sun, from the lighting in the room to the fact that there were so few black folks in the restaurant to the color of the place mats on the table. Everything was worthy of an argument. Jazz couldn't believe it. She just sat there, staring at Pierre. She agreed to have dinner with one person, as she recalled, not three.

But the threesome seemed oblivious to her or her concerns as the waitress brought menus along with their drinks, which prompted them to began new rounds of complaints about that.

"Ha!" the mother said almost as soon as she opened the menu, and then she looked at her trying-to-maintain-his-cool son. "You seen these prices, boy?"

"Mother."

"Well, have you?"

Pierre snapped. "How could I have seen the prices? I haven't even opened the menu!" He said this so violently and loudly that people from nearby tables couldn't help but look his way. Realizing his blunder, he calmed back down. And smiled, or at least tried to. "Now, let's not worry about the prices, Mother," he said.

"Six dollars for a hamburger? *Six dollars?* They must be out of their got damn minds!"

"Mother," Pierre admonished with a smile behind clenched teeth, "watch your language, please. We are in a public facility."

"You ain't got to buy the hamburger," Ferdicky said to Mother. "I don't know why he brought you here. All you gon' do is embarrass us."

"Embarrass *you?*" Mother said. "Now that's a laugh. All that shit you be doing? You embarrass yourself."

"Mother, I am not going to tell you again to watch the language. All right?"

The mother sucked her lips and went back to perusing the menu. Pierre looked at Jazz. And he smiled. "They don't get out much," he said, as if that said it all.

Jazz wanted to look at Thomas, to see if he was watching this horror show, but she was too busy praying that he wasn't.

"I want the steak," Ferdicky said.

"Steak?" the mother asked. "You must be out of your got damn mind! You see the price on that steak, child? Ain't nobody putting out no eighteen dollars for the likes of you!"

"Don't worry about that," Pierre assured them. "Jazz is paying. She doesn't mind."

Jazz looked at Pierre as if he had lost his mind. "Excuse me?" she asked. "*I'm* paying?"

"Why, yes," he said. "What?"

"Where do you get off . . . I mean . . ." Jazz had to calm herself as she was determined not to drag down to their level. "Where did you get the idea that I was paying for this?"

"Did you or did you not invite me to dinner at a time and place of your choosing? Wasn't those your exact words?"

"She tryin' to weasel out of it now," the mother said.

"Mother!"

"Mother, nothin', Peewee. Look at her. She invite us to dinner and then she try to act like she don't know nothin' about it."

"Actually I don't," Jazz said quickly. "Pierre invited *me* to dinner. There may be some debate about who chose the time and location. But he asked me first. I didn't invite y'all anywhere. I don't even know where the rest of y'all came from."

"Where we came from?" the mother asked, taking immediate offense. "We came from the same place you came from. We ain't no aliens! We human same as everybody else. Who you think you are?"

"I told you she was gonna embarrass us!"

"Now, now, Ferdicky," Pierre said. "Let's not raise our voices.

And mother. Please." He then turned to Jazz. "So what you're say-ing," he said, "is that you expect me to pay for all of this?"

Jazz had to look away from the brother, to regain her composure, before she could answer him. "Yes," she finally looked at him and said, "that's exactly what I'm saying."

"She shouldn't have to pay for us anyway," Ferdicky said. "What kind of man are you to even ask a lady to foot the bill? My mama told me y'all was trash. I don't know why she let me even stay with y'all."

"Because she's a crackhead who don't care where you stay," the mother interjected. "And if we suppose to be trash then you must be dirt because you ain't worth sweeping out the door!"

"At least I ain't no alcoholic!"

"At least I ain't no slut!"

"At least I don't pretend like I'm cripple just to get an SSI check!"

"At least my mama didn't name me Ferdicky!"

"That's enough!" Pierre yelled from the top of his lungs and the maitre d', as if on cue, began a quick walk toward their table. By now everybody in the restaurant was staring at Jazz's table, mesmer-ized by this loud bunch, and Jazz decided to take a quick glance at Thomas. She expected him to be staring, too, and he was, but he also sat there with a painfully confused look on his face. So painful and so confused that Jazz wanted to crawl under the table. And to make matters worse, Alex was there. And she wasn't just smiling at them, she was bent over laughing at them, laughing as if they were the fun-niest thing since the Beverly Hillbillies.

"I'm afraid you people will have to leave," the maitre d' said without even pretending to be diplomatic.

"We apologize, sir," Pierre said, "if we got a little loud."

"Sir, you and your party need to leave now."

The mother shot an angry look at the restaurant employee. "No you ain't kickin' us out!" she yelled.

"Mother!" Pierre snapped. "Hold your tongue. Let me handle this."

"Then handle it, dumbass."

"Mother!"

"Please leave," the maitre d' said. "The profanity will not be tol-erated."

"If I can just reason with you, good man," Pierre said as if his sorry excuse for charm was going to convince somebody, and Jazz, knowing that it wasn't, quickly stood up.

"Let's just go," she said bitterly, knowing also that her little scheme to distract Thomas was doing nothing but making a fool out of her, which, she was certain, Alex just loved, and Pierre and his family, seeming to sense defeat, didn't argue with her. They stood, too. They all began moving away from the table to leave the restaurant together, still squabbling as if they just didn't get it, but the maitre d' made a point of clearing his throat loudly enough to get their attention. They all turned and looked at him.

"The drinks weren't free," he said.

Jazz looked at Pierre, expecting him to take care of it, although she should have known better by now, but Pierre, instead, began hurrying his family along. "Come on, Mother," he said. "Come on, Ferdicky. We know when we aren't wanted."

And, of course, now that it was getaway time, they left without the slightest resistance, while Jazz was left holding the bag. She watched the threesome slither their way out of the restaurant as if she were watching snakes crawling across the floor. And that was the man she thought was going to make Thomas jealous. That freeloading mama's boy. Please. She shook her head, angry at her own stupidity, as she reached into her oversized bag and tossed a fifty on the table. And without daring to even look in Thomas's direction, she left.

Alex was, by now, roaring in laughter. Jazz and her *dates* truly made her night. Thomas, however, failed to see the humor. He, in fact, wasn't laughing at all. He was far too baffled for laughter.

Conrad's Jeep drove onto Melrose Drive, where Alex lived, and then stopped two doors away from her home. He stared at the house that was lit up like a fireworks display, and he wondered why he couldn't just forget about her. She was all wrong for him and he knew it. But he couldn't seem to get her out of his head. He couldn't seem to allow his mind a moment's rest ever since she told him to leave her alone. And he knew the real deal. He knew she just used him to clear her sister of those assault charges and to get that legal help her sister needed from Thomas Drayton. She used him and then tossed him aside. She was just like his ex-wife in so many ways and he knew this, too. But unfortunately for him, knowledge wasn't power.

Because all the knowledge in this world wasn't stopping him from wanting her. It wasn't stopping him from driving by her house, like some kind of crazed stalker, just to feel a sense of connection to a woman who wouldn't really care if he was dead or alive.

He shook his head. *What a fool!* he said aloud, and then cranked up his Jeep and drove away.

ALMOST PERFECT

She knew why he was doing it. She knew the moment he phoned and invited her to dinner with him and Alex. After that pathetic display by that trifling Pierre and his ridiculous mama and niece, Jazz was certain that the only reason Thomas was phoning her at all was because he pitied her.

But she still didn't say no. She didn't want his pity, she hated even the thought of it, but she had to accept if only to prove to him that she didn't need his pity. She wasn't poor Jazz after all. She wasn't the thrice-divorced woman with zero luck with men, regardless of how it looked, and she had to let Thomas see for himself. She was still a tough, strong, desirable woman who could attract men far more appealing than losers like Pierre, and Thomas had to understand that. It wasn't about merely distracting Thomas away from Alex. It wasn't about them anymore. After the humiliation of the other night, this was all about Jazz.

She hung up the phone after accepting Thomas's dinner invitation but declining his offer to pick her up and raced from her loft, down the stairs, across the backyard, and up to the back door of the main house. Although she owned the house, she never took any liberties with it. Carmella was her tenant and she respected her privacy as a tenant. She knocked on the door, nonstop, until Carmella finally opened it.

"It better be the police knocking on my door like this!" she yelled as she swung open the door.

"I need a man," Jazz said anxiously when the door flew open. Carmella smiled.

"So do I, sugar," she said. "So do I."

"I'm serious, Carmella. Thomas has invited me to dinner with him and Alex."

"Even after witnessing that Pierre fiasco?"

"That's why I think he's doing it. He pities me."

"Well you are pitiful, girl."

"Carmella!"

"Okay. Dang. Don't get all hot with me. I was gonna set you up before, remember? With a real man who could really make Thomas take notice. But nooo. You wanted to give Pierre a try. It'll be more authentic, you said."

"Okay, okay," Jazz said. "I was wrong, all right? I admit it. Now are you going to help me or not?"

Carmella exhaled. And then she thought about it far longer than Jazz felt necessary. "Come on in," she finally said. "I'm sure I can come up with *somebody*."

They had taken a few sips of their drinks and Alex had excused herself to the ladies room by the time Jazz arrived at the small, Italian bistro in South Beach. Thomas, who had been smoking more than ever lately, doused his cigar as soon as he saw her face and stood to greet her. She looked gorgeous, he thought, even in her less-than-stylish jeans and eyeglasses, and he found himself staring at her so hard that he didn't realize the tall, attractive gentleman walking in behind her was with her until they began heading for his table. And he immediately understood why she declined his offer to pick her up. She knew she would be bringing a date. A *date,* he thought. Jazz with yet another man? What was up with this? he wondered.

Jazz noticed Thomas when she first walked in, too, as he stood to his feet in a suit of fine clothes that screamed super-expensive. He had on his reading glasses, because he'd been perusing the menu, and she liked him like that, although he quickly removed them. This man, this best friend of hers with his low-cut fade, with a smile to beat back blues, with a sexiness that had Jazz's entire body hot just from looking at him, was the reason for the season and she wasn't about to disappoint.

"Hello, Thomas," she said with a grand smile and an extended hand. She was determined to make it clear, by her demeanor alone, that she was in need of nobody's pity.

"Hey," Thomas said as he stared at Jazz's hand before he reluctantly shook it. He found it odd that she didn't kiss him, especially since she'd never offered to shake his hand before. But then again, he thought, she'd never had such a great-looking brother on her arm before, either.

"I hope we aren't late," she said, still smiling, still too upbeat, he felt.

"Not at all," he said. "I'm just a little surprised, I guess."

"Surprised? About what?"

"I didn't know you were bringing a date."

"You didn't? I thought I mentioned it."

"No."

"You sure?"

"I'm positive."

"Ah. That's strange. Well, anyway, let me introduce you now. This is Mark Hartmann. He's a very good friend of mine. And Mark, this is Thomas Drayton."

Thomas was wounded by Jazz's decision not to mention that he was her best friend, but he didn't sweat it. He shook Mark's hand eagerly.

"Nice to meet you, Mark," he said.

"Same here, man. Nice suit."

Thomas looked down at his expensive suit and then looked at Mark. "This old thing? It's nothing."

"It's a Valentino, right? Yeah, that's nothing at all."

Both Mark and Thomas laughed. And then they all sat down.

Alex didn't join them until the waitress had taken and returned with the drink orders for Mark and Jazz, but as soon as she saw the strange man at their table she couldn't help but smile. "Well now," she said as Thomas helped her to her seat, "who do we have here?"

"Alex Mailer," Jazz said, "Mark Hartmann."

"Mark. Nice to meet you."

"Nice to meet you. You must be Thomas's better half."

Alex smiled greatly. That was all she needed to hear. "You must be Jazz's better half," she said.

"From your lips to God's ears," Mark said.

"So you hope to spend more time with Jazz?" Alex asked this all smiles, as if this was the best news she'd come across in a while. And for good reason. That good-looking stranger seated across the table, she felt, could be just what the doctor ordered to get rid of that headache called Jazz.

Mark placed his arm across Jazz's chair and looked at her with a smile. He was putting on this show for Carmella, who promised him a date with *her* if he did this right, and he wasn't about to disappoint. He'd been after Carmella for months now, but she was on one of those hard-to-get trips. One night out with this artist friend of hers, whom, he confessed, wasn't bad to look at either, made Carmella indebted to him—a debt he aimed to collect.

"Well?" Alex asked again. "Can we assume you and Jazz will be an item now?"

"Of course," Mark said. "If she'll have me."

"If she'll have *you?*" Alex asked this as if it was an incredible thought, but when she glanced over at Thomas and realized he didn't find it incredible at all, she eased up. She was winning, she had to keep reminding herself.

They ordered dinner and Mark turned out to be the life of the party. Even Thomas couldn't find a thing wrong with him. He tried, he smoked on his cigar and stared at Mark unceasingly, and then he asked the brother every question he could think up to tarnish his shine. But he shot blanks. Mark was a nice-looking, single man with no children, no current ties to any one woman, and he had a great job as a sports writer for the *Herald*. He was easy to like and easy to get along with. A man perfect for Jazz, which should have made Thomas enormously happy for her. But he wasn't.

He kept looking at Jazz as she responded to Mark's whispers in her ear with a few whispers and then laughs of her own. They shared private jokes that Thomas and Alex weren't privy to, and it bothered the hell out of Thomas. Many times he wanted to ask them what was so damn funny, but he held his tongue. Jazz had apparently decided to get back into the dating game, after many years of relying exclusively on Thomas for her companionship, and who was he to deny her that? He was her best friend, a man who was supposed to be there for her and catch her lest she fall. His job was not, however, to sit up there seething with jealousy because his best friend's finally got a man.

But that was exactly what Thomas was sitting up there doing. His entire body rocked with envy every time Mark's shoulder touched Jazz's shoulder, or his hand rubbed across hers, or his smile caused hers to light up. Mark even took his big hand at one point and pushed her glasses up on the bridge of her beautiful, small, buttonish nose. A nose he had the nerve to criticize.

"I think they can expand those nowadays, you know," Mark said to Jazz.

"Expand what?" Thomas asked in a voice laced with such a bite that even Jazz had to look at him. But Thomas didn't care. The idea of somebody even thinking about tampering with Jazz's perfect nose was more than he could stand.

"Her nose," Mark said as if the concern in Thomas's voice didn't bother him at all. It was his job, after all, to rile the brother. "They can make them more shapely now. Jazz's just too small."

"I think it's fine," Thomas replied.

"It's too small. It's so small she can't even keep her glasses up on it. And speaking of glasses—" Mark took a sip from his beer before he continued. Thomas blew out an impatient breath and looked at Jazz. She was perfect in his eyes—glasses, small nose, and all—and if Mark didn't think so then Thomas could only hope that Jazz wasn't so desperate for bed action that she wouldn't tell that clown to hit the road. But the way Jazz was looking at Mark, so lovingly, so understandingly, made Thomas doubt if she was capable of saying anything negative to the brother. "I don't mean to be cruel," Mark said, having no trouble whatsoever going negative, "but those glasses have got to go."

Jazz smiled. "You don't like my eyeglasses?"

"I do not. Not when you can wear you some fashionable contacts. Girl, they can hook you up now. Get you some blue ones, you know, and you've—"

"Blue?" Thomas asked incredulously.

"Yes, blue. I can see it. Look here." Mark removed Jazz's eyeglasses, revealing stunning dark brown eyes. Thomas's breath caught in his throat.

"See there!" Mark said with a laugh as he pointed at Thomas. "Her beautiful eyes even took your breath away. These eyes don't need to be hidden! And with some blue contacts, man-oh-man, she'll have to beat the brothers off of her! Of course her eyes are a little too droopy for my taste, but some brothers think they're sexy like that."

Thomas looked at Jazz as she removed her glasses from Mark's grasp and put them back on her face. She was always self-conscious about the downward slope of her eyes and Thomas knew it. And the anger he was feeling for Mark began to surface.

"Jazz doesn't need contacts," he said with such restrained anger in his voice that Jazz looked at him. "And she doesn't need a nose job. She's perfect just the way she is. You, on the other hand—"

Alex quickly laid her hand over Thomas's and smiled, effectively stopping him just as he was about to lash out at Mark. Mark was the man to get Jazz out of their lives, Alex felt, and she wasn't about to let Thomas mess that up. "Why don't we all plan to go see the Dolphins play one Sunday?" she asked. "They're supposed to be Super Bowl contenders this year."

Mark smiled, although he was mad as hell at Thomas. "Great idea," he said, and as Thomas and Jazz stared deep into each other's eyes, with feelings they knew weren't commonly found among friends, Mark and Alex talked sports as if they never realized just how close to an explosion they had really been.

After dinner Thomas was stunned when Jazz said good-bye without kissing him. He and Alex walked some distance behind Jazz and Mark as they left the restaurant, and Jazz left his side with nothing more than a smile and a wave good night. And the way Mark placed his hand around her waist as he escorted her to his show-off SUV, some foreign job with thousand-dollar rims, made Thomas's stomach turn. He walked Alex further toward the back of the huge lot, where his Bentley was parked, but he couldn't take his eyes off of the so-called happy couple. He couldn't stop fuming either. Who does this Mark think he is that he can be touching Jazz like that? he wanted to know.

Jazz wanted to know, too, as Mark opened the passenger door of his SUV for her. "You can cool it now, partner," she said to him. "He got the point."

"But I can't cool it, J. Not now. You turn me on too much, girl. You and those hips of yours. And my hand fit so comfortably on you." Mark said this with a smile, and Jazz, ready to tell the brother a thing or two, first glanced over to make sure Thomas was now out of viewing range. Then she slung Mark's grubby little hand off of her.

"I said that's enough," she warned.

But as he left her side laughing at her outburst, Jazz rolled her eyes and sat down in his SUV. And all things considered, she couldn't have been more pleased. The plan had worked. Thomas was beside himself with jealousy all evening, it seemed to her, and the look on his face when she didn't give him even an opportunity to kiss her good night was priceless. She had his attention now, she felt.

But as she watched that trifling Mark Hartmann walk around his SUV to the driver's side door, she also felt an eerie presence of some kind behind her. She felt spooked even, as if she was being watched. She turned around quickly, just in time to see a woman with an unmistakable big-bladed butcher's knife raise up from the backseat like a character out of a horror movie and lunge at her. The blade came within inches of slicing Jazz's neck, causing Jazz to scream *"Thomas!"* from the top of her lungs and sling open the door of the vehicle with the agility of an acrobat. She flew out of the SUV screaming Thomas's name again and again and running toward him, frightened out of her wits. Mark was yelling, desperately wanting to know what had happened, what was wrong with her, and Thomas, on the other side of the massive parking lot, thought he heard her scream his name and turned around.

When he saw that it was indeed Jazz screaming for him and running his way, with a woman, a knife-wielding woman, on her trail, he sprung away from Alex and ran toward Jazz. Mark was running, too, either trying to stop the woman or to help her injure Jazz, Thomas wasn't at all sure. All he knew was that he had to get to Jazz, he had to get Jazz, and his mind was almost stricken with fear. Jazz was fearful, too, as she ran, as she kept looking back at that knife-packing crazy woman who definitely was not a part of the plan. It was supposed to be simple. Distract Thomas with jealousy and maybe that'll give him enough time to come to his senses about gold-digger Alex. A very practical, simple plan that was turning out to be, from what Jazz could see, a very practical, simple disaster.

"Thomas!" she cried as she ran into his arms. He wanted to crush her against him and hold her forever, but he didn't. He quickly slung her behind him and braced himself, in a wrestler's stance, for an attack. But the woman, who looked haggard and wild and just plain tired, took one look at the large, muscular man before her and stopped her pursuit.

She didn't, however, stop her threatening words. "I'm gonna kill her!" she kept yelling. "I'll kill that bitch!"

By the time Mark made it to the scene she was pointing her knife, panting practically out of breath, and crying hysterically. He came up behind her and easily removed the knife from her grasp, as if this kind of activity was nothing new to him.

"Stay away from my husband!" were the last words the woman uttered to Jazz as she collapsed against that husband of hers in sheer exhaustion. Mark seemed to absentmindedly pull her closer to him as he asked if Jazz was all right. Jazz came from behind Thomas and reluctantly said that she was. Mark, seemingly satisfied that no injuries occurred, turned his bedraggled wife around and pulled her against him. And he actually managed to smile. The bastard, Jazz thought.

"Sorry about this, Jazz," he said as if it was humorous. "We had a good night out. It was almost perfect, in fact. And if you don't tell Carmella, it still could be."

Jazz looked at Mark and shook her head. He was sicker than his wife, she thought.

"You aren't going to tell Carmella, are you?" he asked.

Jazz almost told Mark exactly what she felt about his crazy question, but Thomas placed his hand around her waist and pulled her against him, effectively shutting her up. "Just get her away from here," he said to Mark.

"I don't know what got into her tonight. She knows not to follow me like this. But she wouldn't have hurt anybody, if that's what you're worried about."

"I don't care. Just take her back where she came from."

Mark, with his wife in one hand and her deadly weapon in the other, only nodded his head with a kind of twisted smile on his face and began to walk away.

"And Mark," Thomas added, causing Mark to turn back around, "stay away from Jazz."

It sounded like a warning, one Mark had every intention of heeding since Jazz wasn't the one he wanted anyway, and without a word Mark turned around and escorted his wife back to their vehicle.

Thomas exhaled a sigh of relief, as if they truly dodged a bullet this night, and then he looked at Jazz. She was still staring at Mark.

"You okay?" Thomas asked her.

The best she could do was nod. But Thomas kept looking at her, causing her to return his stare.

"Did you know he was married?"

When Thomas asked her this, Jazz frowned. "Of course not, Thomas! How could you ask me something like that?"

Thomas sighed. She nearly scared him to death, how did she expect him to react? "I want you to stay away from that guy," he said, prompting her to laugh.

"No kidding?" she said snidely. "And here I was thinking about how I could get around him again. I mean, no harm, no foul, right? His wife—wife, by the way—didn't kill me. All she did was chase me around the parking lot with a knife. And who wouldn't want to be chased around the parking lot by a crazed killer with a knife?"

"You'd better knock it off." Thomas said this so chillingly harsh that Jazz did just that. She wasn't accustomed to that tone of voice coming from him, and he wasn't accustomed to talking to her that way. He rubbed his low-cut fade and exhaled once again. Jazz, understanding the tension that had filled the air, walked away from him and headed toward his Bentley. Unfortunately for her, relief wasn't there. Alex was. And she was all smiles, as usual.

"My, my," she said, "your dates are the most interesting people, Jazz. A movie couldn't be more entertaining. Who do you have in store for us next? I can hardly wait!"

Jazz ignored the sarcasm and looked at Thomas, who was heading their way, too, his suit coat flapping wildly against the strong night wind and his tie nearly wrapped around his neck. He was walking awkward and slow and Jazz could see the concern still all over his face. And her heart went out to him. The crap she put him through, she thought. "Mind if I catch a ride?" she said gaily, attempting to lighten his mood.

"Not at all," Alex said before he could respond, as she moved to claim the front seat for herself. "We'll be glad to drop you off."

Remarkably, however, given their recent history, it wasn't Jazz who was dropped off, but Alex. She was stunned as the Bentley bypassed the turn to head for Homestead and instead turned onto Melrose Drive and came to a stop in front of her house. When Thomas got out of the car to go and open her car door, she couldn't wait to look at Jazz, who she just knew would be gloating. And she was right.

"What's so damn funny?" she asked her.

"Oh, nuttin'," Jazz said. "We're just glad to drop *you* off!"

Alex gave her a chilling, murderous glare but then smiled greatly as Thomas opened her door. "I think dropping me off first was a very good idea, Thomas," she said as she placed her hand in his and stepped out of the car. "Jazz has been through such a traumatic evening, I'm sure she can use all the support she can get."

"Well, I'm glad you understand, Alex," Thomas said as he placed her arm on his and began walking her to her front door. Alex looked back at Jazz and smiled. Jazz leaned back against the headrest. If it wasn't for bad luck, she thought, as she could see once again that crazy woman lunging at her. And then she smiled. *How was the date?* she could imagine Carmella asking her. *I was nearly decapitated,* she'd reply, *but other than that, it was perfect!*

Thomas unlocked the door to Jazz's apartment and then handed her back her keys. For a moment she just stood there, staring down at her keys, and then she looked into Thomas's face. He stood so close to her that she could feel his warm breath against her cheek. He looked as if he wanted to kiss her, and she certainly wanted him to, but he didn't do it. He just stared at her.

"Well," she said, "good night."

"Good night."

"And thanks for the ride."

"Anytime. You know that."

Jazz smiled. "I don't think Alex was crazy about you dropping her off before me."

Thomas didn't say anything, which made Jazz immediately regret her comment. He never talked about his relationships with his women to her, not ever, and she was disgusted with herself for not remembering that. "I'm sorry," she said.

Thomas frowned. "Sorry about what?"

"Nothing. I just . . . Nothing."

Thomas folded his arms and stared at his friend. She was worrying him sick and he wondered if she even realized it. "Jazz, are you all right?" he asked her.

"Yes. I'm fine."

"Sure?"

"I'm fine, Thomas." The defensiveness in her voice was more pronounced than she had wanted it to be. It seemed to reveal too much, she felt, including why she appeared so unnerved around him lately. And why she was willing to stoop so low, on dates with the likes of Pierre and Mark, to distract him, or, more precisely, to take him away from Alex.

"Anyway," she said, as she began making her way across the threshold of her front door, feeling too exposed for comfort, "good night again." She said this without looking at Thomas, or even bothering to hear his reply, but as soon as she stepped inside her living room, and the quietness of the room overtook her, that intense desire she had for Thomas to hold her and kiss her, desire that had been simmering just below the surface ever since she first saw him at the restaurant tonight, began to bubble over and she hurried back outside the door. "Thomas!" she yelled as soon as she saw him descending the stairs, his straight back wide and strong against his perfectly tailored suit.

He turned and looked at her, his wondrously passionate eyes searing her. "You may as well stay here tonight," she said, and then added, "if you want," when he seemed to hesitate.

Thomas did hesitate, a lot longer than he knew Jazz would be comfortable with, but he was beginning to get confused as hell by all of these mixed signals she'd been giving him lately. One minute she didn't seem to want to have anything to do with him, she couldn't seem to stand the sight of him, and the next minute she was urging him to spend the night with her. He stared at her, at this woman who still managed to throttle his heart every time he saw her, and he knew, despite himself, he could never say no to her. "Why not," he said as if it were a compromise, as he began a slow climb back up the stairs.

He had some phone calls to make and stayed in the living room nearly an hour after Jazz had gone to bed. She laid there stiff as a board, listening to him talk on the telephone in great animation during one phone call, or in almost inaudible whispers during another. Undoubtedly that call was with a woman, Jazz figured. And the entire feel of it depressed her. What in the world was she doing? Here she was, a soon-to-be thirty-five-year-old woman, and she was just realizing for the first time how dependent on Thomas she really was. Tonight crystallized it for her, when she saw that she was in danger. She couldn't get to Thomas fast enough, screaming his name as if he was Jesus Christ himself. And it wasn't until she got to him, and felt his arms around her, that she believed she stood a chance.

When she discovered that Albert, her third husband, was cheating on her, she swore by all that was right and just that she would never depend on another human being again. But as soon as Albert walked out of her life, Thomas came into it. As her lawyer first, and then as her friend. But he'd now become more than a friend, and she knew it. He was not only her best friend now, but her husband, her father, her brother. Her family. That was it. Thomas was her family, the only one she had. And the thought of losing that family, the thought of Alex Mailer working her charms on him to steal him away from her forever, was choking the life out of her. It was turning her into some pathetic, bitter female who would stop at nothing to keep a man. Jazz, the strong one. Sister J, the woman who wasn't about to let some man rock her world, was tossing like a tugboat on an angry sea. And she wasn't strong at all. Or steady. Or some island onto herself as she had thought. Because hard as it was for her to admit, and as bitter the pill was she had to swallow, she knew now, without a doubt, that she needed Thomas Drayton.

But she also needed her pride as her shield, as the last vestige of self-determination she had left. And the thought of him sitting in her living room on the telephone, talking possibly to some other woman when he knew she was back here waiting on his behind, was beginning to bruise that pride. She began wondering why she even asked him to stay the night when it was obvious by his hesitation that he didn't want to. Why didn't she just say forget it when he didn't speak up? That was her normal style. Why didn't she exhibit that style tonight? He, after all, wasn't the only hunk in the hay, he wasn't the only fish in the sea, and she hated being so open to him like this. But Alex wasn't lying. She'd had a very traumatic evening. And whether she liked it or not, she needed to feel his arms around her tonight, to be able to talk to him even if it was just small talk. She *needed* him.

And when he finally made his way into her bedroom, and undressed himself down to his briefs and got into her bed, just the strong sweet scent of him alone made her glad that she had swallowed that foolish pride of hers for once in her life and asked him to stay.

For a few long moments, however, it was tortuous, as he just laid there seeming to stare at the ceiling, as if he was in some deep thought, and she certainly wasn't about to make the first move. She'd exposed enough vulnerabilities for one night, she felt. But then his big arm came curling around her shoulder and pulled her beside him, and she quickly returned his gesture by placing her arms around him, too. Words weren't spoken—there didn't appear to be any need for words, as Jazz was perfectly content to just lay her head on his chest and sleep the night away.

Thomas, however, had other ideas. He placed his hand on her chin and lifted her face up to his. He stared at those lips of hers for what seemed like an eternity to Jazz, and then he looked into her eyes. She could feel desire creep through every fiber of her being as he looked at her, and she felt as if she would die if he didn't kiss her. But he didn't. Not even a peck. He just stared at her and stared at her, unable to unlock the mystery that had become her. He thought he saw longing in her eyes, and great desire, but how could it be? Jazz didn't want him. She was moving on with her life. She was even dating now, although her selections left a lot to be desired, but that was her choice, her business. And besides, she knew he was in a relationship with Alex now, such as it was, and he couldn't be passionately kissing on her anymore even if he wanted to. But he'd also seen more than his share of lust-filled females in his day, and Jazz, it seemed to him, definitely had that look.

He decided to look away from her, and move away, too, but Jazz pulled herself tighter against him and wouldn't let him move. First he looked at the ceiling. What was her problem? She was clinging to him tonight as if she were some scared child, which certainly wasn't like Jazz, and then he realized suddenly that it probably wasn't Jazz at all but the events of the day that were driving her passion. And that was when he looked back down at her. God, he wanted to kiss her, and make love to her, and keep her under his thumb for the rest of her life. But he knew it wasn't going to happen, even if Jazz appeared ready to let it happen, because tomorrow would come, and if he thought she was drifting away from him now, a budding romance would surely finalize the process.

He attempted to move his arms away from her again, but again she grasped hers around him tighter. "Jazz, come on," he said.

"Don't, Thomas."

"You've had a tough night, baby. That's what's going on here. Try to get some sleep."

"Hold me," she pleaded. Then she looked up into his eyes. "I need you to hold me."

Thomas's heart dropped like a brick when he saw the pain in her eyes, pain that seemed to cut to the chase of her affliction the way marrow cut to the bone, and he immediately crushed her against him in a huge bear hug. He kissed her on her forehead and then pulled her on top of him, holding her even tighter. It was easy holding her, he thought, he never had any problem holding Jazz. The trouble for him was that he just wasn't sure if he could ever let her go.

They woke up the next morning still locked in an embrace. Thomas's face was buried in Jazz's hair and Jazz was still lying on top of Thomas, crushed against his chest. Her breasts ached with pinned-up tension of too close contact for too long, and she could feel where Thomas's hand, sometime during the night, had found its way under her gown and was now resting on her bare derriere. She laid still, as that soft hand of his began rubbing her buttocks, and she knew then that Thomas, who had merely stirred awake earlier, then dozed back off, was now becoming completely awake. But his hand felt so good. She closed her eyes and hoped that he wouldn't stop, although she knew he had to.

And he did, as soon as he realized what he was doing. He quickly looked down at Jazz, hoping that she wasn't awake to witness his blunder, and when he saw that her eyes were still closed, he gently, perhaps even regrettably, removed his hand from her backside and smoothed her gown back down.

She opened her eyes. And then she yawned and stretched and looked up at Thomas. He smiled.

"Feel better?" he asked her.

She smiled back at him and nodded. "What time is it?"

Thomas grabbed his Rolex from off of the nightstand and looked at it. "About seven," he said.

"Seven on a Saturday morning."

"Right."

"What's your plans for today?" She asked this with what seemed to him to be excitement and anticipation in her voice. Thomas didn't know how to respond to such emotions from Jazz. He had fully expected that clinging behavior she displayed in the night to be well out of sight this morning, but his expectation appeared to be wrong.

"I don't think I've made any plans yet, Jazz," he said, knowing he couldn't lie to her by making something up.

"Me, either," she said.

Thomas just laid there, absently stroking her soft hair, although he stopped when he realized what he was doing. He would love to spend a day with Jazz. There was, in truth, nowhere else he'd rather be than with her. But was it wise? Was it just a carryover from the trauma of the night, and once she came back to herself she'd become angry with him for taking advantage of the situation? Knowing Jazz, she would. And given the rough way she'd been treating him of late, he wasn't sure if she'd ever forgive him for it, either. But he wanted to be with her anyway. He was willing to take the chance.

But his cell phone began ringing before he could say another word to her. He smiled. It just wasn't meant to be, he figured.

"Hello," he said into his phone as he retrieved it from the night-stand. After a moment he said, "Good morning to you, too," and then glanced at Jazz.

It was Alex, Jazz decided, as she slid off of Thomas and laid on her back beside him. She felt defeated for some reason, cold, lonely, and defeated. She felt better, however, when he took his arm and placed it across her shoulder, which drew her back against him. But when, after a minute or two of conversing, he said, "I'm on my way," into his phone, her heart dropped.

He flipped off his cell phone and then stared at it momentarily, as if trying to decide what to do. Then he looked at Jazz. "That was Alex," he said.

"I gathered."

"She wants to cook me breakfast."

Jazz had that thought in mind herself. But Alex, as usual, beat her to the prize. "That's very nice of her."

"Why don't you join us," Thomas said, sensing Jazz's defeat, although he knew it was an unwise suggestion.

"No," Jazz said. No way, she wanted to say. "But thanks."

Thomas laid there for a moment, as if he was still deep in thought and unsure about his actions, although, it seemed to Jazz, he had already made his decision. Then, as if he suddenly understood it, too, he got out of bed and headed for the bathroom.

By the time he had dressed and was telling Jazz good-bye, she was not showing an ounce of her displeasure. But she was very displeased.

She stood at her front door, accepted a peck on her cheek from Thomas, smiled and waved and played the role of the grateful friend, and then watched with deep-seated sadness as he hurried away from her home. Hurried to fall into the arms of Alex Mailer. That conniving bitch.

She closed her door and plopped down on her sofa. It seemed as if it was over, and Alex had won. She tried to distract him. She tried with Pierre and then Mark. But she failed miserably. She was close with Mark, before knife lady showed up, but close wasn't good enough. Alex seemed to have fate on her side and she was taking full advantage of it. Her seduction of Thomas was well on schedule, Jazz felt; it may even have been ahead of schedule. And he was letting it happen. He was so desperate to find himself a life mate, to finally end that cycle of starting over as he constantly told her he was tired of doing, that he was compromising like hell, settling for what he could get, when a man like him didn't have to settle for anybody.

But fate seemed to have dealt Alex the perfect hand. And she knew how to play it. And Jazz, though disappointed with defeat, should just accept it. And normally she would have. She was never a sore loser. But the catch, the prize, was never Thomas before. And she had already decided this morning, when she felt his warm hand caressing her backside, once again filling her very soul with a passion she thought had long since died, that the answer was no. Just like that. No. Alex or no Alex, fate or no fate. The answer was no. She was not losing Thomas.

NOT EVEN A LESBIAN

Biscayne Boulevard was alive at lunchtime as Jazz worked her way through the press of tourists that cluttered the sidewalks and entered the RCN building within a minute of the time she agreed to be there. She saw Carmella, standing near the elevators in the downstairs lobby, a lobby that was forty-one floors beneath the floor housing Thomas's law offices, and as soon as she laid eyes on the woman standing with Carmella, she knew that her decision to go through with this was a very bad idea.

Carmella, however, was totally oblivious to Jazz's disappointment. She proceeded with introductions. "Jazz," she said gaily, "this is Bridget, the lady I told you about. And Brig, this Jazz, girl."

"What's up?" Bridget asked as she smoothed an overlong artificial eyelash with a finger.

Jazz just stared at her, astounded by Carmella's choice, and then she looked at Carmella. "May I see you for a minute, please?" she asked her and began moving away, toward the water cooler, before she could answer.

Carmella, knowing Jazz all too well, excused herself from Bridget and hurried over to Jazz, trying her best to maintain her calm and not run over the excessive number of people coming in and out of the crowded building.

"Okay, Jazz, what is it?" She asked this as soon as she reached Jazz's side.

"I said a lesbian, Carmella. Not a hoochie!"

"What's the damn difference? She's a woman pretending to be your girlfriend, that's all Thomas needs to know."

"But she's got to look the part, Carm!" Jazz said this with great exasperation. "Thomas is not going to believe for a second that that female with her mile-high-in-the-sky hairdo and block-long nails and can't-get-enough-attention, up-her-behind miniskirt is a lesbian!"

"Oh, so they all look alike now? One can't possibly have any style?"

"You know what I mean, Carmella. I'm not trying to make a social statement here. I'm just trying to stop Thomas from making the biggest mistake of his life. That's all I'm trying to do here. And if he doesn't buy the scheme from jump, then hey. I'm just wasting my time."

"It's gonna be a waste anyway, Jazz, given your track record."

"*My* track record? No you didn't say that. You picked the last one. Remember?"

Carmella smiled. "That fool actually called me last night," she said.

"Mark called you?"

"Yes! Talking about he's sorry about his wife acting a fool but he still think we should get together."

"What did you say?"

"I told him to kiss my ass, what you think I said? Knife lady ain't coming after me!"

Jazz laughed. "I hear that."

Bridget, however, appeared to want in on the fun as she was more than a little perturbed by their neglect of her. "I don't mean to be rude," she said, "but, like, I really got other things to do. Now Carmella said this was a *paying* gig." She said this and looked from Jazz to Carmella and back to Jazz. Jazz sighed. Thomas was expecting her upstairs, she was supposed to meet him at his office so that they could go to lunch together, and Jazz knew the most effective way for her plan to work was to catch him totally off guard. That was why she wanted to have the female with her when she entered his office. The idea that Jazz would bring her "girlfriend" to his place of business, when she knew he didn't play that, would help prove to him just how serious she was. But now, thanks to I*'ve got just the person for the job* Carmella, she had to convince Thomas that, not only was she a lesbian dating another woman, but that the woman she was dating was a lesbian herself! Jazz shook her head. If it wasn't for bad luck, she thought.

"Yes," she finally said to Bridget, "it is a paying gig. You know what to do, right?"

"Yeah. Make some woman jealous. And trust me, I can do that with my eyes closed."

Jazz looked at Carmella. "You didn't tell her, did you?"

"Yes! Okay, I didn't. But I thought you could . . . you know, explain it better."

"It would not have required all of this explanation if you would have gotten a real one to begin with."

"A real one?" Bridget asked. "A real what? What's this about, Carmella?"

"I didn't get a quote, unquote, 'real one,' " Carmella said to Jazz, "because you didn't give me enough time. And in answer to your question, Bridget, what this is not about is you making a woman jealous. This is about you making a man jealous."

"A man? How am I supposed to make a man jealous?"

"By pretending to be her girlfriend."

"By what? Hold up. Hold the hell up! You had me coming all the way up in here, clean across town, to play some woman's woman?"

"That's about the size of it."

"You got to be crazy. You have got to be out of your *f-ing* mind." Bridget said this and then looked at Jazz. "I'm sorry, lady, but I don't do the dyke thing."

"Neither do I," Jazz said quickly, "so don't flatter yourself, all right?"

"I'm out of here, Carmella," Bridget said angrily as she began leaving. "And don't even think about showing your ass at the crib again!"

"Now what am I supposed to do?" Jazz asked Carmella.

"Just stall him," Carmella said. "Invite him to your place tonight for dinner. That's it. Invite him over. I'll have a lesbian for you then, I promise you that."

"A real one, Carmella?"

"Yes, a real one. I'll call you later." Carmella hurried behind Bridget, whose brother owned one of the hottest clubs in Liberty City, and the idea that she was going to shut her out was unacceptable.

Jazz just stood there, shaking her head. She wasn't about to invite Thomas to dinner tonight. She wasn't about to continue this fiasco. She was going to tell him the truth, she suddenly decided. No more games. No more innuendos. She was going to get on that elevator, march into his office, and tell him exactly how she felt about that devious Alex and how she was using him and playing him like a drum and he was too lust-filled to realize it. She was going to tell him the truth. All of it.

But by the time she rode up on the elevator to the forty-first floor, got off, and headed for Thomas's office, she wasn't so sure if she even knew what the real truth was. Was it all about Alex hurting Thomas? Or was Carmella right all along and this was all about Jazz? Did she want Thomas so badly that she'd result to petty games to get him?

No, she decided, as she approached his huge office doors. They had made a conscious decision to remain friends, to protect their friendship from the wavering storms of romance, and even if Thomas made the biggest mistake of his life and married that witch Alex Mailer, their friendship would still be strong. Or would it? Jazz thought, and then she decided to just stop thinking because it was getting her nothing but more emotions to deal with.

Thomas was seated behind his desk talking on the telephone by the time she entered his office. He looked gorgeous as usual, in his shirt sleeves, and she had to fight the urge to run into his arms as soon as she saw him. It didn't used to be this strong, her attraction to him. But now it seemed to overwhelm her every time she looked his way or heard his voice or smelled his scent. She wanted to dismiss it as her friendly love for Thomas trying to assert itself as something else, but it wasn't something that was easily dismissed.

Thomas didn't acknowledge her presence as she walked in; he was too busy listening to a settlement offer he was receiving over the phone. But he did watch her every move as she performed her customary looking around as if she'd never been in his office before, when she'd been there a hundred times, and then she made her way up to the wall-sized window and stared out at the busy streets of downtown Miami. She was wearing shorts today, which he always loved because they revealed those shapely legs of hers, and her oversized shoulder bag seemed to weigh her down less today. Maybe she finally cleaned out the darn thing, he thought.

As his phone conversation began to come to a close, his eyes kept moving downward, to Jazz's tight butt, and he couldn't help but remember how soft and tender it felt as he massaged it the other morning. He had hoped she was asleep that morning and didn't realize what he had done, but now, as his entire midsection tightened with desire just from looking at her, he wished she knew; he wished there was no doubt in her mind whatsoever how much she meant to him.

"Sorry about that, Jazzy," he said cheerfully as he finally ended his conversation and hung up the phone.

"No problem," Jazz said without turning around. Cheerful was the last thing she could manage to be.

"So Gerald finally gave you a day off?"

"Two weeks. And Gerald had nothing to do with it. It's my annual."

"Your annual vacation," Thomas said as he stood and walked toward the window. "And once again you aren't spending it on the beaches of Maui, or on a cruise ship to Jamaica, oh, no. Not Jazz. She's spending it with me. Lil' ol' me." Jazz looked over her shoulder at him. "And I'm flattered," he said, heartfelt.

Then he placed his hand in the small of her back and kissed her on the lips. It was supposed to be a peck, that was as far as they needed to go, and they both knew it. But it wasn't a peck, and neither seemed to have the will to do anything but allow it. Jazz closed her eyes and tilted her head further back as Thomas moved her closer to him and began kissing her in a circular, passionate motion. Her lips quivered underneath his hard kiss, and for the life of her she didn't want it to end. But it did. They were just friends. Thomas had a woman. What did they keep trying to prove?

When the kissing stopped, Jazz fully expected Thomas to not only pull away but move away as well. For the love of mercy she was praying that he would. But he stayed where he stood, his breathing labored, his closeness like an untouchable gem in front of her.

"So," she asked, attempting to lighten the mood, "how's your day going so far?"

"It's all right," Thomas said in an almost strident tone, as if the frustration of never being able to finish what he started, something he'd been dying to finish for far too long, was beginning to anger him. "I settled a case that I thought was destined for divorce court, so that helps."

"Good," Jazz said as she purposely backed away from him.

Thomas's heart pained when she backed away, but he didn't question it. He walked back toward his desk. "Ready?" he asked without looking at her. He, instead, began closing confidential files and removing them from his desk.

"Ready for what?" Jazz asked in such a tone of suspicion that Thomas looked at her.

"Lunch," he said.

"Oh," Jazz said, remembering why she was there, but Thomas's phone began ringing before she could affirm that she was more than ready to get away from there.

Because the ringing was from Thomas's private line, he answered it. When he realized it was Alex, he smiled. At least she wouldn't back away from him, he thought. "Hey, lady," he said into the phone, and Jazz, who already felt uncharacteristically off-balance, felt worse. She just knew he was talking to Alex.

And he actually sat behind his desk and talked with her for a good little while, seemingly with no thought of Jazz in the room, and when he laughed and said he'd see her tonight and she could demonstrate her intentions then, Jazz's stomach muscles knotted up. As soon as he hung up the phone, she knew she had to do it.

"I wanted you and Alex to come to my place for dinner tonight," she said.

Thomas looked at her. "Tonight?"

"Yes."

"We already have plans for the evening, Jazz."

"Oh, did you? I mean, do you?"

Jazz was more off-balance than Thomas was accustomed to seeing her, and it bothered him. "But," he decided to add, "we can move some things around. We'll be there."

Jazz felt as if she was some consolation prize that nobody wanted or campaigned for. "Are you sure, Thomas?" she asked him.

"We'll be there."

"Alex won't mind?"

"It's my decision."

"Really now," Jazz said, unable to resist this rare opportunity to actually talk about his relationship with Alex. "Alex doesn't appear to be little Miss Compliant to me."

Thomas hesitated. "What's that supposed to mean?"

"She's got you snowed if you think she'll jump at your command."

"What are you talking about, Jazz?"

"I'm talking about Alex. I don't think she'll be thrilled to know that you've decided to drag her to my place tonight without even consulting her first. She doesn't seem like that kind of woman to me."

"Let me worry about Alex," he said, and he said it in such a definitive manner, as if Jazz had no right to so much as mention Alex's precious name, that Jazz's balance returned. Alex was winning, big-time, but not for long, she decided.

Jazz opened the door and smiled as soon as she saw Carmella and the "date." Her name was Kim, Carmella said as they entered the loft, and she was everything Jazz was hoping she'd be: butch, down to her clothes, her swagger, the snarly, devil-may-care look on her face. Jazz looked her up and down, and then she smiled.

"She's perfect, Carmella!"

"She's not a lesbian," Carmella said, as if to quickly get it out in the open.

Jazz's smile vanished. "What?"

"She's not a lesbian, but she's played one at a community theater before."

Jazz shook her head. "That's great. She's played one before. That is just terrific, Carmella. Thomas and Alex are on their way as we speak and you're telling me you couldn't do something as simple as bring over a lesbian? One can't be this hard to find!"

"What difference does it make? Look at her."

"You said you would get a real one this time."

"Will you stop complaining for two seconds and look at her!"

Jazz exhaled angrily and then looked at Kim.

"Now," Carmella said, attempting to lower her voice, "is she or is she not a walking stereotype of anybody's definition of a lesbian?"

"And?"

"And nothing. That's why you smiled when you first saw her, Jazz. She convinced you. You even said she was perfect."

"But an actress, Carmella? Thomas isn't gonna fall for this."

"Yes, he will fall for it. Think about it, Jazz. She's an actress. She's somebody who earns a living convincing people that she is who she isn't. Besides, ain't no real lesbian gonna be playing this game with you. Kim here is the best choice all around."

She was Jazz's only choice now, and Jazz knew it. So she decided to just chill. "Sorry, Kim," she said to her silent guest. "I just want this to work, you know?"

"Girl, I know what you talkin' about. Carmella already told me how you was, so you ain't got to be apologizin' to me."

Jazz looked at Carmella. "And just how am I, Carm?"

"Hard to please, that's how. Now tell the sister what you want her to do so we can get this show on the road."

"You didn't tell her?"

"She told me you want me to pretend to be your girlfriend," Kim said.

"Right," Jazz replied.

"You want me to make some hunk named Thomas jealous."

Jazz could do without the hunk reference, but she nodded. "That's right."

"So, what's my name gonna be?"

"Your name?"

"Yes."

Jazz looked warily at Carmella, then she looked back at Kim. "Kim," she said.

"Oh. Okay. I thought you would want me to go by a different name."

Jazz frowned. "Why would I want you to go by a different name?"

"You know. A made-up name. But never mind. Tell me about this Kim person. What's she like?"

Jazz, at first, just stared at Kim, then inhaled in such a way that Carmella, realizing the surfacing anger, intervened. "What Kim is trying to say, Jazz," she said, "is that she needs to know what's the motivation behind the character Kim."

Jazz shook her head in angry confusion. "Look, I don't know anything about all of that Hollywood stuff. I just need you, Kim, to act as if you're my loving girlfriend, that's all I need you to do. Just be a lesbian. That's it. That's the motivation. All right?"

Kim didn't care for Jazz's harsh tone, but she didn't respond in kind either. She was getting paid for this nonsense and she wasn't about to leave in a huff, and thereby empty-handed.

"Now that that's settled," Carmella said as she hurried for the exit, "I'll just leave you two love bugs alone."

Jazz rolled her eyes at her friend and then went into the kitchen to see about her dinner. This had to work, she thought. It just had to. But before she could even explain to herself why it had to work, Kim came walking into her kitchen.

"I have a question," she said.

Jazz shook her head. What did airhead need to know now? she wondered. "Ask away," Jazz said.

"Just what do you hope to accomplish tonight?"

Jazz paused. Good question, she thought. "I want to make Thomas jealous," she said.

"So that what can happen? Carmella said this Thomas dude isn't even your man."

"He's not. We're friends. But he's dating a woman who's up to no good."

"And?"

"And that's it."

"But how are you gonna make a friend jealous by pretending to be a dyke?"

Jazz exhaled. None of your business, she wanted to say. "Thomas and I are very close," she said instead. "We would probably be married to each other, or, at least, romantically involved, if we weren't afraid of what it could do to our relationship."

"What your marriage to him could do to your friendship to him?"

"Right."

"That doesn't make sense. If y'all get married y'all will be more than friends."

Jazz shook her head. "I've been divorced three times, okay? And Thomas is a divorce lawyer. We've seen it all, sister. And we're both old enough and wise enough to know that romantic love never lasts. I mean never."

"Then why you trippin' about this woman who means him no good? Based on what you're saying, it's romantic love, so it ain't gonna last anyway."

"But he may marry her."

"And, accordin' to your theory, which I strongly disagree with by the way, it won't last. So why you sweatin' it?"

"Because she's not worth the pain she'll put him through. I don't want to see my best friend suffer like that. And for what? Some hoochie gold digger? Please. Thomas has never been married before. Never. And for him to marry a snake like Alex Mailer is out of the question. She doesn't deserve the honor of being his first wife."

Kim smiled. "I see," she said.

Jazz didn't like the sound of that. "What do you see?" she asked Kim.

Kim, however, merely smiled even greater and then laughed out loud as she left the kitchen. Jazz wanted to go after her and tell her it wasn't what she was thinking, that no, she was not trying to corral Thomas for herself, but she didn't even bother. She could think whatever she wished, because Jazz knew better. Then Jazz smiled too because, in truth, she wasn't sure what she knew.

Thomas and Alex arrived some twenty minutes later. Thomas was, at first, very kind to Kim, believing her to be just another friend of Jazz's. But after dinner, when they all gathered around in the studio to take a look at some of Jazz's latest work, Thomas's feelings for Kim abruptly changed. Kim placed her hand around Jazz's waist and began whispering sweet nothings in her ear. Alex even elbowed Thomas, to get him to see what she was seeing, and enjoying seeing, but Thomas had already seen enough. He asked Jazz if he could see her for a moment.

When Thomas and Jazz walked across the house toward the kitchen for their private conversation, Alex wormed her way closer to Kim. "So," she said with a grand smile, "you're Jazz's girlfriend?"

Kim looked at Alex and returned her smile. "Yes, as a matter of fact. You got a problem with that?"

"Oh no," Alex said almost laughing. "I think it's rather cute," she added.

"What is it, Thomas?" Jazz asked as soon as they arrived in the kitchen.

"Have a seat," Thomas said, pulling out a chair at the small table.

"I have guests."

"It won't take long."

Jazz hesitated, as if not at all thrilled by this little meeting, although she was. She sat down.

Thomas sat down and pulled out a cigar. It was shaping up to be one of those nights. "Still smoking, Jazz?"

"No, I'm trying to cut back."

Thomas looked at her. "I'm glad to hear that."

"While you seem to be picking up."

Thomas looked at the cigar. "I know. It's been a crazy few months. I'll ease back up."

"What do you want, Thomas?"

"I can't talk to my best friend?"

"Of course you can. But you didn't ask to see me alone just to chat."

Thomas nodded. "True that," he said and then smiled because that was one of Jazz's favorite expressions. "Who's Kim?" he asked her.

"I told you she's a friend of mine."

"She was hugging you pretty tightly, Jazz, for a friend."

"You hug me all the time and we're friends."

"Yeah, that's what worries me."

"What?"

Thomas didn't say anything. He didn't mean to go there. "This isn't about our friendship," he said, to quash that line of talk. "This is about you and Kim."

"What about us?"

Thomas hesitated. "She's gay, Jazz."

Jazz almost laughed. "Oh, yeah?"

"This isn't funny."

"I didn't say it was. But I still don't know what you want me to say. Okay, she's gay. And?"

"And she might have designs on you."

"Designs?"

Thomas took a puff on his cigar then crossed his legs and leaned back in the chair. He pointed his cigar at Jazz. "You know what I'm talking about," he said frowningly. "Now what's going on with you?"

He said this in an angry tone, which caused Jazz's anger to rise, too. "Nothing's going on with me, okay? Kim is a good friend of mine. Somebody's company I happen to enjoy."

"Oh, so you're gay now?"

"And what if I am?"

"Jazz, you're not gay."

Jazz smiled. "How would you know?"

"Because I know. You're just lonely."

"Lonely?"

"Yes. And trying new things."

Jazz shook her head. "Funny," she said, "I can say the same thing about you."

Thomas just stared at Jazz without saying a word. What was she trying to prove? he wondered, as he took another drag on his cigar.

"Is that it?" she asked.

"Jazz."

"Is that it, Thomas?"

"Yeah," Thomas said, dousing his smoke and rising with a sudden flash of anger. Why should he care anyway? he thought. "That's it."

Jazz left the kitchen ahead of him, thrilled by the turn of events. Thomas was so worried he couldn't hardly contain himself. Now, she thought, if Kim could just keep it up for the rest of the evening she would feel triumphant. Because Thomas would not rest, she was certain of it, until he got to the bottom of what exactly was wrong with her.

But Kim played her role too well, from touching Jazz way too much to insinuating all kinds of explicit activities they'd shared. They were all sitting around in the living room, drinking sodas, and Kim was having a field day with graphic details. Alex was loving it—she believed all along that Jazz was butch and therefore was of no threat to her—but Thomas was amazed. Yet, the more graphic Kim became the more relaxed Thomas seemed to be. It wasn't true and he knew it, and Jazz knew he knew it when he leaned back and crossed his legs.

"And Jazz did that?" he asked Kim as he picked up his can of soda from the table.

"Yes. She just couldn't get enough of me. She even wants us to go to Vermont where gays are allowed to have a civil ceremony."

Thomas choked on his soda and then burst into laughter. Everybody looked at him.

"What's funny?" Alex asked. "I think it's so romantic."

"Yeah, it's romantic all right." He then looked at Jazz. "Isn't it, Jazz?"

Jazz tried to smile but couldn't do it. Thomas was seeing right through their act, and she knew it. She could just kill Kim for overdoing it. They had him. They had him right where she wanted him. Now he was laughing at them. "Yes," she said with little enthusiasm, "very."

Kim snuggled closer to Jazz. Jazz wanted to slap her. "But, Thomas," Kim said, "since you're a lawyer maybe you can answer this. Once me and Jazz are married, will I take on her last name, or will she take on mine?"

Jazz rolled her eyes. Thomas could barely keep a straight face. "I don't know," he said.

Alex, however, had an idea. "I would think it depends on who's the man and who's the woman," she said, and Thomas, once again, burst into laughter.

"I'm the woman," Kim said quickly and then everybody looked at Jazz.

"Is that right?" Alex said with a big smile. "That must make you the man, Jazz," she said.

"Yeah, I'm the man," Jazz said and stood quickly. "But listen, it's really getting late and I have to get an early start in the morning."

Thomas and Alex placed their drinks on the table and stood up, too. "We fully understand," Alex said, always glad to leave Jazz's presence. "We know you want to get to your little sweetheart." Then she looked at Kim. "It was nice meeting you, Kim."

"Nice meeting you."

"And y'all have a lovely evening together," she said. "But don't be too naughty." Alex said this and then she and Kim laughed.

Once at the door Alex eagerly told Jazz good night, but Thomas, coming up behind Alex, leaned over and kissed Jazz on the lips. Her lips still quivered whenever he kissed her, and he was glad to know that, but he still had no clue why she was playing this lesbian game. Maybe it was just for the hell of it, Jazz was odd that way, or maybe it was just to trip him up a little because she didn't care all that much for Alex. He wasn't sure. But just the thought of Jazz jetting off to Vermont to marry some female, some *female,* was too much for him to take with a straight face. "Well, Jazz," he said, fighting with all he had not to break down in laughter again, "I wish you and Kim a very happy life together."

Jazz wanted to cuss Thomas out, right then and there. She knew he was trying to front. She knew he knew it was all a scam. "Thank you," she said instead with a strained smile on her flustered face, and as soon as Thomas and Alex cleared the exit, she slammed the door shut. Then she looked at that Kim. "*Vermont?*" she yelled.

CLASSIC ALEX

"He'll see you now," the secretary said to Alex, and Alex and Nikki rose at once and walked into Larry's office. They were in Key Largo, at the Lindsey Bottling Plant, and the last thing Alex needed at this fragile time in her life was trouble with Larry. Things were going great with Thomas; he was falling for her hard, she felt. But he was still cautious with Alex, still feeling her out even though she knew she was pleasing him, and she couldn't very well start asking him for money when her position with him wasn't yet secured.

Now Larry was trying to get on her case. He had phoned earlier in a rage, according to Nikki, and demanded to see Alex as soon as her "tight ass can get here." He wouldn't say what was bothering him, but he was hot. So hot that Nikki was insistent that she come along, too.

"What's she doing here?" Larry asked as soon as they darted the door. "You don't need no damn chaperone."

Alex decided to meet his aggressiveness with a smile. "Well, hello, Mr. Lindsey. How are you?"

"Pissed," Larry said bluntly. He was standing behind his huge desk, smoking a cigarette, and looking at Alex and Nikki as if they were roaches in the room.

Alex didn't care for his tone of voice at all, but she decided to walk over to him and kiss him to calm him down. It didn't work. He, in fact, backed away from her. "I don't want your bullshit, Alex."

"What bullshit?"

"Where the hell have you been? I called you all night, until four this morning, and you didn't answer. I called your home phone, your cell phone, I even beeped your ass, but you was nowhere to be found! Nikki kept trying to make excuses for you but I didn't wanna hear that shit! You were out with some dude and I know it, so Nikki couldn't tell me nothing!"

Alex hesitated. She absolutely, positively could not lose Larry now. Not yet. "Larry."

"Don't Larry me! Just answer my damn question. Where the hell were you?"

"Who do you think you're talking to?" Nikki asked, unable to keep quiet a moment longer. But Alex panicked.

"Okay, Nikki, that's enough."

"Yeah," Larry said, "you'd better get her straight."

"Just stay out of it," Alex said. "I got this."

"You ain't got shit," Larry said. "You ain't handling me. I want to know where were you, and you're going to tell me."

"If you give me a chance to, then I will, Larry, damn." There was a pause, as Larry decided against responding to Alex. But as the pause dragged on, his patience thinned.

"Well?" he asked.

"A friend of mine was sick—"

"Bullshit! Don't give me that bullshit, Alex, and I mean it! Now you tell me the truth!"

"That is the truth."

"I declare if I won't slap the shit out of you, Alex. Don't play with me!"

"Don't play with you?" Nikki asked. "Again I ask, who the hell are you? You are not about to stand up in here talking to my sister any kind of way."

"Nikki!"

"Alex, what's the matter with you? You ain't got to take this from this chump. And I want you to slap her, Larry. I want you to lay a hand on her. Because if you do, boy, I'll lay you out!"

"That's enough!" Alex yelled. Then both Nikki and Larry looked at her. She smiled. "Can't we all just get along?"

"You know what?" Nikki said with great exasperation. "You'd better handle your business, Alex, that's what you better do."

"I am handling my business, okay? Larry just wants to know where I was, that's all."

"And if that sister of yours don't shut the hell up," Larry said, "I'm not gonna care where you were and your ass gonna be on the street again."

"The street?" Alex asked as she placed her hand on her hip and faced Larry. "I wasn't never on no street, okay?"

"Yeah, I forgot. Nikki's john was taking care of y'all."

Nikki attempted to rush at Larry, to hit him, but Alex held her back. "Yeah, I got yo' john!" Nikki yelled.

"Just stop it, Nikki, stop it!" Alex said this and then looked at Larry. Anger was too calm a word to describe how she felt. "My sister is not a ho, do you understand that, Larry?" she asked cooly.

"Yeah, sure she isn't. And you aren't one either."

"I'm not!"

"What the hell you think you been to me? My woman? Get real. You was an easy lay, an expensive, easy lay, and you know it! What man in his right mind's gonna want you for anything other than sex? Talk about not being marriage material, please. You ain't even mistress material! Just somebody to screw. Simple as that."

Alex could not believe the words she had just heard. Nikki wanted to fire back, she was itching to fire back, but she knew she didn't have to. Alex needed to hear this, she felt. She needed to realize for herself that Larry Lindsey never cared anything for her, that he was a dog in the basest sense of the word, and if she wasn't convinced now to leave his stank behind alone, Nikki knew she'd never be.

But she was. She smiled and began slowly walking backwards. "Kiss my ass, Larry," she said.

Larry frowned. "What?" he asked. "How dare you!"

"Kiss my ass. You and your money."

Larry began nodding his head. "Yeah, uh-huh. Don't you come running back to me when the bills are due, you hear me?"

"I won't," Alex said as she and a smiling Nikki began leaving his office.

"Yeah, go run to your other man. Let him take care of your butt for a change! I'm done, you hear me, lady? And I mean it this time. You ain't riding me no more!"

Alex and Nikki laughed, wondering if Larry understood the significance of what he'd just said, but they did not stop as they made their way out of Larry's office. They knew they had just made a hard bed to lie in, but Alex also knew that she couldn't take another minute of Larry's nasty, demeaning tongue. Thomas wouldn't let her lose her home, she felt. If push came to shove, he'd be there for her.

Nikki, however, wasn't so sure. They were in Alex's Saab, driving swiftly through the streets of Key Largo, onto the Florida Turnpike, heading back to Miami. It was a hot, breezy south Florida day and the car's top was down to take advantage of that breeze. Nikki leaned her head back to let the wind blow through her braids. "I don't think he'll do it," she said. "He doesn't even ask how you're surviving when he knows you don't work."

"I told him I was living off of my savings, remember?" Alex said this as she picked up speed along the Turnpike. Traffic was heavy, but she zoomed in and out of lanes with ease.

"I remember. But that was a good while ago, Al. The brother knows you ain't got that much savings."

"He doesn't know anything. He's never asked, and I never told. And I won't tell unless he asks. It's got to come from him."

"Then how is he gonna know that your benefactor just dumped you, again by the way, and I don't have one anymore, and rent is soon to come due, if you don't mention it to him?"

Alex smiled. "Because I'm clever, Nikki. I'll find a way to bring it up without bringing it up."

Nikki shook her head. Alex glanced at her. "What?" she asked.

"I wouldn't advise that strategy."

"What strategy?"

"Thomas Drayton probably seen every trick in the book, Alex. He's not gonna fall for no *if you lend me some money* scheme. He'll show you the door if you try that on him."

Alex sighed. "I thought about that. I never met anybody like him. He doesn't offer me a dime. He buys me dinner and pays for me wherever we go, but that's it. He doesn't shower me with jewelry, he doesn't show his affection by giving me a little 'walk around' cash, nothing. Men usually love to give me money. But not Thomas."

"Maybe he's cheap."

"No way. Not the way he tips, not the way he spends. And he's always doing something for Jazz Walker. He's always quick to put out cash for her."

"She's his best friend, Alex."

"And I'm his woman, damn, Nikki. She ain't on no higher pedestal than me. She thinks she is, but she's not. If he can do things for her, he can do things for me."

"But he's not doing things for you. That's the problem. Now for whatever reason he apparently figures his woman should take care of herself, he don't feel any obligation to her. But he feels a big obligation to this so-called friend of his. It don't make no sense, but there it is."

"So-called?" Alex asked. Then smiled. "If you saw her the other night with her girlfriend you'll know like I do that that heifer can't possibly be anything to Thomas but a friend."

"So she's gay?"

"Yes. I told you she was. And stop worrying. I know I can't just go up to Thomas and ask for rent money, and I know I can't risk being too slick. But I'll think of something. We have a few weeks yet. Something will turn up." Alex said this as she turned off onto exit 17 and drove into a filling station.

"What about Conrad?" Nikki asked as the car came to a stop at one of the pumps.

"What about him?"

"He likes you."

"Please."

"He does. He's a good one, Alex. He'll probably be happy to help you out."

"That man can't pay our rent. He's just a low-level, salaried attorney on Thomas's payroll. And he's paying child support, too? Forget it. He's not even on my radar screen."

"I still say he's a good man."

"I still say he's a chump." She then gathered up her purse and stepped out of the car. "I pay, you pump."

"Yeah, whatever," Nikki said and Alex smiled at her sister and then headed for the store. She didn't notice the young hunk pumping gas into his bright-red Corvette until she had entered the store, paid for her gas, and was heading back toward her car. When she saw the young man, she nearly stopped walking. He was tall and in a tank top that revealed muscles twice Thomas's size, and his face—angular, handsome, and dark-skinned—made her want to kiss him where he stood.

He placed the nozzle back on the pump and twisted shut his gas cap. When he turned to get into his car, Alex was standing beside him.

"Hey," he said with a smile, attempting to shield the fact that he'd been startled.

"Hello," Alex said with a smile. Then she extended her hand. "I'm Alex."

He looked at her small, pretty hand and quickly shook it. "I'm David."

"Like Michelangelo's David?"

David laughed. "I don't think so."

"Oh, but I do." Alex said this as she gave an unabashedly lustful look at his big body. "I like a good-looking man," she said, "and you are that and then some."

"Thank you."

"You from around here, David?"

"Yeah."

"Me, too. That girl over there pumping gas in that Saab is my sister. That's my Saab."

David looked at the car and Nikki and then he nodded. "How nice for you."

"I agree." She then looked at the red Corvette. "This yours?"

"Yes, matter of fact. All mine."

Alex smiled. "I hear that."

"Would you like a spin?"

Alex hesitated. He had money, she could tell, and the way he didn't mind her aggressive come-on made it clear that he could handle somebody like her. Talk about good luck. Just by showing up at a gas station, within an hour of ending it with Larry, she might have stumbled upon the best side show yet. And this one was gorgeous like Thomas, but younger. Very young.

"I'll love to," she said, and then she quickly notified Nikki to drive the car on home.

Thomas was sitting on the sofa in his office going over a stack of paperwork when Jazz entered. She always had clearance, his secretary didn't even have to announce her, and he looked over the reading glasses perched on his nose and smiled. "Hey, lady," he said.

"You look busy," she said as she removed the strap of her shoulder bag from around her neck and sat down in the chair by the sofa. "Your secretary said you wasn't busy."

"I'm not. Not really. How are you?"

Jazz nodded. "Good."

"And how's Kim?" Thomas said this with a smile on his face. Jazz ignored him.

"It was such a pretty day I thought I'd drop by."

Thomas respected her desire to forget about Kim and what went down three nights ago. He wanted to forget about it, too. "Still on vacation and enjoying it?"

"I don't know about all that much joy. But I'm still on vacation."

"I don't know why you don't let me take you somewhere."

"No, thanks. I'm fine."

"I don't know about that."

"Meaning?"

Thomas exhaled and removed his reading glasses. "You know what I mean, Jazz. You've been making some pretty weird choices lately."

"So now you're gonna lecture me? Terrific."

"Come over here and give me a kiss. That'll shut me up."

Jazz smiled, and although she hesitated, she did move over to the sofa and sat next to Thomas. She kissed him, peck-style, but he placed his arm around her waist and pulled her back to him. And kissed her his style, long and passionate. She closed her eyes and enjoyed it. His kisses were becoming impossible for her not to enjoy lately. And when he stopped, she opened her eyes and looked at him. "I don't think Alex would approve," she said.

Thomas looked into her eyes. Then he took his hand and smoothed it across her cheek. "Tough," he said.

"So you fool around on Alex, do you?"

"No."

"This could be construed as fooling around."

"I can show you how I fool around, if that's what you want."

Jazz's heartbeat quickened and her chest heaved. Why he had to say that, she thought. "And what if I do want it?" she decided to ask.

Thomas looked at her, at her hair and then into her eyes. His hand began stroking her back. "I'll give you what you want."

"And then?"

"We'll deal with then then."

Jazz smiled. "I don't think I like those odds."

Thomas exhaled. "Me either, sweet thing," he said and removed his arm from around her. Then he placed the papers that were on his lap onto the table and leaned forward. Jazz could tell something was bothering him.

"What's wrong?"

"Other than my hard-on?" he asked smilingly and looked down at the huge bulge in his pants. Then he looked at Jazz.

"Yes, other than that," she said with a smile.

He paused. "You've got to get to know Alex better, Jazz," he said so heartfelt that she was taken aback by his concern.

"Why is it so important to you?" she asked, terrified of his response.

"You know why."

Jazz's heart dropped. Had he proposed to Alex already? Had it gone that far? "It's that serious?" she asked.

Thomas leaned back, his reading glasses still in his hand. "Yes."

"Marriage kind of serious?"

"Possibly. It's crossed my mind, anyway."

"What do you see in her, Thomas?" Jazz asked this before she realized she had asked it.

"What?"

"Nothing."

"Jazz, what is it?"

"I don't like her, that's what it is."

Thomas blew out an exasperated breath. "You have got to like her. You hear me? I'm damn-near forty years old. I can't keep starting over like I'm some kid who doesn't get it. I'm not going down that road again. I'm not starting over with some new woman for another few months. And then what? You don't like her and I start over again?"

"So what are you saying, Thomas?"

"I'm saying you've got to make an effort to get along with Alex. There's no two ways about this. You've got to do it."

"I see. What you're really saying is that if you receive an ultimatum from Alex asking you to choose between her and me, you aren't choosing me this time. That's what you're really saying, aren't you, Thomas?"

Thomas looked at Jazz, at her eyes now filled with tears, and his very being shook. "Jazz."

"No, Thomas, that's fine. You're right, you know? You shouldn't have to choose. I don't know why you chose me all those other times anyway. You lost a lot of good ladies because of me."

"That's not true."

"It's true."

"No, it's not. There was no way I was losing you."

"Then. But this is now." Jazz said this as a tear began to drop down her cheek. Thomas reached out to hug her, but she attempted to get up and away from him, wanting desperately not to let him see her cry. But he refused to let her go. He fought against her resistance and pulled her in his arms, and he didn't stop pulling on her until she was sitting on his lap. And he held her tightly, her face buried in his chest, his in her hair. The realization of what was happening was burying her. They should have tried, she thought. They should have forgotten about the risks and took the plunge. If it didn't work out, if they ended up enemies, it was a chance they should have taken. But they didn't. Now it was too late.

"Oh, Jazz," Thomas said as he pulled her closer.

"It's all right, Thomas," Jazz said, stopping the tears before they overwhelmed her.

"It's not all right. I never wanted to hurt you."

"You haven't hurt me." She looked at Thomas. "You haven't. I'm glad you reached a decision. It's about time." She said this with a smile. Thomas tried to return it, but he couldn't. "You won't have to choose, Thomas. I'll do everything I can to get along with Alex."

Thomas smiled weakly and began rubbing her hair. "You two have got to get along," he said painfully, "or I don't know what I'll do."

"We'll get along," Jazz assured him, and then she leaned against him and allowed his big arms to wrap around her again. She knew he was asking her to do the impossible. Getting along with Alex was like getting along with a toothache. She couldn't pretend that Alex was this loving woman all of a sudden, worthy of Thomas's affections. She wasn't worthy of a toad's affections. And although Jazz knew she'd sound like a woman scorned if she told Thomas how she really felt, she couldn't just sit back and play the game. She was going to play a game all right, that was for sure. But at the end of that game Alex, without question, had to lose.

Alex felt like a winner as David's big body slid off of her and they lay side by side in the motel room. They were still coming down from the exhilaration of their first time together. He was good, she thought. Not as good as Thomas, nobody was as good in bed as Thomas, but he knew what to do. And he would do nicely.

"I'm glad I met you, David," she said.

"I'm glad I met you," he replied. "And not a moment too soon."

"Why do you say that?"

"My old lady just kicked me to the curb and I was just wondering how in hell was I gonna make my rent. Then you show up."

Alex looked at David. Her heart dropped. "So you're using me?"

David laughed. "Of course not. I like you."

"Then what does your rent have to do with it?"

"I feel like a very lucky man, that's all I'm trying to say."

"Lucky in what way exactly?" Alex sat up on her elbow when she asked this, the white sheet of the motel's bed covering her bare breasts.

"Come on, Alex, you know what I'm talking about here. You're not only loaded, but you're beautiful, too. They don't usually go hand in hand."

"And they don't this time either."

"What?"

"That's right. I'm beautiful, I'll admit that. But that's it, sweetheart."

David smiled. "Don't tell me."

"I'm afraid so."

"No, I didn't. I was hoping you were my next sugar mama."

Alex laughed. It was painful, but it was funny. "I've got a secret, too," she said. "I was hoping you were my next sugar daddy."

Now David laughed. "Ain't this a mess? And here I was getting ready to hit you up for a few hundred."

Alex leaned back down. At least she got some good sex out of it, she thought. "No, boyfriend," she said, "ain't no sugar in my tank either. But it will be soon."

"Yeah?"

"Oh, yes." Then she looked at him. "I've hit the jackpot."

"The jackpot?"

"Yes. The daddy of all sugar daddies."

"All right now." Then he looked at her. "Why were you looking for my sugar if he's such a catch?"

"Because he's not keeping me. He's just falling in love with me. That's why. And soon, very soon, he will marry me. And all that he has, which is substantial, will be mine."

"That sounds like a plan to me. But just who is this big deal anyway?"

Alex hesitated. She just loved saying his name. "Thomas Drayton," she said with great pride.

David looked at her as if she had lost her mind. "Thomas Drayton?" he asked, astonished. "Thomas Drayton the lawyer?"

"Yup."

"Damn, girl. He be on TV."

"I know."

"And you're gonna be Mrs. Thomas Drayton? You're telling me I'm laying up in this sleazy motel with the future Mrs. Thomas Drayton?"

Alex laughed. "That's overstating it a little, but yes, you're enjoying the company of the soon-to-be wife of a very esteemed man."

"That's all right. So what's the deal? He don't mind you fooling around?"

"I'm not his wife yet. I can do what I want. Besides, you won't tell."

"And how do you know that?"

"Because you're no fool. You want a piece of the action for yourself, and telling Thomas about me won't get you a damn thing."

David smiled. "So you gonna hook a brother up then?"

"You keep doing your job and hooking me up the way you just did, and oh yeah, I'll gladly hook a brother up."

David laughed and then moved on top of Alex again. It was a shocking development, Alex thought, as this man she'd just met put on another condom and entered her again. Her prospects were still in dire straits, she was still a few weeks away from potential homelessness, but just the thought of how bad the situation was made her even more resolute to hurry up and secure a claim to Thomas. He was it. He had to come through for her. And as for David. She looked at him. He was too pretty to throw back, she thought. "So tell me," she asked him, "other than gigolo, do you have a profession?"

"Handyman," David said as he pumped, his attention solely on pleasing the woman beneath him, the woman who, if she was telling him the truth, may very well be his meal ticket out.

Alex was also pleased. A handyman, she thought. It seemed only fitting that she should keep him around. He was bound to come in handy eventually.

NO STOPPING SENSE

Stroke, a rough-looking young brother in dreads, arrived at the front door of Jazz's loft on what Carmella told him was a blind date with a "fox." He wasn't hoping for much, as he knocked on the door, but he owed old Carmie a favor—about two hundred favors, actually—so he didn't sweat it. He knocked again.

Jazz opened her door, a little peeved by the excessive knocking, but when she looked at Stroke, who didn't look a day over eighteen, she was satisfied.

"Good evening," she said as she eased her way out of the front door.

"What up?" Stroke said as he looked her up and down, his stance slightly leaned to the side with one hand on his crotch, his clothes a baggy assortment of Fubu where his pants hung off his butt and his belt tied around his blue-and-white-striped boxers. He looked like a straight-up gangster to Jazz, the brother in the alley you didn't want to cross, and she was thrilled beyond words.

"Ready to go?" she asked him when it appeared he was content just staring at her.

"I was born ready to go with you, pretty lady," he said. "Carmella wasn't lyin' though."

Jazz smiled. "Thank you."

"What you say we rain check this bitch you talkin' about going to party at and just chill out here? I can make you feel real good."

Down boy, Jazz wanted to say. "I'm sure you can," she said instead as she began walking down the stairs. "But they're expecting us."

Stroke didn't care if they were expecting them or not, but Carmella had already warned him to be careful, that Jazz wasn't the one to play with. And he decided to heed that advice. For now.

His car, an eighties-model Chevy with the thousand dollar rims and silly hydraulics, bounced along the streets of Miami as Stroke played his block-loud rap music and smoked a joint as if he was alone in his room. Jazz was able to persuade him to kill the dope, that she needed a sober date when they arrived at her best friend's house, and he did, eventually, put it away. But the music he wouldn't turn down and his hip-hop talk that Jazz didn't even understand had her nearly dizzy with anxiety. She knew she told Carmella to hook her up with a real bad boy, not an actor, not one who played one at a community theater before, but she never dreamed she would dredge up someone *this* original. She only hoped the young brother wasn't a criminal, too. But then she smiled. She needed somebody exactly like him to make the evening work, and Carmella probably knew that. Because Carmella knew, like Jazz was beginning to realize, that if a brother like Stroke wasn't able to shock the mess out of Thomas, there was no brother alive who could.

Henry escorted Jazz and Stroke into the living room of Thomas's big house, where they took a seat on the long, white sofa. Stroke began rubbing the leather and then stretched out his long legs and threw his arms across the back of the sofa. Henry stared at him. Jazz looked at Henry. "Where's Thomas?" she asked.

"Still upstairs," Henry said, "but I'll notify him of your arrival."

"No need," Jazz said, standing. "I'll tell him myself." Then she glanced at Stroke. "Henry, why don't you entertain Stroke while I'm gone?"

Keep an eye on this one, he knew was what she meant. "My pleasure, madam," he said.

Jazz hurried up the stairs and began walking toward Thomas's bedroom. She still remembered that day in his office, when the realization that she was no longer the number-one female in his life overtook her emotionally and caused her to break down. He held her in his arms for nearly an hour, without saying a word, just holding her, as she couldn't seem to get a grip on her tears. He all but told her to either be nice to Alex, or get out of his life. And it hurt her to the very core. Alex, of all people, the one female she, at first, didn't even feel threatened by, was the one who'd managed to take Thomas away from her. Now she felt as if she was swimming against the tide, trying to reclaim a spot that she never should have given up in the first place. But Jazz knew Alex's game. She knew Alex was manipulative if she was anything. She wouldn't dare allow Jazz so much as a minor role in Thomas's life, because they'd been too close as friends and a woman like Alex, who had to have complete control, wasn't about to let such a relationship stand.

Thomas would, of course, resist Alex's scheme for a while, Jazz was certain of that, but as he said himself he was not starting over again. And that declaration alone would force him to try and stick it out with Alex. He'd eventually kick Jazz to the curb.

"Knock knock," she said as she tapped lightly on his bedroom door and then peered inside. She could hear the shower running so she walked on in, walked around the side wall, and then plopped down on his bed. She grabbed a book from his nightstand that he apparently had been reading, a book on the Civil War, and lay down on his bed. His pillow, his bedspread, even the book she was holding had that fresh cologne scent that was always so dominant on him. And Jazz sniffed it as if he was standing right in front of her, and then she closed her eyes. She could only imagine how wonderful he looked in that shower, every inch of that beautiful body. But as soon as she heard silence from the bathroom as Thomas appeared to have concluded his shower and was stepping out of the stall, her eyes quickly reopened. And the last thing she knew she needed to see was every inch of that beautiful body. "I'm in here," she yelled to him, "so cover yourself!"

She could hear faint laughter coming from the bathroom as some movements were made, and then Thomas came into the room with a towel wrapped around his midsection. His exposed six-pack abs, however, caused Jazz to shudder.

"You should have surprised me," he said with that gorgeously alluring smile of his. "I would have loved to see your expression."

"No, you wouldn't have."

Thomas laughed and began walking toward his bed. "You're early," he said.

"As usual. I either come too soon or I don't come at all."

Thomas sat on the edge of the bed. Too close for comfort, Jazz thought, although she made no effort to get up. His heart raced as he looked at her. "So," he asked, "what did you do today?"

"Painted."

"And?"

"Painted some more."

"Jazz, you're on vacation, remember?"

"And I'm vacationing. In my studio."

Thomas looked at Jazz and shook his head. "What am I going to do with you?" he asked.

"Darn if I know."

Thomas smiled. "Thanks for coming, Jazzy."

"It's no problem. I know what Alex means to you. She's your lady, and although I have my concerns, I'm willing to try my best to get along with her just as I told you I would."

"You wouldn't have any concerns, Jazz, if you just get to know her."

"I know her."

"You know her type, but you don't know her."

"If you say so."

"Jazz."

"It's how I feel. I can't help how I feel, Thomas. But I said I was going to get along with her, and I am going to try. Besides, who you choose to be with is your business anyway. Right?"

Thomas hesitated. "Right."

"Just like who I choose to be with is my business."

Thomas smiled. "You mean like Kim?"

Jazz rolled her eyes. "She's just a friend, I told you that."

"A friend who wants to fly you off to Vermont and marry you."

Even Jazz had to smile at that. "She has issues, Thomas, all right?"

Thomas laughed.

As the laughter died down, they found themselves staring into each other's eyes. Thomas was conflicted about his feelings for Alex, unable somehow to make it clear to even himself that she was his woman now. But his feelings for Jazz never wavered, never came into doubt, never once gave him a break from the magnitude of their intensity. And he couldn't resist her. Even in the depths of his relationship with Alex, a relationship he was asking Jazz to accept, he still could not resist that pull Jazz had on him.

He placed his hand on her soft, cool cheek and rubbed his thumb over it. Then he leaned down and began kissing her. As usual lately, she couldn't resist the pull he had on her either, and she placed her hands around his neck and allowed his hard, bare chest to crush into her until he was kissing her with even more vigor. She opened her mouth wide and his tongue rammed in, and he stroked her and stroked her and pushed harder into her as the feelings inside his loins inflamed. This was who he wanted, and he knew it, but he wished it was as simple as that. He wished to God it was that simple.

Yet he couldn't stop kissing her. He placed his arms around her and pulled her up to him, cradling her and kissing her even more desperately, and he found himself crossing his legs to fight the urgency of his ever-expanding erection. He rubbed his lips across her mouth, the smell of her sweet breath and the taste of her driving him out of his mind, and he began kissing her all over her face, and her neck, and her ears. He undid the top three buttons of her blouse with an urgency that nearly caused him to snatch one off, and then he began kissing her chest and the top groove of her breast, but it wasn't enough. He slung her bra cup up as if it were a feather, causing her large breast to bounce, and he began kissing that bare breast as it bounced back in place. And he kissed it and sucked it and cupped it with his hand to kiss it some more. Nobody but Jazz made him feel this way, this out of control, this needy for her affection. And she wasn't resisting him, which scared him as much as it pleased him, because he knew, like she knew, that they were treading on dangerous ground.

The danger almost became apocalyptic, however, when the door to Thomas's bedroom sprang open and Alex, like a noisy mouse in the night, walked in. As soon as Thomas heard the opening of his door, he and Jazz, as if by reflex, pulled away from each other, even though his erection was throbbing for release, even though every inch of her body craved his caressing touch. And by the time Alex darted around the wall to where she could clearly see the bed, they had both recovered enough to no longer be embracing. But their erratic breathing and Jazz's disheveled clothes as she quickly sought to button her blouse back up, unable to reassemble her still-lifted bra, made it obvious what they had been up to.

Alex stopped in her tracks when she saw them, and anger swept through her body like a flood, but she knew she couldn't make a scene. Thomas would choose Jazz over her easily, especially since she'd just given it up to him, and it would be her, not that pesky, apparently bisexual Jazz, who would be out the door with nothing. She was angry as hell and would like nothing more than to snatch Jazz by the hair and drag her around that room, but painfully, bitterly, she had to take the long view. Nobody, especially not Jazz Walker, was taking her future away from her.

"There you are," she said with a big smile on her face, as if she didn't suspect a thing. "And you aren't even dressed yet!"

Thomas stood up from the bed, which allowed Jazz enough cover to pull down her bra and better adjust herself. He looked at his girlfriend. His chest was heaving heavily and his face appeared almost dazed, but he managed to return her smile. "Is it late?" he asked her.

"Not really. I'm just early. Like Jazz." She said this as she walked up to Thomas and kissed him on the lips. "How are you?" she asked as she hugged him and looked up into his eyes.

"I'm okay," he said and began rubbing her hair with his hands. Such a sweet kid, he thought, who was always misunderstood. She could have made a scene, she had to know that something was up, but she didn't. And he respected that. And that was why, when she laid her head on his bare chest, he couldn't just stand there. He felt he owed her; he felt the least he could do, after what he'd done with Jazz, was place his arm around Alex's waist and return her hug. But when he looked at Jazz, when he finally allowed his eyes to return her gaze, he could barely contain the sadness that overtook him. She looked bewildered to him as she stood to her feet and continued straightening her clothes. She looked as if she'd just been used and discarded when nothing could be further from the truth. But they had gone too far, and it wasn't far enough for either one of them, and the realization of that sad fact was wrenching both their hearts.

"I'll be downstairs," she said as she began leaving the bedroom, not bothering to look at Thomas or Alex, and Thomas had to fight every urge in his body that wanted to tell her not to go, not to leave him. But Alex was there, and she, as always, demanded attention.

"She's weird," she said when Jazz walked out of the room, her head still resting against Thomas's chest.

Thomas, however, didn't say anything.

Alex looked up at Thomas. "Don't you think she's weird?"

Thomas sighed. "No, I don't."

"Well, she is to me. I mean, come on, Thomas. One day she's a lesbian off to Vermont to get married, then the next day she's got the hots for some thug-looking, straight-up gangster who'll be right at home on a drive-by shooting."

Thomas frowned. "What are you talking about? What thug?"

"Stroke."

"What?"

"I think that's what he said his name was."

"Alex!"

"The dude downstairs."

Thomas released her and looked at her. "What dude downstairs?"

Alex rolled her eyes. "Jazz's old man, Thomas. At least that's who he told me he was."

The jealousy that pinched Thomas's heart annoyed and angered him. If Jazz brought a date along, that shouldn't bother him in the least. She, after all, had every right to bring a date along. And she didn't have to mention it to him, either. But why didn't she mention it? "I'd better get dressed," he said to Alex, unable to hide his sudden anxiousness.

Thomas arrived downstairs just as Stroke was on his feet demonstrating to Jazz and Alex the latest dance craze, his thin body jerking around to the sound of an imaginary beat, his youth so apparent that Thomas almost frowned. What the hell was Jazz up to? He looked at her, who, although smiling, still appeared bewildered to him; she still had the look of a woman trying to go on with her life when life just didn't want to cooperate. He was still recovering from that day in his office, when he held her in his lap and listened to her cry, those tears haunting him still, as she reacted to the way he all but gave her an ultimatum. Be nice to Alex or else, he'd said. Or else what? He'd leave Jazz? Never, he thought. But Jazz seemed desperate now to get on with living and Thomas knew he had to let her. If she had any chance at all he had to stop kissing her the way he did and holding her the way he did and wanting her. He had to let her go. But he couldn't stop thinking about her in his life. He couldn't stop wondering if their decision not to fall in love was as smart as they had thought. Or if they had really pulled it off at all.

"Thomas!" Alex said as soon as the group realized he was standing there. She hurried to his side. "Don't you look nice," she said as she slipped her arms around his big body.

Thomas had decided to wear a suit, one of his most expensive, because he wanted to meet this date of Jazz's looking as powerful as he possibly could. Why he wanted to intimidate the man wasn't particularly clear to him. But that was exactly what he wanted to do. But looking at this Stroke fellow, who appeared to be no more than twenty, if that old, all Thomas could do was sigh with great exasperation. Jazz's picks were going from bad to worse lately, and he aimed to find out why. She was getting back into the dating scene for her own private reasons, he understood that much. But the people she was choosing to date were not only curious to him. The idea that she was seriously considering these people was scaring the hell out of him.

"You must be Thomas," Stroke stopped dancing and said with a big, gold-teeth smile. He moved toward Thomas swiftly and extended his hand. "What up, niggar?"

Thomas hesitated, his eyes refusing to release Stroke's eager gaze, but then he shook the outstretched hand. "How are you?" he asked.

"I'm Stroke, niggar, what you think?" Stroke said this laughingly. "And everybody know Stroke always good."

"I hear that," Alex said, to encourage his sideshow.

Jazz stood up. Since her encounter with Thomas upstairs, her enthusiasm over her plan was waning fast. She wanted Thomas desperately now, and she needed his touch even more than that, but the way he held Alex, even after all of that passion he had just shared with her, from kissing her lips to making love to her breasts, made her desire seem futile. He obviously wanted Alex. It was obviously too late. "Stroke is a friend of mine, Thomas," she said almost in a monotone.

Thomas looked at her, and it was such a disapproving look that Jazz not only became concerned, she became angry. "What?" she asked him.

"This is a friend of yours?"

"That's what I said."

"Since when, Jazz?"

Jazz hesitated. How dare he talk to her in that tone. "Since I saw what I liked and invited him to my place."

Stroke laughed and Alex coughed back a laugh.

Thomas, however, just stared at Jazz. "Come with me," he said as he moved away from Alex's embrace and began walking toward the study. Jazz just stood there, practically immobile, as if unsure what she should do. Thomas, without breaking a stride, looked back at her over his shoulder. "Now, Jazz," he ordered.

Jazz glanced at Alex, whom she could tell didn't like the fact that Thomas was always going off alone with her, and Stroke, who seemed ready to fight somebody as if Thomas's orders were directed at him, and she decided to follow Thomas if for no other reason than to get away from those two.

Thomas was in his study leaned against the edge of his desk, his arms folded, his face not serene as it usually was but hard and stern, by the time Jazz walked in.

"Get rid of him," Thomas said as soon as Jazz made her way up to him.

"Excuse me?"

"You heard me."

"Why should I get rid of my date? Get rid of yours."

"He's a thug, Jazz. And you know it!"

"He's a friend of mine."

"Did you have sex with that joker?"

Jazz could not believe he'd just asked her that. "What?"

"Did you have sex with your date? You heard me."

"Did you have sex with yours?"

Thomas exhaled. The idea of those sweet breasts of hers that he was not long ago caressing being touched by anybody else's hands piqued at him. "Jazz," he said with some irritation.

"Jazz nothing! Where do you get off judging me?"

"I'm not judging you. I just don't want to see you hurt."

"Nobody's going to hurt me, all right? I know what I'm doing. I got this."

"Sure about that?"

"Positive."

"So you saw him on the street and took him home with you?"

Jazz hated lying to Thomas. But she also hated the fact that his do-what-I-say-not-what-I-do macho attitude was all but forcing her to continue with her charade. "Yes," she said.

"Somebody called Stroke?"

"That's right."

"What's his real name?"

"I have no idea, Thomas."

"You don't even know his name, but you bring him to my home?"

"Hey, we can leave," Jazz said and turned to do just that. Thomas, however, grabbed her by the arm.

"Jazz, listen to me," he said, but Jazz jerked away from the grip he had on her arm.

"What is it, Thomas?" she asked with some degree of pinned-up frustration. "You don't feel we're worthy to be in your precious house then we'll be glad to go."

"You know I don't mean you."

"Oh, so you want me to abandon my date? Will that make you happy, Thomas? Will you love for me to go home alone once again and have my paintings to embrace me at night while you and Alex are . . ."

"While we're what, Jazz?"

"Just forget it, all right?" Jazz said this with a wave of her hand and began walking toward the exit.

"Why him, Jazz?" Thomas asked, and she turned around. "You're a beautiful woman. You can have any man you want. Why somebody like Stroke?"

"Because he's a nice guy. Because he's interested. Because he's there. He's a little rough around the edges, but hell, who isn't? Besides, he has his uses."

Thomas looked at Jazz as if she had just lost her mind. Jazz smiled and walked out of the room.

Thomas was on pins and needles all evening as Stroke seemed unable to stop groping Jazz or asking if Thomas could get his hands on some weed or if he'd be willing to "help a brother out" with some cash.

"No, I wouldn't," Thomas said as he sat in a chair in front of Stroke and Jazz, his legs crossed, a glass of wine and a cigar in his hand. Alex, who was determined to stay as near Thomas as feasibly possible, was sitting on the arm of his chair.

"It's to get my career going, dawg, that's all."

"No, thank you."

Stroke smiled. "You don't even know what career I'm talking about!"

"And he doesn't want to know either," Jazz said to Stroke. "So let's move on, okay?"

Stroke looked at Jazz. His look seemed dangerous at first, as if she'd just offended him, and then he smiled. "Anything for my baby," he said and kissed her on the forehead. Jazz recoiled slightly when he kissed her. Thomas's hand rolled into a fist when he kissed her.

"No, but for real," Stroke said to Thomas immediately after kissing Jazz. "I'm gonna be a rapper, that's the career I'm talking about. And not just any old rapper, either. I ain't gonna be standing in front of no bad ride runnin' the lips. I'm gonna have me a twenty-piece orchestra with my set, man. Twenty piece! They gonna play some classical shit, though, real classical, then I'm gonna rap what they just played. Ain't nothing like it out there, niggar. I'll be a trailblazer!"

Thomas could not believe this drivel. He glanced at Jazz, still irritated with her, then he looked at Stroke. "I'm sure you will," he said, "but I'm not interested."

"You ain't righteous, dawg." Stroke said this and everybody looked at him. "I'm sorry, and I know you Jazz friend, but you ain't right. You got a young brother here in need of a helping hand, you rich, it's obvious, so you can help a young brother out. But you act like I'm not good enough for your money. Like you above me. Like your shit don't stank."

"Look," Thomas said in an impatient tone as he uncrossed his legs, leaned forward, and pointed his glass of wine and cigar at Stroke. "Do whatever you like. Thank God it's a free country. Just don't include me in your plans."

"Yeah, whatever," Stroke said contemptuously and leaned back. Then he placed his arm around Jazz.

"And stop touching her!" Thomas yelled violently. Everybody, especially Alex, looked at him, astonished. But Jazz, understanding the tension perhaps better than anybody in the room, eased Stroke's arm from around her. "We'd better go," she said and stood up.

"Do you have to?" Alex asked patronizingly as she stood to her feet along with Jazz and Stroke. Jazz ignored her.

Thomas was the last to rise, as he appeared shaken by his sudden outburst, and as he sat his wineglass on the table and doused his cigar, he could feel the looks now focused on him. But he didn't look at anybody. He just stood there and waited for the group to begin their walk toward his front door and he followed behind them.

Yet everything changed when they arrived at the door and he saw Stroke, once again, placing his arm around Jazz. Stroke even glanced at him, as if he was proving some point, and that did it for Thomas. He walked up to Jazz and took her by the arm. "I'll take her home," he announced.

Stroke, however, couldn't believe his ears. "Are you on dope, niggar?" he asked Thomas. "You ain't takin' her nowhere. She came with me, she's leaving with me."

"That's enough," Jazz said. "Let's just go."

But Thomas would not release her arm. She looked at Thomas angrily, ready to tell him to leave her alone, but the desperation in his eyes stunned her. And she couldn't say a word. Even Alex and Stroke stared at Thomas, and the grip on Jazz he wouldn't let up.

"Thomas," Alex asked, "what are you doing?"

"I'm taking Jazz home."

"What's up with you?" Stroke asked frustratingly. "You lookin' for an ass-kickin', I can see that right now."

Thomas released Jazz's arm. Stroke smiled. "Yeah, I thought you'd get the message then."

But instead of backing off Thomas quickly grabbed his wallet from his back pocket, pulled out a large stack of bills, and shoved them toward Stroke. Hundreds of dollars flapping off his fingertips. "I'm taking her home," he said.

"Are you out of your mind?" Jazz asked Thomas. But Thomas was staring at Stroke.

Stroke stared at the bills, his eyes growing larger as he looked, and he began to rub his chin. "It ain't gonna be like I'm strandin' her or nothin'," he said, and Jazz, offended, looked at him. "I mean, you gonna make sure she gets home, right?"

Thomas, unsure why he was so insistent that Jazz could have nothing more to do with this character when they obviously deserved each other, could only nod his head. But it was enough. Stroke grabbed the cash and took off.

Jazz, however, was beside herself with anger. "What is wrong with you? How dare you bribe my date!"

"He's gone, isn't he?" Thomas said, equally angry. "He took the money, didn't he?"

"But you had no business offering it to him, Thomas!"

"Like hell I didn't. You saw how he was behaving tonight. You saw what kind of man he was. I'll be damned if you was going anywhere with him!"

"It was her decision, Thomas," Alex said, still trying to smile, but Thomas gave her a harsh look.

"Stay out of this," he warned her.

"But why are you so upset about what Jazz is doing? She's not your woman. Why should you care—"

"I said stay out of this, Alex! Now I mean it!"

Alex gave Thomas a cross look, but she didn't lash out. Jazz, on the other hand, headed for the telephone.

"What are you doing?" Thomas asked her.

"I'm calling a cab," she replied as she picked up the phone's receiver. Thomas hurried to her side and snatched the phone from her hands.

"I said I was taking you home," he said as he slammed the phone down. "And I don't drive a cab."

"No, you drive a Bentley. How dumb of me to not realize that? You're the great Thomas Drayton. You get anything you want."

"Don't push it, Jazz."

"Push what? I can't talk now? I can't have my own dates or opinions now?"

"You aren't having anything more to do with Stroke, I know that much."

"He was my date, Thomas. *My* date. *My* choice. I came with Stroke, and I should have been leaving with Stroke!"

"A stroke, that's what you're trying to give me!"

"This is all so ridiculous," Alex said smilingly as she walked toward them. "You're arguing about the most ridiculous thing. Jazz obviously is one of those females who wants a thug at home, Thomas, let's face it."

"Alex," Thomas said in warning.

"I'm just saying," Alex said, not heeding the warning, "that we need to face the truth. A thug is what she apparently wants or she wouldn't have bothered with somebody like Stroke to begin with."

"Knock it off, Alex."

"So I say let her have him. She wants a thug, let her have her thug. Besides, they seem like the perfect couple to me."

"That's it!" Thomas said angrily as he grabbed Alex by the arm and rushed her toward his front door.

"What are you doing?" she asked hysterically. "Thomas, what are you doing?"

"I'm getting you the hell out of my house," he said to her. "That's what I'm doing!" He shoved her outside. "And you stay the hell out!" He said this forcefully and then slammed the door in her face.

Thomas pressed his forehead against the door in total exhaustion as he listened to Alex angrily kick on the door and yell all kinds of profane words at the door before she eventually gave up, got in her car, and sped away.

And then they were alone. Jazz and Thomas. And the room suddenly seemed too small. Thomas just stood there, his back still to Jazz, his head swimming with the terror of what his actions truly meant. Jazz stood still, too, staring at Thomas, still stunned by the emotional events of the night. And the implications of those events. And it humbled her. That was why, when Thomas seemed unwilling or unable to say anything, she felt it necessary to speak. "I'd better go," she said.

Thomas stood erect then. And he turned and looked at her, his heart pounding ferociously, his entire body drained. "You may as well stay here tonight," he said.

FINALLY

The door slammed and Nikki looked up from her math book. When Alex rounded the corner of the foyer and began walking toward the sofa, she shook her head. "What's happened?" she asked her.

"Some damn nerve," Alex said, "handling me like that. Some damn nerve!"

"What is it, Alex?"

Alex plopped down on the sofa and exhaled. "Thomas," she said.

"What about him?"

"He kicked me out of his house tonight." She looked at Nikki. "He kicked me out, Nikki."

Nikki closed her book. "All we need."

"You should have seen him. It was like it wasn't him."

"What happened?"

"Nothing happened. That's the point. He just all of a sudden got all hot because Jazz had a date."

"A man?"

"Yes."

"First of all, I thought you said she was gay?"

"I don't know what she is. She may be bisexual, I don't know. I don't know what that heifer is."

"And secondly—"

Alex looked at Nikki.

"Yeah, I'm learning something at the college, aw'ight? Secondly, I thought they were just friends?"

"That's what they claim to be."

"So why would his friend having a date make him hot?"

"That heifer got him all twisted up, Nikki, you just don't know. Every time she comes to his house she's in his bedroom, got her hands on him, kissing on him. And tonight I even caught them . . ."

"Caught them what, Alex?"

Alex quickly stood up and began pacing. "She knows exactly what she's doing. A straight-up thug she brought to Thomas's house tonight, knowing good and well he wasn't going for that. But that's what she wants, you see. To take Thomas away from me. That's what she's up to. She don't want him for herself, no way, she just don't want me to have him. But that ain't gonna happen."

"But what made him kick *you* out? What did you have to do with it?"

"Because of her, Nikki, listen to what I'm saying to you! Just because I said Jazz and that thug looked like the perfect couple, he's shaking mad."

Nikki laughed. "No you didn't say that."

"It's true. I don't see nothing so hot about Jazz Walker. But Thomas thinks she's a goddess. Just Miss Perfect. But the way he did me." Just the thought of it slowed Alex's walk. "Some damn nerve," she said again and then picked up the pace.

"Why don't you just calm down, Alex. We'll figure something out. Thomas Drayton ain't the only brother on the block."

"You should have seen the way he handled me, Nick. The way he *looked* at me. It was like he didn't . . ."

There was a pause as the truth strained to come out. "He didn't what?" Nikki finally asked.

Alex stopped walking. "It was like he didn't give a damn about me." She said this and looked at her sister. Nikki tried to play it off with a smile.

"That's just your imagination, Alex. The man was angry. It probably didn't have nothing to do with you."

"He'll come around."

"Yes, he will."

"He'll realize how close he came to losing me tonight."

"And he won't lose you. You're his woman, not radio lady."

"That's right. I'm his woman." Then Alex hesitated. "But the way he did me tonight. Damn. Just slammed the door in my face like I had no feelings at all. Like he didn't know who I was. I'm Alex Mailer, dammit. I can have any man I want, what's his problem? And you know what," she said as she hurried to the telephone, "I'm gonna have any man I want. He ain't gonna find me sitting around here crying my eyes out like he's the end of the line for me. Huh! Not me."

Conrad Baines left the evening praise service at his church, All Saints AME, earlier than usual as the tiredness of a long day in court caused him to call it a night. He planned to go straight home but found himself detouring onto Melrose Drive to make what was becoming his customary drive by Alex's house. He parked his Jeep two doors down, his regular routine, and fought the urge once again to go up to the door and knock. He couldn't seem to stop thinking about Alex. He hated it, but it was true. He dreamed about the woman every night. And it wasn't as if she was leading him on. She wasn't. The few times he did try to call her were met with cold responses from her, and every time she made it clear that she just wasn't interested.

But he couldn't stop thinking about her. And wanting her. And wishing he could figure out a way for her to want him. There was no way, he knew it, he wasn't born yesterday. But he still couldn't let it go.

He was about to crank back up and leave, the sting of another unfulfilled night enough to drive him away, but just as he was about to shift his car in gear, the garage door of Alex's house lifted up and her Saab came racing out. Conrad, stunned, stopped everything. Where in the world could she be going, and in such a hurry?

But he didn't wonder long. As soon as her Saab backed out of the garage and began a northerly jot up the road, he followed her. Her speeds were excessive as she journeyed through downtown Miami to a cheap motel near the outskirts. Conrad's Jeep slowed as she pulled into the parking lot of the odd location, which was obviously frequented more by prostitutes than people supposedly of Alex's esteem, and the idea confounded Conrad. He stopped and killed his lights as she parked next to a dark Corvette and hurried up to the room in front of the parked car. She had only to knock on the door once and it was quickly opened by a tall, muscular man, a man Conrad could tell even from a distance was young and gorgeous. He quickly cranked up his car and drove up into the parking lot to get a better look, suddenly not caring if Alex saw him or not. And her lover was even younger and more gorgeous up close. He had already grabbed her into his arms and was kissing her passionately before they even closed the door. Conrad's heart dropped when they closed the door. And then he smiled. Just what he deserved, he thought. Falling for a whore like that. He shook his head, backed up his Jeep, and took his behind home.

After nearly two hours of sitting in the living room watching television, literally staring at the screen rather than each other, unable to laugh at what was supposed to be a very funny movie because their thoughts were a million miles away, Thomas and Jazz finally rose from their seats and took the slow walk upstairs. Jazz walked in front, her stride as unprovocative as she could make it, as if determined not to be the one to ignite any more emotions. Thomas walked behind her, even slower, unable to stop staring at every curve of her body, even though the tension of the night should have been enough. But he knew what he was doing. And his goal was singular. Ever since he got rid of Stroke and forced Alex to leave his home, he'd been unable to focus on anything else, or anybody else, but Jazz. He had to have Jazz. He had to convince her that their love was too strong to falter; that their friendship would survive a romance; that everybody else may fall by the wayside, but they wouldn't. They were going to make it. He had to get her to understand that she could no longer be this once mighty battleship that passed through life afraid to get wounded again, because she belonged to him now. And he wouldn't hurt her. He wouldn't surprise her the way her three ex-husbands had. He would heal her wounds. And that was the difference. That was their saving grace. He had to make her see that now, finally, she had nothing more to fear because her heart would be in good hands with him.

But she was so tense, he thought, as he watched her climb the stairs, as she placed her feet on the second floor landing and just stood there, as if she didn't know the way to his bedroom, a room she'd visited and even spent the night in many times before. But even she sensed this time was different.

Thomas stepped up on the landing beside her and looked at her. "What's the matter?" he asked her.

"Just waiting on you," she said, trying to smile. But Thomas wasn't playing along. He stared at her.

"What is it?" he asked.

"I think I'll sleep in the guest room tonight."

"And why would you do that?"

"Thomas, you know why. It's been an emotional day. I think we need to be alone with our thoughts—"

"Jazz?"

Jazz exhaled. "Yes?"

"We've been alone with our thoughts long enough."

Jazz looked at Thomas. The intensity in his eyes, eyes that bore down on her as if they could see right through her, caused her to swallow hard. And continue her trek to Thomas's bedroom.

Once inside the room she found herself uncharacteristically awkward. She tried not to be, doing her regular routine of grabbing one of his dress shirts and going into the bathroom, but when she got into the bathroom she sat on the side of the tub and covered her face with her hands. The fear that ripped through her was like a torrent of pain. She even clutched her stomach as it knotted up inside. She thought the world of Thomas, and trusted him completely, but she once trusted Andrew, hubby number one, just as completely, too. Until she found him sprawled out on their bed with another woman who trusted him even more. And she thought the world of Mike and Albert, hubbies two and three. But they proved to be liars and users and cheaters, too, who toyed with her heart and then tossed it aside. Now she felt nothing but disgust for them and wouldn't trust them as far as she could throw them, and she rued the day she ever laid eyes on them.

Now it was Thomas. A man who befriended her when she needed to know that all men weren't dogs. So she chose not to be with Thomas. That was the only answer if she was going to keep him in her life. Don't make a commitment to him, because then, she rationalized, he couldn't break her heart. And he'd stay in her life.

She looked at herself in the full-length bathroom mirror across from her. And the terror in her eyes stunned her. Just the thought of being romantic with Thomas was creating upheaval in her life already. Just the *thought* was doing that. And she couldn't have it. She knew she couldn't bear it. She looked away from the mirror and reached her decision. She would get in bed with him, let him kiss her good night, and then do as she had done so many times before and get some sleep. She was woman enough to handle that. She had come to the brink with Thomas more than a few times before and had been able to pull back. Because she knew it would take more than just Thomas, but active participation by her, before anybody was going to change her life.

Yet when she undressed quickly, put on Thomas's shirt, and crawled in bed beside him, the feelings she suddenly felt just from being next to him made everything she had thought about in the bathroom, all of those lofty decisions, seem almost foolhardy.

Thomas, who had been lying on his back smoking, his large body stripped down to his briefs, doused his cigar in the ashtray and then turned toward Jazz. Her entire body clenched when he turned her way, but she decided to play it off with a smile.

"Thought I would have to call 911," he said.

"Why?"

"What took you so long?"

Jazz's smile weakened. She wasn't fooling this man in the least. "I didn't think I took too long," she decided to say.

Thomas exhaled. He knew it would be easier to pull ten teeth out of her mouth than to get her to fess up, so he didn't pursue it. He laid back on his back and, after a moment, took his pillow and moved his body closer to hers. She tensed immediately, and he could feel the tension, but he didn't back off. "You worried me tonight, Jazz," he said.

Jazz looked at him. He was so close they were practically shoulder to shoulder. She thought about moving farther over, away from the intensified feelings his closeness evoked, but she dismissed such a response as childish and ridiculous. She was in control here. He could move over all he wanted. If she didn't like it, she knew all she had to do, at any time, was simply get up and leave.

"How did I worry you?" she asked.

He smiled and looked at her. "Stroke," he said.

Jazz wanted to give her pet line, that he was just a friend of hers, but she couldn't do it.

"You don't play around with people like that, honey."

"Who said I was playing around?"

"Jazz."

"No, I'm serious. Who said I was playing around?"

"I say it."

"Well, you're wrong. Stroke is a very nice man."

"Please."

"You don't know him."

"I think I do."

"I know you don't. He's a good guy."

"Yeah, a good guy who was more than happy to take my nine hundred dollars and get away from you."

"Whatever, Thomas, all right? I still say he's a good guy."

"You can say anything you want. But I'll say again: you don't play around with people like Stroke."

"I'm not playing around with him."

Thomas's anger flared. "What the hell else are you doing, Jazz? You use him as some boy-toy date, then discard him, what else could you be doing with a punk like that?"

"More than just taking him on a date, I'll tell you that."

Thomas shot a harsh look her way and Jazz refused to return his glare. Why she was defending Stroke was a mystery to her, too, and why she was determined to make Thomas's blood boil with innuendo about her and somebody like Stroke was an even bigger mystery. The last thing they needed was more unmitigated gall in the house.

"What's that supposed to mean?" he asked her.

"Nothing, Thomas."

"I asked you this before, Jazz. Now I'm asking you again. Did you sleep with him?"

"What difference does it make?"

"Did you?"

"That is so not your business."

"Answer me, dammit!"

Jazz quickly looked at Thomas. She expected to see anger in his eyes, fiery, hot, green-eyed-jealousy-induced anger. But she didn't. All she saw was pain. And seeing him that way, in such a vulnerable state, caused the anger she was about to unleash to ebb, too. "No," she said calmly. "I didn't sleep with Stroke."

Thomas exhaled. Then he turned on his side and placed his hand on the hand she had lying on top of the bedspread. "Didn't mean to yell at you, Jazz," he said with a smile.

"Yes, you did," she said combatively. Then she smiled, too. "But it's okay."

Thomas paused and then began rubbing her fingers with his hand as he stared undauntedly at her. She wanted to stare back, to prove to him that she could do it, too, but she was shaking too much, afraid of her own emotions, to pull it off. And when his face began to slowly move closer to hers, to undoubtedly kiss her, she thought she would pass out.

"Good night, Thomas," she said as if she were exhaling it out and then looked at him.

"Good night," he said effortlessly, as if her words weren't deterring him at all. He continued his move toward her mouth, and once on it he smothered it with a kiss that took her breath away. She shuttered underneath it, and her lips quivered the way they always did when he kissed her. He continued, drinking up every ounce of her, as if he couldn't get enough, and then, when it seemed he would finally let up, he pressed even harder into her, his tongue easing her lips apart until he was completely inside of her, forcing her to hold her breath even longer as he delved into the far reaches of her soul and released the passion. And she threw her arms around him and matched his hunger, taste for taste, until she wanted to devour him, too. Because, when the intensity slowed, and he began to slowly remove his lips from hers, she wanted more. He indicated, to her delight, that she would get more when he took his arm, placed it underneath her shoulders, and pulled her closer to him, her lips, face, and eyes within an inch of his. She closed her eyes, to experience the sweetness of his breath and smell and the exhilaration of being in his arms again. And when she opened her eyes, he was staring deep into them.

"Stroke may be a good guy, Jazz," he said, "but he's not for you. A brother like that doesn't care how you feel or how desperately you can't bear to be hurt again. He doesn't care. All a brother like that cares about is one thing and one thing only."

Jazz stared at Thomas, at the kindness in his beautiful eyes, and the sincerity, and the pain. "And what is that?" she asked.

Thomas looked intensely at her, at this woman he'd loved from the moment he laid eyes on her, and at her breathtaking body, a body he'd stayed away from to avoid losing forever, a body he would lose anyway if the right man came along. And he kissed her again. Long and longingly. But tonight, this night, he was not going to let it be enough.

He stopped kissing her and began unbuttoning her shirt with a sense of urgency, and he stared at her as he did it, stared into her eyes with a pleading look in his. He was silently begging her not to stop him.

And she didn't. Heaven help her she couldn't. And when he removed her shirt and then his underwear and moved on top of her, the massive weight of him making her want him even more, all she could think to do was hold him as tightly as she could in her arms.

"Condom?" she asked him, as he showered kisses all over her face and neck and breasts and thighs, her breathing an almost hyperventilating pant.

"With everybody else, yes," he said, kissing her inner thigh. Then he stopped momentarily to look up at her. "But not with you."

She hesitated at first, but when a smile crossed her face he moved back up and kissed her on the lips again. And then, as if he would evaporate if he didn't, he entered her, easy at first and then with a thrust that caused her to scream out. It had been so long, she thought, so very long that she didn't know if her heart could take it. She couldn't stop screaming as he pounded her, as the desires she had denied for so long came out in a need too ferocious to contain. She grabbed onto him, as if she was holding on for dear life, and let him ride her hard, the feelings deep within her intensifying with every thrust. And when their eyes met, when they were finally able to remove themselves from the euphoria of their passionate ride and look at each other, neither one of them could take it another second. They came. Like a rocket-propelled release, they came. And even Thomas, who'd seen it all, had never seen the likes of this. He yelled, too, and poured into her, and when it was finally over, when the intensity finally ceased to completely overwhelm every fiber of his being, he collapsed, like a falling rock, into the comforting, open arms of a completely satisfied and completely terrified Jazz.

BECAUSE FEELINGS
GET IN THE WAY

Her eyes opened to the sounds of running water and the smell of Thomas's strong, sweet scent still buried deep within her. She looked around, at his luxurious bedroom, at the Chippendale chest, the Victorian dresser, the Hepplewhite mahogany secretary, the Renoir on the wall, at the empty space beside her, and tears began to appear in her eyes. Neither one of them was casual with sex, and she knew this would not be a casual affair. Nothing about Thomas's life was casual, not even the elegance he surrounded himself in. And certainly not the way he was talking last night, nor the way she was allowing him to talk. It would be all-out. And would change the course of their lives forever. They could sink or swim now. Make it or fail. It was fifty-fifty. That was why she couldn't deal with it now. She didn't like the odds.

She got out of bed, still naked, to search for her clothes. Getting away, to be by herself, was what she felt she now needed most of all. But her clothes were still in the bathroom, where Thomas was showering up a storm.

She found his big shirt she had slept in—for all of two minutes—on the floor beside the bed, and she covered the front of her body with it as she walked over to the bathroom door and eased her way in. She'd grab her clothes, she hoped, without detection, and get away. But she had hoped foolishly. Thomas saw her immediately and opened the door to the shower stall.

"Good morning," he said as he stood there, dripping wet and naked.

She decided to begin grabbing her clothes without looking at him. "Good morning," she replied. She could feel that he was staring, at her half-exposed body, at her, but she hoped to shrug off the awkwardness by hurrying her task along. Another foolish hope.

"Come here," he said.

"I really need to get going, Thomas."

"Jazz."

"I'll call you later."

"Jazz."

Jazz angrily looked Thomas's way, ready to tell him no again, but when she saw him, so big and beautiful, so happy and content, she sighed. She felt as if she was sinking, in too deep, about to lose a perfectly fine friendship because of sex. But then Thomas smiled and spread his arms out wide as if to show her how erected he was, and she couldn't help but smile, too. "What am I going to do with you?" she asked.

"Come and find out," he said. "I can show you better than I can tell you."

Jazz shook her head. What in the world were they getting themselves into? she wondered. But she placed her clothes back where they were and she, without much reluctance given what she had before her and the feelings she still couldn't control, went to him.

Thomas arrived at work late for the first time in his life, and he was thrilled to death. There were no gruff replies to subordinates who spoke to him as was normally the case in the mornings, but cheerful *hellos* and *how are yous* that surprised even Janet, his long-time assistant. She even followed him in his office, asking if he was okay.

"I'm fine," he said as he walked behind his desk.

"You aren't acting fine. You're acting . . ."

"I'm acting what?"

"I don't know. Nice."

Thomas laughed. "What's up?"

"You're late for a meeting with Peter Jordan."

"Peter's here?"

"Yes. But the agenda has changed. He wants to settle all of a sudden."

"No way."

"I told him. But he thinks he can persuade you. Foolish man."

"Where is he? In the conference room?"

"Yes."

"Send him into my office. Tell Wade to handle the Mulberry case today. Tell him to meet with the lawyers, listen to everything they have to say, and then tell them the answer is no to their proffer. And call Bernie Lawrence and tell him yes. And Janet?"

Janet looked up from her writing pad.

"I don't know if I'm nice. But I'm happy."

Janet hesitated, then decided to be bold. "Does . . . Jazz have anything to do with this happiness?"

Thomas didn't respond. He merely smiled.

Janet nodded. "It's about time," she said, and before Thomas could playfully admonish her about getting into his business, she left.

Thomas smiled and shook his head. How did *she* know? he wondered. But he didn't wonder long. He sat back in his chair, unable to stop thinking about last night, and this morning, when Jazz fought against her natural inclination to hide behind her wall again and came to him, her warm body searing his wet one as they touched, and all he could think to do was kiss her gorgeously long, thin neck, and her face, and her lips, until her back was against the wall of the shower and her legs were around his waist. He closed his eyes and remembered how it felt as he entered her, as his body slapped against hers almost as hungrily as it had the night before, his every thrust as exhilarating as a release. And if she was here right now he knew he'd do her again. It was just that good. Just that potent. Just that powerful enough to make him feel as if he couldn't live without her. He opened his eyes. And the reality of what he'd just admitted caused him to shutter. And then to fall into a long, agonizing, heartrending reflection. He was in trouble, he thought.

Jazz arrived at work early for a change and everybody couldn't help but ask if she was okay.

"I'm fine," she said as she plopped down in the chair in Gerald's office.

"You sure?" he asked, sitting behind his desk, his face betraying his anxiety.

"I'm positive. Why is everybody asking me that?"

"Because you look terrible. You look as if your mama died, your daddy died, and your sister is in a coma."

Jazz exhaled. She actually thought she could hide her feelings. "Yeah, well, my parents been dead and I don't have a sister."

"You know what I mean, Jazz."

"I'm fine, G, come on. I've just got some things on my mind, that's all."

"What things?"

Jazz smiled. At least she tried to. "Nothing worth troubling you about."

Gerald hesitated. "Is it worth troubling Thomas?"

Jazz looked at him. "Excuse me?"

"Or is Thomas the trouble?"

Jazz stood up. "Is that all you wanted?"

"I wasn't trying to pry, Jazz. I was just worried about you."

"Thank you. Is there anything else?"

Gerald exhaled. "Nothing."

Jazz turned and left. The last thing she needed, she knew, was to involve somebody else in this mess of her own doing.

"Like it?" Nikki asked as she held a small, blue blouse against her chest. Alex, however, just stood there. "Earth calling Alex."

"What?"

"Like it?"

"Hate it."

"Alex!"

"Well, I do."

"Why?"

"I just do."

Nikki placed the blouse back on the rack. Then she looked at her sister. "You need to get it together, girl."

"He didn't call, Nikki. Not last night. Not this morning. Not today! So excuse me if I'm a little concerned." They were in Mill's, a trendy dress shop in the mall, and Nikki had dragged Alex along with her, not to do any shopping but just to get her out of the house. But even she understood that Alex was right. She needed to be concerned.

"Where did you go last night?" she asked her.

"What?"

"You heard me."

Alex hesitated. "I visited a friend."

Nikki shook her head. "How do you expect Thomas Drayton to want you, Al, if you can't even be faithful to him?"

"I am faithful. As far as he's concerned. Ain't none of his business what I do on my own time. He's the one who kicked me out."

"I still can't get over that," Nikki said as she began looking down another aisle, with Alex willingly following.

"You should have seen him, too. Just because I had the nerve to say something about that damn Jazz, with her weird-behind self. Lives in a loft while somebody else lives in her big, beautiful home. I tell you, she's nuts."

"And Thomas loves her to death."

Alex exhaled and ran her fingers through the warm, silk material of a burgundy strapless. "I know," she said. "He's crazy, too. But dammit, Nikki, why hasn't he called me?"

Nikki stopped walking and looked at her sister. "Call him. And ask him."

"It's not that simple."

"Why the hell not?"

"Because I was hoping not to have to do that. I didn't want to press. He might not like it."

"He liked it when you flew to Tampa to be with him. That's how you wrangled him, girl, so why is he all of a sudden so puritanical now?"

"It's different now. I'm his woman now. And I'm telling you he won't like it. Not with his woman doing it."

"That's stupid," Nikki said as she kept on walking and looking.

Alex saw him from her periphery, but she had assumed he was just somebody in the store. But when she glanced at him once, and then once again, he was still staring their way. He was a short man, balding, middle-aged, but just from the look of the clothes he wore she could tell he was no small deal. And when he smiled, reassuring her that he was indeed interested, Alex smiled back and then elbowed Nikki.

"What?" Nikki said with some agitation as she turned her sister's way.

"Don't look," Alex said, "but a potential is staring at us."

Nikki, of course, began looking. "Where?"

"Nikki!"

"Okay," she said, looking at her sister once more. "You ain't got to holler. Now where is he? Who is he?"

"I don't know who. Just a dude. Over by the hats."

Nikki moved around to where she could casually glance at the gentleman. When she saw him she looked at Alex. "You must be high."

"Just listen to me."

"That man can be our granddaddy. What we want with him?"

"In one week, Nikki, rent is due. One week. Need I say more?"

"I told you I wasn't down with that no more. I'm not trying to live my life that way, Alex. Not anymore. Not since Ray Ray died."

"Will you bury that damn Ray Ray and concentrate on the here and now? We've got a problem, Nikki," Alex said as she looked over at the "potential" and smiled at him again, "and the solution is staring us in the face. Now you can play Miss High and Mighty later. But right now I need you to be nice to the man."

"No."

"I'd do it but you know my situation. I can't risk Thomas finding out."

"No."

"Please."

"I said no!" Nikki said firmly and began moving away.

"Nikki!"

But she wasn't thinking about Alex. She kept walking, without looking back, until she was clean out of the store. Alex looked at the man, who took Nikki's leaving as a green light to head her way, and she knew she had to swallow the anger she felt toward her sister and put her best flirt forward. Not because she liked the man or thought he was interesting or cute. Not for any of the reasons crazy Nikki suddenly felt a necessary prerequisite. But Alex saw herself as a businesswoman first, and she flirted with the willing man for the sake of good, sound business. Namely, the rent.

The judge finally called a halt to what Thomas considered to be dragged-out proceedings anyway and dismissed court for the day. He glanced at his Rolex as he hurried for the elevators. If he hurried, and he planned to, he knew he would get to the station on time. And he did, driving his Bentley through the streets of Miami as if he had no regard for speeding limits, with two minutes to spare. The plan was that he'd pick her up from work and then they'd go to dinner together. But Jazz was already gone.

"Gone?" he asked the production assistant who met him in the hall.

"Yes, sir."

"How long ago?"

"About an hour ago. Or longer. She wasn't feeling it today, not from the way she was responding to her callers, so Gerald decided to pull the show off live and put on a taped rerun. And then he took her home."

Thomas could feel the pang of jealousy that pricked his heart, but Gerald was the last thing on his mind. Jazz was. "What was wrong with her?" he asked.

"She claimed nothing, but I don't know. She just wasn't Jazz."

Thomas exhaled, nodded, and began leaving the radio station. Was making love to him so abominable that it would make her sick? Or was she still on that kick of hers, still blaming him because some other jokers got her to fall in love with them and then broke her heart? He knew it was the latter, he knew it was going to take more than a night of passion and morning of ecstacy to tear down that built-up wall of Jazz's, but his had already crumbled. One night did it for him. But hers was so fortified, so resistant to all manner of penetration, that he began to wonder if hers would ever come down, if she would ever have the courage to let it fall where it may.

Jazz heard his car drive up but she didn't bother to look out of the window. She and Gerald sat relaxed on her sofa, laughing at the pitiful advice she found herself giving today, when in the back of her mind was Thomas. And last night. And this morning. And the terror that she had made the biggest mistake of her life.

"I didn't say that."

"Yes, you did, Jazz. I'll play you the tape. You actually told that woman to beat him." Jazz laughed. "He likes it rough, give it to him rough. The next time he came at her, you told her to take a hammer and beat the paint off of him. That'll show him rough, and those were your exact words."

Jazz shook her head. "I don't even remember that. My listeners must think I'm on drugs or something."

"The station manager told me to pull you off live then. It was funny, but it was scary, too." Gerald said this and looked at Jazz.

"I'll be okay."

"I hope so."

"I know so. Ain't nothing but a thing. I'll get over it."

Gerald nodded as the sound of footsteps could be heard on the stairs outside. He looked toward the open door. The screened door, fortunately, was closed. "Expecting company?" he asked.

"It's Thomas," Jazz replied, without bothering to even look in that direction.

Thomas stood at the screened door looking into the living room at Jazz and Gerald, and their closeness on the sofa didn't sit well with him at all. He tried to shake it off with a smile, but he was fooling no one. "Good afternoon," he said.

"It's open," Jazz said and he walked on in.

She felt a warm flushness as he entered, his big body immediately overwhelming the room, and even Gerald, who had no reason whatsoever to fear Thomas, who had in fact known the man for many years, quickly rose to his feet as if he'd been caught doing something wrong. Jazz wanted to tell him to sit back down, what was he doing, that didn't he know he was her security blanket right now, but she didn't say a word. The look on Thomas's face made it clear why Gerald stood up. Thomas, who was smiling as he entered but his eyes were cold as ice, was royally pissed.

"How you doing, Thomas?" Gerald asked too eagerly and Jazz rolled her eyes.

"Good," Thomas said in his best controlled voice. "And you?"

"I'm cool. Just gave Jazz a lift home, that's all. She wasn't feeling her best today."

"I was feeling fine," Jazz felt a need to interject. Thomas glared at her.

"But she's fine now. That's what we were just talking about. That and work, of course. That's all we were really talking about."

Jazz looked at Gerald. What was his problem? But she wasn't finding out tonight. He began heading for the door, as if he was getting away from danger, as if he couldn't get out fast enough. "I'll see you tomorrow, J," he said as he moved. "Later, Thomas."

"Later," Thomas said as Gerald hurried away.

Thomas stood in the middle of the now-silent room for a moment longer. Then he took a seat beside Jazz. Jazz's entire body tensed at his close presence, which unnerved him even more. But he remained calm.

"Hey," he said as if he was seeing her for the first time. They sat so close their shoulders touched.

"Hey yourself."

"I thought we had said that I would pick you up today."

"I left early and you were in court. I tried to get in touch with you."

"Why did you leave early?" Thomas asked this and looked at Jazz, as if he couldn't wait to hear her response.

"I just did. Was no major reason."

"Why did they pull you off live, Jazz?"

Jazz hesitated. He knew more than she had thought. "You have to ask them that."

"I'm asking you."

"What difference does it make?" she asked snappily and looked at him. His eyes were still cold and angry. She quickly looked away. "They just didn't think the live show was going anywhere. They weren't feeling it so they pulled it. That's all."

"So you left?"

"Right."

"And you got Gerald of all people to drive you home."

She looked at him. "What of all people? What's wrong with Gerald?"

"He's in love with you, Jazz, don't play dumb with me."

"I'm not playing dumb, all right? But forget it." She said this and moved to stand up, but Thomas grabbed her by the arm and pulled her back down. She couldn't believe his reaction, as she looked at his big hand that totally surrounded her small arm, and then she looked at him. "What do you think you're doing?"

"What's the matter?"

"Nothing, Thomas. Will you release my arm, please?"

"Not until you tell me what's going on. Not until you tell me why you're terrified of me."

Jazz laughed. "Terrified of you? Please. Why would I be terrified of you?"

"Because I made love to you, Jazz, you know why. Because you can't stop thinking about me and I can't stop thinking about you. Because our relationship is different now."

"It's not different," Jazz quickly replied. "Don't say it's different. We're still just friends—"

"You know better than that."

Jazz frowned. "What?"

"We haven't been just friends in months. Do you think I French kiss my friends? Do you think I allow my friends to sleep in my bed with me and hold them in my arms all night? Come on, Jazz. Let's stop this ridiculous game of pretense for once in our lives and—"

Jazz quickly snatched her arm away from him and stood up. "I don't feel like . . . I think I'll take a rain check on dinner. I don't feel like going out tonight."

Thomas looked up at Jazz, whose eyes were almost unreadable, and he stood up. "Fine," he said. He stared at her for a few moments longer, his sadness overwhelming his anger, and then he left, the screen door bouncing back open from the impact of the slam.

AGAINST ALL ODDS

He could see Miami, another city that never slept, from his bedroom balcony, and he stood on his terrace drinking sherry and leaning against the rail. It was a breezy night, a typical south Florida spring night, but it could have been snowing for all he knew. Jazz was on his mind. Again. And nothing else, not even the beautiful lights that abounded like stationary fireworks, caught his attention.

She wouldn't face the truth, and that was disappointing. She'd rather pretend that nothing had happened, that having sex with her best friend was an everyday occurrence in their lives. And she wanted him to play along. But he wasn't about to. Their friendship started out innocent enough. They enjoyed each other's company and didn't want to complicate things by injecting sex into the equation. Thomas understood that. And he accepted that. But that was seven years ago. He was a younger man then, with more than a passing interest in several women at the time, and he felt a definite need to separate Jazz from that less-than-admirable part of his life. Now he was almost forty, and tired of going through women the way he goes through suits, and tired of pretending that Jazz wasn't the one he wanted when she was always the one. Even seven years ago, that day in June, when they first met.

Thomas turned his back to the rail as a thought suddenly entered his mind. Seven years ago, he thought. This past June it was seven years. This past June was their seventh anniversary. They always celebrated it. Always. And this year, he suddenly realized, he'd totally forgotten it.

He closed his eyes and leaned back. Not that it mattered now. They had something new to celebrate. A new beginning. Although Jazz was tripping about that.

He picked up the cordless phone off of the table and dialed her number. As expected, she wasn't answering. He tossed it back on the table and went inside his bedroom. The memories of Jazz in that bed began to flood him and prick at his heart. He had to have her again, he thought. Maybe if he did her again she'd realize she was fighting a losing battle. She was his, whether she wanted to admit it or not, and he was determined to make her understand that.

He grabbed his wallet and keys from the nightstand and hurried out of the door. He almost felt as if he should be grabbing equipment, too, because he was going to need all the help he could get when he tried to scale Jazz's mountain.

Jazz was at home painting when the knocking on the door occurred. She sighed, because she hated being interrupted, and looked out of the big window in her studio as she wiped her hands on a cloth. Thomas's Bentley was on her drive. This time of night. She hurried to the door.

"Do you realize what time it is, Thomas?" she asked him snappishly as she opened the door. His expression, a kind of calm but unreadable one, went unchanged.

"May I come in?"

"It's almost one in the morning."

"May I come in?"

Jazz exhaled. And then she stepped aside and let him in.

When she closed the door, she leaned against it. He was in a pair of faded jeans and a torn-collar sweatshirt. She was in her worker jumper. For once, she thought offhandedly, they kind of matched.

"Painting?" he asked her, looking down at her attire.

She nodded.

"We need to talk, Jazz."

"About what? There's nothing to talk about. Since I'm in the land of make-believe anyway, according to you."

"That's not what I said."

"Oh, no, you're right. You're right. I'm phony, that's what you said."

"I said we need to talk. We need to admit the truth and stop pretending our feelings for each other don't exist."

"And then what, Thomas?"

"And then we get on with it."

"Get on with what? Our relationship? Our happily-ever-after romance?"

Thomas paused. "Yes."

"Now that's the fairy tale," Jazz said as she began walking toward her studio. "I can't make believe like that. I know better. Too much experience."

"I'm not your ex-husbands, Jazz," Thomas said as he followed behind her.

"I didn't say you were."

"I'm not deceiving you about anything."

"Neither were they, Thomas, don't you understand that?" She said this as she made it back up to her painting and turned and looked at him. "They were in love, too. At first. It was all good at first. But it never lasts."

"It can."

"Name one."

"What?"

"Name one relationship you know of that has lasted. And I'm not talking about any marriages of convenience either. I'm not talking about those females who put up with everything under the sun and then proclaim how they stood by their man. I'm talking about good, solid marriages built on trust and love. Name one."

Thomas just stood there silent far longer than he had planned to be. Then he folded his arms. "They're out there, Jazz."

"Yeah. I'm sure they are. Just not around us." Tears began to appear in Jazz's eyes. "Our friendship is the only lasting relationship I've ever had. The only one, Thomas. And I was proud of that. Because despite our disagreements I knew I could count on you to be there for me, and understand my need not to explain, and love me and care for me. Now I'm scared to death we just destroyed all that. We'll end up hating each other. And why? Just for a few moments of pleasure? I'm scared to death it'll never be the same again. I've never had a lasting romantic relationship, Thomas. Never."

Thomas grabbed her before she could say another word and pulled her against him. His arms wrapped around her and held her tightly. She attempted to suppress the tears, but they came anyway, and she buried her face in his chest.

"We'll be the first, Jazz," he said calmly. But Jazz began immediately to shake her head.

"Yes," he said, without giving her a chance to speak. "Yes, we will. Because it's been the same for me, too. Our friendship has been the only lasting relationship I've ever had, too. And that's going to make us even more determined to make this work."

"It's rarely planned not to work, Thomas," Jazz leaned her head off of his chest and said. He handed her his handkerchief. "It's not something that's planned. It just happens. And always to me. And what about our friendship?"

Thomas smiled. "Lovers can be friends, Jazz."

"No, they can't. There's too much emotional baggage. Too many strings attached."

"We'll just have to see about that. This will be different."

"No, it won't."

Thomas frowned. "What is it you want me to do? Give you up? I want more than a friendship, Jazz. Much more. And that includes sleeping with you. And I'm not worried about all that other stuff. Yeah, there's a chance we won't make it—"

"A chance?"

"A very good chance. But there's also a chance we will. And I'm willing to take it."

Tears began to appear in Jazz's big, droopy eyes once more. "The odds aren't in our favor, Thomas," she said.

"Are they ever?" he asked. "Especially yours."

Jazz didn't want to smile, but she couldn't help it. Then she laughed. "You're wrong for that," she said.

Thomas laughed along with her, thrilled that she could at least understand that there was some humor in pain. And when the laughter wound down into an almost deafening silence, they both suddenly realized their physical closeness. Jazz quickly thought to move out of his embrace, but her slightest movement was met with a definite resistance by him. She looked into his eyes, and she knew what that look meant.

"Thomas," she said but he wouldn't allow more. He leaned down and placed his mouth over hers, rubbing his lips over hers a few times before kissing her. Her body went limp as he held her tighter and before she knew it herself she had placed her arms around his neck and leaned into him with kisses of her own. How easily he ignited her passion, she thought as she kissed him, as she leaned her head back and allowed his kisses to cover her throat. She had a thousand reasons to say no, to stop him where he stood before they went too far again. But she didn't say no. And she didn't stop him. And when he lifted her in his arms and carried her to the bedroom, kissing her as he went, she wouldn't dream of stopping him. Because she knew, as he laid her on the bed, and undressed her, and moved on top of her as he undressed himself, that she couldn't stop herself, her feelings for him already went too deep and seared too wide, and she couldn't stop those feelings even if she wanted to. Which, at the moment, she didn't, she realized when he entered her, when their flesh collided in ferocious pounding as if they'd never had it so good. Because they didn't. Not like this.

Jazz held on to Thomas as tightly as she could as he pounded her harder and moved deeper into her, the bed creaking and bouncing with the intensity of their joy, and she had to face the truth. It was no secret any longer. She'd never felt this complete. And this intense. And this terrified in all her natural life.

The sun was just coming up when they walked down the stairs of the loft and stood beside Thomas's Bentley. Jazz had on her robe, and Thomas his jeans and jersey from last night. His car phone began ringing as soon as he opened the door, and he leaned inside and answered it. Jazz just stood there as he answered, and thoughts of all kinds clouded her mind. She could just enjoy their newfound romance for the sheer happiness that it was, praying that it would last, understanding that it probably wouldn't. Or she could remain in her shell, scared and comfortable, maybe even content, but a long way from happy. When Thomas hung up his phone and turned her way, she smiled. Looked like romance was winning out, she thought, and happiness, not because the fear was gone, but because it felt too good.

Thomas looked at her, at the front opening of her robe that revealed part of her breasts, and then at her face. And unbelievable even to him, he wanted to do her again.

"I'm sorry, Jazz," he said, deciding to ignore the seemingly unsatiable appetite he was beginning to acquire.

"That phone call? What's to be sorry about? You didn't rudely talk for hours, just a minute or two."

"I'm sorry I forgot about our seventh anniversary."

Jazz paused. "Oh, that."

"Yes, that."

"You were preoccupied, Thomas."

"I guess I was. But that was the reason for your little show of attitude in the art gallery that Saturday, wasn't it?"

Jazz laughed. "Of course it was. You had never forgotten before. Then you meet Alex Mailer and everything goes to hell."

Thomas nodded and looked away, toward the rising sun. Alex, he thought. What was he going to do about Alex? He hadn't even given her a second thought. But he couldn't worry about that now. He couldn't let Jazz see him worrying. He looked at her. "Want anything?" he asked.

Jazz smiled. "What an odd question to ask."

"It's not odd."

"It's certainly general. Anything like what?"

"Anything."

"And you'll give it to me?"

"If I can, I will."

"Since when? You never gave me anything I wanted before."

"You wasn't my woman before," he said just as his car phone began ringing again. "It's different now."

As he reached into his car to answer his phone, Jazz folded her arms. He didn't know it, but he was terrifying her again. She wanted their transition to be gradual, not rushed, because she knew she needed time, and plenty of it, to get emotionally accustomed to this new state of affairs. She was Thomas's woman now, not just his friend, and that elevation alone presented problems of a different kind for them. But he said they would overcome it. He said they would fight against the odds. And she smiled, believing her fears were misplaced, because she trusted his word and knew he understood. He'd give her time to get it together. He was still Thomas Drayton, the jaded divorce lawyer after all, she thought. He knew what she was going through.

When he completed his conversation, he hung up the phone and then looked at Jazz again. His eyes trailed down her again. "Got to run," he said. "Just think about what I said."

"You mean about giving me anything I want?"

"Yes."

"Don't need to think about it. I'm fine."

"Yeah, you would be. Even if you weren't."

Jazz wanted to respond to that smart little remark, but she didn't bother. She allowed him to give her a peck of a kiss on the lips and then sit down in his Bentley. "Be good," he said.

"You be good," she said with a smile. "Don't worry about me. I got this."

Thomas laughed. Then his look turned serious, solemn. "And Jazz," he said before he closed his door, "I'll be picking you up from work this afternoon." Then he looked into her eyes. "Make sure you be there."

It was a direct order, no mistaking that tone, and Jazz suddenly felt queasy. Where does he get off? she wanted to say, she should have said, but she didn't. She allowed him to spout out his command, close his car door, and begin to leave. But as she walked back up the stairs of her apartment, not bothering to even look back, the anger began to rise. Who was he to command her anyway, she wondered. Was this the opening salvo of things to come? Was Thomas some domineering control freak just itching to put her in her place? She decided to shake off such thoughts. You never know a person until you know them, and she understood that. But she was also reasonably sure that she knew Thomas.

She went into her house, showered quickly, and then poured herself a cup of coffee before she began her usual morning routine: a little painting and then a little gardening before time to catch that ride to the station with Carmella.

As she headed for her studio, cup of coffee in hand, she glanced out of her living room window just as Thomas's car was backing away from the main house and driving off. At first she wondered what he was doing all this time, at Carmella's of all places, but then she dismissed that unexpected moment of jealousy out of hand. He was probably shooting the breeze with Carmella, an old friend of his after all, whose usual morning routine was far less stringent than Jazz's. Instead of painting and working in gardens, Carmella simply enjoyed sitting on the porch in the mornings. Besides, Thomas and Carmella? Carmella and Thomas? Jazz smiled. Talk about a mismatch, she said aloud as she headed for her studio door.

NOTHING BUT THE RENT

Denny's was crowded at breakfast time as Alex and Nikki made their way through the buffet line and took a seat near the front of the restaurant.

"You eat like a bird," Nikki said as she prepared her fork to feast on the enormous pile of hotcakes, sausages, bacon, hash browns, eggs, toast, biscuits, and bowl of grits on the side. Alex looked at all that food and shook her head.

"No," she said, "you eat like a football team."

Nikki smiled. "I'm a growing girl," she said.

"You're gonna be a growing linebacker, you keep on."

"Ah, Alex, it ain't even like that. You know like I know that brothers like women with some meat on their bones."

"Meat, Nikki, yes. Not slabs. Not layers and layers of blubber."

"They say all you can eat and I'm gonna eat all I can. And if you don't like it you can sail your little skinny ass on out of my face."

Alex looked at her then they both laughed. "You're sick, you know that?"

"I know," Nikki said, and, after tasting every food group on her plate, she placed her elbows on the table and looked at her sister. "So," she said. "How did it go last night?"

"Don't even mention it."

"Was it that bad?"

"Worse. The man is fifty-nine, has bad breath, and loves to talk about how he pulled himself up by his boot straps and became a success. Before the date was through I was about ready to pull him up by something, too."

"I don't know why you still going down that road. And you wanted me to date him. Please."

"Dating Theophilus—"

"Whew. That's his name?"

"Yep. And you better not call him Theo either. But dating him has its advantages."

"Yeah. You'll only have to entertain him between his naps."

"Nope," Alex said, reached into her purse, and pulled out a check. "*Voila!*" she said.

"What's that?"

"Rent, my dear. Next month's rent."

Nikki was astounded. "He gave it to you *already?*"

"Already, girl. I asked and he whipped it out."

Nikki laughed. "You're the one who's sick."

"Hey-hey-hey. That gives me time, though."

"Yeah, I'll bet." Then she looked at Alex. "Time for what?"

"To win Thomas back, what you think? To get a ring on my finger. To become Mrs. Alexandria Drayton." Then she smiled. "Damn," she said, "that even sounds rich."

"Come on, Al, that man ain't thinking about you. He kick you out his house and don't even give you a call to apologize? Please. You better stick with Theopo . . . whatever his name is because, girl, from what I'm seeing, you can forget about Thomas Drayton."

"I'm not forgetting about nobody. He'll be calling."

"Wanna bet?"

"I don't gamble. It's against my moral code."

Nikki laughed. "Moral code? You ain't got no moral code."

Alex looked at her. "That's not funny, Nikki. I happen to think of myself as a good Christian girl who just so happen to be in a cut-throat business. And Theophilus is business. Pure and simple. Ain't no different than these men in these corporations."

"Don't."

"Don't what?"

"Believe a lie. You're no more a businesswoman than I am. Mama sold us that bill of goods since we were little kids and we bought it.

What you do and what I did for so long ain't no different than what a hooker does, now I'll give you that, but don't try to compare us to no business people."

The wind seemed to go out of Alex's sail. "Speak for yourself," she said.

"Hello, ladies," a familiar voice sounded just above their heads and both sisters turned quickly. When Nikki saw that it was Conrad, she smiled. Alex, however, rolled her eyes.

"Hello, Connie," she said with no enthusiasm.

"Nice to see you, too, Alex."

"Hey," Nikki said, smiling greatly. "Care to join us?"

Conrad looked at her plate of food. "Looks good," he said. "But no thanks, I'm here to meet a client." Then he looked at Alex. "So how have you been?"

"Wonderful."

"So have I."

"Wonderful."

Conrad hesitated, trying to keep his cool. "You still looking good."

"Yeah, well, anyway." Alex said this as if she was inviting him to leave. Nikki, however, quickly interceded.

"You're looking good, too, Conrad. Working out?"

"No, not really," he said, unable to stop staring at Alex.

"Looks like you work out. I tried before but it wasn't for me, you know? All that work."

"That's why they call it a workout," Conrad said with a smile and then looked at Nikki. Nikki smiled in return. "But, hey, I'll see y'all around, okay?" He said as his eyes looked over at Alex again.

"Sure, Conrad, see you around," Nikki said, and then he walked away from their table. Nikki smiled until he had moved away, then she frowned and looked at Alex. "What is your problem?" she asked her.

"What?"

"You were so rude to him. What did he ever do to you except help your behind?"

"Child, please. I ain't thinking about no Conrad Baines. He just wanna get all up in my business so he can run and tell Thomas what's going on, to get his revenge, that's all this about."

"I thought you said Thomas was discreet and Conrad doesn't even know about your relationship with him?"

"He didn't know about it. But it's been two days. He may know everything now for all I know. But it don't even matter. He's a loser and I'm not interested. Case closed."

"Yeah," Nikki said as she watched Conrad pile food on his plate at the buffet across the room. "Case closed."

Jazz, on her knees and in her thick yard gloves, had already pulled a pile of weeds from the small garden behind her house and was digging up earth with her trowel to plant her new azalea seeds when Carmella walked up to her. She wiped her forehead with the back of her glove and looked up at her tall friend, who, against the sun, looked almost too tall.

"Good morning."

"You're out here early."

"I tried to do some painting, but it wasn't happening for me today, so I came on out here. What's up?"

"Just curious."

Jazz squinted her eyes as she looked circumspectly at her friend. "What's the matter? Not going to be able to take me to work today?"

"Of course I will. It's not like I have a job, right?"

"You're an artist. A designer of unique African postcards. Postcards, I'll remind you, that's selling far better than my full-grown paintings."

"Which isn't saying much."

Jazz laughed. "True that," she said. But she knew something was bugging her friend. "So what is it?"

Carmella hesitated then kneeled down to Jazz. She wore a pair of shorts and a halter top and had a bottled water in her hand. She looked like the typical suburban housewife to Jazz, although she wasn't a wife; lived in the country, not the suburbs; and was anything but typical. Which meant, Jazz knew, she wasn't telling what ails her without a whole lot of prodding and pushing first.

"Carmella, what's wrong?"

"I think I'm going to be moving out." She said this and looked at Jazz.

"Moving out? Why, what's happened?"

"Nothing's happened. I just think it's best I move on."

"Move on? Where?"

"Who knows? I just may go back to Saint Croix."

"Please. You're an American girl through and through now. You aren't about to go back there."

"I said I may."

Jazz exhaled and stuck her trowel in the dirt. Then she stood, prompting Carmella to stand, too. "Okay, let's have it."

"There's nothing to have. I've just been thinking and I thought it would be a good idea if I moved on to someplace else."

"And you don't even know where this someplace else will be?"

"Not yet. The brainstorm occurred this morning, okay? I haven't had a chance to iron out the details."

"But what brought on this brainstorm, Carmella? You aren't telling me anything."

"It's really none of your business. All you need to know is that I'm going, okay?"

Jazz should have been offended by Carmella's less-than-grateful remark, but she wasn't. She knew her friend well enough to know that something other than ingratitude was driving this train wreck. "We've been friends for six years now, Carmella. Six years. And I've been up front with you every step of the way."

"This isn't about you, Jazz. You've been wonderful, and I'll never forget it. Don't think I'm leaving because of something you did."

"I need you to be up front with me. I need you to tell me what's going on here."

"Okay, you know what? That's why I don't like secrets because I can't keep any. All somebody has to do is push me a little and I tell all. So I'm telling all." She said this and then exhaled. "It's Thomas," she said.

Jazz frowned. "Thomas? What does Thomas have to do with this?"

"He told me this morning that things have changed between the two of you and he feels it's no longer appropriate for me to be living on your property."

Jazz shook her head in utter confusion. "What are you talking about? What does our changed relationship have to do with you?"

"Nothing."

"Then why is it suddenly inappropriate for you to live in my house?"

Carmella shook her head. "It's a long story, Jazz."

Jazz folded her arms. "I'm listening."

Carmella paused, began moving side to side.

"Carmella!"

"Okay," Carmella said. "Damn." Then she paused again. "Thomas and I were friends, as you know."

"I know."

"Six years ago, as you know, he became my lawyer."

"When you were going through your divorce, yes, I know. That's how we met."

"Right. He introduced us because he thought I would be a good candidate to stay in this house you was wanting to rent out."

"Right. I know that."

"What you don't know is that he was more than just my friend and lawyer."

Jazz hesitated, staring at her friend. She knew exactly what she meant and she had no clue what she meant. "What do you mean?" she decided to ask her.

"Thomas and I were lovers, Jazz."

Jazz actually smiled. "What?"

"Thomas and I—"

"You and Thomas? I don't believe you."

"Fine. But why would I lie?"

"Why didn't you tell me this?"

"Why didn't he? You were his friend first. I needed a serious helping hand, he helped me, I wasn't about to mess that up. Besides, y'all weren't going together then. Y'all were just friends, remember?"

"You slept with him?"

"We had a brief affair, Jazz. I was divorced, he was available, end of story."

"How long was this brief affair?"

"Not even a year."

"But you were his girlfriend when you moved into my house?"

"I was somebody he slept with occasionally, Jazz. I honestly don't think he viewed me as his girlfriend."

"You slept with him in my house. Right?"

"Jazz."

"Am I right, Carmella?"

Carmella sighed. "Yes, you're right. A few times we did have sex in the house."

"Anytime recently?"

"No! I told you that was years ago. And yes, Thomas broke it off."

"Why?"

"He didn't say and I didn't ask."

"And neither one of you thought it would be a good idea to let me in on this information?"

"I don't know what he thought, but I didn't see the point."

"You didn't?"

"No."

"You, the woman who was always so certain that I was in love with Thomas, didn't think that I needed to know that the man I was allegedly in love with was also banging you?"

"Years ago."

"Did he wear protection?"

Carmella's entire countenance changed. "You go to hell, Jazz!" she yelled. "Of course he wore protection! You needn't worry about any STDs of mine becoming yours."

Jazz unfolded her arms. And she felt as if all energy was seeping from her body. Carmella had been his friend, too. And slept with him. And now he didn't want to have anything to do with her. It would be inappropriate for his new woman to have to face the old one, he told her. And when the next one come along, Jazz knew, she'd be the old one.

Why couldn't they just remain friends? Why did they have to go down this emotionally hellish road when she knew this was how it was going to be? And she also knew that this confession of Carmella's was just the beginning of the slide. "I was out of line," she said to her friend. "I apologize."

"Accepted."

"I just . . . I just had no idea."

"It was a long time ago, Jazz."

"I know. But I still should have been told."

There was a long pause. "Sorry, Jazz."

"No need. It's done now." Then she hesitated. "And where does he get off kicking you out of my home? He has no right to do something like that."

"Thomas is very bossy, Jazz, you know that."

"He won't be bossing me."

"And he does have a right."

"No, he does not. You're living in my home. Okay, you slept with him six years ago and I slept with him last night. I would have preferred we not have that kind of association, but there's nothing we can do about that now. But I'll tell you this, Thomas cannot kick you out of any house of mine because it's my house and he doesn't have anything to do with how I handle my property."

"He pays the rent, Jazz."

"What?"

"For the past six years Thomas has paid the rent. Even after he stopped seeing me. So it was more for you than for me, I'm thinking."

"Thomas has paid the rent?"

"Yes."

"Every month?"

"Every month since I've lived in the house. At first I was flat broke after my divorce, remember? So because I was giving him some favors he was helping me out. It was a mutually beneficial relationship. But he kept on paying it after my favors long since stopped. And I kept on letting him."

"Where does he get off!" Jazz said aloud. "How dare he!"

"It's too entangled, Jazz. That's why he wants me out of here. He says the least complication and you might . . ."

Jazz looked at her. "I might what?"

"You might change your mind, that's what he said."

Jazz smiled and shook her head. "My mind changing is the least of his worries. And you aren't moving anywhere, Carmella. Not unless it's what you want to do and how you want to do it. Thomas doesn't run anything around here. Especially me."

Jazz said this and began heading for her loft. She slung off her gloves and tossed them as she walked. She knew Thomas had his share of women, more than his share. But Carmella, too? And in *her* house? She thought they were just friends. She thought their relationship was as innocent as his was with her. What a fool, she thought. And where does he get off paying rent on her house? As if she needed his cash flow to survive. As if she couldn't make it without his macho generosity. If she was upset when she walked up the stairs of her loft, she was outright furious by the time she walked inside the loft. Because he had no right, because she'd fallen in love with a straight-up player, because the unencumbered lifestyle she had worked so hard to hone, a lifestyle she thought she'd never have after her three heartrending divorces, was on the verge of total decimation if she didn't do something, and something fast.

TAKING BACK
THE NIGHT

"Thomas?" Gerald asked, as if surprised to see him at the station. Thomas, who was walking briskly down the hall toward the recording booth, smiled faintly.

"Hello, Gerald."

"She's not here."

Thomas's walk slowed. "She's not?"

"No."

Thomas couldn't believe it, not after he told her to be in place when he came to pick her up. He opened his suit coat and placed both hands on his waist. "When did she leave?"

"No, you don't understand. She didn't come in to work today. She said she wasn't feeling well."

Thomas frowned. "Wasn't feeling well?"

"That's what she said. I just assumed it was a carryover from yesterday."

Thomas nodded. What game was Jazz trying to play? As soon as he thought he'd made a breakthrough—and last night certainly qualified—she erected that damn wall of hers again. He exhaled. "Thanks, man," he said and hurried away from there.

It was turning out to be a very nice day, Jazz thought, as she loaded her big Delta 88 with the potted plants she had just purchased at the flea market. Instead of going to work, she got Carmella to drop her off at the nearest used car lot in town. It wasn't Jazz's normal route—she normally got herself a newspaper and purchased her automobiles from private owners—but she wanted it now, today, and she had no time to shop around.

They ended up at Al's, a buy-here pay-here kind of place, and the only car on the lot that was both cheap and reliable enough for them to be willing to put a thirty-day warranty on it was the very big, very old Delta 88. The asking price was twenty-three hundred financed. Jazz paid a little over a thousand dollars cash and, within an hour, was the car's new owner.

Then she headed for the flea market, a place she'd been itching to visit for weeks now but she didn't want to bother anyone. Now she didn't have to bother a soul, she thought, as she got into her car, rolled down the window to let the built-up heat out (it had no AC), and then drove the long stretch from Miami's huge flea market to little Homestead. She wasn't at all surprised, however, when she pulled into her graveled driveway to find Thomas's car and Thomas himself sitting on her bottom stair, sitting in his suit and sunglasses, looking big and gorgeous, she thought.

Jazz exhaled and stepped out of her car. In direct contrast to Thomas, she wore shorts and a sleeveless tank top and eyeglasses rather than sunglasses to cover her expressive eyes.

Thomas just sat there as she began removing the plants from the car's backseat and placing them on the side of the stairs. He would have helped her, easily, but he knew she'd decline the offer so he wasn't bothering with the drama this time. And besides, he thought, his anger was still too intense. The idea that she would have him show up at the station to pick her up when she probably had no intentions of even going to work astounded him. All she had to do was phone. He wasn't in court at all today and she knew it. But she didn't bother. As if he wasn't worth the trouble. And what the hell was she doing in that big boat of a car, he wondered, when he told her he didn't want her driving again? He sighed and shook his head. He had to set some serious-behind ground rules, he decided.

She walked up to the stairs when the last of her plants was safely pushed up against the side of the garage and looked at him. She couldn't see his eyes but she knew he was fuming.

"Hello," she said as he stood up beside her.

"You didn't show up for work."

"No."

Thomas waited, fully expecting an explanation, but Jazz wasn't giving one.

"What did we discuss this morning, Jazz?" he asked her.

"I don't remember us discussing anything this morning. I remember you barking out an order for me to be in place when you came to pick me up, but I don't remember any discussion about it."

"Why didn't you phone me and tell me you wasn't going to work today? I have better things to do than to be chasing you around."

"And I have better things to do than to be phoning you. Now excuse me." She said this as she sought to scurry past him and hurry up her stairs. But Thomas caught her by the arm and immediately stopped her progress. She angrily looked up at him, wanting nothing better than very direct eye contact, but his dark shades blocked her view.

"Let go of my arm, Thomas!" she demanded, but he wouldn't do it.

"I thought we had settled this, Jazz. I thought your little roller-coaster ride was over!"

"Well you thought wrong, didn't you? Now let go of me!" She said this and snatched away from him. Then she headed up the stairs.

Thomas sighed again, shook his head again, but followed her up.

"We need to talk," he said as Jazz entered her loft and began opening the blinds and lifting up the old-fashioned wood-framed windows, seemingly ignoring his presence in her home. But she couldn't ignore him, of course. Thomas had a way of overwhelming every room he entered, especially hers, and she was so aware of his presence that she could feel flashes of heat searing her body, as if she were middle-aged and menopausal or still burning with desire for his touch.

"Jazz!"

Jazz looked at him. He was hot, too, she could tell, but it had nothing to do with any burning desire. She therefore stopped her almost-manic window lifting and stood in the middle of the living room. "Okay," she said, folding her arms. "Talk."

"Whose car?"

She frowned. "What?"

"Whose car is in your driveway?"

"It's my car, Thomas. Mine. Why?"

"Why do you think, Jazz? We agreed that you were going to wait before you got behind a wheel again."

Jazz laughed. "We agreed? Did we now? I don't know, Thomas. I just can't quite see myself agreeing to give up my right to do whatever the hell I want simply because you agreed that I should. That's just not me, hear what I'm saying?"

"Dammit, Jazz! What's wrong with you? You were fine this morning."

"Was I?"

"Yes! You were! But I stay away from you for a few hours and suddenly you're . . ."

"I'm what? Me, perhaps? Free, perhaps? Unable to bow down to you, perhaps?"

"Jazz."

"Why did you try to kick Carmella out of my house?"

"What?"

"You heard me. Why were you sleeping with her and making me think y'all were just friends?"

Thomas slung open his suit coat and placed his hands on his waist. This was getting to be too much emotion for him. "Why don't you sit down," he said calmly. But Jazz wouldn't budge. He exhaled. "Is that what this is about? Me and Carmella?"

"I would never tell her anything intimate about you. I never even told her that we slept in the same bed sometimes, because foolish me figured that was too personal for her to know. I thought she was just your friend, Thomas. That's what you told me when you introduced her. Your friend. But you were paying her rent, weren't you? And you were sleeping with her, *in my house,* and neither one of y'all even mentioned it to me?"

"You and I weren't together then, Jazz."

"So why didn't you tell me? It was you who said we've been more than friends for a long time now, we just wouldn't admit it. But that little revelation didn't stop you from doing what you do, did it, Thomas?"

"This is ridiculous."

"It's not ridiculous!" Then she shook her head. "Carmella, Thomas? And in my house. How could you!"

Thomas threw his hands in the air. "I'm going home," he said and turned to leave.

"We can't do it, Thomas," Jazz said quickly, causing him to slowly turn back around.

"We can't do what?"

"This. Be lovers. Be together like that. It's tearing us apart already. You're my friend, the closest friend I'll ever have, and I can't lose you. But that's exactly what I'm doing. And every day it's getting clearer to me. We knew what we were doing when we forbid this. We were experienced people, Thomas, we knew exactly what was going to happen. And now it's happening. We'll end up hating each other if we don't stop this madness right now and just be friends again."

Thomas looked at her, as tears filled her eyes, and all he could think to do was go to her and place his arms around her. When she didn't resist, he held her tighter.

"It's going to be all right, Jazz," he said.

"I can't do the romance thing, Thomas. It's too much. We're just getting started and already we're on the verge of a breakup. So let's break up, okay? So we can get on with our friendship. The way it used to be. Because no matter what, Thomas, I can't lose you as a friend."

Thomas rubbed her hair as he held her. She was right. God, was she right. But not even the realization of the truth could lessen the reality of the failure.

Ten days later and Alex, decked down in a provocative, skin-tight, micro-mini leather skirt suit with matching waist-high jacket and a pair of stilettos, peered into Nikki's bedroom, hoping that she had already fallen asleep. But she hadn't. She was reading, as always, one of those college textbooks of hers, this one on biology, the room dark but for the illumination of the desk lamp.

"Alex?" Nikki asked as she looked up from her book, her body sitting slumped over at the desk as if she was stuck in a permanent contortion. Alex shook her head. She could barely recognize this obsessively studious, will-die-if-she-don't-succeed sister of hers.

"You're ruining your posture, Nikki," she warned.

"Just getting in?"

"Just going out. Don't wait up now."

"Just going out?"

"Bye-bye."

"But it's one o'clock in the morning, Alex!" Alex, however, had already closed the door. "Alex!" Nikki yelled again futilely, knowing for herself that her sister was like a bullet out of a gun when she made up her mind.

And Alex's mind was well made up, as she hurried from Nikki's bedroom, totally ignoring her cries for sensibility because she could not be detained a moment longer. It had been nearly two weeks since Thomas kicked her out of his home; nearly two weeks since she heard that reassuring, smooth voice of his; nearly two weeks since he touched her. She had waited and waited and waited. A nun could not have been more patient. Of course having Theophilus in her life now as her new meal ticket/sugar daddy/boyfriend preoccupied a considerable amount of that time, and although Theo was wealthy and generous and easily at her beck and call, he was no Thomas Drayton.

And that was why enough was enough, she thought, as she got into her Saab in the late night–early morning air and pulled out of her driveway. She had to have Thomas. Period. She had to make him love her again.

Her idea was simple and cunning at the same time. This wasn't an impulse that drove her from her home at one a.m. She waited until after midnight before she prepared to leave on purpose. She wanted to catch him off guard. In truth, she wanted to catch him just sleepy enough, and therefore dazed enough, that he would be less inclined to over-analyze her motives and more inclined to just want to take her where she stood.

Her first goal was easily realized. She could tell as soon as first Henry answered the door, and then Thomas behind him, that she had clearly caught him off guard. No way, from the almost disconcerted expression on his face, had he seen it coming. It was her second goal, however, that proved problematic.

Not only had he not been asleep, she quickly learned as he escorted her into his study, but he was knee-deep in work; work that required complete analytical thought. Which meant, not only was he much more inclined to analyze her motives, but he was, mentally, in a perfect position to do so.

And he did. As soon as he sat beside her on the leather couch in his study, a leather that was almost as dark brown as her skirt suit, she could tell without much effort that he was studying her, warts and all, like a book.

"So," she said, trying to smile grandly, trying not to show the horror she felt all over, "how have you been?"

"Okay."

"Good." Then she hesitated, wondering if she should say it. Then she decided to stop thinking so darn hard and just do what she came here to do. "Wish I could say the same about me," she said.

Instead of responding to her obvious self-pitying statement, Thomas pulled a gold case from the pocket of the robe he was wearing and removed a cigar. He replaced the case, pulled out a lighter, and lit up. Alex watched him, watched his massive, bare chest bulging out of the robe's top opening, and she wondered if he had on anything at all underneath. Although they'd made passionate love many times in the past, she'd never spent the night with him to know what exactly he did wear to bed at night: boxers, pjs, nothing? She wanted to find out many times, desperately, but it never got that far. He never saw the point in her spending the night with him, which was an odd decision to say the least, and even in their most romantic late hour, he would always do what he had to do to her and send her on her way. He was great at foreplay, she thought, lousy at after-play, as if the passion left him as soon as he pulled out of her, and he wanted nothing more to do with her. It saddened her now, as she watched him, as she wondered if sex was all there was between them; and if it was, she thought sadly, she was doomed.

"But I'm glad things have been going well for you," she decided to say, to force him to at least respond to her, even if all he had to say was thank you. He responded all right, but not in the way she had expected.

He leaned forward, the lit cigar between his fingers, his face, not on her, but on the enormous amount of paperwork that sat on the table in front of them. "Why are you here, Alex?" he asked without looking at her.

She swallowed hard. It used to be easy for her to deal with him. Now she was nervous and off-balance, as if those two weeks had robbed her of her edge. But she aimed to get it back. "I hadn't heard from you," she said. "I was worried."

"Worried?"

"Yes, Thomas. About us."

Thomas looked at her. She was still pretty, still sexy, although she looked like a hooker to him in that ridiculous leather suit, but she still had an almost wide-eyed innocence about her, despite her poor taste in clothing, that turned him on. If he couldn't have Jazz, and she'd made it perfectly clear that he couldn't, then Alex, he decided, wouldn't be a bad second choice. Yet his heart dropped at even the thought of it. He couldn't have Jazz!

When Thomas just stared at Alex, as if she didn't know if he should hug her or haul her out of his house, she decided to help make the decision almost unavoidable.

"I care a great deal about this relationship, Thomas, you must know that. We had a good thing going. I figured you didn't call me because you needed a little time to yourself. And I respected that. But that didn't stop my love for you. That didn't stop me from wanting you even now." Alex began unbuttoning her jacket, revealing her large, bare breasts in the process. "And I do want you, Thomas. I've missed you so much."

Thomas stared at her breasts, as she slowly unbuttoned and then removed her leather jacket. He'd been lonelier than he'd been in years when he and Jazz, ten days ago, painfully concluded that romance didn't appear to be in the cards for them. He thought about calling Alex probably a dozen times during that period, but he never did. He'd be using her if he had, for the sex, for companionship, when his heart would be somewhere else.

But watching her disrobe—and she seemed so willing to please him, so ready and able to give him exactly what he knew he needed— was a temptation almost beyond his ability to control. But when she stood to her feet and began to unzip her skirt, he took her by the arm. "Alex, don't," he said.

Alex just stood there, her arm seething with fire from the touch of his big hand, and to her own shock tears came into her eyes. The idea of Thomas rejecting her, the way every man in her life had eventually come to their senses and done, mortified her. He was the one. She decided long ago that this smart, wealthy, handsome man before her was going to be the one to make her dreams come true. And to think that he, her last hope for happiness, would turn her away now was too much to take. And that was why the tears came in spite of her preference that she remain unemotional, and they would not ease up.

Thomas looked at her exposed breasts, as they heaved with the uncoordinated breathing that her sudden show of emotion evoked, and then at her eyes, now tear-filled and even more wide and innocent and always so sad; for a woman who had so much going for her she was always so sad to Thomas, and he pulled her between his legs and sat her on his lap. She slung her arms around his neck and laid her head on his broad shoulder, the tears flowing freely now, and in response to her almost-desperate show of affection, he pulled her closer against him and held her tighter.

Thomas ran his hand up and down her spine as her crying became louder, and his heart felt heavy, as if it had been rended in two. He cared deeply for Alex, for this sobbing woman in his arms, but he did not love her.

"Alex," he finally said, softly.

"I didn't mean to cry," Alex replied, attempting to regulate her emotion by slowing to the point of sniffling more than she was sobbing.

"Honey."

"I don't know why I was crying like that. That's not like me."

"Honey, look at me."

Alex hesitated, unsure of the tone of his voice, then she lifted her head from his shoulder and looked into his large, expressive eyes. She batted hers and said, "Yes?" as if she was expecting the worst. She was right.

"I slept with Jazz, Alex," Thomas said.

Alex quickly began shaking her head. "No."

"Yes, Alex, listen to me."

"You couldn't have."

"But I did. I slept with Jazz." Even the thought of it raced Thomas's heart.

"You mean you . . . you mean you laid in the same bed with her?" Thomas wouldn't respond to that lame response, so she continued. "Once?" she asked.

He hesitated. "No."

"More than once?"

"Yes."

"But why, Thomas? You said she was just your friend."

"She is. She was."

"Then why? When?"

Thomas decided to answer the simpler question, knowing that the why was far more complicated than Alex would ever understand. "During our separation, honey. It started the night I asked you to leave the house."

Asked me, she wanted to say. But she didn't. She knew the night. It was the same night she ran to David at that sleazy motel he loved to frequent and slept with him. But that, she quickly decided, was none of Thomas's business.

"I'm sorry, Alex," he said.

"But how could you?" she asked, as if genuinely hurt, which, she realized, she was. "You know how I feel about you. You know how I trusted you. How could you, Thomas?"

The tears began to flow freely again down Alex's lovely face and Thomas sought to soothe her by rocking her in his arms and rubbing her long hair. "I'm sorry, honey," he said over and over, holding her, comforting her. He wasn't sorry that he slept with Jazz, he could never be sorry about that, but he was very sorry that he had hurt Alex. She was a good kid, he felt, somebody generally over her head in life, and the last thing she needed was more heartache from a joker like him.

But then she stopped crying like the strong trouper she always tried to be and looked at him. The pain was still in her eyes. But something else was there, too. If Thomas didn't know any better, and based on his vast wealth of experience he did, he'd call it lust.

"Kiss me," she said softly.

"Alex—"

"Kiss me!" she demanded, and without waiting for him to voice yet another objection, she crushed her lips to his and took what she was asking for. Thomas, to her relief, responded immediately, kissing her until his tongue sunk in. And Alex knew instinctively, gutturally, that she had him exactly where she wanted him. And as he pulled her down to her knees, put on the condom he, to her dismay, never failed to be without, and entered her from the back, she also knew just as definitely that Jazz Walker was now more than just a little annoyance. Jazz Walker was now a serious obstacle to her future with this big, thirsty man who was now pounding into her so mercilessly, so wonderfully that she couldn't help but scream in delight.

But she wasn't so far gone in passion that she could not plot her revenge. And Jazz Walker, for all of her *we're just friends* platitudes, was the target of that revenge. For she was now a clear and present threat to Alex's future, a clear and present threat to everything Alex needed to live the lifestyle she felt she richly deserved. And if Alex was to have her way, and she usually did, that threat was going to be eliminated.

"Ready?" Jazz said to Carmella as she walked up to her in the gallery. She'd just sold three paintings, and she felt good about herself.

"No, I'm not ready," Carmella said. "We just got here."

"Isn't it great? I didn't have to even bargain with the man. He accepted on the spot."

"Yeah, 'cause it's a rip-off no matter how you slice it. You should have let me handle it. You never ask for enough."

"Enough for me."

"Which is never enough."

"Whatever, Carmella," Jazz said, then looked at the painting that had originally caught Carmella's eye. "Ooh, that's most unusual."

"It's unusual all right. Looks like a . . . I don't know. An old junk car. Like that Delta 88 of yours outside."

"Very funny."

"Am I lying? What does it look like to you?"

"It doesn't look like a junk car, I know that much."

"Then what?"

"Just plain junk," a voice from behind them said, and they both turned and looked around. It was David, looking gorgeous in an African safari shirt and jeans, his smile laid on thick and charming. "Hello, ladies."

Carmella smiled. "Well, hello."

David quickly looked at Jazz, to make it clear early on which one he was interested in. "I didn't mean to thrust myself into your conversation. But I couldn't understand that particular painting either. It has no aesthetic value whatsoever. In my humble opinion."

"And your opinion is right," Carmella said, determined to win him to her side, "in my opinion."

David, however, never did anything for the hell of it. He was on an assignment, and Carmella—although, he had to admit, was enticing—would not deter him from his ultimate goal. He therefore looked at Jazz. "What about you?" he asked her.

"She disagrees," Carmella said.

"I didn't say I disagreed," Jazz replied.

"No, Jazz, you're right. You said it was most unusual. Not ugly. Not junk-worthy. But most unusual. Which is so you."

"What is that supposed to mean?"

"You know what it means."

"Jazz?" David said smilingly, to thrust himself back into the conversation. "If I may call you Jazz?"

Jazz looked at him over the top rim of her eyeglasses. Not bad looking, she thought, although she definitely wasn't interested. "You may," she said noncommittally, "since that's my name."

"And my name is David. Nice to meet you. What I've noticed, Jazz, is that you are slightly more of an expert here, somebody who has more than just a passing interest in these works, unlike myself, unlike I assume your friend here has."

Carmella smiled. "Boy did you hit that nail on the head."

"Excuse me?"

"She's a painter herself."

"Ah."

"A painter of some reputation, I might add."

"And you aren't?" Jazz said.

"I draw picture postcards, Jazz, let's not even think about putting what I do in the same category with what you do."

"So you're a painter," David said to Jazz, completely ignoring Carmella.

"I dabble," Jazz replied.

"She more than dabbles. She just sold some of her work to this very gallery."

"Did she?"

"Come back next week. You'll see them hanging around here somewhere."

'Thank you. I'll do that."

"Anyway, Carmella," Jazz said, suddenly very ready to go. "You're ready?"

"Oh, I'm sorry," David said. "I didn't mean to keep you ladies from some appointments."

"We ain't got no appointment," Carmella said, "just going to lunch." Then Carmella smiled. "Would you care to join us, David?"

Jazz rolled her eyes. David kept his eyes on Carmella, although he saw very clearly Jazz's reaction. "I would love to, actually. This is my first Saturday off work in a while and I didn't have anything planned. But I honestly don't think Jazz here would appreciate my intrusion."

Jazz looked at him. "Why would you say that?"

"I don't know. Maybe it was the way you rolled your eyes when Carmella invited me along."

Carmella laughed. Jazz couldn't help but smile.

"Sorry," she said.

"Not a problem. Women aren't usually disgusted by me, I'll admit that, but hey, if you are, Jazz, that's fine. I can live with that."

"Good," Carmella said, placing her arm in his and moving him toward the exit, "because you will all too soon find out that is just Jazz being Jazz, okay? Live with it and you'll be fine."

David smiled and looked back at Jazz as she walked slower behind them, her mind seemingly miles away. Alex said Jazz was going to be a tough nut to crack, and boy she wasn't exaggerating. But that Theophilus character was keeping Alex financially comfortable, and, in turn, Alex was keeping David financially comfortable, so he didn't sweat it when she came to him with this scheme of hers. Because she was right. Because the sooner Alex could get this surprisingly beautiful but baggy-pants-wearing, four-eyed, not-his-type-by-a-mile woman called Jazz out of the picture to where she could wrangle herself the big fish, the elusive Thomas Drayton, then the sooner he could live in his own lap of luxury as the undisputed and, he was certain, well-maintained boy toy of the new Mrs. Alexandria Drayton.

And it started from there. As a friendship. Alex had schooled David well. As soon as they got to the café for lunch, he made it clear to both ladies that he was not looking for another woman to warm his bed, he had too many trying to do that as it was, but he was just looking for a friend. He also made it clear, without any verbal enunciation but nonverbal clarity, that his offered hand of friendship was being extended to Jazz alone. And, to his relief, Carmella, who was far more his type in the real world than the bookish Jazz Walker could ever be, understood when to back off and not hog up the stage from the one being spotlighted. She tried early on, a few times, but when David didn't take the bait she got the message fast enough.

It was just that Jazz was not falling for his charm. Not at all, he felt, after they left the café in the different cars they came in: he in his Corvette, Jazz and Carmella in Jazz's big Delta 88. David sat in his car and shook his head in disgust as they lumbered off, gas fumes from the old car sprouting out from the exhaust pipe and proudly polluting the already stale Miami air. Who the hell was she, he wondered, to be playing hard to get? She should be crawling at his feet, begging for some, the way most of those intellectual females did him. But she barely gave him the time of day. He was gorgeous and easily likable and she was able to laugh at his stale jokes. That, however, was as far as she was willing to take it. But he had an ally in Carmella, who just so happened to mention to him that tomorrow they were going to a gospel concert at the Abyssinia Baptist Church in town, and he took note of it without comment.

And he showed up at the church the very next day. Jazz relaxed more around him during the concert, and soon, after two more weeks of drop-ins and happen-to-be-in-the-neighborhoods, Jazz eventually warmed to him. He, after all, was just looking for a friend, and she, after all, could use one to help distract her from her almost-unending obsession with Thomas. Sleeping with Thomas changed the dynamic, and now she didn't know how to view their relationship. They called themselves friends, still, but it wasn't the same. And David's humor and easy style kept her mind from wondering why things weren't the same and, more painfully, if they ever would be. But she also had to lay down the law to David. And she did. On their first official night out without Carmella.

It was a Japanese steakhouse and they sat in a quiet booth that overlooked a sweeping view of Biscayne Bay. David was dressed in a nice double-breasted suit that did wonders for the muscular strength of his body, and Jazz wore jeans and her Woodstock '69 jean jacket. She was growing on David, because she was not only looking beautiful to him but sexy as well. Something he would have never thought possible when he first laid eyes on her.

"All right now," he said and folded his arms after their finished plates were removed, "let's have it."

Jazz smiled. "Have what?"

"The law that you've been itching to lay down for me. So lay it on me, girl."

"You're a drama king, you know that?"

"So you have no rules for this relationship?"

"We're friends. That's what we both agreed we'd be."

"Right."

"So that's the rule of the relationship. We remain friends."

"Even if it goes in a different direction?"

Jazz laughed. "I doubt if that'll happen."

"Oh, I see. So I'm not good enough for you, is that what you mean, Jazz?"

"Of course that's not what I mean! You've been . . . you've been perfect, David."

"But?"

"But nothing."

"So you agree we won't put any artificial constraints on our time together? We'll take it as it comes?"

Jazz exhaled and looked at him. "Sure," she said, knowing full well that it wasn't going anywhere beyond a friendship, so there would be nothing to take.

"Good," David replied, knowing full well that before the month was out, Jazz Walker, for all of her protective walls and denials, would be curled up in his bed like a clawing cat in heat.

HEARTACHE

The drizzling rain blew all over the Miami skyline and Thomas stood at his office window staring at the sweep. For all of his enchantment, it was just a rainy day, nothing special at all, and although it consumed his sight, his mind was far from it.

Jazz was on his mind. Always on his mind. Even that same night when Alex reentered his life, armed with that aggressive lovemaking style of hers that used to turn him on but now, after sleeping with Jazz, barely gave him a rise, he couldn't stop thinking about Jazz. And comparing Alex to her. Whereas Alex was young and vibrant and eager to please, Jazz was older and steady and smart and funny and would not let him get away with a damn thing. He was fond of Alex, but he respected Jazz and loved her with a love as deep as his soul, and just the sight of her still filled him with the kind of passion that made his heart want to leap from his chest. The way she pushed her glasses up on her face, the way her eyes drooped into a lazy sexiness that made him want to pull her in his arms, the way she bit her lip whenever something troubled her, the way he couldn't stop cursing himself for not claiming that woman as his own seven years ago, when they first met, when they first made that awful, ill-fated decision to just be friends.

Friendship be damned, he thought angrily.

He leaned down from his six-two frame and picked up his desk telephone. He wanted to hear that husky voice of hers again, even though he'd already called her this morning when he first arrived at work, unceremoniously waking her up, but she was nice about it. She was always nice lately. That was what was bothering him. She was polite and nice and treated him as if he were some distant acquaintance of hers in whom she had no emotional stock whatsoever. And they'd talk on the phone, see each other only occasionally, and even there it was only when he couldn't bear it any longer and would go out to her loft or over to the station, just to see her pretty face again, but still the contact was very superficial. He dialed her numbers and leaned back in his desk chair. Their night of passion seemed to have done exactly what they feared it would do, he thought. Sadly, it had drawn them apart.

"This is Jazz Walker," she said lively into the phone after the receptionist at the station dispatched his call through. His heart dropped.

"Hey," he said, attempting to match her elation.

"Hi," she responded, her voice far less excited now, which infuriated him. She was super-upbeat when she thought he was just another one of her listeners, but as soon as she realized it was him, her best friend after all, she became subdued.

"Sorry to disappoint you," he said sadly.

"No, you didn't. I was just . . . So, what's up?"

"I just called to see how you were doing."

"Oh," she said, as if that was the most surprising thing in the world, that he would be concerned about how she was doing, which infuriated him even more. "I'm doing good," she added.

He didn't know what else to say. He still couldn't get over how let down she sounded when she realized it was him.

The door to his office flew open and further distracted him as Alex came sailing in gaily, saying "Good morning!" with such cheerfulness that he wondered if she had lost her mind. His secretary came sailing in right behind her. Only her expression was nothing short of flustered.

"I'm sorry, Mr. Drayton, but I told her you were on the phone."

"It's all right," he said to his secretary.

"What's that?" Jazz asked on the phone.

"No, I was talking to Pamela," he said into the phone as his secretary looked angrily one more time at Alex and then left the room.

"What's all right?" Jazz asked.

"Just something, nothing, just something related to work," he lied. He didn't know why he lied. He didn't know why he wasn't ready to let Jazz know that he was back with Alex.

"Anyway," Jazz said, "I'd better get back to work. Time is money you know. Talk to you later. Bye."

And she hung up. Just like that. Thomas kept the phone on his ear a moment longer, as if expecting her to pick back up and apologize for hanging up so abruptly, but he knew better than that. The new Jazz might have been nice now. But she was still nobody's patsy. He hung up, too.

Alex stood in the middle of the office smiling greatly, and her outfit, a hot-pink, apple-red, eggshell-white pantsuit that reminded him of a peacock, gave an almost eerily bright, glowing highlight to her face. This was his woman now. This lit-up, neon light of a woman-child standing before him was now his woman. And watching her, especially after his conversation with Jazz, which didn't help his dark mood at all, made him wonder why. Why her? Why now? He was pushing forty, and he was absolutely tired of starting over, he understood that much. But was he *this* far gone?

"Good morning," she said again, cheerfully again, and clasped her hands together as if awaiting with bated breath his response.

"Good morning," he said to Alex in the same tone Jazz had used on him, but with even less enthusiasm. "I told you about disrespecting Pamela, Alex."

"She's horrible. She just sits at that desk like she's lording it over somebody. She wouldn't even let me come see you. All I wanted to do was say hello to my man—"

He hated it when she referred to him that way. "I told you not to come on my job with our personal business. I told you that, Alex. Now that I will not tolerate."

"And I know that, Thomas," Alex said and quickly began moving toward him. She could tell he was in one of his bad moods, which she always feared because it made her position in his life far more precarious, so she knew she had to tread carefully. "You made that absolutely clear to me. I never say anything to anybody around here about us. I wouldn't dare. Especially not to these big mouths around here, are you kidding?"

Thomas couldn't help but smile. Perfect, Alex thought as she ran her hand through his soft hair and leaned her hip against his chair. "So," she said. "How are you this wonderful morning?"

"What's so wonderful about it?"

"You're in it."

Thomas was about to make yet another snide remark, but he caught what Alex had said and stopped himself. He looked at her. She smiled so grandly that she almost reminded him of Paula. Could she be as fragile as Paula? God, he thought, he hoped not. "Thank you," he said.

"You're welcome. Who were you talking to?"

He hesitated. "Jazz," he said.

Alex hesitated, too. Jazz was now the elephant in the room of their relationship. She'd had Thomas sexually. She was now Alex's undeniable enemy. "I see," she said. "What were y'all talking about?"

"Nothing. She's at work."

"Ah, yes. *Ask Sister J.* The advice maven. I hear she's practicing what she's preaching now."

"What's that?"

"I say it's about time, too."

"What's about time?"

"I hope it works out for her though."

"Alex, what are you talking about?"

"I'm talking about Jazz. Nikki tells me she's been seeing her around town with some dude. And I think that's a good thing. Maybe she'll finally understand that all of her advice is so unrealistic when emotions are involved. 'Leave him,' that's what she loves to say every time I listen to her program. Like leaving is as simple as picking up a bag and going. Maybe now this dude will teach her a few lessons of her own. And maybe now she'll understand that it's never simple when emotions are involved."

"What dude?" Thomas asked, knowing that he was risking exposure but not caring. He had to know what Alex was talking about.

"Some dude," Alex said and, realizing Thomas's interest, suddenly bounded up onto his lap, forcing him to catch her and embrace her. "Kiss me."

"Alex."

She began planting small kisses all over his face, the whiskers from his day-old beard turning her on. "You didn't shave this morning."

"Alex!"

"What?"

"What dude?"

Alex looked at him. "What difference does it make, Thomas?"

"It doesn't make any difference, but you're the one who brought it up."

"All I said was that Nikki's been seeing her with a guy, that's all."

"Does she know this guy?"

"Now come on, Thomas. Nikki and Jazz Walker don't exactly run with the same crowd."

"Did she describe him?"

"Not really. Just that he was good looking."

Thomas's heart dropped. "Good looking?"

"Very, very good looking. Nikki said he was one of those body-builder types, somebody like that. But who cares? Kiss me, dammit!"

Alex began kissing on Thomas again, and he was holding his face back and allowing it, but he was responding only as he would toward a favorite pet licking on him, rather than how he should respond when his woman was all but begging him to take her. He wasn't thinking about taking Alex. Jazz was on his mind. And this new dude in her life. Maybe it was just a passing thing, like the Strokes and Mark Hartmanns of this world, but maybe it wasn't. Jazz was free now. Totally free. And maybe, just maybe, she was ready to get on with her life. Without him. With the body builder now. Just the thought chilled Thomas. And he politely, but firmly, told Alex to knock it off.

It was intermission at the much-hyped gospel play *Centuries* and Thomas and Alex hovered around in the theater's lobby with a who's who among the black upper class who also felt it their civic duty to support such ventures. Thomas leaned against one of the round, colorful posts and placed his hands in his pants pocket. He was dressed conservatively in a blue Hugo Boss suit, and Alex, who stood beside him as if she were an attachment, was toned down, too, in a beautiful sleek black, knee-length dress he personally purchased for her for the occasion. Alex wasn't crazy about the dress—it didn't show enough skin for her taste—and the idea of wearing just black didn't turn her on either. But it was the first and, so far, only thing Thomas had ever given her, and she cherished it. He was beginning to fall in love with her, she believed, and she relished in the thought that soon and very soon, if she continued to play her cards exactly right, and if David did his part, too, which, at any moment, she was about to find out just how well he was doing that part, then she'd be walking down the aisle ready to take her place as the first and, hopefully, last Mrs. Thomas Drayton.

"I don't believe it," Alex quipped and touched Thomas's coat sleeve.

Thomas, who was bored to tears by the play itself, too much drama for him, and had welcomed intermission, looked at Alex smilingly. "Yes, love," he said.

"Look who's here, Thomas."

He followed her eyes to a couple directly across the room and he couldn't believe it either. It was Jazz, with a man on her arms, and they stood in the middle of the lobby as if they were posing for the next edition of *Vanity Fair.* Especially Jazz, he thought, who had done the unthinkable. Her hair wasn't natural anymore but permed and curled now and flowing all over her sexy little head in a beautiful winding bob. And she wasn't in jeans tonight but a rich, white, beaded dress with singular hem shrills that touched at the knees and made for perfect viewing of her wondrously shapely legs. She looked beyond perfection, Thomas thought. Nobody could look more radiant. And she was on another man's arm.

"Finally they look this way," Alex said as she began smiling and waving them over. Thomas stood erect, his heart racing faster with every step that brought Jazz closer to him. Her dress was sheer and seemed to hug around her thighs as she walked, causing a burning sensation deep within Thomas as he watched her. And her walk was so graceful now, so swan-like, that he wanted to grab her and hold her and beg her to stop torturing him like this.

"Well, good evening," Alex said smilingly as the couple made their way in front of them.

"Hello, Alex," Jazz said warmly but with her characteristic cool. Then she looked at Thomas. And it was only then that he realized she wore no eyeglasses, but contacts, beautiful brown contacts within her beautiful droopy eyes. His breath caught. "Thomas," she said.

"Hello, Jazz," he said stiffly composed as he leaned over to kiss her. She immediately turned a cheek to him, which caused his jaw muscles to tighten in anger, but he obliged her, giving her as austere a kiss as he could possibly muster. But not before he placed his hand on her soft, thin, bare arm and held it there even after his kiss was complete. She smelled of fresh soap and a kind of sweet, endearing perfume, one he'd never smelled on her before. Nothing about her, in fact, was the same. "What brings you out here tonight?" he asked her, as it took every ounce of courage he had to smile.

That smile, Jazz thought, as she tried to conjure up one herself. Her heart still melted from just the sight of his smile. He'd undoubtedly won over countless women with that smile. Women like Carmella. Like Alex. She didn't even know he was back with Alex. But she wasn't surprised. Given Thomas's libido, he probably ran back to Alex the same night they decided to call it quits. But she was disappointed. Still making the biggest mistake of his life, she felt. But what could she do? "David's the reason," she said in answer to Thomas's question, and just saying David's name actually helped to calm her down. "He likes these sort of things. This is David, incidentally. David Murray. David, this is my friend Thomas Drayton, and his friend Alex Mailer."

Alex wanted to say "that's *girlfriend* to you," but she didn't. She knew better now. The last time she even deigned to say something negative to Jazz, Thomas did not hesitate to kick her out of his life. So she bit her tongue and said nothing. After the marriage she'd talk. After her last name was Drayton, too, she'd have her say.

David smiled and shook hands with both Thomas and Alex, careful not to do or say anything to make it appear even remotely that he and Alex were acquainted. Especially in the way that they were acquainted.

"Wait a minute," David said, looking at Thomas. "You wouldn't happen to be THE Thomas Drayton? The attorney?"

Thomas studied the handsome young man carefully. And he was young, Thomas decided; he could not have been a day over twenty-five. And when Alex said Nikki described him as a good-looking, body-builder type, she wasn't exaggerating. "Yes," Thomas said after a moment. "I'm guilty."

David laughed. "No way, man. I'm impressed. So many marriages end in divorce, as I'm sure you know. You've chosen a lucrative trade. I had the law school option myself, among others, but it wasn't for me. Too seamy for my taste."

Thomas had a sense that he'd just been bitch-slapped, but he didn't respond in kind. The young man was obviously trying to impress Jazz. And trying to tear down any man who had so much as a passing interest in her.

"How do you guys like the play so far?" Alex asked. "I love it."

"It's great," David said. "True to life."

"Jazz, what about you?" Alex asked, and Thomas looked at her.

"It's okay," Jazz replied. In truth, she hated it. True to life my foot, she wanted to say.

"Thomas doesn't like it either," Alex pointed out. "He's bored."

"Bored?" David responded. "Are you kidding me? That crackhead character alone is worth the price of admission. What don't you like about the play, Mr. Drayton?"

Thomas could do without the Mister part, he thought, as David's subtle little insults were beginning to agitate the hell out of him. "I guess I just didn't get into it," Thomas said in an almost dismissive tone. "But Alex is enjoying it so that's good enough for me."

Alex smiled greatly and snuggled her arm even tighter around Thomas's. Jazz looked away.

"I'm enjoying it, too," David said. "I love plays."

"Did you see the way that fat one sang that song?" Alex asked him.

"Lord, yes," he replied. "I almost broke down and cried. And I'm a man." He said this and looked at Thomas. "No doubt about that."

He and Alex laughed. Jazz smiled mildly. Thomas rolled his eyes.

"And what about when your boy tried to con his way back into that woman's life?" David asked Alex, glad to know he was riling the big man. "I was so glad when she didn't fall for that game."

"I know. That was one of the best parts. And that poor crackhead!"

And on and on it went. David and Alex played goo-goo eyes over a play both Thomas and Jazz thought was a cross between over-the-top melodrama and pure nonsense. Jazz, however, listened intensely to the back and forth anyway, as if trying to determine if maybe she had simply missed the point of the thing, but Thomas couldn't take his eyes off of Jazz. She didn't appear happy to him, she rarely appeared happy to him, but there was a contentment about her. A warm, almost comforting contentment. He always admired the way Jazz could make a decision and stick with it, no matter what, no matter if the pain was more than the change of mind, no matter what her true feelings on the issue really were. They were friends, and that was the bottom line. No room for maneuverability. Because as soon as they tried to become more than friends, the first sign of upheaval had her running back for the cave, for shelter, for the solid ground of yet another inflexible position. She even told him once that life wasn't supposed to be flexible, not because she was rigid but because she was experienced, and because the only thing flexibility ever got her was a bad back.

He remembered laughing heartily at her little joke then. He never could have imagined how serious she really was.

The two-minute warning was issued and patrons began heading back into the theater.

"We'd better get back," Jazz said to David, thrilled to finally end the endless dribble about the play that was coming out of their mouths. You'd think they were attending Shakespeare, the way they went on. But they were also very anxious to see the second half and Jazz therefore got no argument from David.

"You're right, *babe*," David said to Jazz as he placed her arm over his, "we certainly don't want to miss the rest of it."

That four-letter word, babe, stuck like a chicken bone in Thomas's throat. The idea that such an upstart little punk like that would be calling Jazz babe, as if she was indeed his babe, as if she was *his,* made Thomas's blood boil. If she belonged to anybody, he wanted to tell the boy, she belonged to him. But he'd sound like a fool. David was the one *with* Jazz after all. David was the one going back into the theater *with* Jazz. David was the one who would soon be going home *with* Jazz, inviting himself in for a nightcap and then relaxing on her sofa and, who knows, relaxing someplace else. Not Thomas by a long stretch. David.

"We'd better get back, too, Thomas," Alex said to him.

"You go on in," he replied. "I'll be there."

"You okay?"

"I'm fine. Go on in."

Alex stared at Thomas a moment longer but she knew, when he was in one of his moods, that she was better served just doing what he said and not questioning him. So she headed for the theater, too. Jazz, however, heard their little exchange and looked back at Thomas just as he was turning away, an oddly dejected look on his face, as he quickly made his way out of the lobby doors.

Thomas did make it back into the theater, but only near the very end, and even then he was angry with himself for not showing up *at* the very end, as he had intended to do. When the play did finally end, Alex, as expected, was disappointed to see it go and she was on her feet, along with almost everybody else in the theater, giving the cast a rousing ovation.

Thomas tried mightily to search out Jazz, wanting desperately to brand her with his kiss before she left with that clown, but the crowd was too massive and moved too slowly for him to adequately search her out. Alex noticed what he was trying to do—he wasn't exactly trying to hide it—but she and David had already discussed the evening's end. His job was to usher Jazz away from there as fast as he could. And he had. Thomas would, they hoped, finally come to terms with what was obvious all night: his precious Jazz, the woman who was the only real obstacle now to Alex's future, was no longer his.

Thomas, however, wasn't ready to come to terms with anything yet, as he was so disappointed that he barely said two words to Alex during the entire drive home. She even offered to come over to his house, to "relax" him a little, but he turned her down cold. He was tired, he said, and was going straight to bed. But by the time he had dropped Alex off at her place, and kissed her good night, he knew he wasn't about to get any rest until he had a talk with Jazz. He headed, not home, but for Homestead. He was not about to allow Jazz to sleep with some body-builder muscle man who would only use her in the end. Jazz may hate him for his intrusion, and would certainly find him overbearing again, but he didn't care. On this, he decided, he was putting his foot down.

Jazz, however, wasn't too thrilled with that foot. She slung open the door of her loft with a look of pure befuddlement on her face. "What are you doing here?" she asked him, unable to shield her annoyance.

Thomas, however, was looking beyond her. For David.

"May I come in?"

"What do you want, Thomas?"

Thomas looked at her. "You aren't going to invite me in?"

"What do you want?"

"I saw his car downstairs."

Jazz hesitated. Then frowned. "Whose car?"

"Muscle man. Body builder. The Corvette."

"And?"

"So where is he? We're all adults here. He doesn't have to hide from me."

Jazz could not believe her ears. She stared at him intensely. Who was this man, she wondered. Certainly not Thomas! She was so concerned, in fact, that she stepped out of her home and closed her front door, leaving David, who was in the kitchen making himself some coffee, safely inside.

"You don't have to protect him, Jazz."

"Protect him? Thomas, what are you doing?"

"What do you think I'm doing? Who is this David anyway? We don't know anything about him. He could be an ax murderer for all we know, yet you invite him into your home!"

"It's my home. And he's not an ax murderer."

"Are you sure?"

"An ax murderer, Thomas? Surely you can be more original than that. Now he may be a chainsaw murderer, now he may be that. Or a screwdriver murderer. Yeah, something original. He is a handyman, after all. Maybe he'll take one of his screwdrivers and screw my eyes out."

Thomas didn't see that line coming, and it threw him. He stared angrily at her. "He might," he said with clenched teeth.

Jazz hated that she was hurting Thomas, but he should have known better than to come at her this way. "So what difference does it make, Thomas?" she asked him. "Either way I'm screwed."

Thomas looked into her eyes. Was she giving up now? Was she ready to settle for a toy boy like David just to prove she didn't give a damn anymore? Was it Thomas's fault? Had he done this to her? "I don't believe I'm having this conversation with you," he decided to say, a sense of guilt and unexplained moroseness weighing heavily on him.

"You don't believe it? Well I don't believe you would even come here with this nonsense! Who I date is my business, Thomas, I told you that."

"Even a screwdriver murderer?"

"Yes! It's my life, my decision, my business."

"I just don't want to come here in the morning and find your eyeballs hanging off your face."

Jazz laughed before she could stop herself and shook her head. Even Thomas had to smile at that one. "You're crazy, Thomas," she said. "You know that, don't you?"

"I've been told," he replied, his wonderful smile warming her back over to his side. But there was no clever followup, as the pain of her earlier words still stung him, and then the conversation died.

Thomas placed his hands in his pockets and Jazz folded her arms. The cool night air was cutting through their clothing, but neither seemed ready to say good night and leave. Especially Thomas, who couldn't get over how fidgety he felt.

"Well," Jazz finally said. "I'd better get back inside."

Thomas tried to smile again. He failed. "You aren't going to invite me in?"

"I don't think that would be a good idea."

"Because of David?"

"David has nothing to do with this, Thomas. I don't know why you keep acting as if you don't understand that."

Thomas stared at Jazz, as her beautiful hair glistened in the night, and his soul shook with the thought that some other joker would be the first to feel the warmth of the softness there. Her hair was always soft, even in its natural Afro style, and he could only imagine what it felt like now. But of course David would soon find out, Thomas was certain of it, if he hadn't already. "Don't let him sweet-talk you, Jazz," he said to her.

Jazz looked his way, ready to pounce. How dare he say such a thing to her? she was gearing up to respond. But when she actually looked at him, when her angry eyes looked deep into his, her heart dropped. To her shock and equal amazement, his very expressive, wondrously caring eyes appeared just an exhale away from watering up. Just the thought of Thomas breaking down on her, something he'd never, not ever, done, forced her to grab hold of the rail. And to acquiesce. "I won't," she said to him.

"He'll try."

"Understood."

"Just don't let him."

Jazz said nothing. What could she say?

"And . . ." Thomas said this but didn't finish. Jazz stared at him, her look a combination of pity and pain.

"And what?" she asked him.

Thomas looked at her. And exhaled. "Make him wear protection."

Any other time, any other moment, and Jazz would have been all over Thomas. She may have even gotten defiant and told him something really good, but she couldn't bring herself to do it. Not this time. Not at this moment. Not when Thomas didn't even look like himself anymore. "Okay," was all she could manage to say.

Thomas nodded, as if he was suddenly admitting defeat, then he moved up to her, to kiss her, but just his overwhelming presence caused her to take a step backwards. Thomas, however, took another step forward, overwhelming her once again. And when he leaned down to kiss her, he wasn't about to accept a cheek. She knew it, too, and didn't quarrel; how could she when she looked into those sad eyes of his? And when his lips met hers, and she quivered the way he loved it, he fought every urge to pull her into his arms. He simply placed his hands in hers, their fingers intertwining, as he kissed her, as his lips probed around and around hers begging her to open up. She wanted to. She always wanted to. But she wouldn't do it. She couldn't. It would only make it worst.

Thomas understood. That was why he didn't force it. That was why his probing eased up, his frustration only making him even more hungry for her, and he opened his eyes.

She opened hers, too, and, stunning, but not surprising, there was water in his. She felt burdened by the sight, scared; she'd never seen Thomas quite like this. And she moved to get away. But he wouldn't let go of her hand.

"Good night, Thomas," she said, pulling away once again. But again he would not release his grasp. She looked down at his hand, so firm and warm and strong, so everything she needed and didn't need in her life. And then she looked up at him. "Where's Alex?" she asked him.

He exhaled. Sometimes he felt as if life was mocking him. And he was tired of it. But what could he do?

He let her go.

CHOICES AND CURVES

Less than a month later and it was Alex's twenty-eighth birthday party. Nikki, of course, was there, being the sweet little sister-hostess as she brought the guests drinks and laughed at the jokes and made sure the music kept the party lively. Jazz and David were also there, reluctantly on Jazz's part, but David pretended to be too thrilled when they got the invitation for Jazz to turn it down.

Alex, however, wasn't thrilled with David. After all this time he still hadn't managed to seal the deal of his relationship with Jazz by getting her in the bedroom, but he kept assuring Alex that it was just a matter of time. She was frigid, he said, not the kind of woman who jumped in bed with just anybody, but Alex wasn't impressed. She wanted no curveballs at this delicate stage, no change of heart by Jazz Walker, and a sexual affair with David, she felt, would ensure that hope. But time was on her side. Thomas was warming to her nicely and Theophilus was showing no signs whatsoever of stopping her cash flow, so she kept supplying David with whatever he needed, kept dividing her time between the very eager Theophilus and the mildly eager Thomas, and kept her fingers crossed.

Thomas was also in attendance, having bankrolled the little get-together when Nikki phoned him and told him that such a party would be a nice gesture for Alex. So they invited twenty or so of Alex's closest friends, including Jazz and David, at Alex's urging, and pulled it all together. And it worked, as everybody appeared to be having fun. Including Jazz, Thomas was quick to point out, who danced with David most of the night and seemed to be actually happy. Thomas sat back in the chair in Alex's living room and watched Jazz nearly all night. He couldn't get over the happiness he saw in her eyes, as if she had come to terms with life and told it to just leave her alone, she was having too much fun. And, oddly enough, it did.

Although jealousy had been stalking him like a bear lately, rearing its ugly head every time he so much as thought of Jazz with another man, he was nonetheless glad to see her happy. Her happiness alone put it all in perspective for him. Because if it wasn't clear to him before, it was clear to him now that Jazz was right, and whatever they thought they had wasn't what she needed. David was giving her what she needed. David was. The young man who was turning out to be all right. The young man who managed to do in one short month what Thomas couldn't do in seven years. He put a lasting smile on Jazz's face. Talk about a painful realization. Talk about a humiliating consolation. But it was the truth.

"Enjoying yourself, darling?" Alex came up beside his chair and asked him.

Thomas smiled, moved the glass of wine into the hand that also held his cigarette, and placed his arm around her waist. "I should be the one asking you that question."

"Oh, Thomas, are you kidding? This is wonderful. I just love it."

"Nikki thought you would."

"Oh, you guys did a wonderful job. I feel so blessed. Nobody has ever been this nice to me before. Thank you." She said this and threw her arms around his neck.

"You're welcome," Thomas said, and he meant it. This was his woman now. Alex. Not the one dancing across the room. Not the one laughing coquettishly as David whispered something in her ear. She made her choice. And Alex's warmth and kindness and endearing gratitude were making Thomas's infinitely easier, too.

Even at the end of the evening, when Jazz made a point of coming over to Thomas's chair and bending down and kissing him good night on the cheek, before he could even rise to his feet and wish her farewell, he knew he was dealing with another man's woman now. And when he did manage to sit his drink on the table and rise to his feet, he felt big and bulky and old around the exuberantly youthful Jazz and David, as if they'd found the answer to the mystery of life while he was still asking questions. He felt awkward, unsure of himself. For the first time ever, he felt inadequate.

"You didn't have to get up, Thomas," Jazz said politely.

He wished he hadn't. "Just want to see you to the door," he said as he escorted Jazz and her date—her *date*, he thought—to the front door.

Jazz brushed past him as they made their way out of Alex's front door, and Thomas wanted to grab her by the arm again, the same way he did that night he first saw her with David, and look her squarely in the eyes just to make sure that the happiness he thought he was seeing from across the room was really what it appeared to be. But David was right behind her, with his hand on the small of her back as if asserting some possessive, macho stance, and Thomas let it slide. He still had her friendship at least. It wasn't as strong as it used to be, not nearly, but at least again, as Jazz loved to say, they didn't hate each other.

When the last of the guests was gone and Nikki had, as was her way, excused herself to her room to catch up on her school work, Thomas dropped down on the sofa, leaned back, his legs stretched out across the floor and crossed at the ankles, and he watched Alex work.

She had the place looking great in no time, he thought, as she continually declined his request to help her, and by the time she plopped down on the sofa next to him, he understood why. She loved impressing him, doing what she could to make him proud of her, going that extra mile to make him comfortable even when she was dead on her feet. Like most women he'd had in his life, she was anxious to please him, but it went even further with Alex. She was desperate to please him, as if he was the answer to her prayers and she would stop at nothing to get him to understand that. He understood it.

He looked at her. She immediately smiled at him. "You okay?" he asked.

"Oh, yes. I'm more than okay. I'm happy."

Thomas's heart tightened. He would move mountains before he hurt her. "The house looks lovely, Alex."

"Thank you."

"It always does. You work so hard and always do a wonderful job."

Alex held her hand to her chest. "Gosh, Thomas. You're making me blush."

"Come here," Thomas said huskily and Alex, knowing that tone of voice very well, moved closer to him. He wrapped his arm around her waist. "Alex?"

"You smell good," she said. "Did you know you always smell so good?"

"You don't smell bad yourself," he said with a smile. "Now listen to me."

"Yes, sir," Alex said playfully and looked up into his eyes.

Thomas swallowed hard. "I've been thinking a lot about our relationship," he said.

Alex's heart almost skipped a beat. "You have?"

"Yes. I have." Thomas paused. "I'm not the easiest man to get along with, Alex. I'm moody, I'm bossy, I'm everything probably a husband should not be. But I care a great deal about you. I think you're a wonderful woman with a big heart." He placed his hand on the side of her face. "And I would love for you to be my wife."

Alex's heart did skip a beat. "You would?"

Thomas nodded. Then he reached into his coat pocket and pulled out a small case. "Alex," he said, and she immediately became so overcome with genuine emotion that she buried her face in her hands. Never had it gotten this far. Never had one of those men she'd been with, not one of those numerous men who so gladly graced her bed, ever deemed her worthy of this.

"Oh, God!" she yelled, and then looked back up at Thomas. Wonderful Thomas. The best man she'd ever known. And her hands began shaking uncontrollably and tears filled her eyes.

"Alex," he said again, touched by her incredible excitement, "will you marry me?"

Alex leaped from her seat and jumped into his arms, her face rubbing against his as if she had to feel him to believe he was real. "Yes!" she yelled. "Yes, I'll marry you! I'll be honored to marry you! Of course I will, darling. Of course I will!"

She kissed all over Thomas's face, in a kind of nervous elation, and Thomas had to smother his lips over hers just to calm her down. She groaned her approval as he kissed her, her mind filled with the wonderful possibilities of what being Mrs. Thomas Drayton truly meant. She couldn't wait to see the ring. She couldn't wait to see how big and expensive and gorgeous she just knew it was. But she would wait until he revealed it to her. She would not let him see, not for a moment, what she was really after. "I'll make you so happy, Thomas," she leaned back and said. "I promise you I will. You're perfect. You're exactly who I want. I love you so much!"

She fell into his arms again. And Thomas held her as tightly as she held on to him. He would not lie to her. He would not tell her that he loved her, too, that she was exactly who he wanted, that she was his perfect ending. He cared about her, deeply, and that would have to be enough. Because he was getting too old to keep starting new relationships only to end them a few months later when Jazz once again consumed his thoughts. It was Alex who proved herself to be stronger than all the others. She could tolerate Jazz. She understood the depth of his feelings for Jazz and didn't question it. He loved that about her. And he had slept with Alex, something he never took lightly. She had willingly given her body to him, her mind, her soul, her everything. Asking for nothing. Not ever. And he showed no mercy, he took from her and took from her. And now, finally, it was she who deserved something special in return.

Jazz, after all, was spoken for.

The woman of his dreams was now somebody else's perfection.

He didn't see where he had a choice.

The morning after Thomas was knocking on Jazz's front door.

"Come in!" Jazz yelled from the studio. She had already looked out the window and saw Thomas's Bentley. She had already braced herself for yet another one of his powerful appearances in her life. They were getting rarer lately—he didn't drop by practically every day the way he used to—but when he came he still had the same debilitating effect on her and her now-racing heart.

She was standing at her easel painting, wearing her beloved work jumper, her beautiful, curly hair concealed by an African-styled head wrap. To Thomas's delight, she was wearing her glasses again.

"Good morning," he said as he leaned against the doorjamb of the studio.

She looked at him, looking fresh and gorgeous in a blue warm-up suit, and she gripped her brush tighter to discourage him from walking farther into the room and requesting their customary hello kiss. Looking at him now, and the way he looked last night, made her question if she could handle just a simple kiss from him. "Good morning."

"Working hard I see."

"Yeah. I woke up with an inspiration."

"I see that." He pushed his large frame from the doorjamb and walked slowly toward Jazz, studying her and her painting as he moved. "What is it?" he asked her.

"A cool day."

Thomas nodded. Then smiled. "A cool day, eh? I see." Then he shook his head. "How in the world do you paint a cool day?"

"Very carefully, I'll tell you that," Jazz said, and they both laughed.

Thomas ended up standing just behind Jazz, so close that she could feel his cool breath blowing gently against her neck.

"I don't know, to tell you the truth," Jazz said, as she stroked lines on her painting, not daring to so much as turn toward Thomas. "I'm using soothing colors and quiet lines and eventually, hopefully, a day will burst through."

"A cool day."

"Right."

Thomas nodded and, before he realized what he was doing, he moved closer to Jazz, his chest touching the top back of her shoulders. Oddly, Jazz didn't move away as he had expected but actually leaned back against him. Thomas welcomed the contact but sighed anyway. It was far too late now.

"Well, I hope a day does burst through for you, Jazz," he said.

"I hope so, too," she said, but her instincts told her it was not a casual comment she was responding to. She paused. "What's wrong, Thomas?" she asked.

Thomas exhaled. How could she know, he wondered. "Nothing's wrong."

"No?" Jazz said this as she dabbed more yellows onto the canvas.

"No. I just came by to tell you the good news."

Jazz smiled. "Oh," she said, still painting, still avoiding any eye contact with him. "I can always use some good news. What's up?"

Thomas paused. "I proposed to Alex last night."

Jazz almost smeared paint on the canvas. Her hands went numb. Her breathing became so unregulated that she wondered if she would faint. This should not be news to her. She should have seen it coming. Thomas was no monk; he had to have a woman in his life. And he told her long ago that he wasn't starting over again.

She sat down her paint supplies and she closed her eyes before gathering all the forces within her to put on a grand smile. Then she turned and faced her friend. When she looked into his eyes, eyes that weren't happy or excited but almost expressionless, her heart pounded against her chest and, although she'd never know it, so did his.

"Well now," she said, trying her best to maintain her calm, "that's certainly news."

"Yes, it is."

"And she accepted, I take it?"

Thomas nodded. "She accepted."

Jazz's eyes fluttered nervously, a reaction Thomas had never seen in her before. "Have you guys set a date yet?"

"Alex says she can pull it all together in a month or so. We'll make the official announcement this coming Friday. At a big dinner party at my place."

"Oh, okay."

"Alex very much wants you to be there."

"I'm sure she does."

"And so do I."

Jazz nodded and began looking around the room, as if she'd forgotten something. But clearly she hadn't. She remembered all too well. She looked at Thomas. "I'm so happy for you, Thomas," she said.

"I'm happy for you, too," he said. "You and David. He seems like a good guy."

"Yes, he's been very nice."

"Good."

"And Alex, she . . . she seems to love you very much. I hope so anyway."

"Thank you," Thomas said, and then they both found themselves just standing there. Although they were singing the praises of happiness, although they were congratulating each other endlessly on their supposedly perfect mates, when the words stopped coming they both appeared to be in a state of suspended disbelief. It seemed so final now, so complete, but neither one of them seemed ready for it. They suddenly didn't know what to do, or say, or feel. Yes, they did know what to feel, they just didn't want to deal with what they were feeling, and almost simultaneously, as if they had been programmed that way, they both looked away.

It was their weekly brunch at Denny's and Alex hurried in, smiling from ear to ear. Nikki rolled her eyes and prepared to hear it again. She had to hear it all last night after Thomas Drayton left, and this morning before she left for class, and she knew, given that exuberant look in her sister's eyes, that she was about to hear it again. And again. And again.

"I'm gonna be a Sadie, Nikki!" Alex said happily as she arrived at the table and plopped down. Nikki shook her head.

"Yes, you told me," Nikki said. "About two thousand times."

"Did I show you my ring?" Alex asked and tossed her hand out to give Nikki an excellent view of the beautifully rich diamond ring on her finger.

"Yes, Alex, you showed me."

"It's so heavy," Alex said and laughed. Nikki couldn't help but smile, too.

"Go to the buffet and get you something to eat," Nikki ordered, but Alex shook her head.

"I couldn't eat a thing, girl. I just left Theophilus."

"Oh, Lord," Nikki said, wiping her mouth with a napkin. "How did it go?"

"Awful. You should have heard him. Called me everything but a child of God. But I was ready for his ass."

"What you did?"

"I reminded him that he was a married man, married with children I might add, and if he even thought about getting ugly with me, I would easily pick up the telephone and give old wifey a call."

"You went there, girl?"

"Hell yeah I went there. I ain't thinking about that trifling Theophilus. He knew this was just a meal-ticket thang, wasn't nothing permanent about our relationship. And I told him I was capable of feeding myself now, thank you. And that's what really got him going."

"So it's over then?"

"Completely. Nothing's messing up my wedding plans, you hear me? Especially no cheese-eatin' joker like Theophilus."

Nikki played around with the eggs on her plate. "What about David?" she asked and then looked up at her sister.

Alex waved her hand. "David's nobody's business. He's a handyman. My personal handyman. I'll take care of him."

"So he won't get kicked to the curb?"

"Not yet, he won't. He's doing what he needs to do. You saw how tamed Jazz Walker acted at my party last night. That's because of David. He's turning out to be all right."

Nikki shook her head. "You gamble too much for me, Alex."

"What gamble? I'm handling my business, I don't call that gambling."

"You've managed to get the catch of the century. Thomas Drayton. But is that enough for my sister? No. She's got to have some musclehead handyman around. She's got to invite this muscle head and Jazz around every chance she got, as if to tempt fate. Thomas isn't stupid. What you think will happen if he finds out just how close you really are to your handyman?"

"He won't find out. I'm not telling and David certainly won't. He knows the big money is just around the corner. And besides, after I get married to Thomas, it doesn't matter anyway. I ain't about to sign no prenuptial agreement. And even if Thomas decides to kick me to the curb after we're married, I'll still be sitting pretty. So, you see, either way I've got it made."

"Too much gambling for me," Nikki said again.

"Yeah, whatever. You just eat up. We've got a lot of arrangements to make for the party Friday night. That's when we're going to make the big announcement. Nobody knows, you know, except Jazz I'm sure, so you keep it buttoned up."

"How many people are y'all planning on inviting?"

"Everybody from Thomas's firm, definitely. And a few of my friends and his friends. It won't be a small gathering, but it won't be oversized, either. The point is, everybody is going to be so surprised. Especially all those women in Thomas's firm, all those frustrated old maids who thought they would win him over some day. I can't wait to see their faces!"

"Why can't you just be happy for you? Why is it always about showing people something?"

"Because it is, Nikki. People look down on us. We ain't good enough. Well, guess who's wearing Thomas Drayton's ring? Not the high and mighties. Me. And hell yeah I'm rubbing it in." Alex smiled and began gathering up her purse. "I'm wallowing in it, too. So excuse me so I can go and freshen up. I gots to look pretty while I wallow."

Nikki laughed as Alex stood to her feet and hurried for the ladies room. Then Nikki shook her head and began eating heartily again, the idea of Alex taking such foolish chances with her happiness not making any sense at all to her. But that was Alex. Always willing to roll the dice.

"Hello again," a strong voice was heard just above Nikki's head and she looked around and smiled. It was Conrad.

"Hey there," Nikki said. "I didn't know you were in here."

"Over there," Conrad said, pointing to a booth near the window. "I was hoping Alex would leave. She doesn't seem to like me anymore."

"She's okay. But sit down. Join us."

"I can't. I'm going over notes for court. I just wanted to holler at you."

"Well, thanks for hollering."

"I also wanted to congratulate you, Nikki. I meant to do it a long time ago, but your sister kind of kept me at bay."

"Congratulate me for what?"

"Getting it together. Going back to school. I hope I'm not offending you, but you're a far cry from that young lady I got out of jail for fighting."

Nikki laughed. "The truth can't offend me. And that ain't nothing but the truth. And thanks. I feel much better about myself now."

"Good. Good for you. And if you ever find that you need some help, some tutoring, some financial assistance, whatever it is, please feel free to give me a call."

"What a nice offer. Thanks. I'm okay, but I appreciate the offer."

"Any time, Nikki. But hey, I'd better slip away before Mama Alex gets back here. But you take care now. I'll see you around."

"Sure thing, Conrad," Nikki said, and Conrad walked back to his booth.

Nikki exhaled and watched him leave. And she smiled. Conrad as tutor sounded like a plan to her.

*   *   *

Jazz was dressed and still sitting on the examining table when Dr. Cooper finally came back into the room. She really didn't like doctors, finding them on whole way too greedy and egotistical for her taste, especially when they left her waiting and waiting as if her time wasn't valuable, too. But she hadn't been feeling well lately, not well at all, and she was no fool. She was well overdo a checkup.

"You're pregnant," the doctor said as soon as he walked back into the room.

Jazz just sat there and stared at him. Her mouth was gaped open but she didn't realize it.

"Did you hear me, Miss Walker? I said you're pregnant."

Jazz continued staring at him, at his large head and small eyes, his thick mustache and flat nose. His wild Afro. And she blinked. "Come again?" she asked.

Dr. Cooper smiled. "You're pregnant, Miss Walker. That's why you haven't been feeling like yourself lately. You're going to have a baby."

"A baby?"

"Yes."

"Me?"

"Yes."

"But . . . Wait a minute. You're saying that I, that I'm . . . going to have a *child*?"

"That's exactly what I'm saying."

"Whoa, doc. Just hold on. There has got to be a mistake."

"Oh?"

"Absolutely!"

"The test wasn't ambiguous. I made sure of that. There's no mistake here."

"But you don't understand what you're telling me," Jazz said with a tinge of anger. And then she shook her head and looked up at the ceiling. And then she laughed. "This is too much," she said. "This is too much."

"It happens every day."

"Not to me it don't! But it's typical of my life. That it is. Always some curve waiting to greet good ol' Jazz." She shook her head again. "Unbelievable."

"Miss Walker?"

"If it wasn't for bad luck, doc, I wouldn't have any luck at all."

"We have counselors on staff, Miss Walker. Very good, very experienced counselors. Perhaps you'd like to talk to one. You seem to be a little shocked."

Jazz just sat there. And shocked wasn't the word. She was mortified. Stunned. Stupefied. And the timing, she thought, which dazed her even more. On the very day that Thomas had told her about his engagement to Alex, she was sitting in the doctor's office pregnant with his child. Pregnant. With *his* baby. And yes, she reminded herself, it was definitely his. Thomas was the only man to touch her in years. And although David was asking almost every day for the opportunity, she refused him every time. David was sweet, and she enjoyed his company immensely, but she just didn't see herself going down that road with him.

Ironically, Jazz had never been all that big on premarital sex. She was seventeen when she married her first husband and waited until the wedding night to indulge even then. Thomas was, in fact, her first sexual encounter outside of marriage. But such a saintly track record made her want to laugh out loud now. Because she was pregnant. And nowhere near married. And dating a man who wasn't the father of her child. And in love with a man who was the father but was about to marry somebody else.

And yes, she finally said to herself, she was in love with Thomas. Deep down, heart aching in love. She knew it for some time but refused to admit it. She'd been in love too many times before and all it got her was broken heart after broken heart. And a hatred and disgust for the man she once wanted. But when Thomas gave her the news of his engagement and left her house, leaving an emptiness inside of her she thought was going to do her in, she finally decided, her past notwithstanding, to stop hiding the truth and admit for once, as she did to herself, almost dispassionately, that yes, dammit, she was in love.

But now, this bit of news the good doctor so easily waltzed into the room and told her had changed everything. She was in love with a man she couldn't have. Dating a man she didn't want. And pregnant. She was in trouble.

"Miss Walker?" Dr. Cooper finally asked. "Miss Walker, are you all right?"

Jazz heard the doctor, but she didn't respond. Mainly because she couldn't. Mainly because all right was the last thing on earth that she could claim to be.

LEARNING TO LEAN

The party downstairs was filling up fast with guests and Thomas knew he needed to hurry. But he didn't. He sat out on the terrace off from his bedroom, fully dressed in his white tux except for the jacket that hung in his room, and sipped more wine. The sun had gone down and the night was darkening fast, and the breeze from the blue Atlantic made him hate himself for not even trying to look on the bright side. He would have never dreamed that he'd end up like this. Engaged to a woman he didn't love. Somber on the night of the big announcement. And still aching, badly, for Jazz.

But the way she looked that morning after he told her that he was marrying Alex made him know that he was doing the right thing. She was actually happy for him. She could actually manage to smile and she even seemed relieved. Unburdened by him now. Able to go on with her freedom in style.

Damn her, Thomas thought as he sipped more wine. Why couldn't he just forget about Jazz, once and for all? Why couldn't he get it through his thick skull that he was a man desperately in need of settling down, but the woman he couldn't seem to leave alone had already made it clear that she wasn't settling with him? What part of "no, you can't have her," was he not understanding? His fiancée, for Christ's sake, was waiting downstairs. Every member of his law firm showed up tonight, thinking it was just another dinner party, about to be stunned out of their pants that Thomas Drayton, after all these years, was finally jumping the broom. And he was sitting on his terrace smiling within himself at the way Jazz was always pushing her eyeglasses up on her cute little nose.

"Don't get drunk, Thomas," a soft, husky voice said behind him, and he smiled. So much for not thinking about her, he thought.

"And what would you know about that?" he asked, without turning around. "Miss Clean and Sober for six years now."

"And I owe it all to you," Jazz said as she walked from behind his chair, past him, and leaned against the rail on the terrace. "I was an alcoholic before you came along, as I'm sure you recall since you were the one collecting me from bars. I know the signs." She said this with a smile and turned and looked at him.

Thomas was about to take another sip, thought about Jazz's words, then sat the glass down on the floor beside him. "I guess you're right."

"I know I'm right. And don't worry, Thomas, it's only natural what you're feeling."

Thomas looked at her. She looked gorgeous, in an evening dress and heels no less, her hair up this time in a beautiful french roll. He wondered what power David had that would pull her out of those jeans. And he also missed the jeans. "What I'm feeling is natural?" he asked. He knew she had no idea what he was feeling, but he couldn't resist seeing if, possibly, there was some way that she, too . . .

"Yes," she said. "This is your first engagement. The first time you've come anywhere near asking a woman to marry you. And now you're about to make it public and official. You're bound to have the jitters."

"Yeah, I guess so."

"I should know, Thomas. I've been around this block a few times myself, don't you know?" Jazz said this and smiled. Thomas was annoyed by her relaxed, easy manner, but he was relieved to see it, too. For Alex's sake if nothing else. She certainly was only helping the odd situation he found himself in. So he smiled, too.

And he stood up. "Guess I should get on with it, eh?"

"I should think so."

Thomas stood there and stared at her. She was in contacts again. Looking even more gorgeous than he could have imagined possible. He began walking back into the bedroom and heading for his tuxedo jacket.

"You look spiffy," Jazz said, following him, "if I may say so myself."

"And you," Thomas said, glancing back over his shoulder. "I used to feel honored when you graced my presence in a jean jacket. Those days are gone, I see." Jazz laughed. "What's David's secret?" he added.

"David?" Jazz said, as if offended. "David has nothing to do with it. I just thought it was time to make changes in my life, that's all. Although David's been very supportive, it has nothing to do with him really."

Thomas began putting on his jacket. What, he wondered, she didn't think he'd be supportive? He loved her just the way she was. And if she felt she needed changes, then he would have supported that, too. But she sounded as if he wouldn't approve or would have battled her about it. But forget it, he said to himself as he snatched on his jacket. What difference did it make now?

Thomas went over to the mirror to make sure everything was in place, and Jazz walked up beside him. When he glanced over at her through the mirror, her look had turned decidedly somber. He turned and looked at her.

"Here," she said, pulling a cigar with a ribbon tied on it from her small clutch bag.

Thomas smiled. So typically Jazz. "A congratulatory cigar," he said. "Thank you, Jazz." Thomas said this and hugged her. She wrapped her arms around his neck and leaned into his ear. She was now near tears.

"I've got to tell you something," she whispered softly, and before he could react, his bedroom door flew open and Alex came inside.

"Thomas!" she said, and Jazz quickly released him. "Do you realize what time it is? Hello, Jazz."

"Hello, Alex," Jazz said, now able to ward off the tears.

"Why aren't you downstairs yet?"

"I was just finishing up now, Alex."

"I'd better get down myself," Jazz said, moving away from Thomas. "David is probably wondering where I got off to."

"Yes, he is," Alex said snidely as Jazz walked past. When she left the room, Alex smiled. "You look lovely, darling, but people are beginning to ask about you."

"Okay."

"I just want everything to be perfect tonight, Thomas."

"I said okay, Alex."

She knew the tone. She knew to back off. She left the room.

Thomas moved to the table next to his bed and began putting on his Rolex. He looked at the gift cigar Jazz had given him and smiled again, and then began stuffing it in his inside coat pocket. Leave it to Jazz, he thought, to come up with a gift like this. But then, as if he was having a sudden, shocking realization, a first befuddled then startled look crossed his face. She had something to tell him, she had said. And the cigar she had given him. And the tears she had tried to conceal.

He sat down.

The party was in full swing, as everybody was dancing and relaxing and having seemingly a ball, while Thomas stood back against the wall, his hands in his pockets, his head tilted back and his eyes nearly hidden from sight, as he stared at nobody else but Jazz.

She was dancing with David, as was becoming what Thomas felt was her favorite thing to do at parties, and just watching David swing Jazz around made him cringe. Jazz was laughing and enjoying the swings, but she had been near tears in his bedroom. Tears of joy for his decision to finally settle down, maybe. But somehow he doubted it.

Then another man, Thomas's senior partner, Wade Cobb, tapped David on the shoulder and took over dancing with Jazz. Thomas felt better about that move. Wade was always making the right moves. David, however, immediately went over to Alex and then began dancing with her. Oddly, Thomas didn't even care. His eyes swung back to Jazz.

"Wonderful party, Mr. Drayton," Conrad said as he walked up beside Thomas.

Thomas glanced at him then returned his gaze toward Jazz. "Where have you been keeping yourself, young man?"

Conrad smiled. "Buried in that Washington case."

"Oh yeah," Thomas said and looked at Conrad. "Wade told me about that one. One of our pro bono cases."

"That's the one. Kid accused of murdering his grandmother." How's it going?"

"Tough. The prosecution won't even plea bargain. Or when they did it was so outrageous."

"What was the proffer?"

"Twenty years."

"Is the kid guilty?"

"Yes. He admitted it to me. But he's only nineteen, sir."

"And he'll be pushing forty when he gets out. My age. It beats the hell out of the death penalty."

"I understand that. But I just . . ."

"Has he been in trouble before?"

"Yes."

"What for?"

"Oh, you name it. Robbery, burglary, assault, attempted rape, attempted murder. All as a juvie."

"Until he turned eighteen and murdered his grandmother."

Conrad hesitated. "Right."

"Why did he do it?"

"Sir?"

"Why did he kill his grandmother?"

"Oh. She was . . . it's crazy. But he said she was snoring too loud."

Thomas stared at Conrad. And his anger was a kind of controlled rage. "Has he had a psych eval?"

"Yes. He's typically antisocial, but he knew what he was doing."

"You go to your client first thing tomorrow morning and you tell that little murderer that he'd better accept the prosecution's proffer or find himself another lawyer. Do I make myself clear?"

"But I think I can get the prosecution to go a little easier if . . ." Thomas stared at Conrad. And he knew that look. "Yes, sir," he said.

"You mean well, Conrad. But he killed somebody. And he did so maliciously. He'd better be glad to get the twenty years. That's enough leniency for him."

"Point taken," Conrad said. "I'll get on it on first thing."

"Good man," Thomas said and then began looking around the room again. Jazz and Wade were no longer dancing but were talking in a corner. He kept searching the room until he saw Alex still dancing with David. She was happy, which pleased him.

Conrad, who looked at Thomas and then in the direction of Thomas's eyes, smiled. "There's Miss Alex," he said.

"Yep. There's Alex."

"Feisty, isn't she?"

Thomas nodded. Then he looked at Conrad. He should have apologized to the young man a long time ago when he knew Conrad had the hots for Alex. But Thomas just came along and took her, believing Alex, believing that they were only friends as she had proclaimed. But even Jazz warned him not to fall for that. "I'm sorry, Conrad," he said.

Conrad smiled. "About Alex and me, you mean?" he asked. "I'm not. I'm glad it didn't work out between us."

"No," Thomas said, ready to correct Conrad's misinterpretation. Thomas wasn't sorry that it hadn't worked out between them, he was sorry that he had taken Alex away from Conrad to begin with. But then he looked at Conrad. "Why are you glad about that?" he asked.

"Because of the kind of woman she's turned out to be. I never would have guessed it in a million years. She put on such a sweet little act, you know."

"Excuse me?"

"I caught her red-handed, Mr. Drayton, that's what I mean. I caught her in some sleazy motel with some young buck, kissing all over him like she was his whore."

Thomas just stared at him. "Did you?" he asked.

"I still had some feelings for her then, you know? So every now and then I'd drive by her house, just to, I don't know, just to do it. And one night I caught her leaving for her little rendezvous. I lost my appetite for her real quick after that." He said this with a laugh. "I hadn't even thought twice about the whole thing, to be honest with you, until I saw the dude here tonight."

The first chink in Thomas's otherwise expressionless armor came now, when he frowned. "He's here?" he asked.

"Yes! That's what I'm talking about. The one Alex was groping at the motel is at your party. Right over there," Conrad said and pointed in David's direction.

"Where?" Thomas asked nervously, praying that it wasn't the person it appeared to be.

"The brother over by the band," Conrad said. "Alex is dancing with him now."

It was David. Conrad, who was, in Thomas's view, the personification of integrity, was pointing out David. Jazz's David. Thomas's heart dropped.

"Thank God her sister is nothing like her," Conrad said. "You know Nikki, don't you? I guess that's why you invited them, because you had helped Nikki out. She's my date tonight. Now she's a special lady."

"Excuse me, Conrad," Thomas said seemingly absently and he walked slowly but deliberately toward David and Alex. His heart was beating faster, and his rage was on the verge of an explosion, but he knew better than to fly off the handle without all the facts first.

They didn't see him coming. They were laughing and dancing and having a big time of it when Thomas tapped lightly on David's shoulder. And David, thinking Thomas wanted to claim his woman for a dance, gladly stepped aside. But Thomas kept his eyes on him.

"May I see you in the study?" he asked him.

David at first glanced at Alex. Then he smiled at Thomas. "What's this about, Mr. D?" he asked.

Thomas didn't say anything, afraid that his anger would unleash if he spoke another word. Alex smiled. "I know what he wants," she said. "He wants to make sure you mean to do right by his best friend, isn't that it, Thomas? I don't mind. I know how much Jazz means to you. But go on with him, David. He won't hurt you. I promise."

David smiled, relieved. "If that's the case, sure, I'll be glad to talk with you about Jazz. My intentions are honorable, I can tell you that now."

Thomas and David began to move toward the study. Alex grabbed Thomas by the arm of his white jacket. Thomas looked at her hand on him, then at her.

"Need my help?" she asked, all smiles. Thomas's stare was ice cold. He was more mad than sad by her betrayal.

"No," he said, "I can handle it." Then he and David walked away.

Alex watched them leave with just a bit of trepidation. She thought she saw, just for a second, a chilling hatred on Thomas's face. But it left as quickly as it had come. And maybe it wasn't there at all. She shook her head. Why was she worrying? She had nothing to worry about. David wasn't going to tell him anything, and he certainly had no reason to suspect anything. She was just overreacting. It was just nerves. And that was why she decided to go into the kitchen to see how dinner was coming along and stop sweating every little thing. She was doggedly determined to not let anybody rain on her parade and that determination alone, she was convinced, would help her to overcome any storm clouds gathering.

"Nice room," David said, looking around.

Thomas, with arms folded, leaned against the edge of his desk, his long legs stretched out across the floor. "I want to know the full extent of your relationship with Alex," he said without hesitation.

David swallowed hard. Then tried to smile. "You mean my relationship with Jazz."

"I mean your relationship with Alex."

David hesitated. How much did he know? he wondered. "I don't know what you're talking about, Mr. Drayton."

"You've been spotted kissing her, rather passionately I might add, at a motel, David. I think you know exactly what I'm talking about."

He had a private dick following them, David thought. That had to be it. He told Alex it was possible, that a man like that was used to spying on people before he put them in his trust. But Alex insisted that it wasn't possible, that Drayton wouldn't waste his money like that. Yeah, David said to himself, sure he wouldn't.

"I still don't know what you're trying to prove here," he said, deciding to see just how badly Drayton wanted a confession. If the jig was up, he may as well get *something* out of it.

"I want the truth, that's all I want. I want to know all about your relationship with Alex and, more importantly, your intentions regarding Jazz."

David smiled. "My intentions regarding Jazz are more important to you than whether or not I've been kickin' it with your old lady? Now that's a switch."

Thomas stared at David, studying him. He was a punk. He could see it now. Had that hustler smooth all over his pathetic face. Why he didn't catch it before was a mystery to him. He could have saved Jazz an awful lot of heartache. Damn, he thought. *Jazz.*

"How long have you known Alex?"

"Let me see. We were at that gospel play, remember? At intermission. It was called *Centuries,* I believe."

"How much?"

Now he was talking, David thought. "Sorry?"

"How much, David, don't play games with me. How much will it take for you to tell me the truth and get out of Jazz's life?"

"How much cash you got around this joint?"

Thomas exhaled. He had wondered, for a brief moment, if David would continue the charade. But, as expected, his instincts were right. David was a hustler, not a gambler.

"I can write you a check," Thomas said.

"I'm sure you can. And for a lot of money. And when I go and cash that check the feds will be waiting right at the bank for me. And I get ten years for extortion. You ain't dealing with no dumbass, Drayton. How much cash you got around here?"

Thomas hesitated. "I think I can pull together a couple thousand."

"Pull together five thousand and you've got a deal."

Thomas paused. It was a lot of money but certainly not a lot to pay to get a vermin like him out of Jazz's life. He walked behind his desk, called up Henry's quarters on the intercom, and instructed him to pull five thousand out of the safe and bring it to the study. Then he lit up a cigarette, walked back around to the edge of his desk, and stared at David.

"Now let's have it," he said.

"Money first."

"Story first."

David paused. He knew he was taking a chance, that Drayton could hear the whole story and then kick him out on his ass. So he decided to compromise. He'd tell part of it. But leave the best for last, *after* the money arrived.

"I met Alex at a gas station."

"When?"

"Oh, right about the time she first started dating you. She called you her sugar daddy." He said this and looked at Thomas to see his reaction. But Thomas's expression was as unreadable as a rock's. David exhaled and continued. "And since I was without a sugar mama at the time, we sort of hooked up. Became friends, you might say."

"Lovers?"

David smiled. "Oh, yeah. Very close, personal, passionate lovers. She's not bad either. You made a good choice in wife there. She should give you many years of pleasure." If David thought his vulgarity was going to elicit anything from Thomas other than impassive listening, then he was rudely mistaken. Thomas already knew that Alex had betrayed him. Conrad's word was good enough for him on that score. It was David's intentions regarding Jazz that was fueling his interest.

"Where does Jazz come into this neat little picture?"

David shook his head. "When I get my money in my grubby little hand, I'll be more than happy to tell you." He continued, just as Thomas was about to protest. "Why wouldn't I, Drayton? I told you everything else. I exposed Alex, and she was my moneybag, not Jazz. So why wouldn't I tell you the rest?"

Thomas didn't argue with him. He just stared at him. When Henry finally arrived, the money in an envelope inside his coat, discreet as always, and when Henry looked hard at David and then left, Thomas told David to continue.

"The money first," David said.

Thomas smiled. Can't put anything past a hustler, he thought. But as he began handing the envelope to David, the door of the study opened and Jazz walked in. Both men looked at her, as both men still had their hands on the cash.

"What's going on in here?" she asked. "I saw Hank hurrying in and hurrying out. What's the matter? And what's that?" She asked this as she walked farther into the room, staring at the white envelope.

Thomas released it, and David began hurriedly counting the money stuffed inside. "Tell Jazz what you were about to tell me," Thomas instructed him.

"Tell me what?" Jazz asked with a frown. "What is it now, Thomas?" she asked suspiciously. "And what are you doing, David?"

"Getting paid," David said with a smirk on his face. "Sorry, sweetheart, it's been fun, but it was a matter of business."

Jazz hesitated. "What was a matter of business?"

"You and me. Alex was taking good care of me, so I felt I owed it to her."

"Owed what to her? What are you talking about?"

"Come on, Jazzy, you ain't that far out there. You're out there, but you ain't that far out. Alex was paying me to distract you, to keep you out of Drayton's life so she could claim her rightful place. She set it up for me to meet you at that boring gallery and all those other places I just so happened to drop by. She got me the tickets for that stupid play and she told me all about what it would take to please you. And it was all good, actually. You ain't a bad-looking lady, a little boring, but you look good. But you just wouldn't give it up in the bedroom. That was the only drawback."

Jazz stood there stunned. Talk about another blow. It almost took her to her knees. She looked at Thomas, who was about to propose marriage to a woman like that, a woman she herself tried to warn him off a long time ago. And the pain in his eyes couldn't compare to the hurt in her heart. She looked at David. "You were using me?" she said, as if it needed saying.

David exhaled. "I was taking care of business, Jazz. Didn't mean to hurt nobody. This was a matter of business for me."

She looked down at the money. "So Thomas is paying you now?"

"He wanted the truth. There's a price for truth."

Jazz smiled. "Tell me about it."

Thomas, now unable to conceal the devastation from his face, moved over to Jazz, to hold her, but she pulled her arms away.

"No!" she said angrily. "Just leave me alone, Thomas."

"Jazz, please."

"No!" she said again and this time began heading for the exit. She could barely breathe, could barely think, could barely face another heartbreaking scene again in her life. She had to get out.

Thomas watched her as she left, his heart as knotted up as hers, and then he looked at David. "I don't expect to see you anywhere near Jazz ever again," he warned.

David nodded. "You don't have to worry about me. I'm very good at moving on."

"I'm sure you are," Thomas said and then waved David away from him. David smiled, as if glad to be getting away, and hurried out of the study.

Thomas began pacing around, unsure what his next move would have to be, then he walked over to the window and looked out. Jazz's big Delta 88 had already gone, he didn't see it anywhere, and he knew she needed some time alone, to cool down, to nurse her wounds once again. He was so angry with himself, for not seeing this coming, for taking some gold digger like Alex at her word when her word was poison oak right in front of him. Jazz tried to tell him, but he didn't listen. Now he'd not only brought trouble into his own home, but he brought it right to Jazz's front door too. And she was gearing up to crawl right back into her protective cave. The wall was going up again. The mountain would be even harder to scale.

But he had to try. He gave in to Jazz too easily, too many times before, but not this time. .

He hurried out of the study and walked swiftly for his front door, ignoring the guests who still whirled around his house as if they had no clue what was really going on.

"Thomas!" he heard as soon as he opened the front door. Alex had grabbed his arm and was standing just behind him. He turned and looked at her with such a chilling glare that Alex herself took a step back.

"What?" he responded.

"What's the matter with you?"

The chill turned to ice. "Ask David," he said, removed her hand from his arm, and walked on out of the door.

The wind and the crickets competed in the silence and Jazz sat on the bottom stair outside her garage apartment with a bottle of brandy in her hand. She was barefoot and anxious to get stoned, but just the thought of her condition kept her from acting on her anxiety. Then she smiled. Barefoot and pregnant. What a sight she must be to behold.

It didn't take long for Thomas to get there, and it wasn't a surprise to her when his Bentley cruised up her graveled driveway and stopped alongside her Oldsmobile. He got out, still looking gorgeous in his white tuxedo, still looking worried and devastated by David and Alex's mess. She looked away from him. Not to mention her own mess, she thought.

Thomas just stood before her, staring, and then, without a word, removed the bottle of brandy from her hand. She started to protest, but she didn't. She smiled instead.

"I'm entitled to fall off the wagon at least once in six years," she said.

Thomas sat down beside her, setting the bottle on the ground beside him. "No, you're not," he replied.

Then she sighed. "I tried to shield it, Thomas. I tried to shield my heart from a wonderful man like you, while some joker like David

Murray drops by and tramples it anyway. But that's the story of my life, you know? Bad choices."

Thomas hesitated as he sat next to Jazz, the closeness of the stair causing them to be thigh to thigh. "How long have you known?" he asked her.

"I just found out in your study. I didn't know anything before. I didn't suspect anything."

"How long have you known about the pregnancy?"

Jazz exhaled. "Oh, that."

Thomas looked at her. "Yes, that."

Jazz smiled. "So you got that cigar reference? I thought you had lost a step, Thomas."

Thomas was deadly serious, almost painfully so. "How long, Jazz?"

"About a week ago. The morning you told me about your . . . I found out that day."

"When did you plan to mention it to me? After the announcement?"

"No! Yes! What difference did it make? It was my problem."

Thomas couldn't believe he heard that. "Your problem?"

"You know what I mean. And don't worry, I can take care of this baby by myself and you needn't feel obligated in the least. I don't want child support or none of that. This won't affect your lifestyle at all."

Thomas just sat there, hurt beyond words that Jazz would even suggest that he wouldn't stand by her at a time like this. He stood up.

"Where are you going?"

"I think it's best if I leave. Staying here might cramp my style. You might want child support from me. I might feel an obligation here."

"I didn't mean it like that, Thomas."

"Let's get one thing straight, Jazz, and let's get it straight right now. You're pregnant. Which means you're carrying, not your child, but *our* child. And not only will I be there for my child but I will be as big a part of his life or bigger. Do you understand me? Your hang-ups about romance and love will have nothing to do with how we raise this child. It's our problem, not his."

Jazz smiled. "Oh, so you saw the ultrasound?"

Thomas smiled. "It doesn't hurt to wish."

"True that."

"I'm just telling you to knock it off. Stop being so afraid. All right?"

Jazz nodded. "Yes. All right. What I said was wrong. I just didn't want to burden you."

"You can't burden me with my responsibility, Jazz. That baby inside of that stomach of yours is my responsibility. I helped get it there. I'll take care of my responsibility."

"I know you will. I was just . . . You know how some men are, Thomas, let's be real here. Some guys don't go for that father thing."

Thomas shook his head. "You will not let up, will you? How many times do I have to tell you that I'm not like those losers of your past? I'm Thomas. Not anybody else. Thomas. And you know me better than that." Then he shook his head. "But forget it. I'll talk to you tomorrow."

Thomas was about to leave, about to get away for good perhaps, but Jazz placed her hand in his and looked up at him. And he looked down at her. And they both knew, instinctively, that the choice they were about to make at this one moment in time would set the course for the rest of their lives.

And that was why Jazz pulled him back.

"You may as well stay here tonight," she said.

THE EVERLASTING ARMS

"*Ask Sister J*. This is J. What's up, Miami?"

The caller hesitated. "Is this Sister J?"

Jazz smiled. "Yes, it is. What's up?"

"My boyfriend is putting pressure on me, Sister J."

"What kind of pressure?"

"Marriage pressure."

"He wants to get married but you don't?"

"Right."

"Why don't you?"

"Because I'm not sure if he's the one."

"You aren't sure if he's Mr. Right?"

"Right."

"How long have you dated this man?"

"Four years."

"You've *dated* him for four years?"

"Yes. We were friends first, but then we became more than friends."

"I see. Do you love him?"

"What's love got to do with it?"

"Everything, my dear. Do you love him?"

There was a pause in the caller's voice. "Yes."

"Is he faithful to you?"

"Oh yes, he's a good man."

"No abuser or anything like that?"

"No."

"No addictions or anything like that?"

"None."

"Have any children by him?"

"Yes. One."

"So this good, faithful man you love, who also happens to be the father of your child, is good enough to lay up with and date, but not good enough to marry?"

"He's good enough. He's more than good enough. But how do I know he's Mr. Right?"

"Because he's good, faithful, and you love him."

The woman hesitated. "But it can't be that simple."

"Why not?"

"Because it can't be! What if I marry him and then Mr. Right comes along?"

"What if you marry him and Mr. Right doesn't come along? Look lady, you want to have your cake and eat it, too. You want the man but you want to keep your options open. That's fine, but it's not fair. If you want to waste your time looking for this great Mr. Right, then do so. But you should tell your boyfriend to stop putting pressure on you because you don't think he's good enough. That'll release him to go on with his life and that'll release you to keep searching for this man who's supposed to be so right. But I will tell you this, my sister, a good man is hard to find, and when you find one you'd better snatch him while you can. Or somebody else will. Now he may not knock your socks off, I'm not going to lie to you, but he can warm your feet just the same. And remember, a man in the hand is better than ten Mr. Rights in the bush. Have a good one. And to all my listeners, may God bless you, may God love you, and may you find a love of your own. Later!" Jazz said this and effectively switched off her show for the day.

Knocks were heard on the booth almost immediately and Gerald, along with a small group of high school students, opened up and walked in. "Got a minute, Jazz?" he asked, and Jazz took a quick sip from her cup of coffee and then turned her chair to face the crowd. She smiled.

"Sure. What's up?"

"These young people are on a tour of the station and the first personality they said they wanted to meet was you. And here she is folks, our very own Sister J, Jazz Drayton."

The students actually applauded. Jazz felt foolish, but she smiled anyway.

"Mrs. Drayton is about to celebrate her eleventh year doing the *Ask Sister J* radio program, a program we are delighted to report is now number one in the ratings." The students applauded again. "But we won't keep her," Gerald said as he began to usher the students out of the booth. "Her ride is waiting."

"Her ride?" one student asked. Then she looked at Jazz. "Don't you drive?"

"I try to avoid it."

"Really? Why?"

Jazz glanced at Gerald, who she knew wanted to laugh. "Let's just say it makes my husband feel better."

The students just stared at Jazz, completely oblivious to what she could possibly mean. All they know was that she was successful, was well known, and could probably afford any bad ride she wanted. The idea that she wouldn't even bother to drive astounded them. Gerald, understanding their confusion, ushered them on out of the booth. "Yes, yes," he said as they walked away. "She's not your typical personality."

He looked back at Jazz and smiled. Jazz shook her head and left for the day.

Gerald was right. Her ride was waiting as Thomas's SUV sat idly in front of the station. When he saw her, he immediately stepped out of the vehicle. Thomas Jr., their six-year-old, got out, too, as he bolted from the backseat and ran up the steps to meet his mother. Jazz smiled vigorously as he jumped into her arms. "Hello, Tommy, sweetheart!"

"I got an A!" he yelled.

"Really?" Jazz said as she began walking down the steps with little Tommy in tow.

"I got an A!" Tommy said again. "All of my spelling words were right. I was the only one."

"Good for you," Jazz said as she ran her hand through his soft mat of jet-black hair, his large, bright brown eyes and velvety brown skin making anyone who'd ever seen Thomas Drayton know immediately that this active little boy had to be his son. Then she looked at Thomas himself, who stood beside his SUV like a chauffeur as he opened the front passenger door for her.

"Hi," she said as she approached him.

"Hi yourself," he replied and then smiled that drop-dead gorgeous smile of his that still caused her heartbeat to quicken. "Put that big boy down," he said.

"Ah, Daddy," Tommy said disappointedly as Jazz put him down.

"You are getting too heavy to carry," Jazz admitted.

"Really?" Tommy said, his eyes brightening with excitement.

"Yes."

"Heavy like Daddy?"

Jazz smiled. "Just like Daddy."

"That means I'm a man then." He looked at Thomas. "I'm a man, Daddy."

"Yeah, you're a little man. Get in the truck."

Tommy, feeling triumphant now, hurried back into the backseat. Jazz and Thomas looked adoringly at their son and then at each other. Thomas's heart raced.

"You look beautiful," he said.

"So do you."

Thomas smiled and then walked up and put his arms around her, holding her tightly in a warm embrace. "Love you," he said as he kissed her on the lips.

"Love you, too," she replied.

"Get in," he said, "so I can love you real good at home."

"Let me kiss the baby first." She said this as she moved away from him and got into the backseat of the vehicle, past Tommy, to their one-year-old who sat patiently in her carseat. A grand smile came on her fat-cheeked face when she saw Jazz. "Hey, baby," Jazz said, kissing her on those cheeks. "How's my little girl?"

"Bad," Tommy said. "She threw her rubber ducky at me."

Jazz laughed. Thomas, who had closed the passenger-side doors, got into the driver's seat.

Jazz looked at him. "I think I'll sit back here, honey."

Thomas smiled. "Wonder why I'm not surprised?"

Jazz reached over and slapped him playfully upside the head. He laughed, then cranked up and drove home.